CW00865744

WUNDERKIDS
PART ONE - WILDWOOD ACADEMY

WUNDERKIDS

PART 1: WILDWOOD ACADEMY

BY JACQUELINE SILVESTER

Lonewolf Press

ISBN: 978-1-9997346-0-2

Edited by Abigail Willford
Cover art by Sarah. N
Cover design by Captcha Studios
Interior design by Shayne Leighton

For mom and dad,

thank you for everything.

Dear Nat!
thanks
for being
a Wunderkid!

CONTENTS

1

Creditors Don't Use Fancy Envelopes

Nikka stared at her empty, raided living room. "Help! We've been robbed!" she exclaimed, with false alarm.

We've been robbed, she repeated silently, in a very slow and legal kind of way.

Nikka let out a measured breath and continued packing. She gathered her collection of American postcards, gas station magnets and wrinkled family pictures, and unceremoniously dumped them all into a large zip-lock bag. She contemplated the cavernous living space once more. Their creditors had wiped the place more thoroughly than expected; all that was left in the Beverly Hills condo now were cardboard boxes stuffed with clothes, zip-lock bags full of documents, and her mother's sketch books. Not even the old popcorn machine they used on lazy Sundays had survived the so-called "seizure of assets."

At first, Nikka fought hard to hide the material attachment she felt to all that was being taken away from her, and she hid it well, especially from her mother, Daria. Nikka didn't want Daria feeling any more guilt than was necessary. Los Angeles was supposed to be their final stop. After moving through 11 states in 13 years, it would have been the first time that they truly settled down somewhere since the death of Nikka's father. All the signs were there; Daria had scored an amazing job as a designer at the luxury hat company *Beau Chapeaux*. The large salary had afforded them a down payment on a condo, and nice furniture that didn't come from a yard sale. *This* was going to be the first time that Nikka would return to the same school for a second year running. This would have been the year she managed to keep friends she had made, maybe even the year when the local coffee shop would know her by name. Daria, however, had a tendency to uproot plans; after six successful months at Beau Chapeaux she quit her job, took out a series of loans and launched her own collection of hats.

That's when all the trouble had started.

It had been three weeks now since the first balding middle-aged creditor with narrow mud-colored eyes and a matching briefcase arrived at their door. Since then, two other similar men had followed, and slowly but surely, Nikka had become immune to the whole process, stopping herself from saying silent, melancholic goodbyes to every item that disappeared. Nikka hated those men; the men who touched her things, took diligent notes on cardboard clipboards, and every so often pointed at an item and yelled, "Auction!" - a command for the muscular men, who carried away their possessions and piled them into a navy blue van parked by the curb.

The hat collection, which Daria had created using the borrowed money, had been stolen, along with the delivery truck that had been transporting it to its very first show. Following this disaster, the bank was quick to decide that Daria would never be able to fully repay her debt. It did not help her cause that she had poured every cent of her own savings into the stolen collection. Once the decision was made, creditors descended on them like vultures, ready to pick the carcass clean.

Nikka scowled as two bulky movers walked by her, carrying a fragile art installation her mother had purchased with her first paycheck. A little piece broke off in the mover's hand. He stared at it in a moment of worry, then shrugged his shoulders, dropped it on the floor, and walked on. Nikka was glad that Daria was not there to see it. The bank was also foreclosing their home and, come the weekend, they were going to be evicted. Nikka knew that there was no point in doing so, but she began to clean the house. She took out the trash and on her way back, out of sheer habit, she opened their metallic mailbox and pulled out a heavy stack of mail. Since the process of their eviction had begun, Nikka had developed a habit of quickly collecting, and discarding the mail before her mother could notice there was any. This was one of the numerous ways in which she protected Daria. Nikka went upstairs and sat on her bed, one knee folded over the other, Indian style.

She flipped absent-mindedly through the stack of white envelopes with large red writing splashed across them, reading "URGENT" and "RESPONSE NEEDED." Nikka knew what they would say but opened them anyway, hoping that maybe one would contain something different from the rest. There were letters from banks, the gas company, the landlord, the landlord's lawyer, and the electric bill. Nikka ripped, shredded, and discarded each letter in a meticulous set of motions, until she came upon the last in the pile and stopped. This envelope was black and the contents felt heavy in her palm. It grabbed her attention for two reasons; first, the envelope was made of thick, rich, textured paper, not the cheap, almost translucent kind used by banks. Second, the envelope was addressed to her, *Vierranikka Mason,* personally. Bills were never addressed to Nikka because she was a minor. She flipped the envelope around; two words were written across the back: *Wildwood Academy*.

Nikka quickly tore the envelope open, pulled the letter out and began to read.

Dear Vierranikka Mason,

It is my pleasure to inform you that you have been accepted to the Wildwood Academy for Talented Youth. Wildwood Academy is undoubtedly one of the most prestigious boarding schools in the country, and we carefully recruit our students from all over the world.

After careful consideration of your talents in the field of technical drawing, we firmly believe that Wildwood is the ideal place for you. Our Academy will provide you with the opportunity to refine and expand your creative potential, as well as equip you with the tools and guidance necessary to improve your abilities. Our establishment is very competitive and just a few spots are offered each year, to a select few talented students. Additionally, we provide full room and board, as well as prospective financial aid in accordance with each student's individual needs. In order to maintain the integrity and anonymity of our selection process, we do not maintain a website or establish phone contact prior to acceptance and orientation.

If you accept our offer of admission, you and your parent(s) or guardian(s) will be picked up by our complimentary car service on 3rd September at 16:00, and delivered to the Academy for Orientation, at the central campus. Wildwood Academy is located near the town of Wildwood, in the San Jacinto Mountain region. We sincerely hope you will consider our offer, and we look forward to welcoming you to our campus.

Sincerely,

The Admissions Committee,

and Dean Steven Edison

Nikka read the letter a second time, but it still didn't make any sense. Yes, she drew, and by all accounts she drew well. Two years ago, she had won the National Monuments Arts prize - a competition where she had to commit a bunch of national monuments to memory and then sketch them. A year before that, she won her school's art fair. Still, how would some prestigious academy located in the mountains know about that? A school she had never applied to, nor even heard of. Nikka stroked the soft paper with her index finger. *Is this a scam?* She wondered, amused that someone would go to such creative lengths. *I do draw, that part can't be a coincidence,* she reasoned, *and they're not even asking for money; they're offering free room and board!* Nikka was still for a moment, her mind somehow blank, yet at the same time overwhelmed. *That's how all scams start,* she reminded herself wisely, *with an offer too good to be true.*

She spun the letter around, again and again, as if the twisted blur of words would suddenly reveal its true motive. There was a logo at the bottom, a circle with the letters *W* and *A* creating a small pyramid inside it. *W.A...*

Wildwood Academy. Her eyes fell and focused on the date and time; 3rd of September. *In just two days?*

"It's a scam," she said determinedly, and pushed the envelope away with disgust. Gloomily, she remembered that no school would want her if they were to see the recent streak of Ds and Fs that she had earned following the stress of Daria's hat disaster.

Nikka was already due to change schools this year; the loss of their condo in Beverly Hills meant she had also lost her place at the local public high school. This year she would be attending a school downtown, near the home of her aunt, Sonya, who was temporarily taking them in. This new school was equipped with metal detectors at all entrances, ringlets of sharp barbed wire lined the fence, and there were metal bars on all ground floor windows. Nikka didn't know if the bars were there to keep people in or to keep people out, but she knew that she was not looking forward to attending. She tried to picture the faraway Wildwood Academy and failed; she no longer had room in her head for daydreaming. Tomorrow they were moving into Sonya's small apartment, and between then and now there was still much to be done; she tossed the letter in the bin.

×

Early Saturday morning Nikka woke for the very last time in her beloved condo, inside her sun-filled bedroom. Her silk curtains had been seized, but the rods remained awkwardly framing the incoming light. Downstairs she found her mother, sitting crossed-legged by an upside down cardboard box, in place of the kitchen table. On the box stood her 'I Heart NY' mug filled with Americano, and the three latest editions of Women's Fashion Daily. Daria was frowning at the jobs section in deep concentration.

"You should give it a break with that thing," Nikka said. She threw a concerned look at the magazine, and flicked the kettle on.

"I can't. They have some great job listings here," said Daria through chewed up fingernails, "one in Seattle, high pay!"

Nikka rolled her eyes at the word *Seattle*. She knew that her mother would have difficulty finding a new job, in Seattle or elsewhere, at least until the hat scandal had blown over, and someone else's disaster occupied the gossip-loving tongues of the fashion industry.

"Sounds great, Mom," she responded robotically. The same response she had given when her mother proposed moving to Los Angeles for the film industry; moving to San Francisco for the nature; New York for the fashion; Miami for the beaches; and Chicago before that, for... well, no particular reason.

"It rains there... a lot. You love the rain," Daria said, animatedly.

"We could have matching umbrellas," she continued. "You know the vintage ones they sell downtown with the ruffles. It's very *'Gone With The Wind.'* And they have great coffee in Seattle. The best! We could have coffee in the rain, every day." She tugged at a strand of her short blond hair. When the going got tough, Daria liked to cut her own hair; it relaxed her. Right now it was cut at different lengths and stuck up on all sides, like the straw hair of a stylish scarecrow.

Nikka affectionately pulled the hair out of Daria's hand. She looked down at her mother, a look of half-love, half-irritation. No matter what mess they got themselves into, Daria's eyes were always gleaming with the promise of a better tomorrow. Daria looked up and met Nikka's gaze.

"Is there any mail?" she asked.

"No, not today." Nikka lied.

"Yesterday?"

"No."

"The day before?"

"Nope."

"Odd, barely any mail these days." Daria's voice carried a smidgeon of sadness. Nikka gave a nervous cough, and poured her tea.

"Well, there was this one thing. It's stupid...or funny, depends on how you look at it. It was this elaborate scam about a boarding school... offering me a full scholarship," Nikka forced a laugh.

Daria's hand froze, her coffee mug mid-air.

"A boarding school?" she asked, incredulously.

"Yes, and without a website. I'm not sure how they try to get money out of you, but there's probably a follow-up letter that asks for a social security number or a sample of your DNA," Nikka chuckled.

Her mother had stopped listening.

"Where is it?" she whispered.

"What?" Nikka took a step back.

"The letter!"

"I threw it away... Upstairs"-

Daria bolted out of the room, the train of her green silk kimono billowing behind her. She ran back into the kitchen seconds later, triumphantly clutching the crumpled piece of paper.

"This. Is. Amazing," she said, trying to iron it out over the edge of the cardboard box.

She finally got it flat and read the entire thing out loud. Nikka waited patiently for her to finish, silently cursing herself for ever having mentioned it.

"There's a financial aid proposal!" yelped Daria as if she were announcing that they had just won the lottery.

"...They would cover room, board and tuition in full! And they included a pamphlet with pictures!" she continued, enthusiastically. Nikka looked back at her, dumb-founded. She hadn't even bothered to see what else was inside the envelope before throwing it away.

Like a small child admiring a Disneyland advert, Daria

pointed at the pictures of smiling students as if they were tangible proof that the place represented in the photos existed. Daria's smile was bright and hopeful. Nikka reminded herself that Daria wasn't the gullible type, but she did believe, genuinely, and perhaps at the most hopeless of times, that problems have a tendency to solve themselves. The letter she held in her hands was her idea of a *solution*.

Daria was beaming. She tossed the pamphlet at her daughter.

Nikka stared reluctantly at a picture of a dense redwood forest on a mountainside. Inside, the pamphlet was littered with captioned pictures: teenagers conducting science experiments in high-tech labs; life models posing in luxurious art studios. The pamphlet reeked of achievement, excellence and superiority. Nikka discarded the brochure and turned away.

"It's a scam," she said, with fake disinterest.

"It is not," Daria spat indignantly grabbing the brochure back.

"I never even applied to any school, so how would they know I exist? You are so *naïve,* Mom," Nikka's voice grew increasingly frustrated.

"No, I'm not, and *this* is real," declared Daria with resolve.

"How would you know?" snapped Nikka.

Daria blinked nervously. She fidgeted for a moment

and then pretended to notice something on the hem of her kimono.

"Mom?"

No answer. Daria fidgeted some more. She grabbed a nearby rag and started wiping the kitchen countertop. This was a rather uncharacteristic move for her, and Nikka was instantly worried. Her hand drifted towards the center of her chest, where she could feel her father's dog tags tucked under her shirt; she always did this when she felt anxious.

"MOM!" she yelped impatiently.

Daria sighed. "When all of these..." she paused, searching for the appropriate word, "*unfortunate events* started happening, and right after we toured your new school..." Daria selected her words carefully, biding her time, like a guilty child. "I may have submitted a few last minute applications on your behalf to a couple of art schools and boarding schools around the country."

She waved her hand in the air dismissively, as if what she were saying were no big deal at all. Nikka stared at her mother, stunned.

"You did what?"

"Listen, I know you worry about me, and everything that happened was my fault," Daria continued. Nikka opened her mouth in an attempt to protest, but her mother raised a silencing hand.

"I submitted applications for you because I didn't

want you to have to stay at Aunt Sonya's house in a small room." There was a long, pregnant pause.

"Let's face it, Sonya is not the most *normal* relative out there, and I didn't want you to have to go to that horrible school," Daria added, miserably.

A hundred thoughts ran through Nikka's head. *What sketches did she submit? When had she had time to do this? How did she manage to keep it a secret?* Daria stared at her daughter expectantly, waiting for her reaction.

Nikka walked over and squeezed her in a tight embrace.

"It's really sweet what you did," she said and smiled. Then she turned and took a sip of her now cold tea.

"But I wouldn't leave you. Not until I knew you were back on your feet."

Daria's smile faltered like a deflating balloon.

"Well, I would get back on my feet faster if I knew that you were somewhere safe and beautiful. Why shouldn't you at least consider this? You deserve it. Have a little faith," her mother murmured, grumpily.

She tilted her head to look at her daughter sideways.

"You can't be this pessimistic at fifteen. You're so talented, you deserve to be somewhere where they recognize that, not shut up in some dirty school with bars on the windows."

"I'm not leaving you at Sonya's by yourself," Nikka insisted. "And all of this still seems a bit odd. I mean, no phone number? Come on! They don't even have a website... and it's *free*." Nikka rolled her eyes.

Daria looked as if she were about to say something else, but then thought better of it.

"Fine. We have to finish packing and head over to Sonya's before five o'clock," she said, flatly.

Her mother walked out of the room. Nikka followed her up the spiral staircase. Both women spent the morning cramming the last of their possessions into suitcases, and in the afternoon the downcast pair reluctantly locked the door to the condo for the very last time, climbed into their Ford, and headed south to a much less pleasant part of town.

×

Sonya's place was small and sad. The 5th floor downtown apartment overlooked a garment factory and a steaming burrito truck. The inside of the apartment was grey and barren; there was a moth-eaten couch that smelled of smoke and musk, a boxy '90s television, and a Greek marble garden statue that Sonya had won in her divorce, stood watch in the corner. It was one of the last two unsold items that remained from her divorce, that and her fully kitted-out orange Jeep; two tokens of her previous life as a banker's wife in Malibu, before the break-up and her rapid descent into alcoholism. Now there was nothing Sonya loved more than drunk-driving her Jeep through the Malibu canyons and cursing at oncoming traffic.

Sonya was a large and rather masculine woman. Her hair was always oily and her voice raspy. She wasn't Nikka's actual relative; she was Daria's stepsister from her father's re-marriage. Daria had looked her up when they first moved to Los Angeles, an act she soon regretted when Sonya crashed her Jeep into their garage on her first visit. Nonetheless, she was the only 'relative' they had in Los Angeles, and the only person they could now turn to for help.

That first morning, when Nikka and Daria woke up on the wiry pullout couch in the living room, Sonya was already flat-out drunk.

"Morning, girls," she whispered hoarsely as she dragged on a cigarette, her eyes bloodshot and bleary.

"Who wants to go for a little drive?" Sonya was looking straight at Nikka, which made her nervous. Nikka shot a desperate look in Daria's direction, but Daria was pretending to be fascinated with the hideous view out the window.

"I, umm..." Nikka stumbled over her words. "Mom, can I go for a drive with Aunt Sonya?" Nikka expected her mother to provide a valid excuse for why Nikka wasn't allowed on the terrifying joy ride. Daria locked eyes with her.

"Sure you can, *honey*," she cooed in a fake sweet voice.

Nikka's eyes widened. "Are you sure it's okay, Mom?"

she stressed.

"Yes honey, I'm sure it will be fun," said Daria, dismissively.

Nikka was shocked at her mother's betrayal, but Sonya's strong manly hand was already ushering her out the door. She threw a final glance back at her mother. Daria was smiling.

×

Nikka's hair was windswept, her face and lips dry and cracked from the air that beat against the open sides of the Jeep. She closed her eyes as Sonya let out a battle cry and raced through the serpentine green cliff sides of Malibu. The hard gusts of warm wind beat against the sides of the car and caused a deafening roar. Nikka closed her ears and jammed her legs forward, slamming into the invisible brakes.

Giant waves crashed against the surfing beaches in the distance. Sonya swerved so dangerously close to the cliff's edge that Nikka saw nothing but jagged rock through the space where a normal car would have had a door. Finally, she let out a scream. Sonya roared with laughter and accelerated.

Nikka made it back to Sonya's hours later. She walked into the apartment furious with her mother.

"How was it, dear?" cooed Daria, knowingly. She looked up from another copy of Women's Fashion Daily. There was a sly sparkle in her grey eyes.

Nikka looked back at Sonya, who had just stumbled through the door, belligerently drunk. The large woman fell onto her couch with a loud thud and fell instantly asleep.

"How do you think it was?" Nikka hissed angrily, once she had made sure that Sonya was completely out of it. "At one point she ran over a skunk, and she just kept driving. She threatened the clerk at 7/11, called him a *'towel head.'* Oh, and she downed six beers in less than 5 miles! Should I go on?" Nikka was breathless with anger.

"Well, I told you it was going to be like this," said Daria, smugly.

Nikka stared at her mother in disbelief.

"You did this to prove a *point*?" She screeched.

Sonya stirred. Nikka lowered her voice.

"That was low, even for you."

Daria brushed the comment off and shrugged, turning her attention back to her magazine.

Nikka was so angry with her mother she could barely contain her rage. *Risking my life just to manipulate me?* She sat down to unpack her bag, and tried to make her disapproval clear through a series of grunts. Suddenly, the front door buzzer rang.

Daria walked over to it briskly and buzzed in whoever was at the other end.

"You should really ask who it is, especially in *this* neighborhood," said Nikka grumpily. She unfolded a sweater and tossed it aside. Daria stared through the peephole.

A minute later the front door rang. Daria looked at Nikka.

"Mom, who is it?" she asked, suspiciously.

Daria didn't answer. She took a deep breath, ran a hand through her hair and opened the door.

For a moment everything was quiet. Then a melodious voice sounded from the other side of the door. Nikka strained her neck, but she couldn't see who the voice belonged to.

"Hello, my name is Stamos Lederman. I'm from the Wildwood Academy for Talented Youth. I'm here to pick up Vieranikka Mason. You must be her mother?"

"Yes, I am. Of course, please come on in," said Daria in a tone more jovial than Nikka had heard come out of her mouth in months.

Stamos Lederman was a tall, handsome Asian man in his early thirties. At first glance he reminded Nikka of an Anime character; his face was very symmetrical, he was lean, and had a complex haircut. He wore an exquisitely tailored suit and smelled of cloves.

He smiled widely, exposing the expensive shine of his veneers. His smile was perfect and commercial, his slanted brown eyes excited.

"Good afternoon, Nikka, my name is Stamos," he said. The sound of voices made Sonya turn over and mutter something indecipherable, but Stamos's eyes didn't even flicker towards the woman slumped on the couch.

"Nice to meet you," Nikka said, shyly. She was aware that her mouth was hanging half open in amazement. So was her mother's. Suddenly, Sonya sat up, eyes still closed, and grunted; everyone in the room ignored her.

"Are you all packed?" Stamos asked, in a smooth and gentle voice. Nikka opened her mouth, but nothing came out. After a long pause she finally responded.

"I'm so sorry that you've had to make the trip, Sir...but I cannot attend your Academy. This is not the right time for me." Her mother began coughing loudly, probably to signal something to her, but Nikka didn't even look her way. Her eyes wandered, she called the stranger's attention to the small room and the many bags and pieces of luggage that stood inside of it, far too many for just one girl. She was trying to silently explain her situation to him, why she couldn't leave, and she hoped she wouldn't have to voice her reasons out loud. Sonya was fully awake now; she squinted up at Stamos.

Nikka hadn't noticed Daria disappear into the living room closet until she re-emerged from it wearing one of her finest hats, an excessively large red number. Nikka noticed now that Daria was also wearing makeup, and her finest couture shoes; clearly, she had prepared for the occasion. Nikka scowled.

Sonya pointed silently at Stamos, her head drunkenly

swaying from side to side. Nikka inched her way towards her, trying to block her from view.

"She's just kidding! What a sense of humor that child has. Of course we are going!" exclaimed Daria with a chuckle. "As you can see, her bags are all packed," she gestured around the room. "I'm coming with her, of course, like the letter says," she announced. Nikka shot her mom a warning look.

"Great!" exclaimed Stamos; his smile widened, but Nikka had the feeling he knew exactly what was going on. He did a great job of ignoring Sonya, who grunted and attempted to shove Nikka out of her way to get a better look at the handsome stranger. She pushed harder and Nikka stumbled to the side.

"Who...who is this *spring roll*?" asked Sonya, sweetly. She hiccupped. For the first time, Stamos looked at her. There was the faintest hint of disgust on his face, masked by a perfect dimpled smile.

"Excuse me?"

Nikka turned red. Sonya looked him up and down. She seemed to like what she saw.

"Did I bring you here?" she asked. She flashed him a drunk and flirtatious smile that showed off her yellow teeth. Stamos regarded her for a second. Nikka and Daria were horrified, afraid of what Stamos would say, and even more afraid of what drunk Sonya would say in response.

"Oh no, I should be so lucky," said Stamos, amused.

Nikka exhaled a sigh of relief. Stamos turned back to face her.

"I will be waiting for you in the car. My driver will come up to collect your bags," and with that, he walked out of the apartment, throwing a cheerful "Ciao, darling!" in Sonya's direction.

Nikka watched him disappear, and tried to comprehend what had just happened. She looked at Daria, who was smiling from ear to ear.

"Well, that went well," she said.

"I can't..." began Nikka, but she was cut off.

"Yes, you can!" Daria whispered furiously. "This school is amazing, they probably have huge studios and all the materials you could possibly need, plus all the food you can eat." Daria stroked Nikka's hollowed cheek. "I'm not letting you pass on this opportunity for *this*." She looked around the room with distaste.

"Please, let's just go see it," she begged, and gave an excited little jump. "If I know that you're taken care of, I can get back on my feet faster and make things good again, and then if you don't like it, you can come back to our new home." Nikka was prepared to say no again, but then her mother took hold of her hand.

"It would take some of the guilt away," pleaded Daria, knowing just which buttons to push. Nikka didn't want to leave her there, didn't want to leave her behind with Sonya, with the debts and the court dates, but Daria was right, she would not be much help if she stayed. She could help, however, by leaving; one less mouth to feed, less guilt, and more time for her mother to start fixing their life.

Nikka didn't need to pack; she had only unpacked two sweaters, which she quickly shoved back into her bag. Sonya was now on her feet and stumbling around the room like a bear coming out of hibernation. She didn't even notice a large bald man enter and wordlessly collect Nikka's bags. Daria checked her reflection in the mirror and applied some red lipstick to match the eccentrically large red hat. They turned to leave, but Sonya suddenly towered in front of them, blocking the door.

"I'm coming with you," she sputtered, in between hiccups.

"I'm not sure that's the best idea," Daria suggested, sweetly.

"I'm going to drive you; I won't take no for an answer!" roared Sonya in response. Nikka took a step back. When Sonya raised her voice, it was a scary sight. They both stared up at her, considering their options. Surely they couldn't move her, *could they?*

"Oh, I have just the thing," cooed Daria suddenly. She walked back to the room, opened a suitcase and pulled out a bottle of bourbon.

"I completely forgot. We need to celebrate us moving in here!" She waved the bottle before Sonya's eyes.

Sonya quickly forgot why she was blocking the door. She stumbled forward and grabbed the bottle hungrily before heading to the kitchen.

"I'll get three glasses! We'll pop this baby open," she called from the other room.

"That was a cheap shot," Nikka whispered, feeling guilty.

"I knew I would have to use it at some point," Daria replied, nonchalantly. "Now let's go!"

Nikka followed her mother out the door on tiptoes. Once they were clear they sprinted down the five flights of stairs.

Beside the car, which was a limousine, stood the same exceptionally large man who had collected Nikka's bags. He resembled Frankenstein, both in his towering immensity and in the slightly Neanderthal accents of his face and jaw.

"All your bags are in the trunk, Miss," he said, and opened the rear door, revealing the tips of Stamos's lacquered boots; he was sitting sideways, legs crossed. The girls climbed inside the limousine, which was spacious and smelled of new leather.

"Champagne?" asked Stamos. He indicated toward a freshly poured flute next to Daria. A flute of juice stood next to Nikka.

"Don't mind if I do." Daria smiled and gave a small flirty chuckle. Stamos waited for Nikka to pick up her glass.

She did, but she had a burning question first.

"Mr. Lederman, can I just ask...how did you know I would say yes? I mean, I didn't contact you or send in my acceptance. Actually, there wasn't anywhere to send the acceptance to, so how would you even know if a student has accepted your offer?"

"We don't get many rejections," answered Stamos, and for a split second his smile grew wolfishly wider. There was a pause. Nikka wondered if she had misread his look.

"And of course, your mother called us and let us know where to pick you up," he added playfully. Daria and Stamos roared with laughter and toasted. Nikka smiled, turned around, and watched Sonya's industrial apartment building disappear from view.

2

Inside the Wild, Wild Wood

The roads that led to the school were rough and jagged; Los Angeles and the thick cloud of smog that permanently sits above it disappeared in the rearview mirror as the limo headed farther up into the mountains. During the drive, Stamos chatted with Daria about politics and fall trends. Nikka watched him talk, hypnotized by the graceful, measured manner of his speech.

In the armrest beside her there was a thick stack of magazines and an impressive assortment of candy. Nikka snacked on Belgian chocolates shaped like hearts as the limousine glided effortlessly up the winding roads, higher and higher, until the scenery outside their windows grew raw and even more beautiful. About three hours into the drive, the limousine crossed the cloud line. A thick blanket of cloud poured in, and swallowed the neighboring peaks.

Nikka felt like she had transcended some earthly barrier, as if they were headed for Mount Olympus and had left all of humanity behind. *Left all of our problems behind,* she corrected herself, and threw a guilty glance at her mother, who would be returning to those problems in due time.

Finally, they reached Wildwood, and Nikka turned her attention to the small town that stretched out beyond her window. Wildwood was a quaint, woodsy village. The town's 'Main Street' was lined with charming log cabins that had been converted into small shops. Their wooden porches were littered with wicker baskets full of crystals, salt lamps, dream catchers, organic soaps, and hanging hemp bags swaying in the gentle breeze. Daria inched forward to get a better view.

"This is the cutest little town!" she declared.

They passed a group of boys with dreadlocks playing the bongos outside a shop called "Ye Olde Ice Creamery." Main Street was only a few blocks long, and soon the limo plunged once again into dense forest. Nikka watched the magnificent passing tree trunks; they were a dark shade of red, and so thick she was sure it would take five people holding hands to form a ring around a single trunk. The limo followed a tight, secluded path until it emerged into a large, well-maintained clearing. In the middle of the clearing was a smooth, white boundary wall with an imposing iron gate, and Nikka could not see whatever it protected.

Two guards clad in black and red uniforms stood watch. They spotted the limo; the one on the left spoke into his headpiece and the gates opened. The limo pulled through the gates and now Nikka could finally see *it*. It was a small, but impressive structure; two cube-like buildings, connected by a suspended glass walkway. The building gleamed in the sunlight, and the smooth round-edged cubes reminded Nikka of the stones she used to collect from the San Francisco beaches, silky and even, molded with time and water. Large glass windows were scattered all around the building, some oval, some round, and some that stretched from ceiling to floor.

Straight from the pages of Architectural Digest, thought Nikka, impressed. Cast iron letters on the side of the nearest building spelled out the words, *House of Dean,* and the school's winding *W. A.* logo was emblazoned upon each side.

"Welcome to Wildwood Academy! Time for the first part of your orientation," Stamos announced energetically. "This particular building was designed by the famous Japanese architect, Niyazaki Ishiguro," he boasted. Nikka and Daria nodded with feigned recognition. The car pulled to a stop and they climbed out. They followed Stamos up the path to the house, which was paved with vibrant redwood chips, kept from spilling out by two lines of solid marble. Nikka noted the striking contrast, *like blood on pale skin*.

The trio traversed a spacious all-white foyer and walked through the glass walkway, which gave Nikka slight vertigo, and entered what appeared to be a waiting room. The room was furnished with expensive-looking minimalist white furniture, which gave it the appearance of a very fancy and futuristic psychiatric ward. One of the walls was covered entirely in golden picture frames. From this angle, Nikka could not see what was in them.

In the corner of the room a prim, attractive secretary sat at a white desk, typically diligently. When she noticed Stamos, she stood up with a jerk.

"Hello, Mister Lederman," she said in a sweet, servile tone.

"Hello, Emily," Stamos nodded curtly in her direction. "This is Daria Mason and her daughter Vierannika, the newest addition to our Wildwood family."

Nikka and Daria shook hands with the dainty girl, then Emily stood there, staring at them.

"Refreshments please, Emily," urged Stamos. With gentle irritation he glanced at the empty coffee table.

"Oh, yes. Of course!" Emily quickly vacated the room.

Stamos glanced at his Rolex. "Ladies, it was an absolute pleasure to meet both of you. *Daria...*" he kissed her on both cheeks in the French manner, "regrettably, I must be going now. Vieranikka, good luck with your first day, you will do just fine."

"Please, just call me Nikka," she responded. "Thank

you so much for picking us up."

"Yes, well, I don't usually pick students up in person," said Stamos amiably, "But *you* are special."

Nikka reddened up to her ears and gave a mumbled "Thank you." She wasn't the shy type, except when it came to accepting compliments, then her face would resemble a tomato. Daria, on the other hand, looked extremely pleased with this exchange, as if in that single moment, all her parental efforts had been validated.

"It was great to meet you, I hope to see you again soon... perhaps at one of my shows," Daria purred.

Stamos walked over to another door labeled *Files*. There was a small coded lock on it and Nikka saw Stamos punch in the numbers *624376* before the door gave way. Nikka would remember those digits for a long time to come; attention to and memory of detail had always been her involuntary forte. She looked away quickly, afraid Stamos would think she was prying.

Once alone, Nikka observed the room with hungry interest: a Cubist painting hung on the wall behind the secretary's desk, a few bonsai trees lined the spotless windowsill, which looked over a spectacular Zen garden. Daria drifted through the room, examining and touching everything, as if to make sure it was real; there was a dreamy half-smile on her face. Nikka walked over to the frame-covered wall for a closer look. The frames were digital, and pictures flashed across the small screens before melting into the next set. Most of the pictures were not of the school, but of people. Smiling people. *Famous people.*

Amongst the faces, Nikka recognized a Hollywood actress, a country singer and a Bollywood star. One man was present in all of the frames - shot after shot, the same lean, older man posed with a multitude of famous, smiling faces. Daria arrived next to her, surveyed the revolving loop of images, and gave Nikka a sly, satisfied wink, as if to say, *we're in the right place now!*

Emily re-appeared and set a tray of elderflower lemonade and mint macaroons on the coffee table.

Nikka sat and took a sip of cold lemonade. She remembered the time her mother was summoned to the Principal's office at her last school. He had lectured Daria on how to improve Nikka's floundering grades, and his secretary had served tap water in Styrofoam cups to ease the blow. This recent memory felt worlds away now. The sun began to set beyond the window, and was pink around the edges. Emily returned to her desk and resumed her quiet typing. A few moments later, her phone rang.

"The Dean will see you now" she announced after hanging up.

Emily led them through the final door, and up a winding staircase. Each step tightened the knot of anticipation in Nikka's stomach. Nikka crossed the threshold into a lavish office and came face to face with the man from the golden photos; he smiled at her kindly The Dean's office had two glass walls, a stunning redwood cabinet, and three spider-like chairs. The sunset behind him had turned from pink to red as he stood to greet them.

"Welcome to Wildwood Academy," said the Dean. "Please, take a seat." The man was wearing a sharp blue suit, and was slightly balding. Daria sat first.

"Daria Mason," she said proudly. "So pleased to meet you."

"Dean Steven Edison, but please, call me Steve," he said, his voice like smoke and honey. He reached out his well-manicured hand to shake Daria's.

Nikka noticed that Daria had worn her old diamond rings for the occasion. The same ones she had successfully hidden during the seizure of their assets, and had refused to sell because they were her only gift from Daria's father. Daria only wore her rings when she was feeling so happy that the memory of her late husband uplifted her rather than dragged her down with sadness. Nikka instinctively felt to check that her dad's dog tags were still intact. She probed the sharp edges that protruded through her sweater and relaxed into her seat. She turned her attention back to the man before her. She could tell that the Dean was a man who took care of himself; his body, his clothes, his office - everything about him and his environment was polished and tailor-made.

"And you must be Nikka," the Dean observed her with keen interest.

Nikka coughed a slightly nervous "I am, it's very nice to meet you," and shook his hand. She assumed he was over fifty; even though he looked younger, small signs of age-reversal gave his true age away. Nikka had seen many women at her mother's work with Botox faces, and she could easily spot the slightly unnatural way the Dean's skin tightened above his brows, and the way his cheeks barely creased when he smiled.

"How was the drive?" he asked.

"Beautiful! These woods are gorgeous," said Daria.

"They truly are," responded the Dean. His small brown eyes fixated on Nikka.

"You, my dear, have been invited to Wildwood Academy because we have taken note of your exceptional gift. The sketches your mother submitted were some of the finest I have ever seen."

Daria nodded along in proud, excessive agreement, the bobble head figurine version of a satisfied parent.

"But I must warn you, Wildwood is not an easy school." His beady eyes briefly searched hers. "And we have many rules."

Nikka shifted in her seat, unsure of whether she was meant to respond or not. She had never had a problem with rules, as long as they were reasonable.

"I understand," she said simply.

"We expect the best from you, and there is no room for failure here," he continued.

Nikka could tell that the speech had been practiced and perfected over several years, but Daria looked so impressed that Nikka feared she would break into applause.

"Talent is fleeting; it must be cultivated and harnessed," he added, warmly. He waved his fingers through the air, as if catching a thread of fleeting talent. "Otherwise it could be lost to us, forever."

"I agree with you completely. Practice makes perfect," Daria interjected eagerly. "My daughter is very talented and a hard worker. She will do very well...in a place like *this*."

"I do not doubt it one bit," said the Dean, his cold voice suddenly chipper. He smiled at Nikka, in a way that seemed to suggest ownership, as if she were a prized horse at a derby; *his prized horse*. Nikka flashed her best 'humble' smile in return.

"There's just one more thing," said the Dean.

Nikka's stomach knotted further; now that she knew the school was real she was suddenly terrified that something would happen, and she would have to leave; terrified that the meet and greet was somehow an interview in disguise. As if on cue, Emily walked in and set a pile of documents in front of Daria.

"These are our terms and conditions that require your signature," explained the Dean. "Take your time going through them," he added kindly before turning on Nikka.

"On a side note, we apologize that your acceptance letter came so late. We just received a generous donation from a benefactor last week, a former student, which meant we could accept scholarship students of our choosing. This all happened in a matter of days. I imagine this was all quite a shock?"

Daria looked slightly irate at the mention of the scholarship, as if this made her less than the man's equal. She flicked through the documents as a ritualistic gesture and then did what she did with most legal documents - signed without reading.

"That's it, we're done," said the Dean, looking both pleased and oddly hungry.

"Just like that?" Nikka blurted out. "A free ride? What's the catch?"

Daria shot her a reprimanding look. The Dean chuckled.

"I know it's hard to believe anything can be free, but we are able to offer scholarships because the students who pay to be here provide us with the means to fund those *less able* to do so. If we only catered to those with both talent and wealth, our Academy would be largely empty. People usually have one or the other," he explained gaily.

"So no catch, then, nothing in it for the school?" Nikka pressed. Her pessimism always got her in trouble. Daria shot her a quelling look.

"Well, if you were to become the next Banksy, that would likely encourage more full-tuition students to attend the Academy in the future. Our scholarship program is largely to thank for our impressive alumni list."

Nikka beamed, satisfied with the honest answer. The Dean rose. Clearly he had decided that the meeting was over, and Nikka and Daria followed suit.

"So cautious for such a young girl," said the Dean amiably. The door to the office opened and Emily stood next to it, expectantly.

"A classmate of yours is waiting outside to give you a tour of our humble establishment," said the Dean, and laughed gently. After a series of thank yous, goodbyes and see you again soons, the man sat back down whilst the three women made their way out of his office. Nikka turned for one last look and caught sight of the Dean's thin mauve lips, stretched as far as his artificially youthful face would allow, just as the door swung shut.

×

Their tour guide was a girl named Eloise. The girl looked so out of place in the Dean's fancy lobby that Nikka struggled to swallow the laugh that rose up in her throat. Eloise was wearing a faded jean jumpsuit paired with stripy yellow socks. She leaned against a wall with one hand in her pocket and the other twirling a braid of blond and blue hair. She looked a little like a blond, punk version of *Pippi Longstocking.*

"Hello! I'm Eloise, and I will be your guide," she said cheerily, and gave a theatrical bow. They made their introductions and Eloise guided them back to the limo.

"How do you like being at Wildwood?" quizzed Daria.

"It's alright. Some parts are archaic, others amazing," confessed Eloise. "But I wouldn't trade it for the world."

"And what do you study?" Daria probed further. In lieu of an answer Eloise opened her mouth and let her soprano fill the car. Her operatic voice shook the tinted windows, and Nikka's skin came up in goosebumps. Daria was beside herself with excitement. When Eloise was finished Nikka applauded but was inwardly alarmed - *I hope they're not all this talented. Otherwise I'm screwed.*

As the limo did a slow circuit of the campus Eloise named the buildings. "That's the Performance Art building, and that's the Music Hall. Oh, and that's the Art Gallery over there. We also have a pool, tennis courts, and off-campus stables. Personally, I'm no fitness buff, but some people find these things exciting."

"Off campus stables," Daria repeated. She elbowed Nikka in the side, unable to contain her excitement.

"Mom, I've never even ridden a horse," said Nikka, as she absent-mindedly rubbed her now sore rib. Nikka was distracted; all she wanted to do was find the art studios from the pamphlet and paint until she couldn't stand.

They drove past the library, a large, square, glass building, in front of which stood a Zen garden, similar to the one by the Dean's House, with precise rows of sand and cacti. All the buildings at Wildwood Academy were modern, each unique and geometrically complex. The car pushed its way uphill and slowed in front of three large white buildings.

"That's the older girls' dorm, *Chadbourne*," explained Eloise, pointing to the first house. "That's where all the cool kids live," she winked.

"I'm guessing that's your dorm?" asked Nikka, grinning.

"You guessed it! That over there is *Blackstone*. Boys' dorm," she pointed at the slightly larger building in the middle.

"We are not *really* allowed in," she said in a mocking voice that suggested this was not a rule that many kept to.

"And this..." she said, as the limo came to a halt in front of the third building, "is your dorm. *Roseland*."

Nikka liked the name. To the side of the building there were rows of cherry trees, and the path to the modern four-story building was lined with blossoming rose bushes.

"It's too bad you have to wait a few years before you can relocate to Chadbourne," said Eloise with obvious distaste.

"What's wrong with Roseland?" asked Nikka.

"Pink just isn't really my color."

Daria and Nikka looked quizzically at her, confused.

"You'll see what I mean in a second." The three women were making their way up the steps when Eloise suddenly stopped and whirled around, clearly having remembered something.

"Oh! I forgot to tell you, only students and staff are allowed inside the dorms. You know...for security reasons. The official orientation finished a few hours ago, so I completely forgot to say." Nikka could tell that Eloise felt genuinely bad about having failed to mention this detail sooner, thus leading Daria to believe that she would be able to see Nikka's room.

"You can see the dorms on pick up day, or Parents' Day," Eloise consoled hastily.

Nikka thought Daria would feel disappointed, hurt, or rejected but when she turned around Daria only looked happy; happier than she had looked in a very long time.

"You are going to do so well here," Daria whispered excitedly. She hugged her daughter tightly, and Nikka took a moment to savor the smell of her hair - Lavender and Chanel Number 5. "This place is so beautiful. Please enjoy it, have faith, grab the opportunity, and take chances," Daria whispered furiously into her ear. Eloise stepped back a few feet and examined the roses, to give them some privacy. Daria squeezed Nikka one more time before walking down the steps.

"It was nice to meet you, Ms. M," Eloise called from the top of the steps.

"You too!" She yelled back. She looked back at Nikka. "I told you everything was going to be alright." Daria winked triumphantly and boarded the limo.

There was so much Nikka wanted to say to Daria; that she was sorry things had to be this way, that she felt guilty that she would be here while her mother would have to return to Sonya's, that she loved her more than anything or anyone, but they had an audience, so all Nikka could muster was, "See you soon!"

"Don't forget to call me later and tell me everything!" Daria called out of the rolled down window as the limo sped off. Nikka's eyes followed the car until it turned and disappeared from view, and then wandered over the horizon. In the distance, Nikka spotted something yellow. It looked like a large tent suspended in between the trees, like an enormous banana-colored hammock. She made a mental note to go and find it at some point and discover what it was. She turned and followed Eloise, who slid a plastic card through a wall-mounted device by the front door, and the entrance to Roseland gave way.

"I don't want to be a buzz kill, but that might be a bit difficult. Calling your mom, I mean," said Eloise. "Wildwood is a cell phone dead zone."

"What do you mean?" asked Nikka incredulously.

"They blame the mountains, but I think they've probably found some way to stop cellphones from working here. If you ask the Dean about it he'll say *'Cellular devices distract the youth from achieving their full potential and developing their capabilities.'*" Her impression of the Dean's commanding tone was perfect.

How will I reach my mom? Nikka panicked briefly. *There must be a landline somewhere.* She glanced around as she followed Eloise through the wide, luxuriously furnished common room; the walls were covered in light pink wallpaper, and scattered with empty corkboards clearly meant for flyers and school announcements. A few girls were sitting in a corner and giggling amongst themselves. Paying them no attention, Nikka and Eloise took the elevator up to the third flour.

"This is the one," said Eloise with little enthusiasm, after they had left the elevator and stopped by door number 5, standing aside for Nikka to enter. She entered a pink sitting room, fitted with shabby chic wooden furniture and behind a half-open door in the back, Nikka could see a bedroom with two neatly made beds, covered in lilac floral quilts.

"I'm beginning to detect a theme," she admitted.

"I told you!" exclaimed Eloise. "The benefactors choose the decor, and the woman who funded this house was some high-tea loving housewife with a paid-for

Duchess title. Basically, she was massively overcompensating, and had a thing for roses and the English countryside. *Et voila,*" Eloise gestured demonstratively to the floral room.

"The other houses are completely different," Eloise continued. "Ours was funded by a German design company, so naturally it's a bit cooler. You should come visit sometime and see for yourself."

Nikka smiled at the invitation. She looked around; despite the outpour of pink fabric and pastel florals she found her new room stunning. More importantly, it was hers! She felt like jumping on the bed and screaming like a child. Nikka noticed another door in the bedroom, with a silver decal shaped like a girl. Behind it, she heard running water.

"Who else is here?" she asked. She hadn't yet given any thought to who she might be living with.

"Um..." Eloise consulted a folded piece of paper, "*Stella Weinstein,* first year, fashion major." Nikka threw a nervous glance at the bathroom door when she heard the word *fashion*.

Eloise handed her a key card. "This is your access card; you'll need it to enter your room, and some school buildings. It's how they keep track of you and make sure you haven't missed curfew or gone missing. You will get in *a lot* of trouble if you miss curfew, or if you scan someone else's key card to get in somewhere. If you lose your card, report to the Main Office right away," she stressed, and her expression became serious for the first time that night.

"I will," Nikka nodded and took the card carefully, as if it were fragile.

"I'll let you settle in," said Eloise, "If you have any problems or questions there is a button by your armoire, it will call your House Matron who will be able to help you."

House Matron? Nikka repeated to herself, testing out the old fashioned word. *What's a House Matron?* She didn't bother asking, because Eloise was shifting from one leg to the other and looked like she had somewhere else to be.

"My dorm-mates are planning this semester's flashmob," she explained, "I'll see you around?"

"Yes! Definitely, and thank you so much... For the tour, for being so nice, for everything," said Nikka. Eloise smiled.

"My pleasure. You can just name your first born after me and we'll call it even," Eloise grinned cheekily and walked out.

The room was quiet except for the distant clanking of the shower. Nikka strode around, taking in each and every item. There were two matching wooden armoires, a plush purple couch, pink and purple carpets and smaller wooden cabinets. She walked over and sat on her bed, sinking pleasantly into the soft layers of expensive bedding. Nikka thought she recognized the pattern, *Windsor and Well,* a fancy English fabric company her mother used sometimes. She checked the tag and smiled at the familiar logo. Her memory never betrayed her.

The bathroom door opened and in came a girl wrapped in a baby blue towel. When she saw Nikka her brown eyes grew wide.

"Hello!" she beamed. "I'm Stella, are you Nikka?"

"Yes, I am. Nice to meet you," Nikka sat up and smiled in return.

"They told me your name this morning on the way over here. You're going to be in the Art Department, right? Oh my god, me too!" Stella shrieked before Nikka could answer. Stella was petite, with small perky lips, simple coffee-colored eyes and a generously sized nose that, in profile, seemed a little too big for her face.

She walked over to her armoire and pulled it open. Nikka's new roommate was already unpacked; the armoire was full of rows upon rows of neatly folded clothes, accessories and handbags.

"So, how excited are you? From one to ten?" Stella hid behind the armoire door so that she could change.

"A solid 10," responded Nikka, "But it all happened so fast, I'm still adjusting."

"What do you mean?" Stella re-emerged in a pair of brand new jeans and a white silk top. She threw the tags into the bin.

"I only got accepted three days ago," said Nikka.

"What? But acceptance letters went out back in May. Three days! How could they do that to you? That's not even enough time to pack! That's just criminal!" Stella ranted, appalled.

"No, no, it's not their fault. They got more funds in recently so they could give out another full scholarship at the last minute," Nikka explained. Stella's eyes widened further.

"*You're* a full scholarship student?"

Stella's tone, and her stare, made Nikka feel uncomfortable; she didn't like where this was heading.

"Yes, I am. So what?" she countered, a smidgeon of challenge in her voice.

"Wow," said Stella, as she sat down on her bed. "You must be really, really talented."

Nikka blinked in surprise. She could hear the envy and longing in her roommate's voice. She lowered her guard. On the wall behind Stella there were a few small drawings scotch-taped to the wall; design sketches. Nikka noticed them and understood. She looked back down at Stella, who was also surveying her sketches.

"Those are really nice," said Nikka encouragingly. This seemed to cheer Stella up.

"Really? You think so? Thanks!" Stella beamed. "I want to be a designer."

For a moment Nikka didn't say anything. She couldn't bring herself to muster any fake enthusiasm for fashion design.

"My mom is a designer," she said reluctantly.

"Oh my freaking god!" Stella squealed like an over-caffeinated Chihuahua. "This union was meant to be! You have got to tell me everything about your mom over dinner?" Stella half asked, half demanded.

Even after the tour, Nikka still knew very little about her new school. She didn't know where they ate, or what they would be eating. A dinner companion seemed better than no dinner companion; that was just high school 101.

"Dinner sounds good," said Nikka.

×

The Wildwood cafeteria was at the bottom of the hill. A line of students had formed by the entrance and Nikka tensed up a little at the sight. Stella gave her an encouraging smile. The line moved swiftly through the door, and soon Nikka was facing the buffet.

Nikka gawked at the food, rooted to the spot. The buffet began with an appetizer stand, loaded with melon and prosciutto parcels, ringlets of cured fish, and mini sashimi towers. Next to it was a cheese table, laden with cheese wheels, olives and jams. Nikka kept walking, trying to keep pace with the moving line. She hungrily surveyed the entrée tables, which were covered with sizzling steaks, sea bass, and herb-coated lamb chops. There was a small stand in the corner of the room where a hefty chef popped thin crust pizzas into an authentic stone-oven.

Nikka looked around at the faces of the other students, but none seemed to match her excitement. Stella was busy examining a tomato and mozzarella platter with contempt.

"Not the freshest *Caprese,* if you ask me," she said dismissively, before making her way to the salad bar.

Once her plate was fully loaded, the food titling sideways like the leaning tower of Pisa, Nikka joined Stella at their table.

"So, what kind of art do you do?" Stella asked.

"You know how when you look closely at a flower petal, or if you put tree bark under a microscope, you see that it's made out of thousands of smaller, intricate parts?"

Stella nodded, looking unsure.

"That's what I like to draw. Details. I also like to sketch things from memory and see how close to the original I can get."

"I just design outfits," said Stella, perplexed, as if she were wondering whether she too should start drawing bark.

"So, do you have a boyfriend?" asked Stella, her face brightening instantly.

"No," Nikka blurted out awkwardly. She couldn't remember the last time she had even liked a boy, perhaps in middle school.

"You?" she asked.

"Well..." Stella straightened up. She seemed happy to finally be asked something about herself.

"I have a few potential suitors back home," she said, coyly, "but I'm going to keep my options open here. There are bound to be some interesting guys, and it's not like I'm going to settle for the first one that walks by, you know? I mean, the boys back home are great, but it's always smart to seek variety, and boys like 'hard to get' girls," she said, smartly. Nikka had a feeling that she was quoting *Cosmo*.

Stella looked as if she was waiting for Nikka to ask more about the boys back home, or at least about where back home was, but Nikka was momentarily distracted.

The Dean had walked in. He was circling the room, shaking hands, and engaging in pleasant banter with the surrounding students. Everyone seemed to want to talk to him. They gravitated toward him.

"What do you think of the Dean?" she asked Stella.

Stella looked disappointed that the subject had changed from boys to faculty members.

"He's nice. A bit scary, but nice."

"Did he... Sort of keep staring at you, like you were a trophy?" asked Nikka. She quickly realized how strange her question sounded.

"Umm, no. He didn't," answered Stella. She pushed

her salad around her plate, as if she were practicing Feng Shui with her vegetables, and shot Nikka a curious sideways glance.

"So what's your story anyway?"

Nikka looked away from the Dean, this was the question she always dreaded. She could just answer truthfully, but whenever she told people the truth, it was always followed by an array of stupid or uncomfortable questions. *What did your dad die from? What do you mean moving from state to state? Wasn't that hard on you?*

"Well, I'm originally from Boston," answered Nikka.

"I knew it!" exclaimed Stella buoyantly, "I thought I detected an accent there."

"I moved when I was three," continued Nikka, "and ever since my mother and I have been traveling around the States," she said dismissively. She wanted it to end there but Stella looked engrossed.

"What do you *mean* traveling around the States?"

"We moved from city to city," said Nikka nonchalantly.

"But why?" Stella persisted.

Nikka was expecting this; people always thought there must be some exciting reason as to why she and her mother continually moved around; maybe they were missionaries, or salesmen, or part of a traveling circus.

"Well," continued Nikka, reluctantly, "we get sick of

being in the same place, and we just move on," she lied.

The truth was that Nikka's mom got sick of places; sick of apartments, sick of boyfriends, and then *they* had to move on. Stella looked at her, doe-eyed.

"That has got to be the coolest thing I have ever heard! I'm not even allowed to go to Cabo!" Stella lamented enviously. The overhead lights dimmed a few shades.

"I think that's their way of saying the cafeteria is closing," said Stella. Nikka was glad. *Saved by the lights!*

The pair dropped off their empty plates and trays by the kitchen and made their way back to Roseland.

×

It was 11 o'clock. Nikka had read and re-read the welcome packet. She learned that her classes would be structured differently each week, a mixture of general requirements and something called 'Workshops'. She also learned that there would be a welcome assembly the next day. Nikka finished unpacking whilst Stella sat on her bed, dog-earing the latest issue of *Cosmopolitan*.

A small intercom on the wall sounded, *"Lights out please."* Nikka obediently climbed into bed. Stella yawned a few times, fighting off sleep in hope of more gossip from her new roommate, but when it didn't come she whispered, "Sweet dreams," turned and fell asleep. Nikka stared up at the rose-colored ceiling above her and thought about whether or not her mother would approve of the color choice, *if she had been allowed in*, she added guiltily. *I'll tell her what it's like on the phone.*

With a jolt, Nikka was wide-awake and sitting up. She had forgotten to call her mother! Nikka quickly climbed out of bed. She crouched down on the floor, dug through her bags and pulled out her cellphone. She switched it on. *No service.*

She looked over at Stella, hopeful. Stella was sleeping; her mouth was half open, emitting little snores. Her pink cellphone was charging on her bedside table. Nikka tiptoed over and took the phone. Stella's phone had a bundle of sparkly charms hanging off it, which jingled loudly when she picked it up. She held them in her fist to silence them. Cautious, she looked at Stella, who was still safely asleep.

Nikka checked the bars - zero. *Cell phone dead zone,* she remembered Eloise's odd warning. On a whim she opened the window and stuck her hand out. *Maybe Stella has a better provider.*

She held the phone out and watched the bars. The cold wind blew on her hand. Suddenly a bar appeared. Nikka struggled to stick her hand farther out the window. She typed in the number and pressed dial, it rang through, *one ring, two rings;* suddenly the phone slipped out of her hand and plummeted toward the ground. Nikka stifled a yelp. *What have I done?* She looked down, afraid she would see a heap of broken phone parts on the ground.

At first she could see nothing but the dark, then her eyes adjusted and she caught sight of something shiny dangling in a tree. *The charms!* They had caught on a branch.

Nikka grabbed her identity card and bolted out the door.

She walked through the shadowy hallway and into the elevator. Next to the front door, Nikka stopped abruptly. She looked at the keycard in her hand and remembered Eloise's other warning. She didn't want to be caught breaking curfew on her first day, or for her new roommate to know that she had dropped her phone from a third story window. She felt a cool breeze lick her shoulders and turned around. The living room window was slightly ajar. Without a second thought, Nikka walked up to the window, pushed it open and jumped out. The landing was nasty; she lost her balance and scraped both of her bare knees. She brushed away the gravel and ran towards the trees. With alarm, Nikka spotted the phone high up in the branches of a large redwood. She had no choice but to climb.

Nikka dug her hands into the bark and pulled herself up, higher and higher. Soon she was within arm's reach of the phone. Suddenly she heard a voice; she was startled and nearly fell. She steadied herself and looked down. A boy had emerged from the woods. He stopped and leaned his back against her tree. He was talking to someone.

"Look, I don't feel like being here. I've made that

clear," she heard him say. "You said it would just be a year, it's been two now."

The voice paused, as if waiting for a reply.

"Listen," the boy growled. "I don't *want* to talk to *you*. You are nobody. I want to talk to my UNCLE. Get it? He's *my* uncle and your freaking boss. And I don't care if he's in a meeting. It's midnight! I haven't spoken to him in months." The voice grew angrier and angrier, like a kettle slowly coming to a boil.

"You know what happens when I don't get what I want, right?" said the boy.

Nikka could only see the boy's head. The branch she was perched on was starting to tilt and she was losing her grip. She reached for Stella's phone, snatched it up and quietly pocketed it. The branch shook like a trembling limb and so did the muscles in Nikka's legs. She had no choice; quietly, she began to climb down.

"Why won't he ever talk to me?" said the boy, this time sadly. He was starting to choke up and Nikka could hear the pain draining the anger from his voice. "I DON'T WANT TO BE HERE," he growled murderously. Then the boy hung up his cellphone, turned and kicked the tree. Nikka was almost on the last branch; she prayed he wouldn't look up and see her. She shifted and tried to find her balance, but suddenly she was sliding down. Nikka grabbed another branch but it broke with a loud CRACK, and before she knew what was happening she had landed on the ground with a loud and painful THUMP. Nikka closed her eyes, wishing she would just cease to exist. Then she stood up timidly, brushed herself off and met the stranger's stare.

The boy was frozen to the spot, eyes wide with shock, as if an alien had just landed in front of him. He had high cheekbones, a sharp jaw line and bright green eyes. His hair was jet black and combed back. He was much taller than her, with wide shoulders and thin legs. He was wearing tight low cut jeans with a slim leather jacket and grey hoodie.

His eyes glistened with the promise of tears.

"What were you doing in the tree?" he asked slowly.

Nikka hesitated. "I was looking for a phone," she spluttered without thought.

"You were looking for a phone in a tree?" the boy repeated. His voice was now void of emotion, and laced with mockery. He smiled at her, a striking white smile. A moment later his smile faltered.

"You were there the whole time," he realized.

"I'm sorry-" she started.

"Sorry for what?" he snapped. "Sorry for eavesdropping on someone's private conversation?"

Nikka felt guilty, even though she hadn't done anything wrong. She changed the subject.

"How are you able to make calls?" She asked.

"That's kind of what cells phones are for," he

answered sarcastically.

The wind blew hard and Nikka suddenly felt conscious of her exposed shoulders and cropped pajamas. He was looking at her, his handsome face curled into a predatory grin.

"You know what I mean. I thought it was a cell phone dead zone or whatever?"

"Dead zones don't apply to some," said the boy, looking smug.

Nikka rolled her eyes. She started to walk away, but he caught up with her.

"Didn't your father teach you not to eavesdrop on the conversations of men?" he teased.

This was the final straw; maybe it was the mention of her late father, or the long and overwhelming day, or the fact that she was tired and had just fallen out of a damn tree. She quickened her pace. He caught up with her again and this time grabbed her by the wrist. His touch sent electric currents all the way down her spine.

"It's just a joke," he said.

She jerked away from his grip, *"I don't want to be here, why won't my uncle talk to me?* " She mimicked his phone conversation in a pathetic teary squeal.

"I don't see any *men* around here," she spat.

The boy took a step back, as if she had slapped him. For a second he looked vulnerable. Nikka felt a smidgeon of remorse before walking off. She did not risk a look back.

3

Everything Will Be Just Fine

The next morning Nikka woke half expecting to find that Wildwood had been nothing more than a dream, but as she listened to the peaceful silence that resounded beyond her soft duvet, she knew instantly where she was. Nikka noted that this pleasant morning did not feel like the typical, stressful first day of school; there was no ringing alarm, no sense of urgency, and no smell of burnt coffee, and blind panic permeating the air. Nikka sat up and smiled at the pink, sunny room. After a quick shower, she dressed and excitedly contemplated her class schedule: 9am - Algebra. Her face fell, she hated math.

She glanced over at Stella, who was still sleeping peacefully, her mouth ajar. There was a brief knock on the door, followed by the sound of someone swiping their ID card. In came an unfamiliar older woman clad in a white work tunic, similar to a beautician's. The woman held a silver tray in her papery hands and a garment bag hooked over her index finger. She had long dark brown hair intermeshed with streaks of grey, tightly bound up in an unforgiving bun. She had olive skin and a hunched posture, as if she had been carrying a heavy weight her entire life.

"Good morning, Miss Vieranikka." Her voice was like a lullaby.

"My name is Magdalena. I will be your House Matron for the year." Nikka noted a trace of an accent, which she placed as Eastern European.

"Nice to meet you, Magdalena." It felt odd for Nikka to be called Miss, especially by a woman old enough to be her grandmother. Magdalena began to make her bed, and Nikka awkwardly hurried to help.

"It's nearly 9:00, Miss. You must leave for class soon. Once you've eaten something." Magdalena gestured at the tray. Nikka threw a sideways glance at the golden croissants, small jars of jam, blueberry muffins, bowl of fruit and small floral teapot that now sat on the coffee table.

"Woah," she gushed, "Is it like this every day, or is this the special welcome spread?"

"I could bring it to you this way every morning. Or, if you prefer, the cafeteria serves a full hot breakfast with many more choices," answered Magdalena, so compliantly that Nikka grew red around the ears.

"No, oh no, that's alright. I'll go to the cafeteria from now on," Nikka said hurriedly. "Should I wake Stella up?"

Magdalena looked at a still snoring Stella with concealed displeasure.

"Her first class is at 11:00," she said, in that judgmental way you tell someone about another person's nasty habits. Magdalena unzipped the garment bag and laid out the carefully ironed contents on Nikka's bed.

"A school uniform!" Nikka beamed.

"You are happy about this?" Magdalena's milky blue eyes studied Nikka skeptically.

"Yes! I've always wanted one! Not having to worry about what you're going to wear every morning? Amazing!" Nikka stroked the pleated blue skirt placed atop her bed with admiration.

Magdalena surveyed her curiously and then laughed, a quiet lulling laugh that reminded Nikka of fairy-grandmothers.

"Weekends are casual days, you can wear what you like then," Magdalena added. "I will see you in the evening, Miss," she called over her shoulder, as she gathered the used towels from the bathroom floor.

"Magdalena," Nikka called after her. "Please, just call me Nikka."

"Alright, *Nik-ka,*" she responded slowly, over-enunciating the two syllables. Magdalena looked pleased.

"And you can call me Magda," she concluded, and disappeared behind the door.

After Nikka had devoured a triple portion of croissants she skipped down the curved path that led to the heart of campus. Every now and then she paused by a passing window to admire her brand new uniform: crisp white button-down, a blue blazer patched with the Wildwood logo, a pleated grey skirt and blue knee socks. Nikka consulted a campus map and found her way to a building called Edison.

The Edison building was a small red brick structure with one hollow hallway and a cold classroom at the end of it. The dark building and its single classroom were both a little glum, and Nikka felt this was a fitting atmosphere for her most hated subject. The classroom was jam-packed with students.

Nikka walked through the backpack littered rows and sat down next to a heavy boy in one of the last remaining seats. His round glasses were slipping down his nose, and he was sweating at the temples. His eyes were light blue and his expression eager and kind, framed by swollen pink cheeks. He had a full head of blond curls and little to no neck. In her peripheral vision Nikka saw him not so subtly observing her; he repeatedly turned toward her, apparently wanting to say something, then thinking better of it and turning away. This bird-like dance continued for a while.

"Hi there," he finally mustered a few minutes later, "I'm Sums."

Sums, Nikka repeated to herself. *Peculiar name.*

"I'm Nikka. Nice to meet you," she gave him a friendly smile. The boy looked exceptionally pleased that he had been the one to initiate the conversation.

"You too," he responded, and pushed his thick-rimmed glasses up the bridge of his nose. Unable to think of anything else to say, he turned his attention back to the heap of textbooks weighing down his desk. Nikka read them off in order: Advanced Calculus, Theoretical Physics, Robotics.

A mousey brunette dressed in a pressed blue skirt-suit walked into the classroom and arranged her things on the teacher's desk. She contemplated the class with an *I don't know you but I already don't like you,* sort of expression.

"My name is Martha Leving, and I am your math teacher. This is Algebra 101. Please attempt to keep up," she said unceremoniously.

The stern-looking woman dove straight into a detailed PowerPoint presentation that outlined her personal biography and qualifications. Afterward, she read out the extensive syllabus, and recited the strict class rules to the room full of bored-looking students. The lecture dragged on and on, and Nikka felt herself zoning out. She stared out the window and daydreamed about the art supplies she would soon have access to.

"Vieranikka?"

Nikka was brutally pulled from her fantasy. She looked up and met Mrs. Leving's expectant stare.

"Yes, Professor Leving?" she asked politely.

"The board?" she said and pointed behind her at a mathematical equation scribbled in chalk. Nikka stared at the numbers and realized with horror that she didn't even recognize the form of the equation. The class remained still. Everyone stared.

"We've just gone through the demonstration," said Mrs. Leving, exasperated. "A number of times."

Mrs. Leving stared at her hard. Nikka felt as though the room was being drained of air, she pulled on the collar of her button down.

"X=3629," answered Sums, bored. Nikka looked back at him. Sums smiled; two deep dimples formed tiny pot holes in his round, pink cheeks.

"Thanks," mouthed Nikka. A distant bell rang, marking the end of first period. Nikka huddled her backpack close to her chest and, without making any parting eye contact with Mrs. Leving, quickly exited the classroom.

After consulting another map, Nikka made her way down the forested path that led to the science buildings. She heard someone walking behind her, his deep breaths becoming short pants. Nikka slowed, and allowed Sums to catch up.

"You got science next?" he tried, in vain, to catch his

stuttering breath.

Nikka nodded.

"Me too!" Sums beamed.

"Thanks for helping me back there," said Nikka. "Math is kind of my kryptonite."

"No problem! I can help you in Mrs. Leving's class any time. That's why they call me Sums; I'm pretty good with numbers, but it's also short for Simon," Sums ranted nervously.

"If you're so good at math, how come you're in Algebra 101?" Nikka thought back to the manuals she had seen on his desk.

"I was recruited two years earlier than the other freshmen, when I was in 6th grade, because I had already completed the 8th grade curriculum. I finished all of the available math levels here at Wildwood in my first two years, and it's too early for them to send me to college so they've got me taking refresher classes until they design a new, more difficult curriculum just for me. They said it would only take a few weeks. Poor planning, if you ask me; I mean, they had all summer," he explained in one quick burst of words. He seemed a little reluctant to admit his age, but also proud to show off how advanced he was. Nikka stared at him in awe.

"I guess 'Academy for Talented Youth', is not just a hopeful slogan" said Nikka. Sums reddened and pushed his glasses up.

"Would you like the 411 on the school? You know, the who's who and the what's what," he asked, as they found themselves in a bright clearing facing the four modern Science buildings. Nikka was about to answer, when a distant shiny object nestled in between two buildings caught her attention.

"Excuse me," she said, and headed toward the black box; she grabbed the receiver, hit the buttons and waited, but there was no ring. Nikka stared at the receiver dumbfounded. Nikka slammed the receiver back onto its hinge, frustrated. Her eyes stung with the tension of promised tears. She hated to think about how she was making her mom feel, alone and easily forgotten.

Shoulders slouched, she walked to her next class. Inside the bustling classroom, Nikka spotted Sums, his backpack protectively occupied the seat next to him. He gestured for her to take it.

She sat down and shot him a grateful look. A tall, green-eyed boy walked into the classroom, and Nikka recognized him instantly. *Cellphone Boy* - she had no name for the stranger she had encountered, and insulted, the night before. A short girl with steel blue eyes and raven hair trailed closely behind him. Nikka noticed that the noise in the buoyant classroom died down ever so slightly as the pair made their way toward the back.

"Did you know Violet's pieces were displayed in a real gallery over summer? In New York!" Nikka heard a girl excitedly whisper to her friend in the row behind her. Nikka began rummaging through her backpack on the floor. From that angle she could see his fast approaching sleeves. She did not look up, not wanting to meet his eyes, not wanting to remember falling out of that tree right at his feet. Suddenly, she noticed a small black object wrapped tightly in his hand. As he walked by Nikka's chair he dropped the phone into the open bag that she was pretending to search through. Did he mean to do that? Nikka looked back at him but he was already sitting in the back row, engulfed by a group of friends. There was a piece of paper wrapped around the phone. Nikka unfolded it inside her backpack, careful not to let anyone see. "Use me," it read.

At the front of the classroom, a short, middle-aged man walked in. He clutched a briefcase in one hand and a coffee in the other; the coffee spilled out as he trundled along. He surveyed his students with surprise, as if he hadn't expected to see them there.

"I'm Mister Howards, and this is..." he nervously consulted a piece of paper on his desk, "Science class 103. Welcome, welcome." He gave a little bow to both sides of the room. "Science," he began sleepily, "is the root of everything..."

As Mister Howards continued to recite 103 reasons why science was the root of everything, Nikka watched the large clock mounted on the wall and counted out ten minutes, until she felt like it was appropriate to step out.

She slid the phone up her sleeve and walked past Mister Howards, apologetically mouthing the word 'bathroom.' In the hallway, she searched for a safe spot and settled for an unlocked supply closet. She pushed past the brooms and shelves of cleaning products, punched in the numbers and listened until Daria's voice echoed down the line.

"Daria speaking."

"Mom," relieved, Nikka sighed into the phone. "I'm so sorry. It's some sort of phone dead zone and I found a payphone but it didn't work..." Nikka hurried to explain herself before her mother could jump in with accusations.

"Darling!" her mother's high-pitched voice cut her off mid-sentence. "Stop worrying! What it's like over there? Tell me everything!" Nikka grew still, wary of the jovial nonchalance in her mother's voice, which for the last few months had been glum and lifeless.

"Mom, is everything okay?" she asked slowly.

"Of course, everything is fabulous, my love," responded Daria commandingly. "Three sugars, skimmed milk," Nikka heard her say through a muffle.

"Mom," she whispered nervously into the receiver. "Who is that?"

"The secretary. I'm at a job interview."

"What job interview? Where?" Nikka tried to shift her tone from disbelief to curiosity.

Daria lowered her voice. "I am capable of getting a job interview, you know. In fact, I have another one lined up later today," she whispered indignantly.

Nikka sat still; she didn't breathe, afraid her mother would hear the doubt in her breath. She believed in her mother's talent, she truly did, but after what had happened, it didn't make sense. Nikka calmed her nerves, and silently reprimanded herself for her paranoia.

"That's amazing news."

"Oh, they are calling me in, honey, I have to go. But I want to hear EVERYTHING! Call me when you can."

"Okay. I will, as soon as I can," promised Nikka.

"And, darling," Daria whispered. "I'm so happy that you're there. Everything will be just fine! No, not fine..." she retracted, "fabulous!"

With that, the line cut out.

She contemplated the semi-darkness of the supply closet and felt like a fool for having manically searched for a phone. *Mom is okay. Everything will be fine* - she repeated her favorite mantra. Suddenly the door to the supply closet swung open and the white hallway light washed over her like a nauseating wave. Nikka squinted up at the figure in the doorway. He walked in, closed the door and switched on the overhead light. *Cellphone Boy* looked down at her, taking in the sight of her sitting Indian-style on the floor.

"You hang out in the weirdest places," he said coolly.

His bow-shaped lips curved into an amused, winning grin. "Trees, supply closets..." He reached a hand out to her. She took it and he lifted her up. She ended up inches away from his face, and stumbled back clumsily.

"I didn't want to be caught making a call," she explained. He continued to stare at her, amused, and Nikka suddenly felt about as ridiculous as a clown at a funeral.

"Anyway, here is your phone." She handed it to him. "Thank you, I appreciate the umm... Kind gesture." Nikka realized that she sounded too formal, too nervous. He nodded, took the phone and dialed. Nikka didn't know what to do. She heard the line ring through. He covered the receiver for a moment and looked at her.

"You want to listen in again?" he asked, and grinned.

Nikka was suddenly all too aware of him, herself, and the tiny closet.

"No... I... I'll go. Sorry," she said, and shuffled out of the closet. Her palms were sweating and she couldn't quite figure out if Cellphone Boy had just been nice or rude.

When the bell rang, Nikka was one of the last people out of the building. She spotted Cellphone Boy outside, staring at her. He stood with his back slightly arched, which stretched the leather of his jacket tightly across his wide shoulders. The blue-eyed girl stood next to him, and Nikka noticed her black high heels. The jacket and shoes were both flagrant violations of dress code. The arrogant line, *"Dead zones don't apply to some"* rang in her head. *How the hell does his phone work on campus?* She wondered with frustration.

The boy towered above the six people gathered around him. The skinny girl held his hand. Violet, Nikka reminded herself of the name that Mister Howards had called from his student roster. She tasted the word, sized it up, and for some reason hated it. The girl was pale and beautiful. Her hair was jet black and reached almost down to her waist. Their friends were clearly enthralled, as if the pair were magnetic. His eyes glowed an even brighter shade of green against the backdrop of trees. Nikka looked away.

Someone tugged on Nikka's blazer. Sums was hopeful and hesitant.

"So, see you tonight at the welcome assembly? Maybe I'll save you a seat?" he asked, seeking her approval.

Nikka smiled. "Sure thing."

×

By the end of the day Nikka was excited about the assembly, even though she wasn't sure exactly what it would entail. All she knew was that everyone on campus was talking about it. Nikka and Stella polished their evening meals off quickly, whilst Stella described in great detail every cute guy that she had seen throughout the day. Nikka didn't tell Stella about Cellphone Boy; she didn't want to admit to having dropped Stella's phone out of the window, and the whole story would just sound strange out loud. She wanted to keep this story, and her exchange with him, to herself.

When the cafeteria loudspeaker announced "15 minutes until general assembly," Stella and Nikka disposed of their trays and followed the path that led to the auditorium. Finding it was easy; crowds of buzzing students were all heading to the same place, like bees returning to their hive. The atmosphere crackled with excitement. Nikka recalled how at her previous schools, general assemblies were only called to discuss who had graffitied the Principal's office, or thrown toilet paper up on the roof; they were not an exciting affair, but she reminded herself that everything was different at Wildwood. Her classes that day might have been the usual mundane blend of subjects, but the people, the buildings, the nature, it was all... *Special*. The Auditorium was a stunning, part glass amphitheater that glowed like an orb, illuminated from within by the soft light of chandeliers. In the lobby, Nikka spotted Sums, who wobbled towards her happily.

"Fancy meeting you here," he quipped loudly, before he was quite close enough. A few people turned around.

"Sums. This is Stella. Stella, Sums." Sums and Stella regarded each other cautiously. "Nice to meet you," said

Stella dryly.

"The pleasure is mine," answered Sums, the enthusiasm draining from his eyes. Nikka didn't have time to analyze this exchange because the student body was being ushered inside the auditorium. Soon they were seated. Nikka had Sums one side of her, and Stella the other.

The stage, like the rest of the building, was perfect - tucked velvet curtains framed the stage and orchestra pit, soft golden light spilled from the theatre lights onto the stage. All of the lights dimmed, and the noise in the room dissipated like an exhaled breath. A slow clap began somewhere in the corner of the room and spread like wildfire, crackling as it grew louder. Nikka began clapping too, and then she saw what, or rather whom, they were all clapping for - the Dean. Dapperly dressed in a fine grey suit, he made his way onto the stage, calm and just as elegant as he had been when he had met Nikka one-to-one. He waved at the students, visibly humbled by their wild applause. He stopped by the microphone and raised two silencing hands; the noise stopped immediately. Nikka felt like she was a member of a cult. Never, in her many schools, had she ever seen a Principal command such respect from the student body.

The Dean spoke:

"Welcome to Wildwood Academy. Some of you I happily welcome back, and some I welcome for the first time. As most of you know, and as some of you will soon learn, Wildwood is not like other schools..."

The Dean was loud and commanding, but somehow soothing at the same time. Nikka felt goosebumps prickle on her arm and rubbed them away.

"Wildwood is special," he said. "Being here is a privilege, not a right. There are rules that come with privilege, and so before we delve into an evening of art and entertainment, I would like to take a moment to go over these rules." The Dean's tone turned cold as iron. Nikka looked at Sums, he smiled and rolled his eyes; this was his third general assembly, he was used to the theatrics.

"There are five cardinal rules at Wildwood; the first being that no illegal substances of any kind are permitted at the Academy. We have a zero tolerance policy for drugs and alcohol. Anyone caught breaking this rule will be immediately and severely punished. I trust this rule requires no further explanation. The second rule is no stealing, which should also be obvious. Theft is considered a grand infraction at Wildwood and will be met with immediate punitive action and/or expulsion. I would like to add here that plagiarism is a form of theft."

There was a moment of silence.

"Violence," he resumed, "is by far the most punishable offence. Our zero tolerance policy extends to violence. Keep your hands to yourself. Bullying, both psychological and physical, is a form of violence and will be treated as such."

Suddenly the Dean smiled, turning his charm back on full force.

"Fornication..." he began. Laughter and snickers erupted throughout the room. Nikka could feel Sums fidgeting uncomfortably next to her. Stella joined in with the immature giggling.

"Fornication," the Dean repeated, after the laughter had died down, "is not necessarily bad in nature, like theft or violence is. Of course, we understand that you are teenagers with raging hormones, but you are also minors entrusted into our care, and so for your safety, punitive actions will be taken against any pupil caught..." the Dean paused for emphasis, "fornicating." More laughter erupted in the room. "And since we are in the 21st century, I would remind you that same sex relationships are not an exception to this rule."

Nikka was in awe of the man, the comfortable way in which he spoke to his students, so open, yet so demanding of respect.

"Lastly," the Dean resumed, "it is against the rules to socialize with the Wildwood locals." The room went still. "We have had many problems in the past thanks to turbulent relationships between our students and the Wildwood youth. The sad truth is that Wildwood students have a lot to lose; the locals, in most cases, do not."

Nikka cringed. This seemed a harsh comparison. What was so bad about the locals? She turned to Sums and whispered in his ear.

"What's up with the segregation rule?"

"The townies have unhindered access to illegal substances, violence, and fornication," answered Sums, grinning.

"Any reports of fraternization between our students and the locals will be taken very seriously," the Dean concluded sternly. Then his smile again returned, charming as ever.

"The world has gifted you with talent, and in return, I trust you will gift the world with a worthy legacy. I sincerely hope that this legacy will begin here, in the halls of Wildwood Academy. With that said, should you need anything, my door is always open." The Dean paused and smiled mischievously; he controlled the room and its emotions like a puppeteer. "During my office hours, between 3:00 and 3:30pm on Wednesday afternoons," he added and the room erupted in another wave of laughter.

"Without further ado, here to introduce tonight's acts, the man beloved by all of our student body, Creative Director of Wildwood Academy and Events Coordinator, Stamos Lederman!" he roared, and the room shook with applause.

Stamos, dressed in a perfectly tailored maroon suit, made his way onto the stage.

"Good evening, ladies and gentlemen," he said softly. "For those of you who don't know me, my name is Stamos and I am the Creative Director of Wildwood. I also occasionally dabble in events," he added coyly.

"Stamos, King of Parties!" someone yelled from the back of the auditorium. Stamos smiled.

"Yes, I've been called that as well. First things first, I would like to welcome the incoming Freshman Class, and add that this year we have seen and accepted some of the best, most promising talent we have ever encountered. We already had one of the most impressive student bodies in America, and this year we are even more complete." Stella beamed, as if Stamos were talking directly to her. Sums rolled his eyes.

"He says that every year," Sums whispered into Nikka's ear. She smiled, but could not look away from Stamos. He was so vibrant, so hypnotic.

"He's gorgeous," whispered Stella giddily. Nikka realized it was the first time Stella had seen Stamos.

"I met him yesterday. I drove here with him," Nikka whispered back, but immediately felt worried that this could come across as showing off. Stella's jealous sideways glare confirmed that Nikka might have over shared.

"And since we are on the subject of talent," resumed Stamos. "I think it is high time that we introduce the first act for the evening. This young lady has won the National

Competition for Classical Music two years in a row, and she is also the worthy recipient of the coveted Tchaikovsky Grant. Please welcome Aika Tanaka, on the violin."

The crowd clapped for Aika, a young, plain Japanese girl, who took a seat on the single chair set out for her on the stage. She held her violin and bow in a protective and elegant way. Nikka noticed the bruise on the girl's neck - the mark of a dedicated violinist. Aika adjusted her seat, took a deep breath and began to play. Aika was brilliant and Nikka was quickly overcome. The music overwhelmed her, and she felt every beautiful chord vibrate in the pit of her gut. Pride swelled up inside her; pride that she had ended up in the same school as this talented girl. She closed her eyes and let herself go for the duration of the classical piece. When the performance reached its dramatic climax, Nikka glanced over at Stella to see her reaction. Stella was busy chewing on a hangnail; she looked nervous and intimidated.

The next act was a young Russian boy on the piano. Nikka didn't recognize the piece; it was modern, experimental and fast. It wasn't her type of music, but she could tell that this boy was equally as brilliant as Aika.

Four performances followed; an original monologue delivered by a bearded ginger boy who looked more like a full-grown man. He screamed most of his lines, but the words were beautiful nonetheless. After him came two boys on saxophones, a girl on the flute, and another writer reading her latest short story. After a while the acts began to fuse in Nikka's mind; even though they were vastly different, they all had one thing in common, the sheer talent they exhibited. For Nikka, this was both amazing and exhausting to witness. Stella had dozed off in the seat next to her. Sums had a small notepad open in his lap and was writing some numbers down. Nikka was just beginning to doze off too when the next name called jolted her awake.

"Eloise Mendel singing, 'It's a Hard Knock Life', from the musical *Annie*," announced Stamos.

Eloise skipped up from the corner of the stage. She was oddly dressed, just as she had been the day before. Eloise adjusted the microphone and launched herself into a rendition of 'Hard Knock Life' that was perky, fun and utterly flawless.

'"I know her," Nikka whispered to Stella excitedly, "She gave me my orientation tour."

Stella's smile was envious and tired. When the song came to an end, Nikka cheered loudly for Eloise, who gave a theatrical bow before happily walking off stage. Stamos resumed his place by the microphone.

"Thank you, Eloise," he said. "One of our students achieved an impressive feat this summer. Her photographs were exhibited at the SOHO Modern Art Gallery in New York City. Please give a loud cheer for

Violet Hendricks!"

Students cheered from every corner of the room; some called out Violet's name. Nikka located where most of the noise was coming from. Cellphone Boy sat in one of the front rows, his arm slung lazily around Violet's chair. Violet rose and bowed in each direction of the auditorium.

"To conclude this fabulous evening we will show you a slideshow of Violet's exhibited works," said Stamos. The lights in the auditorium went out completely and the room was plunged into darkness. A powerful projector cast the first image onto a white screen that had unrolled during the brief blackout. The first photograph was of a diamond ring, *an engagement ring*, thought Nikka, set on its own, on a patio table by a swimming pool. The picture was black and white, and to Nikka it conveyed wealth, loneliness, abandonment and carelessness. Nikka was annoyed to admit that the pictures were pretty. More detailed shots followed; a silk robe, a dead bug, a shopping bag poised on a dirty sidewalk. All of the shots were pretty, yet vapid. *Warhol would be proud*, thought Nikka bitterly. Suddenly, Cellphone Boy's face filled the screen. Nikka sat up a little taller. There were pictures of his hands, of him looking off to the side, both angry and beautiful, of him writing in what looked like a diary. There were close-ups of his face, with its razor-sharp angles and reproachful scowls.

The final picture was of him getting out of a pool. He

was flawless, contemptuous, and his superiority shone. *These are not art*, thought Nikka, irritably. The shots were self-indulgent, vain, and she liked them more than she wanted to. Stella stared in awe, whilst Sums had ceased paying attention all together. Nikka looked away, annoyed, her eyes searched the semi-darkness until she found him. He was looking back at her. He held her gaze for longer than was appropriate, sizing up her reaction to the images. Nikka stared back, stubbornly. When the projection went out and the lights came back on, he had looked away. Everyone cheered Violet's name, and he was whispering something in her ear.

Afterward, everyone hurried out of the auditorium, eager to enjoy the last half hour before curfew. The entirety of the student body dispersed in different directions and Nikka caught sight of Cellphone Boy again, unwillingly; he was leading Violet into the woods. A few members of their fan club followed suit.

"Where do you think they're going?" asked Stella, who had followed her gaze.

"Where they always go," said Sums a little enviously, "in pursuit of illegal substances, violence, and fornication.

4

A Beautiful Battle

"I still owe you that social breakdown," said Sums, as he swiftly polished off his tower of pancakes, raspberries and maple syrup. Nikka rolled her eyes; she had never been that interested in school hierarchy, why should she start now? She gleefully dug into her own highly piled plate of Eggs Benedict, sausage, and hash brown. It was the fourth day of school, and Nikka still couldn't get enough of the rich buffet.

Her art classes hadn't started yet, but geography and biology had already been added to her daily workload, so food was what she was most excited about each morning. That, and spending time with Sums. Over the course of the four days she had been at the Academy, she and Sums had become inseparable; they were together for their meals, for the walks to and from the dorm, and they sat together in all of their shared classes. Nikka didn't mind this sudden closeness; she had a feeling that Sums had not made many friends in his two years at Wildwood; no one greeted him in the halls, no one joined him at lunch. It was like he had been there physically, but had failed to leave any kind of mark, which was something Nikka could empathize with. He was also intelligent and a very knowledgeable gourmand, which made for great table conversation.

Since the school year had started Nikka had only spoken to three other students aside from Sums. *Cellphone Boy*, who had ignored her since the assembly, Stella, and Eloise, with whom she had shared a few passing exchanges.

She looked around; there he was, sitting at his usual table, his hand permanently attached to Violet's waist as if superglued there. He always looked faintly disinterested in what his entourage were saying.

Stella was sitting at *his* table today. She had decorated her uniform with a carefully selected assortment of pink accessories and a large peach velour bag, with her initials stitched in gold. Stella spent a small part of each morning trying to convince Nikka to add some 'colorful touches' to her uniform, and each morning she expressed her shock that Nikka, a designer's daughter, showed so little interest in her clothing. The only thing Nikka wore other than her uniform was her father's dog tags, but they were buried under her shirt, resting against her skin where no one could see them. Nikka found herself wishing she had been more accommodating of Stella, because now her only other friend was off trying to impress Violet's crowd instead. Sums bent his head sideways, catching her stare.

"Earth to Nikka. Earth to Nikka," he said, robotically.

"I'm listening," she replied.

"Okay, well the guy you were just staring at is Izaya. It's common knowledge that he is really well off, but no one really knows who his family is. Apparently he doesn't like to talk about them," explained Sums. He threw a discrete glance back at the pancake table, weighing up whether or not to go in for seconds.

"I was not staring," said Nikka defensively. Sums continued.

"The girl across from him is Violet. Her mother is one of those escorts-turned-housewife-turned-millionaire divorcee lingerie designers. When Violet got here, her art was crap, but at the end of her sophomore year she suddenly got good. Just proves that Wildwood know what they're doing," he concluded.

"Violet's dad is a big deal in Silicon Valley," he continued. "He actually created some pretty impressive software." Sums paused for a moment. "I don't know why the smart guys always go for the bimbos," he said with a frown, throwing another glance over at the pancake table.

"Maybe because by the time they make it big they are so sick of being ignored by all the pretty girls that they go for the prettiest dumbest one they can possibly find?" offered Nikka, flashing him a teasing grin. Sums looked like he was briefly contemplating Nikka's theory, and grinned.

"That's probably it! Promise me that when I am a big deal mathematician you won't let me go after some yellow-haired bimbo with a Chihuahua in her purse?"

Nikka burst out laughing. "I promise."

"And speaking of silicone," said Sums, interrupting her train of thought, "Some people believe Izaya and Violet started dating after Violet got her share of silicone as a birthday present for her sweet sixteen last year, which if my memory serves me correctly..." he glanced at his electronic watch, which looked like it had come from a cereal box, "was exactly 263 days ago." He shot an obvious look toward Violet's chest and wiggled his brows.

"Sums, how rude!" Nikka flashed Sums her best attempt at a reprimanding look, which was wholly ineffective, as she was laughing so hard.

"What?" he exclaimed, "I might be a math genius, but I'm still a guy."

×

Nikka could barely contain her excitement as she walked downhill to the lower part of campus. The San Jacinto Mountains were glowing red in the sunlight, majestic boulders hovered above the sandy winding paths, and she honestly could not remember having ever been somewhere so beautiful. Above all else she was excited because she was headed to her first art class. Nikka felt her hands flex, aching with the desire to hold new pencils, a paintbrush, a nice canvas.

Nikka walked on until she came upon a series of small oval buildings, each named after a different artist. She consulted her schedule, and found the building she was looking for. *Picasso* was a white textured dome, like a golf ball sliced in half. It had a red wooden front door; Nikka pushed the heavy door open and walked straight into a large studio.

Soft rays of light shone through the glass top of the dome and reflected off the clean, red wooden floors. Nikka thought that the building looked more like a dance studio than an art studio; there were no paint flecks on the floor, no noise, and she was alone. There was, however, positioned smack in the middle of the room, a single large easel. Nikka dropped her backpack on the floor and walked towards the large, beautiful object. She traced her fingers over the sanded surface of the wood. The easel was brand new. She stretched up towards the top unable to reach it.

"It's American oak," came a woman's voice from behind her. Nikka jumped, startled.

"I know," she replied. "I've seen them online." Who in the art world hadn't seen them? They were handmade in Italy, giant six-by-four easels. *Just 'cause you drive a bike, doesn't mean you don't know what a Bentley is,* Nikka thought to herself with a half smile. She turned to look at the woman standing by the door.

"My name is Ann De Grenoble, and I will be your *Major* advisor this semester," the woman said, in a thick French accent. She stretched out a thin diamond covered hand for Nikka to shake. The woman looked to be most likely in her mid-sixties, but with enough facial reconstruction to pass for a very unnatural looking 30-something. Her hair was artificially red, her eyes green; her thinly plucked winding eyebrows looked like small whips, and what remained of them was penciled in with red. She wore a moss-colored pantsuit, and looked serious, very serious. Nikka shook the woman's bony hand, introduced herself, and anxiously looked to the only chair in the room, the one facing the easel.

"That's for you, sweetie," Grenoble confirmed, gesturing at the seat. Nikka sat down compliantly. Madame Grenoble pulled out a small remote from her pocket, pointed it towards the middle of the room and pressed a button.

"Let's get right to it, shall we? No time to waste! Have you ever heard of *Bataillisme,* darling?"

Before she could respond, a thick black mechanical screen unfolded over the skylight. Then, blackout curtains dropped over all of the windows, plunging the room into complete darkness. A small red security exit light flashed by the door, and two small projectors descended from the ceiling at opposite ends of the room. They switched on with an audible click.

Nikka stared in disbelief.

"No, I haven't," she managed.

"Bataillisme!" exclaimed Madame Grenoble passionately, "Is an art form that requires sharp eyes, keen memory and..." she paused, "fearlessness!"

"All the great leaders of the past, Napoleon Bonaparte, Alexander the Great and so forth, wanted their conquests to be remembered in history, and for that they had to be recorded. So they hand-picked a select few talented artists to accompany them when they went off to war. The artists would stay far enough away from the action to remain safe, but close enough to record all of the glory of the battlefield," she explained.

Nikka gawked at her, mouth ajar.

"A Bataillist..." Madame Grenoble continued, "must observe, remember and record every detail possible. Sketch after sketch, nothing is to be omitted. Later on, should their party win the war, the artists would return home and paint magnificent panoramas memorializing the battles," she said, waving her hands towards the walls, as if she were imagining panoramas adorning them. "Surely you've covered the Stalingrad Panorama in your previous studies?"

"No, I haven't," Nikka admitted, timidly. Madame

Grenoble arched her thin brow.

"So...you want me to draw battles?" Nikka stuttered.

"Precisely," responded Grenoble, "You're going to watch the videos that I will play for you and record as much detail as you can; the pieces of the puzzle, if you will. Then, once you have all the necessary pieces, you will combine them into a panorama for one of your mid-semester projects," she explained. "It's all in the syllabus." Grenoble waved her hand dismissively, as if to indicate that she thought paperwork was a waste of time.

"Umm..." Nikka opened her mouth to try and form one of the dozen questions that were circulating in her head, or to at least point out that she had not yet been given a syllabus. The words *battle, puzzle, panorama* and *mid-semester project* were buzzing around her head like scattered beetles as she tried to make sense of it all.

"Why battles?" she asked.

"Because battles are living, breathing things. They are fast, painful, beautiful and real long after they end. A battle is the most interesting thing one can draw," explained Grenoble, as if it were the most self-evident thing in the world. Nikka had more questions, but Madame Grenoble raised a silencing finger to her thin lips.

"Just watch the video, sweetie. Remember, record as much as you can." With a few loud snaps of her stilettos against the floor, Grenoble was back by the door. She hit one last button on her remote.

"See you soon. I'll come to check on your progress in a little while," she called out. The door slammed behind her.

Nikka slowly turned back to her easel. There was a long roll of fine paper draped around it, like a toga. She stared at the friendly giant in front of her, in awe of the towering piece of equipment that most artists could only dream of using.

Battles? She mouthed to herself. *How?* As if in answer to her question, the projectors came alive with a feverish buzz. The room lit up; images spilled onto the round walls, encircling Nikka, which made her feel like a fish in an aquarium, looking out at the world outside. Nikka saw a clear blue sky, a desert and a decrepit town. There were a few burning cars scattered in a sandy street. Then the footage showed a town square where some sort of standoff was taking place. Nikka was so preoccupied with watching that she forgot to draw. On one side of the square there was a formation of light-skinned men, dressed head to toe in camouflage. On the other side was a disheveled gathering of what Nikka assumed to be locals. Their clothes were dirty and the looks on their faces enraged, betrayed.

The other men stood immobile in careful rows like tin soldiers, neat but menacing. Nikka gulped nervously and watched as tensions rose. The space between the two sides closed, little by little, and then someone threw a grenade. There was an explosion, followed by screams. Nikka closed her eyes tightly just as the two forces collided.

When she finally looked back, all that was left was a thick cloud of dust masking the outlines of colliding bodies. Nikka glumly reminded herself that she was supposed to be sketching this. The easel drawer before her was littered with an assortment of pens, chalks, coals, pencils and markers of all kinds and sizes. She picked the simplest pencil; Nikka had a habit of keeping the best things for last. She then, somewhat unwillingly, began to sketch everything that caught her eye.

Her trained hand moved fast and furiously. She drew every detail that held her attention, except for the blood, even though it was everywhere. She tried hard not to pay attention to how easily the explosions and guns seemed to pierce flesh, as if the men were all made of ripe fruit. Nikka felt the nausea rise up from the hollow of her stomach.

It's just a movie, she tried to convince herself, but she knew the footage was real. She refocused and drew the tears in the fabric of the men's uniforms, the slits in the bloodied camouflage. She shaded the expanding stains on the grimy clothing of the fallen. She drew the footprints that steel-toed boots left in the sand. She drew the shadows that the flailing bodies cast upon the ground. She tore out the finished sketches and let them flutter to the floor like dry leaves.

Nikka then focused her attention on the sand. She sketched the way the soldier's legs sunk into it, the way it buried them in a cloud of dust once they fell, and the way it shifted and swayed like waves, to the rhythm of the fight. She drew and drew and drew, tirelessly, until the video finally dimmed.

Nikka put the pencil back in its place. She stared down at the pile of sketches she had dropped on the floor; there were so many. She gave her aching back a long stretch. *What now?* She wondered, and looked expectantly at the door. She stretched out again in a futile attempt to relieve the knots that had tightened in her back and her right wrist. She sat still, under the red light, and attempted to push away a thought that had been lurking in the back of her mind. All that blood, and the pained expressions on the soldiers' faces, had reminded her of her father. Her father, a soldier who had left home when she was three and had never returned. They were told he had died on a mission, but they weren't told how exactly it happened, no details. Now, after watching the footage, Nikka could imagine that her own father had died similarly, pierced like a bag of meat, discarded and trampled in the aftermath of something grander than him. Her hands unconsciously drifted again over the dog tags under her shirt.

With every minute that she waited for Grenoble to

return, Nikka grew more and more anxious. Thoughts of her father kept pushing their way back into her head, and suddenly she began to cry. She tried desperately to stop the tears with her shirtsleeve, but they kept on coming. *I can't let her see me like this*, she thought. Nikka got up quickly and walked out of the dome. For a moment the blistering sunlight outside blinded her. She gulped for air, and tried to calm down, but her body shuddered with more waves of tears. *A panic attack. I'm having a panic attack*, she thought. Terrified that Grenoble would see her and take her for an unstable wreck, Nikka ducked into the next-door building. It had a sign on it that read *please remain quiet if filming*.

She made her way down a linoleum hallway. The classroom at the bottom of it was empty, so she walked in, sat down in the front row, and buried her head in her arms. For a few minutes she just sat there, crying. Then, suddenly, there was a loud crack, followed by the sound of shuffling. Nikka wiped her eyes and made to leave, but more noise kept her glued to the spot. Stunned, she realized that it was coming from behind her. She turned around slowly; there was nothing there. Nervously, she glanced around the empty classroom until her eyes settled on a supply closet in the corner. The rumbling inside grew stronger. She heard a loud "Ow!"

The supply closet door burst open and a boy emerged, his back to her. He was around her height, with ruffled chestnut hair that poked out from under a grey flat cap. He appeared to be clutching something heavy. He backed toward the teacher's desk next to him, and gently placed a cardboard box on it. The open box was filled with wires and camera equipment. The boy ruffled through the box and shook his head from side to side.

"Well," he muttered, "not going to bring much online, is it? Best work something out in town then..." The boy had an Irish accent and as he turned, Nikka recognized him as one of the boys Sums had pointed out in his social breakdown. *"See that guy in the flat cap? He's new. European. I heard a rumor he's the richest guy at school, richer than Izaya, even..."* The boy was vigorously sorting through the box's contents like an old woman at a flea market.

"Huh," he said, "*Nikon*, that's more like it." He grinned widely. The boy began to stuff his pant pockets full of the contents of the box, tossed a few remaining wires unceremoniously back in and put the box back into the closet, slamming the door shut and whistling merrily. Nikka decided to announce her presence, but then the boy did something that silenced her. A thick padlock hung on the supply closet door. Nikka noticed that there were two picks sticking out from the key slot. The boy removed the picks, placed the lock back on the door, and snapped it shut. He spun around, looking pleased with himself. Then his eyes met Nikka's and his crooked grin faded instantly. He stood there, frozen, and glared at her for a few moments.

"Hi, my name is Nikka," she offered hesitantly. Her voice sounded shaky after the crying.

"Are you alright, love?" the boy asked, seeming concerned. He tilted his head and observed her.

Nikka looked at the classroom window and saw her reflection; she had black mascara circles under her eyes from crying and looked like a distressed panda. She tried to wipe away the smudges from under her eyes, and looked away, embarrassed. Very few people had ever seen her cry, and she didn't like the idea of adding a complete stranger to that list.

"I'm fine," she said, more defiantly than she had intended. The boy reached into the back pocket of his pants and rummaged around for a bit. He pulled out a something small and shiny and handed it to Nikka.

"I was raised by three sisters and my mum, so I quickly learned to always have chocolate to hand, for emergencies," he said jovially, and handed the bar to her.

Nikka took it. Her lips buckled into an unintentional smile. The boy smiled back, revealing two rows of slightly crooked teeth. His eyes were a wonderful shade of dark blue, calm and sincere. Nikka unwrapped the chocolate bar and took a bite.

"You know, I was just *fixing* that lock," he said, carefully. He nudged his head towards the supply closet and took a bite of the chocolate bar right out of her hand.

"Are you a locksmith?" asked Nikka. Her eyes fixed on his. It was a loaded tease, and he knew it.

"When I need to be," he said. For a moment, the boy was serious, then he smiled again, a crooked, mischievous smile. Nikka could tell that he found the whole situation highly amusing.

"My name is Tristan, by the way," he added merrily. He stretched out his hand; it was large and bore a few brass rings.

"Nikka," she repeated. He took her hand and pulled her towards him, planting one kiss on each of her cheeks, in the European greeting. Nikka was momentarily taken aback. He let her go.

"I have a lifetime's supply of chocolate stacked under my bed, should you ever need any," he said to a still stunned Nikka. He looked amused.

"It was nice to meet you, I must be going now," he said.

He walked towards the door and stopped.

"Would you mind not telling people about my locksmith services? I have enough clients as it is," he said. He was still joking around, but there was something serious in his tone now.

"I'll forget I ever met you," said Nikka. He smiled one last time.

"I hope not," he said with a wink.

And with that he disappeared behind the door, leaving Nikka speechless. She realized with a sudden jolt that she had been absent from the dome for too long. She made her way back to the red room and found Madame Grenoble by the easel.

"You are not supposed to take breaks unless I tell you to," she said, grumpily.

"I'm sorry," whispered Nikka. "I just..."

"Never mind," interrupted Grenoble. She began leafing through Nikka's sketches.

"These," she said slowly, "are good." Nikka noticed a distinct sparkle in the woman's eye. Madame Grenoble was visibly pleased. She stroked the sketches with the long nail of her index finger. "Sit down, there is much to do," she commanded, with a satisfied purr. This time she did not leave. Instead she switched the projector back on, walked over to the corner and watched Nikka draw, for hours and hours on end.

5
Townies Tell the Truth

"Please tell me that's not what you're wearing?" said Stella with obvious disgust, looking Nikka up and down. Nikka looked in the mirror: a vintage yellow skirt, an oversize cut-off Rolling Stones t-shirt, and a pair of ballet flats.

"This is not what I'm wearing," she answered testily.

"No, ABSOLUTELY it's not! You're not wearing that if you're going with me!" Stella shouted unhappily over the pop music coming from the pink speakers in the corner.

"But don't worry, I'm here to help!" she added theatrically.

Stella rolled her sleeves up like a chef and disappeared behind the door to her armoire. Each hanger was weighed down by a mass of glittering and patterned fabrics, which caused the wooden hang bar to bend inwards. Stella diligently picked out a few pieces and flung them backwards onto her bed. Then she stood, one arm poised on her hip, as she contemplated her selection. Her focused stare, and the way she chewed the corner of her lip, reminded Nikka of the look Sums got when he was trying to solve a particularly difficult equation.

This was one of many similarities that Nikka had drawn between her two unlikely friends. At first, when confronted with Sums, Stella would jerk away from him as if he had bird flu. In response, Sums always spoke to her slowly, making sure to enunciate each and every syllable, as if speaking to a child. Eventually Stella refused to sit with them altogether, under the pretext that doing so would cause irreparable damage to her social status, but they were now two weeks into the semester, and despite Stella's desperate efforts she was rarely invited to sit at Violet's table. In fact Sums, Stella and Nikka had spent their first weekend at the Academy exploring the school grounds, collecting red leaves, and making hot chocolate; not exactly what Stella would call a blossoming social calendar.

Sums was equally as unimpressed with Stella as she was with him, and he couldn't understand why Nikka chose to be friends with her at all, but Nikka knew that behind the shallow first impression Stella gave, her roommate was a sweet, naïve, and kind girl.

"You. Are. Wearing...THIS!" yelped Stella triumphantly. She threw a short corseted leather dress onto Nikka's bed and paired it with a long red blazer and black suede boots.

"I'm not working the late shift on Hollywood Boulevard," protested Nikka.

"Look, this is the first party of the year and I wasn't even *really* invited," whined Stella. She looked up at the ceiling, embarrassed at her own confession. Nikka knew Stella had only been invited because Marcus Jenkins, one of Izaya's sleazy buddies, had his prowling eye on her, and even then Stella still had to *ask* to be invited.

"It's a miracle I can bring you in the first place, and worst of all you insisted on bringing Sums! That's not going to make us look any better. So can you please do this? For me?" pleaded Stella.

"Fine," Nikka grimaced.

Unwillingly, Nikka put the tight leather dress on and zipped up the long suede boots. Then she threw on the blazer, happy to be at least partially covered up. She ruffled her long blond mane of hair and combed some water through the kinky curls.

"Wow! You know, you're actually very pretty when you try," teased Stella.

"Gee, thanks," muttered Nikka sarcastically. Stella flicked back her pink wristwatch and checked it.

"It's almost time," she said.

It was an hour past lights out, which was irrelevant, because as Nikka had quickly found out, no one in the dorm really cared about this policy. Most girls in the dorm, including Stella, had brought lamps from home, so they weren't dependent on the overhead dorm lights that switched off automatically at 10:00pm. Yes, it was against the rules, but it's not like sweet Magdalena, their House Matron, would ever tell.

It seemed like the entirety of the student body was buzzing about the upcoming party in town, although no one actually knew where it would take place, and not everyone was invited. Because of the Dean's strict rules the invitees would receive an address scribbled on a piece of paper on the day of the party. Marcus Jenkins had slipped Stella her invite at lunch and Stella had clung to it like it was gold. The scrap of paper didn't even have an address on it, just geographic coordinates. Apparently this was how all parties at Wildwood were organized. They had decided to wait two full hours after lights out before attempting to sneak out. Precisely at midnight, a quiet knock resounded on the other side of the door. Nikka crept over to it and shot Stella a playful look.

"Password, please!" she whispered through the keyhole.

"Password?" came a confused muffled voice. They could hear Sums digging through his pant pockets in search of a password he may have written down and forgotten. Nikka took pity on the boy and opened the door.

"Sums, it's a joke," she said beaming at him. Sums exhaled deeply, clearly relieved that his supreme intelligence had not been tested by something so simple. He flashed an anxious smile at each girl.

"Oh no, you're not *really* wearing that!" hissed Stella, looking horrified.

"Here we go again," muttered Nikka.

"What's wrong with it?" asked Sums. He turned to look at his green cargo shorts and Hawaii-patterned button-down in the mirror, and then at Nikka, questioningly. She rolled her eyes in response.

"Purple! And Hawaii print, Sums? Really? It's not 1995 anymore," complained Stella, and she disappeared back into her closet. Seconds later she reemerged and handed Sums a shirt. Sums stared at it, and then at Stella, dumbfounded.

"An ex-boyfriend, okay? Sentimental value. I kept it...so sue me!" mumbled Stella, looking slightly embarrassed.

"At least he had taste," she added resentfully, after Nikka and Sums had both swallowed a chuckle.

"I don't need taste. I'm a math protégé," said Sums grumpily.

"I'll be right back," he added shyly before walking into the bathroom and locking the door. Sums reemerged dressed in a navy polo that brought out his blue eyes but clung very tightly to his full frame.

"I look like a retired polo player," he said with irritation.

"No, you look great!" reassured Stella, shoving Sums toward the door. Nikka followed them out into the dark quiet hallway.

When they had tiptoed all the way down the stairs and up to the front door Nikka stopped abruptly.

"The windows are locked," she said, pointing.

"Damn," whispered Stella, "And the front door alarm rings if anyone uses it after 10:00. How the hell are we supposed to get out of here unnoticed?" Stella gestured at the small blinking device mounted above the door.

"That's not really a problem for me," responded Sums. He pulled out an ID card, scanned it by the door and the light flashed green. "I hacked the school system so my card registers as staff instead of student. I can come and go when I please."

The girls stared at him in amazement.

"Most people scale the wall, or bribe staff to let them out, but my method is more sophisticated. I'm a pretty decent hacker," he bragged. Stella and Nikka stared at him for a few seconds, dumbfounded, then hurried after him into the chilly night air.

It took a half an hour's walk through the forest, and the use of a compass on Sums' cellphone, before they finally arrived at their destination. *No associating with townies. No drinking*. The Dean's two most fundamental, and punishable, rules. Of course. it made sense that Wildwood students would take such precautions.

The log cabin where the party was being held was at the end of a quiet suburban street on the edge of town. There were more similar cabins nestled in the distance, but this one stood a good way away from the residential cluster, right by the forest, conveniently placed for a party. Music roared from the windows and the heavy bass shook the pine-covered sidewalk. A group of teenagers huddled outside, smoking cigarettes and dancing.

Suddenly Nikka felt shy, she looked down at her short leather dress and felt herself growing more self-conscious with every step. Stella, on the other hand, was discreetly pushing up her breasts. They walked past a group of boys chatting on the porch, one of them was playing the guitar, and Stella waved at him flirtatiously as they passed. Sums pushed the screen door that led into the house. Once inside, the three friends squinted through the cloud of smoke. Nikka couldn't see much except for Sums at her side. He shot her a nervous look.

On the left of them was the kitchen. People were popping open beer, tapping the keg, gulping back shots and pouring foamy champagne into red plastic cups. Sums handed her and Stella a couple of beers from a cooler on the floor. After they had made a few rounds of the house, and after Markus Jenkins had led Stella off to "show her the patio," Sums and Nikka ended up downstairs by the sofa area. That's where she saw *him*. As usual, Izaya had one hand wound tightly around Violet's tiny waist; he was smoking a cigar with the other. He was chatting to a couple of boys sitting across from him while Violet's girl gang crowded loyally behind her. Nikka was surprised to see Violet's 'casual wear': a black velvet dress, heavy, dark eye make-up, and lacy black cut-off gloves. She was pale as ever, and her jet-black hair was tied up in a tight ponytail. She looked like a burlesque star.

Izaya's eyes wandered across the smoky room and widened at the sight of Nikka. Nikka desperately wanted to turn around and pretend she hadn't seen him, but that would make her look like a coward. Sums attempted to dance and stumbled into Nikka by accident, pushing her straight towards Izaya and his crowd. Decisively, she closed the remaining few feet between them and stood facing the circle of strangers. They all shifted their expectant gazes towards her.

"Hello," she mustered feebly. Nikka could instantly tell that the two boys sitting across from Izaya were townies. The distinction was easy to make - the boy closest to her had a plethora of facial piercings, and the boy who sat farther away had a shaved head and two sleeve tattoos. These physical features were not forbidden at Wildwood, but at a school filled with the children of America's elite, they were rare. The heavily pierced boy observed Nikka's legs with hungry interest.

He put his drink down on the table in front of him, which was littered with ash and empty shot glasses.

"Hey, doll, come join us," he said and fiddled with his lip ring.

"Ignore him," said Izaya. He disentangled his hand from Violet and reached it out for her to shake. "My name is Izaya," he looked amused as he took in her outfit.

"I'm Nikka," she answered, stunned for a moment by his lack of recognition. *We've met twice,* she wanted to add. Violet simply looked bored by the exchange.

"I'm Violet," she said importantly. "That's Cher, Aubrey and Lauren." She waved her hand dismissively in the direction of her fan club.

"That's Zac and Alex," said Izaya matching the disinterest in Violet's tone and pointing at the opposite couch, where the two townies sat.

"This is Alex's house," added Izaya matter-of-factly.

"Great party," said Nikka politely in the direction of the hairless townie.

"All the credit there goes to Izaya," responded Alex hastily.

He had blue eyes and colorful tattoos that wound up from his wrists to his shoulders. The boy seemed reluctant to receive praise for the party that was taking place at his own house.

"This is Sums, by the way," added Nikka.

"Oh, we all know who he is," said Izaya. The group

laughed. Nikka did not laugh; she shot Izaya a questioning look. Although Sums was smiling brightly at the mere mention of his name, something told her Izaya's words were not meant as a compliment.

"Sums, why don't you take a shot with us!" Violet suggested, in a sickly sweet tone. She suddenly seemed interested. Sums briefly hesitated, then nodded. Violet look pleased. Zac got up and disappeared into the kitchen, reemerging with an array of shot glasses and a large frosted bottle of brown liquid.

"House special," said Izaya. He smiled a perfect white smile, and poured out the shots.

"To new acquaintances," he said, and looked straight at Nikka.

Nikka forced down the brown liquid and grimaced as it burned in her throat. Sums too attempted to discreetly repress a coughing fit. Izaya watched Nikka, that air of amusement in his gaze; as if she were a form of light entertainment.

"Nice dress," he said, running his eyes over her.

"How do you like the Academy so far?" asked Alex. Nikka broke eye contact with Izaya and faced him.

"It's amazing," said Nikka happily, "It's still hard to believe I even ended up here."

The boy observed her, seeming irritated.

"That's what they all say, *at first*," he mumbled glumly, and took a heavy swig from the dented can of beer in his hand. He looked away from her.

"What do you mean?" inquired Nikka politely. The boy swayed in his seat, he was visibly drunk and seemed already to regret what he had let slip.

"It's nothing," he said.

"Alex here hates the Academy, because of our townie rules," said Izaya patronizingly.

"It's not that," growled Alex. He looked embarrassed and angry. "They just do things...the wrong way," he explained, fidgeting with frustration. The boy seemed to be having a hard time picking the right words.

He steadied himself on the arm of the couch, in an attempt not to seem like he was drunkenly ranting.

"Sums, darling, time for another shot!" cooed Violet seductively, and her entourage broke into a fit of giggles. Sums obeyed and reluctantly knocked back another glass before being seized by another aggressive coughing fit. Nikka turned her attention back to Alex.

"What exactly do you mean 'the wrong way'?" she asked, intrigued.

"Don't listen to him," said Izaya dismissively.

Alex seemed annoyed by this, he inched closer to Nikka, determined to finish vocalizing his opinion.

"Did you know Wildwood expels about five students each year?" he asked, and waited for her reaction.

"We have a really strict code of conduct," retorted Izaya.

Alex ignored him. "Whatever, Wildwood is immoral, everyone knows it," he snorted.

"You're starting to sound like your uncle, dude," said Zac, a smidgeon of warning nestled in his voice.

Alex looked livid; he grabbed a shot off the table and gulped it down effortlessly. Then he got up and walked off without another word. Nikka watched the boy stumble away and wondered what had caused him to become so upset.

"Don't mind him," said Zac, tilting his head toward her as if they were having an intimate conversation.

"For him it's personal," he explained. "His uncle was jailed multiple times for trespassing on your school. He's a journalist who always thought there was a story there, and turns out there isn't. Now he lives in Alex's basement. When he's not in jail," explained Zac.

"Poor guy," said Nikka.

Zac inched closer; Nikka could smell the cheap beer on his breath. He seemed less interested in their conversation and more interested in staring down the neckline of her dress. Nikka tried to move away in a subtle manner. Something behind her caught Zac's eye.

"I think your friend has had a little too much," he said, looking over at Sums. Nikka had been so preoccupied with the conversation with Alex that she hadn't noticed what was happening behind her. Sums had clearly surpassed his low alcohol tolerance threshold. He was now balancing on one foot, a shot poised on his head, while Violet happily called out math equations for him to solve.

"674" he yelled eagerly in response.

"85643."

"14."

Sums wobbled heavily and slipped off balance, which caused the shot on his head to spill across his face. Lauren, one of Violet's lackeys, quickly refilled the glass and placed it back on his wet and sticky curls. Sums blinked like mad, his eyes burning from the dark liquid that had spilled into them.

"Don't give up," cheered Violet over the laughing crowd. "We believe in you."

Sums obediently began to balance on one leg again. He was sweating profusely and his blue eyes were drifting in and out of focus. The one leg that was supporting him shook weakly. The surrounding crowd snickered; Violet and her friends laughed the loudest. Izaya, too, was grinning.

Nikka walked over to Sums and gently tugged on his arm.

"246738," he yelled loudly.

"Sums, you're drunk, let's go," pleaded Nikka.

"No," said Sums, "They dared me. I'm having fun," he explained, seeming unconvinced.

"Could you please move? We can't see the show," came Violet's commanding voice from behind her. Nikka turned around and shot her an angry look.

"Sums, they're making fun of you," she whispered gently. Sum's bright smile faltered momentarily. He glanced at the surrounding crowd, seeming unsure.

"No" he snapped back. "I'm fine. Leave me alone," he slurred his words.

Nikka looked desperately at her friend, then at the crowd, and realized there was nothing she could do. She stormed off and shot Izaya a disgusted parting look. Nikka walked off quickly, not looking where she was going, and collided hard against an oncoming body. She looked up to apologize, and her eyes settled on Tristan, who was smiling widely; he reached out and steadied her.

"You're a dangerous pedestrian," he said, and laughed warmly.

Nikka smiled back, "I'm so sorry, I was just..." she looked back at the sofa room. "Distracted."

Tristan observed her carefully.

"Would you like to play pool?" he asked. Nikka noticed that there was a large pool table behind him.

"I don't know how," she admitted.

"I'll teach you," he countered instantly, and smiled his signature crooked smile.

Tristan came up behind her and gently positioned his arms around hers. He pulled her hand back and shot the ball into the colored mass, causing a few balls to sink into the holes.

“There you go. Now you try it,” he said, and let go of her hands. Nikka hit a single ball, which sunk into a corner hole. She yelped happily.

"I got one in!" she squealed, proudly. “How many points do I get for that?"

"Well..." Tristan scratched the top of his head, "you’ve actually got the black ball in, which I’m afraid means you’ve lost the entire game." Tristan stifled a laugh as he watched the surprise register on Nikka’s face.

"That’s not fair," she said and pushed Tristan away playfully.

"You know, alcohol has statistically been proven to improve people’s pool playing skills. I’ll go grab us a drink,” said Tristan with a teasing grin.

He disappeared into the kitchen.

When Tristan returned he handed Nikka tall glass of something pink.

“It’s delicious,” said Nikka with surprise.

"I spent all of last summer bartending," he explained.

Nikka couldn’t help but wonder why someone would bother spending a whole summer working if they had the luxury not to.

Nikka shot the first ball and landed one in. She looked up proudly.

“Told you,” said Tristan. “Pool is the only sport where alcohol can be a performance enhancing substance.” They took turns, and even with her inferior knowledge of pool

Nikka could tell that he was an exceptional player. They played two games, and Tristan replaced Nikka's drink twice. The room was starting to spin a little and the music sounded better to Nikka than it had before.

"So, how come you are so good at this?" asked Nikka as she prepared to shoot. Tristan put his arms around hers again and repositioned her hands into the proper form. She could feel his warm breath on her neck.

"Pool, poker, blackjack, roulette. I'm good at all my vices," he said cheekily and smiled. He pulled back her hands and shot three balls in. He lingered for a moment and didn't take his arms off hers. The room was dancing before Nikka's eyes. Tristan was inches away from her. His breath was hot and it smelled of whisky.

"A gambler and a thief," she whispered. "How very poetic."

Tristan smiled. His face got a little closer.

"I have many other fundamental flaws left for you to discover," he whispered. Nikka was about to answer, but she was cut off.

"Wow, you really choose your company poorly," came a velvety voice from the door. Izaya was leaning against the doorframe and watching them. Nikka realized he was talking to her. She was just about to respond that the company she kept had absolutely nothing to do with him, but Tristan was quicker.

"Why don't you go stare at yourself in the mirror, or

whatever it is you do for fun," he said, dismissively, not even looking at Izaya. He let go of Nikka, fixated on his pool cue, and potted three balls with one shot. Izaya took a slow swig from his tumbler and then a step forward.

"That really is a ridiculous accent for someone from Massachusetts," he said, venomously.

This time Tristan looked up.

"Not that it's any of your business, but I went to boarding school in Ireland," he said, and he looked at Nikka, as if he were justifying it to her, rather than to Izaya.

"Yeah, well I went to boarding school in France. Doesn't mean I speak like a Parisian pastry chef," said Izaya.

"You trying to say I'm faking it?" asked Tristan struggling to remain calm. He balled his fists.

"No, I'm trying to say you're unsuccessfully faking it," said Izaya calmly. The angrier he made Tristan, the calmer he seemed to be.

"Right, well you're doing a very successful impression of a trust fund baby who's never been denied anything in his life," said Tristan.

This comment struck a nerve with Izaya. Nikka could see anger spread across his face like a brewing storm.

"Don't try to act all holier than thou just because you're trying to impress *her,*" Izaya accusingly jerked his head in Nikka's direction.

"You're no hard-working scholarship kid either," he added.

Tristan observed Izaya with a mixture of annoyance and pity. Nikka had the feeling that the two boys did not know each other well, but had heard just enough through the grapevine to be able to insult each other successfully. This particular standoff, she realized, had been brought on by her presence. She tried to think of the right thing to say to calm both boys down, but before she could come up with anything useful, a strange sight through the window caught her eye. Nikka watched as four masked figures approached the house; their appearance was followed by an earsplitting scream.

A sense of panic overwhelmed Nikka as more screams sounded from the other rooms. Suddenly she felt herself being grabbed by both Izaya and Tristan, one on each arm. Both boys dragged her towards the crowded back door exit amidst erupting screams of "run!" and "guards!" Midway out the door Nikka realized that she was leaving an unknowing Sums and Stella behind. Izaya had lost hold of her arm and was being pressed back by the panicked crowd as people pushed and shoved in their attempt to make it out the back door. Sirens echoed in the distance and Nikka dived to the right, headed straight for the sofa room.

Nikka searched the passing faces for a sign of her friends. The guards had entered the house and were closing in on her. She didn't know what to do or where to run; all she knew was that getting expelled over a stupid party would be the worst possible thing that could happen. Tristan appeared behind her.

"Jump, I'll distract them," he urged, shoving her in the direction of the open first floor window. Nikka hesitated, not wanting to leave Tristan behind. She looked back at him but he pushed her more persistently.

"Trust me," he pleaded, and with one more push she was off.

Nikka landed hard on the muddy ground of the backyard. Commotion and the sound of breaking glass resonated behind her and she worried about Tristan. In the distance she could see the approaching police lights. They lit up the dark suburban street in a cascade of red and blue. A few remaining students ran past her, headed for the woods. She followed them. Once concealed in the shelter of the trees the students scattered in different directions, laughing wildly. Nikka could not take the path they had used to get to the party because it was too close to the main road, so instead she just ran in the general direction of campus.

She ran for a few minutes until her sides hurt so much that she had to stop. She inhaled rhythmically in a futile attempt to regain her composure. The cold night air prickled her throat and caused a dull ache in her ears. Her lungs felt like they had overextended themselves, like they were balloons about to burst.

There was a noise behind her. Nikka held her breath.

It was the sound of crunching leaves below someone's feet. Nikka pressed herself tighter to the tree, digging her nails into the bark. As the footsteps got closer, Nikka prepared to run. She pushed herself off the tree and lurched forward but was grabbed from behind. A hand covered her mouth and muted her scream. The strong figure wrestled her to the ground. Both of them collapsed on a bed of dry leaves and Nikka jerked furiously in attempt to push him away, but she was immobilized by his weight on top of her. When her eyes finally settled she saw that the figure was Izaya. He pulled his hand away from her mouth and smiled.

"Gotcha!" he said and laughed loudly. With every inch of strength in her body Nikka threw him off her, as violently as she could. Izaya landed on his back with a thump.

"Was it you the whole time?" she snarled. Izaya laughed.

"Oh, you should have seen your face! I saw you running past me and I followed you," he explained merrily, as if it were the most normal thing in the world for a person to do.

"And at what point did you decide to assault me?" she hissed. She looked at him with fury in her gray eyes.

Suddenly, there was another noise.

Izaya drew a finger to his mouth to hush her, and when Nikka reluctantly went quiet she heard voices; a group of people were approaching. Izaya grabbed her by the hand and she followed him. He crouched and walked slowly. They made their way in the opposite direction to the footsteps, which seemed to grow closer with every second. Izaya led her downhill till they reached a decaying tunnel, hidden from view by surrounding foliage. Once inside, Nikka realized that they were in what used to be a water drain. She wanted to ask Izaya how he had known about the random water drain in the middle of the woods, but she kept silent and listened to the footsteps approach.

Harsh, low voices sounded from just a few feet above them.

"You think anyone is trying to run away this time?" asked a rasping male voice.

Another responded. "Not if I can help it."

"Call the Dean, tell him we've cleared the party up," said a third.

*Guards...*Nikka realized with horror as she watched the shadows approach.

Nikka felt Izaya's hand push her gently, deeper and deeper into the shadows of the drain tunnel. She was so absorbed in listening to the footsteps, her back pressed against the cold, damp surface of the tunnel wall that she barely noticed how close to her Izaya was standing. A moment later, his lips touched hers. It was over in a second, and Nikka felt like she had been zapped with a live wire. The loud crack of a breaking branch resounded in the distance and the guards sprinted off in hot pursuit. Nikka pushed Izaya away.

"What on earth did you do that for?" she asked. Her hand flew up to her lips, which felt like they were burning. She desperately hoped that in the darkness Izaya would not see how red she had gone.

Izaya seemed entirely unfazed; he leaned against the opposite wall of the tunnel and lit a cigarette.

"You breathe loudly," he said nonchalantly, "it was the only way to shut you up." Nikka looked at him, shocked. He smiled briefly then turned and walked away. Nikka struggled to keep up with him; despite her anger, the last thing she wanted was to be left alone again in an unknown part of the woods.

"Why do they wear masks?" she asked, after a long period of silence. The pair walked side by side on what Nikka hoped was the way back to the dorms. She had been contemplating why she had felt so afraid of the very people that were supposed to protect them. Izaya looked at her.

"The children of some pretty powerful people attend this school. I think the masks are meant to protect the guards' identities from the mommies and daddies that might be inclined to do something if their children got expelled."

"They are afraid of retribution?" asked Nikka, shocked that such intricate politics had any place at a high school.

Izaya nodded.

"It's also a useful intimidation technique. You'll get used to it," he promised. Nikka did not see how she could ever get used to masked figures chasing her through the woods.

When they reached Roseland, Izaya's demeanor turned callous again.

"Goodnight," he said, coldly.

He turned away from her and stood silently, waiting for her to leave.

"Goodnight, and thank you," she mumbled, through gritted teeth. He might have been the most insolent, arrogant boy she had ever met, but he had led her out of the forest safely and hidden her from the guards, and for that she was grateful.

"The pleasure was all mine," he replied, so smugly that Nikka instantly regretted thanking him.

There was no longer a need to disable the alarm, which meant it was past 5:00am and Nikka quietly and warily climbed up the stairs to her room. Nikka's body was buzzing - the running, the drinking, and the sheer adrenaline had shaken her to the core, but she had liked it. Her hazy mind was addled with questions; she wondered about Alex's attitude, about Izaya's unexplainable actions, and about how Violet would feel if she knew that he had kissed her. She worried about what had happened to Tristan, and felt guilty that she had been with Izaya during it. The only solace her mind found was when she walked through her dorm room door and found Stella comfortably snoring in her bed, with Sums safely curled up in a blanket on the floor.

6

Remember This

The last two last weeks of September rolled by. Wildwood slowly succumbed to fall foliage, and the grounds faded from green, to yellow, to brown, with occasional bursts of bright red. Nikka had not thought much about the odd party that had taken place over a week ago; or at least she had tried not to. Her mind, and the minds of many Wildwood students, were now preoccupied with the announcement of the 'mid semester showcase.' On the Monday of the last week of September, the Dean had sent out a newsletter, which had informed all Wildwood students that they would be showcasing their work at the end of October. For Sums that meant proving a theory for the math department; for Stella it meant presenting her designs; and for Nikka, it meant exhibiting her artwork at the school Gallery, for the whole student body to see. Furthermore, the newsletter informed them that at the end of the semester the Dean himself would evaluate their progress in a one-on-one consultation.

"End of semester evaluations are the 'make or break' moment," Sums had told her that morning at breakfast, "if the Dean isn't happy..." Sums drew a finger across his throat.

End of semester evaluations were still a good three months away, and Nikka had only recently started her second workshop class, with two more scheduled for that very day, so it seemed premature to worry. But the idea that she only had two months left to do something impressive terrified her.

Nikka pushed her pancake around on her plate. Sums was content to eat in silence, he had a lot to worry about too. Nikka pulled out her class schedule and studied it. Sums had been helping her in math, but she also had an upcoming science test, and Madame Grenoble's weekly Bataillisme classes had grown more intense with each session, which were now bi-weekly. She had also started a simple technical drawing workshop with Stella, which involved self-portraits, ruffled fabrics and brass bowls of fruit.

"Don't worry too much," said Sums catching her gaze. "You're very talented, they'll keep you either way."

Somehow the idea that she could be kept or not kept, like a pair of shoes, did not make Nikka feel better.

"Thanks," she mumbled, half-heartedly.

"Stella, on the other hand..." joked Sums, but Nikka shot him a warning look and he stopped. Nikka looked across the cafeteria. Ever since the party Stella had eaten all her breakfasts with Marcus Jenkins. The two were an item now. Stella was overjoyed, but Nikka didn't like the boy. Something about him was *off*.

Nikka waited for Sums to finish his hearty meal of eggs and chorizo, then the pair made their way out of the cafeteria. They were strolling down the familiar spiral path that connected the cafeteria and their classrooms when they noticed a commotion up ahead. A group of students had formed a half-circle by a large building on the border of the school grounds, facing the southern edge of the forest. Nikka spotted the familiar faces of Izaya and Tristan amidst the crowd. She wandered closer and craned her neck like a bird to catch a glimpse of the scene that had them all so captivated.

Two bulky guards, dressed in the usual red and black Wildwood Security uniforms, with monstrously large arms, were holding a thin spectacled man. The man was thrashing about like a fish out of water, in a manic attempt to escape the guards' grip. The man groaned as they pushed him against the nearby fence with a degree of violence that made Nikka cringe. In the process they nearly smashed the large camera that hung around the man's neck.

"I know what's going on here!" The man yelled. His

voice broke down to a squeal as he was shoved against the wall again and again. He waved a thin finger at the crowd of watching students.

"40 expulsions in the last 5 years alone?" He spat. The guards were trying to drag him away and cover his mouth at the same time, but the man seemed to be stronger then he looked, for he continued to thrash back and forth vigorously despite their efforts. His giant camera lens slapped against the guards' faces and he managed to escape from their iron grasp long enough to yell at the crowd.

"I'm going to get to the bottom of this. You can't do this. I won't LET YOU!" he screamed at the top of his lungs.

Suddenly, the man dropped to the floor and began to shake violently; a cloud of dust rose above him as he was overtaken by a seizure. Nikka looked up just in time to see one of the guards stash a Taser back into his pocket before they both seized the limp man and began to drag him away. Moments later, the only trace left of the disturbance was two winding trails in the dusty path left by his dragging feet, and a few scattered shards of broken camera lens.

To Nikka, the wrinkled middle-aged man had seemed disturbed in every sense of the word. Seconds before he fell Nikka had watched his face contort in sheer agony, and she knew that whatever pain this man was in, it went well beyond the realm of the physical. She felt sorry for him, and outraged at the guards' violent behavior towards someone who was clearly distraught. Nikka was surprised when she looked around and found the rest of her classmates looking amused. A little way away, Izaya was laughing with his friends.

"That gave me a strange feeling in my stomach," said Sums; he laid one hand on his inflated gut and looked like he was about to be sick. Nikka nodded, feeling sick herself.

"Don't worry about it. That guy comes round here all the time," came a sudden voice from behind them, and Nikka knew from its velvety tone to whom it belonged.

"He's a journalist, and a nut job." Izaya said the two words as if they were one and the same. He approached her slowly; a small, almost cruel grin on his smug, perfect face.

"He comes around every now and then talking about conspiracies. Man never landed on the moon; JFK was killed by the C.I.A; the Academy is evil, etcetera..."

He chuckled at his own wit. Nikka glared back at him.

Zero compassion, she said to herself with irritation. She was reminded that this was the first time Izaya had bothered to address her since their forest encounter. She pushed away the sudden wave of hurt the realization caused. Izaya stared back comfortably, without blinking. The corners of his lips twitched into another winning smile; he was amused by her anger.

"Doesn't mean he has to be dragged away like an

animal," she replied, calmly. "But I guess the guards *also* suffer from a superiority complex." She spat, clearly indicating that the 'also' was targeted at Izaya.

Izaya had an intrigued look on his face. He looked surprised, as if no one had ever spoken to him in that way. He looked her up and down, studying her. Nikka felt her cheeks flush from his overtly intimate gaze, and turned to walk away.

"You sure told him! He's such a jerk," said Sums, struggling to catch his breath as he caught up with her. He looked at her with wide-eyed admiration. Nikka glanced over her shoulder just in time to catch a glimpse of Izaya safely back in Violet's arms. She promised herself to never think of the forest night again, and wondered what Sums would think of her if he knew that, for the briefest moment, she had allowed herself to think that Izaya was something more than the school snob. The two of them stopped to consult their new schedules, which had been handed out that morning.

"Alright I'm off to *M.D.*," said Nikka, reading the name of her new studio class list. "Whatever that is," she added.

"Good luck. They've got me on statistics duty," said Sums.

It took ages for Nikka to locate her new classroom, and when she tried the door to the small log cabin, it was locked. She sat down on the stoop and opened her sketchbook with the intention of drawing until the instructor arrived.

Suddenly, she heard giggles and hushed voices resounding from behind the cabin. Curious, she got up quietly, circled the cabin and peeked around the wall. Behind the cabin Izaya was with a girl, kissing her. His frame leaned into her, pushing her towards the wall. She came up for air and giggled again. Nikka recognized her instantly: *Jordan,* Violet's best friend. Nikka gasped, and they both looked up. Jordan met her eyes and instantly looked guilty, scared and pathetic, like a dog caught stealing food. Nikka backtracked and quickly returned to the front of the cabin. Jordan shuffled past her and muttered something in passing.

"I...umm...was just looking for my class. Sorry," she said over her shoulder, and ran off. Nikka hugged her backpack to her chest, unsure of how to feel about the scene she had just witnessed. Izaya appeared behind her. He looked a little flustered, his hair was ruffled and his shirt out of place. He smiled down at her as if nothing had happened.

"I didn't see anything," said Nikka, facing away from him.

"I don't..." started Izaya, but she cut him off.

"You don't owe me an explanation!" She snapped. Izaya smiled.

"I wasn't going to give you one," he said slyly, re-buttoning his top button. Nikka watched his Adam's apple bob up and down as he swallowed.

"Why are you lingering?" she asked, annoyed.

Just then, a short man came down the path in front of them. He was clearly a teacher. He wore glasses, had simple rigid features, a briefcase and a suit.

"Good morning!" he said pleasantly. "You must be Izaya, and you must be Vieranikka. Pleased to meet you both," he nodded curtly. "My name is Adam Jones. Come in, please."

Nikka looked at Izaya, dumfounded. Izaya had a glint of mischief in his eye. He stifled a laugh as he watched Nikka's face as she realized that they had a class together, *that's why he was lingering, you idiot.* Her face flushed.

"You have got to be kidding me," she muttered under her breath before entering the classroom. Izaya followed her with a chuckle. Inside the room there were three computers and three desks. Adam Jones sat in front of the farthest desk.

Izaya and Nikka took the two other seats silently.

"So I'm going to be teaching your *M.D* workshop, which stands for memory development. There will be four sessions altogether. I'm a computer developer, and my company is currently developing software that trains people's memory, visual recognition and image awareness. This workshop will mainly consist of the two of you using this software."

Izaya sighed, displeased. Nikka suddenly remembered

the first time she had ever heard his voice: the conversation she had overheard, in which he said he didn't want to be at Wildwood in the first place.

"Oh, give it a chance," the professor picked up on Izaya's irritation. "People are going to be paying thousands for this kind of self-improvement software. And it's in the form of a game, so it's fun."

"And why is this useful for us, specifically?" asked Nikka. *Why are there just two of us,* was her real question.

"The board decided this would be *particularly* useful to the two of you," he paused. "And because we want to try this software on people from both technical and art backgrounds."

Izaya snorted.

"Welcome to Wildwood Academy, where students and lab rats are one and the same," said Izaya rudely.

Nikka squeezed back into her seat uncomfortably. She had never heard someone be that rude to a teacher before. *He doesn't care about consequences,* thought Nikka bitterly. Kissing Jordan, kissing her, mouthing off to a teacher he had just met. Adam seemed annoyed, but reluctant to pursue the conversation further. He wasn't much older than Izaya, and he didn't look like he liked conflict. After an excruciatingly long explanation of what the exact benefits of this intricate software were, a speech, which served as his revenge for Izaya's snide commentary, Professor Jones launched the program and

Nikka got to work.

While Nikka wasn't quite sure why she was playing this game, she had to admit that it *was* fun, although it got more challenging as they went along. There were two pictures, each of cathedrals, forests, and cities, and Nikka had to spot the differences between the two frames, like the 'spot the difference' games at the back of most children's magazines.

A branch here, a gargoyle wing missing there; frame by frame they came and went, lightning fast, and Nikka was acing it, rearranging the pictures, finding the errors again and again and again. She relaxed and enjoyed the Indian music Adam was playing in the background. Every now and then came a frustrated grunt from where Izaya was sitting. Nikka smiled; pleased that it was he who was frustrated for a change.

They wrapped up two hours later. Nikka felt stimulated and sharp, the way you do after seeing an interesting play or reading a good book. They said their goodbyes to Professor Jones and walked out. Outside of the cabin Violet was sitting on the steps, one leg crossed seductively over the other.

"I saw your new schedule. This room is hard to find," she said. Then she spotted Nikka behind Izaya and her smile faltered. She looked past Nikka and into the cabin, "there's just the two of you in this class?"

"Don't ask," said Izaya crankily. He lit a cigarette and

walked right past her towards the woods. Violet looked a bit surprised. She hurried off the stairs and scurried after him, throwing an irritated look back at Nikka.

Nikka walked slowly through the bush-ridden path to her next class. She reached a small peaceful meadow framed by an array of oddly shaped studio buildings, and made her way to the very last studio in the long line-up. On a disheveled hedge next to the building sat a thin ginger-haired girl wearing a turquoise bohemian-style dress over ripped purple pants and gladiator sandals. Part of her red hair was sloppily braided; the rest was slightly matted into a bun and rested over her left shoulder. A thin crystal pendant hung around her neck.

Nikka recognized the girl as one of her classmates from *Technical Drawing*. The odd girl was using a stick to draw in the dirt beneath her feet, and in the dusty mess, Nikka could make out the outline of a winged creature.

"Hello, my name's Nikka," she said, reaching out her hand. The girl looked up distractedly, and her large green eyes settled on Nikka. She grabbed her hand and held it for while, a gesture that was a little different than the standard handshake Nikka had reached for.

"My name's Amber."

The girl looked back down and continued to draw details on what Nikka now recognized as a fairy's wings. Nikka took a place on the hedge beside her.

"Where's your uniform?" asked Nikka curiously, as

she took in Amber's funky outfit.

"I've misplaced it," said Amber casually. Nikka nodded, but found that odd, *how do you misplace an entire uniform?*

"Any idea what F.D. is?" she asked, as she too picked up a stick and began to draw small flowers in the dirt a little distance away. There was a long pause.

"I'm hoping it means Finish Draping, or Folklore Drawing, or Flower Design," said Amber, as she absentmindedly drew roots onto Nikka's flowers. Nikka started to laugh, but saw from the girl's unchanging profile that she was being serious.

"I'm guessing your workshop classes are as weird as mine?" asked Nikka.

"If you consider sketching live animal sacrifices weird, then I would say *yes*," answered the girl pensively.

Nikka didn't move, unable to muster up an appropriate reaction. Amber nudged her gently in the rib.

"*That* was a joke," she said softly and grinned. Nikka exhaled a sigh of relief, then burst out laughing.

"They mostly make me draw boring sceneries and stills," Amber clarified.

A group of girls had appeared in the meadow, sitting down a few yards away from Nikka and Amber. Amongst them Nikka spotted Jordan, Violet and Lauren, the other 'best friend'. Nikka frowned at the realization that they were waiting for the same class.

"Great, my day can't get any better," she mumbled sarcastically.

"Not a fan of Violet's group?" asked Amber.

Nikka watched Jordan closely. Jordan threw a cautious glance her way, then turned around quickly and hid behind her hair to avoid further eye contact with Nikka.

"Not really," said Nikka. "You?"

"I think those girls are nicer to look at than they are to talk to," said Amber earnestly. Nikka nodded; that was a good way of putting it. Violet noticed Nikka looking at her and whispered something into Jordan's ear. Jordan gave a nervous high-pitched laugh.

The door to the studio behind them opened. A middle aged ash blond woman walked out and stood on the studio stairs, wiping her coal-stained hands on a wet towel. She was wearing a loose peach-colored kimono, a prayer bead necklace and a headband that exposed her forehead wrinkles. She looked like someone who would have attended Woodstock. The woman smiled warmly at Amber as she took in her equally eccentric appearance, as if silently acknowledging that they were both cut from the same cloth.

"Come on in, everyone," she urged in a soothing voice.

Amber and Nikka greeted the woman and made their way into the studio, followed closely by Violet and her gang. There were no boys in this class. There was a chalkboard mounted on the wall and, on it, scribbled in chalk, were the words *Welcome to Figure Drawing*. In front of the board there was a stage, and in front of the stage was a semi-circle of eight easels and eight matching chairs. Nikka and Amber picked two seats next to each other and sat down.

"Figure drawing, that was my next guess," whispered Amber. Nikka chuckled.

"I'll make this short. My name is Mrs. Soraya Camden, and I will be your figure-drawing instructor. Please don't be timid, and let the sheer beauty of movement transport you to another plane. Welcome, and enjoy. *Namaste*," she said and gave a little bow. "*Namaste*," responded everyone in unison, except an unknowing Nikka.

"Please welcome, Kaira, our first model for the semester," said the Professor, before retreating from the stage. A young woman a few years older than Nikka walked in, took the stage and dropped her robe. She stood proud, emotionless and naked before the class. Then she sat down, and assumed her first pose.

Nikka was very impressed. Figure drawing models were a luxury most high schools couldn't afford; or perhaps public high schools were not allowed to show naked people to minors. Either way, Nikka thought she would have to wait until college to experience her first figure drawing class.

There was some brief hustle and bustle as the students reached for their pencils and coals, but a moment later stillness washed over the room. The studio was tense with concentration and inspection; the juvenile discomfort of seeing someone naked had quickly melted away and was replaced by curiosity and focus. There was only the dry sound of coal on paper.

An hour later, Nikka was finishing her last coal sketch. The professor walked up behind her and observed her work.

"Wow," she said encouragingly, "you really captured the individual poses. Good job, Nikka."

The compliment made Nikka grin with pride. She saw Violet purse her lips at the other end of the room, displeased. The professor walked up to Amber. "Good. Great work on the muscles," she whispered. Violet was next.

"You need to practice the hands, darling," she cooed, pointing at something on Violet's easel. "But other than that, it's *fine*," she added sweetly. A bell rang in the distance and students in the studio began packing up their supplies. Nikka tucked her coals back into the easel drawer and went to wash her hands. The hot water ran black. A saccharine voice sounded over her shoulder.

"I like your drawing," said Violet. "Not bad for a *freshman.*"

Nikka turned around to face her. Violet smiled,

revealing two rows of perfect teeth framed by her plump lips. She was wearing a dark shade of burgundy lipstick; her eyes were a cold, muted blue against the pale backdrop of her skin.

"Thank you," said Nikka coolly. She dried her hands off and Violet took her place at the washbasin. She washed her carefully manicured hands, taking care to lather each finger individually.

"I'm sure it will improve by the time I'm a *junior*," said Nikka cuttingly. Nikka was referring to the professor's earlier comment on Violet's work. Violet smiled, a mean little smile.

"Of course it will!" she said sweetly. "If you're still here, that is."

Violet dried her hands and walked off. Nikka had a strong urge to say something about Izaya having kissed her, or about him kissing Jordan earlier that day, but she wasn't that vindictive. Nikka packed up her things and left, and was surprised to find Amber waiting for her outside the studio.

"Would you like to get some lunch?" asked Amber.

"Gladly!" Nikka beamed. The two girls headed for the cafeteria, where they were joined by Sums and Stella.

"So you had a class with just Izaya?" asked Stella with great interest when they had all put their trays down. Nikka nodded.

"What's he like?" asked Stella eagerly. "I mean, I've

sat with him at lunch and all, but he never talks. He just observes..."

"He's alright. I don't really know," lied Nikka. Her stomach tightened a little as she thought of him kissing Jordan that morning. Sums looked at her, knowingly. He was strangely astute for someone with no love life. Nikka squared her soldiers and took a bite out of her Quiche Lorraine.

"I bet Violet wouldn't like that. Izaya in a class with just one other girl, and someone as pretty as Nikka," said Stella pensively.

"Oh, she didn't!" said Amber perking up. She looked up from her assortment of tofu and veggies.

"She was staring daggers at her the whole duration of our class. I thought she was going to challenge her to a duel or something. She looks *stressed,* if you ask me. I would recommend an energy cleanse," Sums looked at Amber, she smiled at him, and he instantly reddened and turned back to his lasagna.

Stella was looking at Amber with a little distaste. The hippie girl, with a sleepy manner, beaded braids, an absent uniform and arms stacked with prayer bracelets was the type of person Stella would expect to see at a music festival as she looked down from the VIP area, and not someone she would choose to share lunch with.

"So you said your class was taught by a programmer? What was his name? Where does he work? What did he say about himself?" asked Sums impatiently.

"Relax, question police," said Stella. She turned to Nikka. "Was he good looking?"

"Not your type," said Nikka with a chuckle. "He was a brainy sort of good looking."

"Nerds are always good looking. You can see intelligence on someone's face; it's like this special glow. It's very attractive," said Amber convincingly.

Stella looked at her like she was a crazy person. Sums swallowed uneasily, and glanced at Amber. Nikka knew that he was wondering whether he had that *glow*. Amber caught Stella gawking at her.

"You don't agree?" she asked.

"She's more into the type that can't read," said Sums, and Stella punched him lightly on the arm.

"I'll have you know, Marcus is going to be inheriting his father's company," said Stella importantly.

Everyone at the table looked at each other. There was a moment of quiet before the gang broke into a fit of laughter.

"You understand inheriting a company doesn't make you literate," said Sums. Nikka stifled another chuckle. Stella looked irritated.

"He wouldn't be inheriting it if he couldn't read! That was the point!" she said defensively.

Nikka changed the subject.

"Well, Violet is the 'don't talk to my boyfriend or you

won't be at this school next year type,'" she explained. "She basically implied that I wouldn't make it to Junior year."

"Oh my god, what did she say?" said Stella injecting more drama into her voice than was necessary.

"Maybe she's just having a bad day?" offered Amber.

"She probably just meant the high expulsion rate," said Sums comfortingly.

Is that what Violet meant? Wondered Nikka nervously. Did I misunderstand her?

"One violation of the cardinal rules and you're out." Sums continued obtusely. "It's like survival of the fittest out here."

"So in this weird scenario, having no social life makes you the fittest?" asked Stella.

Everyone laughed. Sums glowered at her.

"I have a social life," he said indignantly.

20 minutes later, and about three more helpings on Sums's part, the four of them made their way out of the cafeteria. Nikka said her goodbyes to Sums and the girls, and headed off to her geography class.

She was walking down a winding path when suddenly a man in a Wildwood staff uniform blocked her way. Nikka yelped out in surprise, and backed away a few steps.

"School messenger," explained the man formally. He handed her an envelope and marched off.

Nikka opened the envelope and pulled out a small

piece of folded paper. The note simply contained her name and summoned her to the nurse's office the next day for a check-up.

"They have weird way of doing things around here, huh?" said a familiar voice from behind her. Nikka turned around to face Tristan. He was wearing a gray flat cap hat, from which a few strands of wavy brown hair were escaping.

"Understatement of the century..." said Nikka wryly.

"The other day a 'messenger,'" he said, making air quotation marks around the term, "Brought me my rucksack, which I had actually left in the classroom on purpose so that it could serve as an excuse to not do my homework. He appeared out of bloody nowhere, handed it to me, and disappeared. I think they're trying to pretend that they are secret agents just to ease their own boredom."

Nikka laughed. "Listen," she said, shifting her weight from one leg to the other. "I never got a chance to thank you for what you did at the party..." she added, her voice trailing off mid-sentence.

"Don't worry about it," he said warmly. "If they had caught you they would have expelled you."

"Because I'm a scholarship kid," Nikka voiced the uncomfortable truth; scholarship students paid a heftier price for breaking the rules. Tristan nodded, but didn't seem condescending in the slightest. Nikka smiled at him gratefully. She was impressed that he had been so willing to take the fall for her. Nikka was just about to ask what had happened to him when the guards caught him, when Tristan consulted his pocket watch.

"I'm really late," he said, sounding disappointed. "I've got one of my eight detentions to do," he added gaily. Nikka suddenly felt terrible about what she had cost him, and Tristan saw this.

"I'll survive a couple of detentions," he said, kindly, just as Nikka was about to thank him again. Then he added cheekily, "I'm a sucker for a damsel in distress," and with that he walked away, leaving her with flushed cheeks and late for geography.

7

A Not So Healing Hand

After her classes finished the next day, Nikka made her way over to the nurse's office. Sums, a hypochondriac and rather frequent Health Center visitor, had pointed her in the right direction. When Nikka pushed through the double-glass entrance to the Health Center, she found herself tapping away down a long linoleum hallway, the walls of which were plastered with informative mental health posters.

Nikka inhaled the sterile air and grimaced; being there was making her feel anxious. She shuffled quickly past the numbered doors until she reached the nurse's office at the very end. The door gave way to reveal a large, fancy waiting room. A petite, mousy concierge sat behind a desk and fiddled with her cuticles. When she spotted Nikka she immediately pretended to be working. The woman gestured to the expensive leather chairs that encircled a glass coffee table in the middle of the room, and Nikka obediently took a seat. Seconds later, another woman emerged from a door in the corner of the room.

"Nikka Mason?" asked the woman.

"Yes," Nikka countered, feebly.

"The nurse will be right out, sweetie." The woman sized Nikka up for a second too long; almost as if she were trying to calculate her weight just by looking at her.

Nikka sat still for five more minutes and contemplated why it took two people to admit one patient to the nurse's office. In the end, she arrived at the conclusion that Wildwood was generally overstaffed for the sake of comfort and flash. A third woman, dressed in black scrubs emerged from the same door. Nikka observed the ogre-like woman with surprise; the nurse was muscular, very tall and with hands the size of Nikka's head. When the woman's icy blue eyes locked onto Nikka's, her thin, manly lips curled into a smile. Her face was a blunt-edge square, and her skin, as in Madame Grenoble's case, seemed unnaturally stretched over her face. Nikka thought again how many of Wildwood's staff seemed to be fond of plastic surgery, and how many of them seemed able to afford it. The woman seemed pleased to see her.

"Hello there, I'm Nurse Smith," she barked in a cheery alto, "and you must be Nikka!"

"Nice to meet you," said Nikka, forcing herself to

smile.

The nurse gestured for her to follow. Nikka hadn't been to many hospitals in her life, but as she followed Nurse Smith back into her office she knew that this woman didn't possess the comforting, gentle presence of the stereotypical nurse. In fact, her intimidating frame reminded Nikka more of an asylum nurse from the movies, the ones in charge of holding patients down. Nikka tried her best to breathe evenly as she followed the woman into her office. Medical check-ups had always made Nikka nervous.

The office, like most of the facilities at the school, was entirely different to what Nikka had expected. At her last middle school, the nurse's office was a long room vaguely reminiscent of Snow White's cabin, lined with short colorful beds, on which ill students could rest. The counters in that office were covered in cheerful Band-Aid choices, cartoon ice packs and sheets of stickers. The office she currently found herself in was the complete opposite. The metal shelves that lined the walls were meticulously stocked with hundreds of marked medicine bottles protected by locked glass cabinets. Two wide touch-screen computers hung on the walls and a small plastic red bin stood in the corner, stenciled with a black propeller type logo, and the word "hazardous."

In the middle of the white room stood one rather eerie recliner chair, the likes of which you would see in a dentist's office.

"Sit down, please" said the nurse.

Nikka walked hopefully towards another chair in the corner.

"No, not that one," said the nurse.

Nikka sighed and reluctantly climbed onto the recliner chair, the curvature of which forced her to lie down.

"So..." said the nurse, slipping on a pair of crisp plastic gloves with an audible slap, "How do you feel?"

Right now? Silly and terrified, were the first words that sprung into Nikka's head. Nikka's mother didn't like doctors, and rarely took Nikka for check ups; the anxiety in Nikka's stomach came from a lack of experience.

"I feel fine. No different to usual," she answered carefully.

"That's good," said the nurse. "So, I'm just going to do a couple of routine check-up tests, blood work, that kind of thing." She unpacked a few utensils by the counter. Nikka's head spun at the words *blood work* and she gripped the arm of the chair. Nurse Smith took her pulse and listened to her heartbeat.

"So, tell me, how is the new school treating you?" asked the large woman chattily as she prepared the blood work equipment. Nikka cranked her head to examine what the nurse was doing. She quickly looked away when she spotted the glimmer of a needle.

"It's great," answered Nikka uneasily. "It's hard to

believe a place like this even exists."

"It's the only place like it," said the nurse proudly.

"How are you doing with your classes? Are you focusing well? Are you finding everything easy to remember?" she asked encouragingly.

"Yes, haven't had much trouble," responded Nikka, growing wary of the orchestrated small talk; she was more focused on when the needle would be going into her skin. "Yesterday I had my first figure drawing class."

"And are you finding the material easy to *memorize*?" stressed the nurse.

"Pretty easy so far."

"We require a lot from our students," Nurse Smith explained gently. "And it is important that you let me know if you're struggling to remember all of it, or to focus. Or if you're struggling with your work load."

The nurse smiled, steadied Nikka's arm and put the needle in. She did it so quickly and expertly that Nikka didn't even realize it was happening.

Nikka watched the nurse take her blood. The thick scarlet mass poured from her arm effortlessly. The nurse pulled the needle out and applied pressure to the tiny wound.

"I'm especially good at remembering pictures, faces and numbers," Nikka bragged, and flinched as Nurse Smith pressed harder on her arm. Nikka attributed her good memory to the fact that Daria lost things, all the time. From Nikka's birth certificate to her own car, in Daria's case nothing was too small or too large to misplace.

The nurse seemed pleased with Nikka. She smiled and put away the small cylinders filled with Nikka's blood.

"Alright, I'm going to perform a couple of standard memory tests now," she said, and pulled out a fat stack of papers from her cabinet.

"I'm going to show you a few pictures, and you tell me what you remember seeing on them. Try to be specific," she instructed.

"That's kind of like what I do in Professor Jones's class," Nikka noted.

"Yes, it is," confirmed the nurse. "I'm actually doing research parallel to him."

Izaya's comment, *Welcome to Wildwood, where students and lab rats are one and the same,* briefly popped into her head, but as long as there weren't any needles involved, she didn't mind.

The nurse waited for Nikka's approval, then she flashed the first picture and, after a moment, put it face down back on the table.

"What was in the picture?" asked the nurse.

"A farm" responded Nikka instantly.

"Yes, and?" urged the nurse, irritated.

"And a red shovel, a tractor."

"Uh huh?" Nurse Smith nodded her head

encouragingly.

"A cat in the corner with six white dots on it, a green door with the screen in front of it bent slightly out of shape and ripped in the right corner. The top window on the right is slightly ajar, and the path leading to the farm is crooked in two places. There is a blue Ford parked outside with the license plate 10D6574."

The nurse beamed. She flashed her another picture, a construction site. This time, Nikka recalled everything from a dent in one of the trailers and a green hardhat that lay abandoned in a small ditch, to the serial number on the drywall packaging. The exercise was repeated tirelessly for 32 frames until, finally, the nurse put the stack aside.

"That will do. Bravo!" she exclaimed.

Nikka had thought the visit might be coming to an end, but the nurse rose from her chair and pulled a cluster of wires from a nearby drawer. Each wire was connected to a small, black disc. This didn't look to Nikka like something that belonged in a medical office, and she started to panic.

Nurse Smith stuck a disc on each of Nikka's wrists, and two more on her temples, before tracing one sausage-like finger along each cord to make sure they were properly attached to her computer. The tiny discs began to vibrate.

Nikka shrunk back in her seat, in shock.

"What's happening? What is this?" Her voice rose to

a high-pitch squeal.

"Oh honey, don't be afraid," said Nurse Smith dismissively.

"It's just to monitor your stress levels; we want to make sure we aren't overworking you. We do it for all the students. It's pretty run-of-the-mill," she said, and Nikka noted her condescending tone.

Although the wires and discs were giving her vivid flashbacks of documentaries she had seen on alien kidnappings, Nikka didn't want to come across as paranoid, so she commanded her restless body to stay still. Again, Nikka felt the alarming buzz on her skin, and both computers in the room came alive with black and white x-ray style scans. She tried to decipher the nonsensical lines, but the images disappeared before she had the chance to get a proper look. Nurse Smith was already tugging off the silicone discs from her wrists and temples.

"That's it?" asked Nikka incredulously.

"Yes, darling. Very advanced technology," said the nurse giving her the sort of look that said, *oh you poor, ignorant thing.*

"So... how are my stress levels?" asked Nikka.

Nurse Smith looked at her, bemused, as if she had never been asked that question before.

"They're great, dear. You seem very relaxed."

I don't feel very relaxed, Nikka thought to herself, as

she massaged her wrists.

"This is the very last step," Nurse Smith cooed reassuringly, but when she turned around she was holding a syringe. Nikka felt herself shrinking back deeper into her seat, willing herself to disappear.

In Nikka and Daria's life, doctors weren't common. They moved far too often for such a luxury, and Daria adopted a more holistic approach to their health, anyway. At times she used old world methods, such as lowering a temperature by rubbing vodka on the skin, or using a mustard compress to suppress a heavy cough. Nikka wasn't quite sure if Daria used these methods out of holistic principle, habit, or because their budget didn't allow for a real doctor. Nikka's legs shook and she shut her eyes tightly.

"Please take off your shirt," said the nurse. Nikka obliged and felt her joints go cold and stiff. She put her button down aside and tried to even out her breath again.

Nurse Smith noticed. "It's just a new vaccine, darling, required by the school and the state. It's very useful," she added, off-hand.

Before Nikka could protest, Nurse Smith had already sunk the long needle deep into her shoulder. Nikka yelped at the pain as the last few drops were pushed under the surface of her skin. She felt her palms moisten with sweat. The nurse pulled the needle out and Nikka breathed a sigh of relief.

"Now, you might feel drowsy or nauseous for a bit, but that's completely normal," said Nurse Smith. She helped Nikka to her feet and stuck a plaster on her arm. Nikka put her shirt back on and just stood there for a moment, recovering. Nikka had a sudden desire to ask more questions about the vaccine, but before she had a chance to say anything she was already being ushered out the front door. Nurse Smith croaked her goodbyes, abandoning all niceties, and shut the door behind her.

Nikka stumbled down the linoleum hallway. Her head was spinning and the walls swayed a little. The forest, visible behind the double glass doors at the end of the hallway, glowed like a green beacon of hope. She staggered out of them, desperate for fresh air. It was dusk when Nikka exited the Health Center. She felt the promised nausea coming on. She clutched her stomach, which felt like it was turning inside out, and trekked up the path that cut through the forest.

Nikka first realized she was walking the wrong way when she wandered past a small one-classroom cabin she had never seen before. She approached the cabin, hoping to find a building name and thus figure out where she was. She stayed close to the shadows, and risked a quick peer through one of the windows. The classroom she saw was brightly lit. A thin, weasel-like professor sat at his desk near the blackboard and stared at the people in front of him silently and blank-faced. The classroom was packed with students; they all sat there glumly, either mirroring the old professor's expression or staring at the surrounding walls. Everything at Wildwood was so unlike the norm, so far removed from mediocrity, that it took her a moment to recognize a good old-fashioned detention hall. *They got caught at the party,* Nikka realized as she took in the bored, pampered faces that lined the rows of desks. *If the Dean had made good on his promises they would have all been expelled for being at the party,* Nikka reasoned curiously. Were the Dean's policies not as ironclad as she had thought? Again, Izaya's words rang through her head. *The rules don't apply to some.*

Nikka peered through the window again and located the boy she was looking for. Tristan sat there moodily, looking like a wild animal stuck in a cage. His face was one of pure misery. His token flat cap was tilted low over his eyes and he was frowning. Nikka could see him carving a small piece of bark with a Swiss Army knife. *They would have expelled you.* Tristan's self-sacrificing words echoed in her mind and filled her with guilt. She noticed that Tristan was sitting just inches away from the back door.

She didn't know if it was the dizzying effect of her shot, or Tristan's gloomy face, but Nikka was suddenly seized with an overpowering urge to take action. She grabbed a heavy rock and hurled it toward the window closest to the professor; it flew through the air and the window shattered into a dozen pieces.

A few of the girls screamed out in shock, and the professor nearly fell off of his folding chair. Once he had regained his composure, he examined the broken window, his back to the class, and nasally demanded the class all settle down. Suddenly, and rather unexpectedly for a man of his weedy physique, he bolted for the front door to find the culprit. *This* was Nikka's chance. She snuck around to the other side and pushed the back door open just wide enough for Tristan to notice. He spotted her immediately and grinned. Without a moment's hesitation he swung his messenger bag around his shoulders, and, unnoticed by his frenzied classmates, slipped out of the back door. He clasped her hand and the pair broke into a quiet sprint away from the cabin. Tristan took care to avoid the most frequented paths, just in case the professor could walkie-talkie security. Instead, they cut straight through the forest. Nikka had no idea where he was leading her until she saw the yellow parachutes floating above the trees in the distance.

Soon they arrived at a large grassy dip, which Wildwood students simply referred to as *The Valley*. The Valley was mostly used by the Academy for graduations and summer concerts, but it was also rumored to host secret rendezvous with townies, or the occasional illicit cigarette break. The Valley was a steep grass-covered dip, which was special only because a few massive yellow tent-like pieces of fabric were suspended above it, and in the daylight, cast the area in a golden glow. They were like giant flowers and when the night wind blew, the yellow peaks lifted gently towards the skies.

There were no lights nearby and Nikka could barely see in front of her. Tristan tripped, and she came tumbling after him. They spiraled a few feet down into the darkness of the dip before Tristan caught her by the shirtsleeve and pulled her back up, so that they were both laying flat on their backs. They laughed wildly and stared up through the gaps between the yellow parachutes at a star-studded sky.

Tristan was lying close to her, and she could feel the warmth emanating from his body. Tentatively, he closed the distance between them and now their sides were touching. Nikka had complex feelings; part of her felt like she was doing something she shouldn't, like she should be cautious; the other part was too busy enjoying it. Tristan loosely wrapped his arm around her. For a moment Nikka didn't say anything, she just sat there, inhaling his scent and losing herself in the sharpness and unfamiliarity of his cologne. Tristan broke the silence first.

"I can't believe you got me out of detention. You're *amazing*, Nikka. You know that?" he said warmly, and laughed.

"I'm a sucker for a damsel in distress," Nikka countered. There was a moment of quiet, and Nikka could see him grinning in the dark.

“I barely know anything about you," she blurted out suddenly. Tristan sighed gently, and for a moment looked uncomfortable.

"Okay, ask me anything.”

Nikka thought hard for a moment.

"Alright. Name one thing you like, one thing you dislike, and something you love," she asked.

"That’s easy. I like poker. I dislike pepper. And I love my mum and sisters."

“*Loved* my mom,” he corrected. “She’s not around anymore.”

“I’m so sorry,” said Nikka. Tristan looked like he had just realized something important, he bit his lip.

“Would you mind not telling anyone at school about that?” he asked.

“Of course,” Nikka nodded.

"Your turn now. But tell me something no one knows," said Tristan, resuming his usual mischievous expression.

"I like memorizing maps. I dislike war movies. And I love...” she paused for a moment, and felt the thin pendant tucked under her shirt. “My father’s dog tags,” she admitted, wanting to tell Tristan something personal, something important. Like he had told her.

“He’s not around anymore either,” she added.

Tristan didn’t ask to see the dog tags, or how her father died, and he didn’t say anything deep or sentimental. Nikka liked it that way. He just caressed the back of her head and allowed his hand to dip through her curls. Tristan turned sideways and his warm blue eyes set on hers. For a moment, Nikka couldn't speak. She felt shivers travel down her collarbone. Tristan picked a strand of hair off her face and held it up to the moonlight. For a moment they stared at each other. Nikka laughed nervously, then shivered again.

"You're cold," said Tristan suddenly. He took off his tweed jacket and put it around her shoulders. In one swift movement he was back on his feet and brushing off his pants. He pulled her up, and without letting go of her hand led her in the direction of the dorms. They didn't talk much as they strolled back through the overgrown paths, which were clearly lit by the moon.

"You seem very well acquainted with the grounds," said Nikka somewhere between The Valley and the dorms.

"I like to know all my escape routes," he responded, and smiled playfully.

"That reminds me," he said. "Did you find your way back to the dorms alright after the party, all on your own?"

"I did," Nikka lied.

"You weren't scared?"

"No, it was completely fine," she lied again.

Tristan squeezed her hand. Soon they were back at

the dorms and approaching Roseland. There was a crowd gathered by the entrance, and Nikka realized with a jump that Izaya was amongst them. Izaya spotted her instantly. His piercing green eyes narrowed, closed in on their interwoven hands and his bow-shaped lips pursed with disgust. Izaya slowly, almost menacingly, straightened out to his full height from his prior position leaning against the wall. For a second, Nikka thought Izaya would walk over and say something rude, maybe even yell at her. His chest was pressed out and his jaw tightened. His eyes locked on hers.

Nikka looked away, inexplicably embarrassed. Her cheeks burned. Izaya's dark stare was somehow enough to make her feel ashamed, for what, she didn't know. When she finally looked up again, his back was turned, and she watched him storm off towards *Becks*.

She turned her attention back to Tristan. For a moment she had forgotten he was even standing there. Nikka desperately wanted to say something to break the awkward silence between them, but she was now aware of their audience. She could feel Izaya's friends watching their every move and listening for whatever came next, eager for some juicy gossip to pass along later. Tristan had noticed, but didn't seem to care who was watching. He reached into his front pocket and pulled out a small wooden ring. The top was flat and carved; the edges were smooth and curved inwards. He handed it to her.

"I carved this for you," he said, his voice low. "Out of a walnut shell."

He flashed her a crooked and warm, but slightly troubled, smile, then walked away, whistling as he went. Nikka smiled at the small brown object nestled in her palm. She slipped the ring into her pocket, and walked back to Roseland, happily ignoring the spiteful snickers that resounded in her wake.

"I carved this for you," he said [illegible]. "Out of [illegible] tree."

He flashed her a wide [illegible] and warm, and slightly crooked, smile, then walked away, whistling as he went. [illegible] at the small [illegible] object [illegible] in her hand. She slipped [illegible] into her pocket and walked back to Rosebank, happily [illegible] the spiteful [illegible] [illegible] in [illegible].

8

The Rat

That morning, in her memory development workshop, Nikka was distracted. She stroked the ridges of the wooden ring and moved it up and down her finger, back and forth, back and forth. She stared out the window.

"You're too good for him," declared an icy voice from across the table. Nikka looked up and met Izaya's intense green eyes. She had been doing her best to not engage with him since the professor had stepped out of the classroom. This was their third sorting class; Nikka still loved it, but Izaya seemed to grow angrier each time. He couldn't understand why he had to tell apart, combine, sort, unsort and memorize a never-ending sequence of shapes and pictures. Moreover, how would this ever prove useful to him?

"How would you know?" It was more of a statement than a question. Nikka liked the idea that Izaya had noticed the ring, and had figured out its connection to

Tristan. Izaya seemed to notice everything.

"Maybe the dozens of girls you kiss are too good for you," said Nikka spitefully. Izaya smiled.

"Thinking of anyone in particular?" He teased. Nikka looked away. She could only deal with Izaya in small doses. Otherwise her disdain for him melted away and was replaced with an airy, jittery feeling in her stomach- a feeling she hated. Mostly she hated that Izaya was someone she had to *remind* herself to dislike.

"There's a party tonight..." Izaya started, but he was interrupted by the return of Professor Jones, who trekked across the room, looking wet and disheveled, coffee in hand.

"Sorry, I took so long. This freaking dead zone is a nightmare! How do you students cope with it?" He mumbled irritably. "I had to go take a call in the central office!" Izaya's eyes locked knowingly on Nikka's, invoking a shared memory: the tree, the phone, the first time they met. Nikka smiled unwillingly, as she remembered how she had fallen out of that tree.

"You guys can go now, I will review your progress later," added the professor grouchily. Nikka quickly gathered her stuff and headed out the door. Izaya followed her. The air outside was cold.

"See you at the exhibition," said Izaya, as he lit a cigarette. Nikka's worried eyes traveled to the classroom behind him.

"You're worried I'll get in trouble," he noted, "that's cute." Izaya took another relaxed puff. Nikka ignored his comment.

"See you at the exhibition. Violet's work is in the second room," she added matter-of-factly.

Izaya shook his head at her, as if she were a child who had just missed the point. He turned around and walked away, leaving small ringlets of smoke in his wake. Nikka sighed and walked off in the opposite direction towards her Bataillisme class. Halfway there she ran into Eloise.

"Hey, girl!" said Eloise croakily; her voice had gone.

"Hey, are you Okay?" asked Nikka, concerned. Eloise was wearing her school uniform, which was decorated in every way possible: punk rock band pins hung on the lapel, a small skull patch was sewn onto the sleeve of her blazer, there were doodles drawn on her shoes in permanent marker. To top it off, there was a fresh streak of purple added to the underside of her blond hair.

"I lost my voice. It's a cold or something," croaked Eloise. "You know, I've barely seen you around since the tour."

"I know! This school really takes over your whole life," said Nikka.

Eloise was the one person she had wanted to get to know, but hadn't yet had the chance. Eloise checked both sides of the path to make sure they were alone.

"There is a townie bonfire tonight, these are the

coordinates. Come along and we can finally, properly hang out," Eloise slipped Nikka a curled up piece of paper and Nikka pocketed it straight away.

"Thanks! I had heard about it, but tomorrow is my exhibition, so I'm not sure yet. Are you going to go, despite your voice?" asked Nikka. She knew she wouldn't go. The truth was, Nikka didn't want to be near Izaya when he was with Violet, and she did not want to risk another brush with expulsion.

"I don't have to talk to have a good time, I just need to dance." Eloise smiled warmly. She coughed again. "Suit yourself, but I will most definitely come see your exhibition!"

"That's great, thank you," beamed Nikka. She checked her watch again. "Oh no, I have to go. Madame Grenoble is not one to tolerate tardiness."

"Tell me about it," croaked Eloise. "She's tough. I had her for voice development workshops last year. Anyway, I have to get to the nurse's office. See you later."

"Feel better!" called Nikka as Eloise hurried off.

Odd, thought Nikka. Why would the same person teach art and voice development?

Nikka rushed into Oval Dome with seconds to spare. There it was, perched on the giant easel, her first Wildwood painting. She had worked on it for a whole month. It was a representation of the battle she had watched over and over again, a mass of destruction engulfed in the beige colors of the land. Madame Grenoble was standing next to it, dressed in a silk black pantsuit.

"It's ready for the gallery," she announced with satisfaction. Nikka surveyed it. It had been framed. She had never seen one of her works framed.

"You're very talented," said Grenoble from behind her.

"Thank you," said Nikka, as she stroked the side of the frame.

Nikka stared at the colors of her work. Something that she had created, had been framed, and would now be seen by people in a real gallery setting. Something fluttered in her stomach; she was happy, and it was the most tangible happiness she had ever felt. It felt like no matter what happened next, no matter where her mom chose to move, or whatever life threw at them, *this*, the painted, framed piece in front of her, and the feeling it gave her, could never be taken away. It could never be undone, unlike friends, homes, or even the memories of her father that she now struggled to recall. This was a happiness that she would carry with her forever. She had created a small sliver of happiness that belonged to her alone.

×

"You *must* be nervous," declared Sums. He sat on Nikka's bed with his computer in his lap. "You're actually taking the time to pick what to wear," he elaborated.

"It's like seeing a unicorn," said Stella grumpily. She was sat on her own bed, flipping through a magazine, annoyed that Nikka hadn't asked for her help yet. After dinner Sums had snuck into Stella and Nikka's room because Nikka needed to use his phone for her weekly call to her mother. She didn't like using the phone in the common room; it was almost always occupied, and it was right next to the communal couches, so there were constant prying ears. The phone was also only active during the *social hours* of 7-10:00, so unless you got there early you had no chance of using it.

On the phone, Daria had said that what you wore to a gallery was crucial, so Nikka stood facing her wardrobe, baffled, like a deer caught in the headlights.

"Why are you trying so hard, anyway? It's not like you're going to a *party*," continued Stella resentfully. She was tiptoeing around the fact that Nikka had mentioned during dinner that she had been invited to the bonfire. Stella hadn't been invited. Nikka sighed and reached into her back pocket. She pulled the piece of paper out and put it on Stella's bed. Stella yelped excitedly as she looked at the coordinates. She slipped into her maroon leather jacket and grabbed a purse.

"Don't get caught!" warned Nikka.

"Thank you! Thank you so much. I won't!" she screeched and hurried over to the door just as there was a knock on the other side. Sums quickly grabbed Nikka's quilt and covered himself with it. Nikka threw a few decorative pillows on top of him to cover the bulge his body made under the blanket.

"Come in," said Stella and Nikka in unison.

Magda came in with a tray. She smiled at both girls and put the tray down on the coffee table, two cups of herbal tea and biscuits. She stared at Stella questioningly. Stella looked down awkwardly at her leather jacket and purse in hand.

"Umm, hey Magda. I was just...headed out for a little fresh air. I'll be back before curfew, of course," said Stella in her best innocent voice.

"Of course," echoed Magda. Stella smiled and walked out. Magda rolled her eyes ever so slightly.

"Your exhibition is tomorrow," she said to Nikka.

"Yes, it is. I'm so nervous."

"Nerves are no good," said Magda sternly in her thick Eastern European accent. "You just need a little bit of *luck*." She reached into the pocket of her work tunic and pulled out a silver chain with a coin on it.

"Silver coin, for good luck," she explained.

Nikka smiled with delight. She turned around, pushed her thick hair aside and Magda closed the small chain around her neck.

"Thank you so much, Magda," she said earnestly. For a brief moment, she held Magda's hand. There were four floors at Roseland, and one House Matron for each floor. Nikka had met them all, but none were as sweet, as understanding, or as open, as Magda.

"I wish I could come," said Magda. Nikka knew she had to work; her daily shifts were long. For a second she wondered what Magda was like in her free time, what she did then? The Magda she didn't know. She vowed to herself that she would get to know her House Matron better in the future.

"Me too," said Nikka. Magda smiled and turned to leave.

"No boys allowed," she said in passing, and pointed at the lump on the bed.

"Sorry, Magda," came Sums's muffled voice from under the quilt. He came up for air, red and sweaty. He did not look Magda in the eye; he was a little afraid of her. Nikka stifled a laugh; she could tell by Magda's amused expression that she knew the pair were not up to any mischief, that they were just friends, no *fraternizing* going on here. Sums stood, and with his head hung low he walked out the door. Magda smiled at Nikka and followed him. Nikka was left alone, full of excitement and anxiety over the coming day.

×

The gallery was beginning to fill with guests. Nikka checked her reflection in the glass entrance. She had decided on a vintage blue chiffon dress. Her hair was down with a few braids in it, courtesy of Amber. She had borrowed a pair of heels from Amber too, since she hadn't seen Stella all day. Nikka went to stand a few feet away from her painting. She stood proud and straight, her hands gracefully clasped before her stomach, just as Madame Grenoble, the exhibition curator for the night, had instructed her. Violet stood a few feet away from her own painting, doing the same.

"For the first part of the exhibition, stand close to your work so that you may enter into discussion with interested guests," instructed Madame Grenoble when the art students had arrived early to help set up. "Afterwards, circulate and socialize."

The first thing Nikka had done upon arriving at the gallery was look at Violet's piece. She knew that was vain, but she couldn't help it. It was even more vain that Nikka had been pleased to see that Violet's oil painting of the redwood forest, much like her other pieces, was beautiful, but void of originality or emotion.

Nikka stood and watched people arrive. The room slowly filled with sound as groups of students, teachers, staff and esteemed guests arrived. They did their rounds, one polite, contemplative pause at each spotlit artwork followed by brief analytical chatter, before moving on. In her peripheral vision Nikka watched as visitors stopped by her piece, commented to their friends, then moved onward, past her and onto the rest of the white, maze-like gallery. She saw Amber across the room and waved to her. Amber was also standing close to her piece, an elaborate coal drawing of a fairy colony.

A few minutes later, she spotted Sums by the buffet table. He saw her and walked over happily, a wide smile stretched over a mouth full of food. He was carrying an assortment of cheese, grapes, and crackers on a paper plate.

"Really nice," he said and pointed at her painting. Nikka smiled.

"Cheese?" offered Sums.

"I can't eat," said Nikka. Her stomach was full of butterflies that fluttered each time another group of unfamiliar faces stopped by her painting and examined it. A few moments later Tristan walked in. He looked very dapper, clad in a red bow tie and a tweed blazer. His chestnut hair was ruffled and for once he was not wearing his signature flat cap. He was carrying a rose. His eyes searched the crowd; he spotted Nikka, walked up, and handed it to her.

"*Madame*," he said in French accent.

"Thank you," she said shyly.

Tristan turned towards the paintings and made a serious face.

"The composition! The lines! The colors!" he exclaimed theatrically. *"Bravissimo!"*

Nikka and Sums laughed. Nikka pointed to the

painting next to the one Tristan was looking at.

"*That* one is actually mine. But I will tell Jeanine that you like her work." Tristan frowned a bit.

"Thank god, because I actually think *that* one is rubbish," he said pointing at the painting he had just been complimenting.

"Yours is wonderful. Good job, Nik. You even make war look good," he said. Nikka smiled up at him, relishing her new nickname.

"Thank you for the rose," she said, running her finger up the thorn-less stem. Tristan allowed himself to stroke her shoulder, his way of saying *you're welcome*. Sums stared at his plate of cheese, uncomfortable with the intimacy of the gesture.

Nikka noticed Izaya walk through the front doors and her stomach clenched, unwillingly, she took a step back, away from Tristan. Violet ran over to Izaya, took his hand, and led him straight to her piece. She was explaining something to him and he was nodding along, but his eyes traveled the room and settled on Nikka. Nikka looked away.

"I'm going to go get some cheese," she said to Tristan and Sums.

After she had half-heartedly picked at some cheese and made small talk with a few of the other art students, Nikka returned to her painting. Tristan and Sums had gone, probably to explore the rest of the large and winding gallery. Instead, she found Izaya standing next to the piece, his hands folded behind his back as he leaned in towards it. Nikka took a deep breath and walked up to him. He didn't turn around, but she knew he had seen her. His black hair was carefully swept to one side and he was wearing a black blazer over a white button-down adorned with silver cufflinks. He straightened back out and towered over her, his lips pursed in concentration. Nikka desperately wanted to know what he was thinking.

"I'm not in the mood for any snide comments," she said preemptively.

"It's stunning," he said, quietly.

"Thank you," Nikka whispered, stunned. She didn't know why they were whispering. Maybe because the room was nearly empty, as visitors had migrated on. Nikka heard a cello player begin to play in one of the other rooms.

"Sell it to me," said Izaya.

"Excuse me?"

He turned to her. His green eyes glowed in the dim light of the room. He looked serious.

"Sell it to me," he repeated.

Nikka was momentarily taken aback.

"Umm, I don't know...I'm not sure what..." She stuttered, unable to form a sentence.

"You're an artist," he said.

"I am," she answered hesitantly. She wasn't sure if he

was asking her, or telling her.

"And this is a gallery..." He pressed.

"Well, yeah, but..." she began, but he cut her off.

"*So*, sell me your piece," he insisted.

Nikka took a step back; she didn't know what to say. She looked up at him and searched his face for a sign that he was joking.

"Why?" she asked incredulously.

"It will be a worth a lot some day," he said dryly.

"And besides," he continued, "I want to own your first ever gallery piece. Promise me that you will sell it to me?"

Nikka was equal parts blown away, flattered, and a little insulted. She didn't understand whether or not he was making fun of her. Or trying in some way to own a piece of her, to prove that he could. At the same time, what he was asking her felt good. Better than good. No one had ever asked to buy her art, and it was a feeling like no other in the world – satisfaction, validation, bewilderment and pleasure. He had given her all of that with one arrogant request.

"I promise," she said, without thinking it through. He reached his hand out to her. She shook it. Izaya smiled a triumphant smile and walked away. *What just happened?* Nikka asked herself. *Was it business, insolence, a compliment, affection?* She had absolutely no idea. Tristan walked up behind her, a plate of cheese in one hand.

"What did *he* want?" he asked irritably. Nikka did not like the entitlement in Tristan's voice.

"Nothing. He just asked what the subject matter was," said Nikka dismissively. For a second she was surprised at her own lie.

"What an idiot," said Tristan. "It's clearly a battle scene."

Nikka nodded, but she wasn't paying attention to Tristan any more. Nikka had noticed Stella standing in the corner of the room, and instantly she knew that something was wrong. Stella did not look like her usual self; her eyes were bloodshot, her hair messy, her outfit disheveled, and it looked like she had been crying for hours. Nikka went to her.

"Stella, are you okay?" she whispered.

"I'm fine," said Stella unconvincingly. There was a pause, a sniffle.

"Tell me," Nikka pressed.

"That bonfire we went to last night, it was raided by the guards and I spent half of today being questioned by the Dean," said Stella.

"He questioned you? About what?" asked Nikka.

"About last night; who was there, who drank..." Stella admitted. "But I didn't tell him anything!" she added defensively.

Tristan had walked up behind them and was standing quietly by Nikka's side.

"So why have you been crying then?" asked Nikka.

Stella looked up at Tristan hesitantly, as if she were embarrassed to explain in front of him.

"Marcus broke up with me," she stuttered. Her pretty face contorted with the promise of more tears.

"What? *Why*?" asked Nikka angrily.

"He said that I shouldn't have come to the party, that he didn't invite me," said Stella. Her bottom lip quivered and she began to cry quietly. Nikka stepped forward and stood in front of her so that no one could see. She put her hand on Stella's arm and squeezed lightly.

"I'm going to have a chat with him, teach him some manners," said Tristan.

Both girls gawked at Tristan in surprise.

"No, that's okay," said Stella carefully. "I really wanted to come to your exhibition, but is it okay if I come back and see your piece tomorrow? The gallery will still be open, right?" Stella's voice shook. Nikka threw a hesitant look in Tristan's direction.

Would you mind taking her home?" she asked, guiltily.

Tristan looked like he really wanted to stay, but then he sighed.

"Of course I will."

"Thank you," Nikka whispered gratefully.

Gently, Tristan offered Stella his arm and led her out. Nikka stayed late to help the gallery staff clean up. Once the gallery was clean she said her goodbyes to her classmates and the staff, and took out the trash in passing. On her way to her dorm Nikka shivered; it was almost the end of October, and the nights were getting colder every day. She heard a rustling sound behind her and turned around. Violet stood facing her, with Jordan flanking her side.

"Good evening," said Violet. Her voice was syrupy as always.

"Hello," answered Nikka coldly. Two other girls approached Nikka from behind. One of them Nikka recognized as *Cher*, Violet's friend from the party, the other one Nikka could not recall. The girl was fat, tall, and intimidating. Violet took a step forward and the others closed in on Nikka. *I'm surrounded,* the alarming thought sounded in Nikka's head like a siren.

"What do you want?" she asked Violet.

"You know that there was a bonfire last night?" said Violet.

"So what?" asked Nikka.

"Eloise invited you and gave you the coordinates," Violet pressed on.

"*Again*, so what?"

"And then *you* gave the coordinates to Stella."

Nikka rolled her eyes and nodded. "Get to the point, Violet."

"You know we are not supposed to give anyone

coordinates when invited to a party," continued Violet her voice laced with accusation.

"I don't see what the big deal is, Eloise gave me the coordinates, I passed them down," said Nikka shrugging her shoulders. Her eyes met Jordan's. Nikka stared back at her knowingly, Jordan looked away quickly, with an expression vaguely resembling shame.

"Did you tell anyone else? About the party," asked Violet. Her glare was vicious now and Nikka had had enough.

"Are we done with this inquisition?" Nikka asked sarcastically. She tried her best to act nonchalant, unthreatened. But the larger girl had come a little too close to her. Nikka's body was going into fight or flight mode, but her rational mind forced her to stay in place, to wait.

"Someone *ratted* us out," spat Violet.

"And you think it was me? I didn't even go to the stupid bonfire," said Nikka, relieved that Violet didn't have anything legitimate to accuse her of, like kissing Izaya, for example.

"That's precisely the point," Violet snapped, her voice venomous. The girls closed in a few more steps. Nikka contemplated her options. She wasn't the fastest runner, and she definitely couldn't fight four girls at once.

"It wasn't me," she repeated calmly. There was a boulder behind her, in one quick step Nikka climbed up and sat down.

"What are you doing?" asked Violet incredulously.

"It just seems as though we're going to be here for a while, so I might as well sit," Nikka willed every inch of her body to stay relaxed, and injected her voice with fake boredom. It was cold outside; they wouldn't want to stay too long, she figured. *They wouldn't pull me off the boulder, would they?* Nikka rationalized, only half-convinced. The four girls all stared at her. The large one smacked loudly on her gum.

"I *will* find out if it was you," said Violet. "And I don't like rats," she warned.

"Your friend Eloise got expelled," added Jordan maliciously, knowing that this would strike a chord with Nikka. Nikka nodded, acting disinterested, pretending she already knew. The large girl took another step towards her and Nikka balled her right hand into a fist, ready to fight if necessary.

"There's only one way to get rid of a rat, Nikka," said Violet.

"Oh yeah, and what's that?" Nikka replied defiantly.

"*Poison*," said Violet sweetly. She smiled at her, a nasty little smile, and with that, she and her friends walked away.

Nikka sat there for a few minutes, waiting for the shaking to pass, she didn't know if it was from the cold or from the fear.

Nikka dismounted from the boulder and walked towards her dorm, thinking about Violet's threat. What did she mean by poison? And why does she think I'm the rat? And did Eloise really get kicked out? Or was that just a vicious lie? It was too close to curfew to go to Chadbourne and check on Eloise; Nikka would have to wait until the next day. It upset her deeply to think that Eloise could have gotten expelled; if anyone truly belonged at Wildwood, it was her.

Nikka found Tristan by the dorms, waiting for her.

"Hey there, where were you? I looked for you. I was worried," he said in a rush.

"Hey," she answered. Nikka kept walking and he fell into step with her.

"Stella talked my ear off for hours. By the time I went looking for you the gallery was shut. Where did you go?"

"Just a walk," said Nikka absent-mindedly. Tristan stopped. Nikka turned to face him.

"What's wrong?" He asked.

"Nothing," Nikka lied.

"You're shutting me out," said Tristan.

"Because you're pushing your way in," Nikka snapped defensively, and instantly felt guilty. Tristan's blue eyes were soft; his hair fell over his face and he pushed it back. For the first time he looked serious, and remained silent.

Nikka didn't know why she did it. Maybe she was still running on adrenaline caused by the events of the evening, but she crossed the distance between them, took his face in her palms and kissed him. She felt his stubble press against her cheek, his kiss soft and warm. When she pulled back he smiled at her.

"Ignore me, I'm tired," she whispered.

Tristan pulled her into his arms. Nikka felt drained by the combined fear and excitement of the night. She burrowed her face into his shoulder. Tristan stood there silently and held her, for as long as she needed to be held.

9

All Hallows Eve

Nikka and Stella merrily walked down the twisted path that connected the cafeteria to the log cabin studio where their technical drawing class took place. It was a sunny day, but the October mountain air was cold and Wildwood students had begun wearing winter coats over their uniform blazers. Stella smiled and pulled her pink parka tighter around her skinny frame; the shift in weather meant she had a new opportunity to escape the dreariness of her uniform. Stella caught Nikka's eyes and smiled brightly. She was in better spirits now that a full week had passed since her *break-up*; in Stella's world, a week was more than enough time to suffer for lost love.

It had been a good morning thus far; Magda had delivered their *Review* letters following their exhibitions, which congratulated Nikka and Stella on the successful completion of their mid-semester projects and announced that they had both *passed*. This was paired with a note from the Dean, in which he wrote that he was pleased with Nikka's efforts, but that she should continue striving for improvement. The short impersonal note felt a little anticlimactic to Nikka, who had worried about the Dean's decision for weeks. Nonetheless, she was elated.

But it was the second piece of mail delivered that morning that really put a spring in Stella's step: an invite to the much talked about Wildwood Academy Halloween party. The invite was a small black envelope decorated with a lacy skull; inside was a piece of aged parchment paper stating the date, time and location: a *mansion* on the school grounds. Stella was beside herself with excitement.

"I brought my pirate costume and nurse costume with me from home," she said giddily on their way to class. "What about you?"

"I didn't bring a costume," said Nikka coolly. Wildwood had come into her life so unexpectedly, the last thing she would have remembered to pack was a Halloween costume.

"What are you going to do?" said Stella with such a degree of seriousness they could have been discussing terminal illness.

There were a few clusters of students waiting outside the cabin, chatting. Stella followed Nikka into the circular studio. In the center of the room was a table covered with the items they were to draw that day: bronze candleholders, scattered pomegranates, and a few patterned silk scarves. Nikka's eyes fell on a halved pomegranate; she admired its symmetry and the rhythmic, interwoven pattern of its seeds and flesh, and decided she would draw that alone.

"Nikka, what are you going to wear for Halloween?" Stella persisted.

"I'm not sure," said Nikka. "I'll probably just make something."

"Don't worry," said Stella attempting to sound comforting. "You can borrow whichever costume I don't wear. I'm sure Tristan would love you as a nurse," she teased.

Nikka smiled half-heartedly; the prospect of dressing as a sexy version of Mrs. Smith for Halloween didn't appeal to her that much. She thought back to the night in the woods when she had kissed Tristan, and the skin on her face turned hot. For a second she was lost in a daydream as she tailed Stella over to the corner of the studio where their easels stood side by side. A sudden, shrill scream pierced the air and brought her back to reality, disoriented. *What is it? What's going on?* She glanced around in a panic.

The screams continued, and with alarm, Nikka realized that it was Stella who was screaming.

Stella stood there, paralyzed. Nikka took a step

forward and came face to face with what had provoked Stella's scream. There was something fixed onto Nikka's easel; it took her a moment to realize what she was staring at: a dead rat with a tiny noose around its neck, hanging limp across her easel. The perfect white surface of the new canvas was stained with a cascade of red streaks, and the word *Rat,* was scribbled in blood.

×

"A dead rat?" asked Sums disbelievingly at lunch later that day. He pushed his food away, his unconquerable appetite suddenly gone. Tristan was next to Nikka, his arm hung loosely over her shoulder. Stella was sitting across from her, pale and anxious.

"Are you feeling okay?" asked Tristan. He rubbed her shoulder lightly. His touch felt warm and safe, just as it had after the exhibition. Nikka nodded.

"Well, I'm not!" whined Stella from the other side of the table.

"A *dead* rat! It was *so* disgusting; you can't even imagine. I'm scarred for life. And do you know what Nikka did? Do you have *any* idea what *your girlfriend* did?" Stella quizzed Tristan hysterically. Nikka gently shrugged Tristan's hand off her shoulder. She didn't like someone else labeling whatever it was that she and Tristan had.

"What did *she* do?" asked Sums, interested.

"*She* picked up the damn rat with her own bare hands, took it outside and buried it behind the building! Then she washed her hands and changed her canvas; as if it was the most normal thing in the world."

"Wow, that's grim, *Nik*. I'm impressed," joked Tristan. He grinned at her. She smiled back, albeit weakly. The incident had shaken her up, and it had scared her, but in response she had employed one of her mother's favorite life lessons: *when someone frightens you, do the unexpected*.

"So did you, like, have a sermon at hand? Did you sing *Amazing Grace*? I'm not really familiar with rat funerals," Sums teased. His appetite was suddenly back, and he dug into his plate of chicken tacos. Tristan chuckled.

"I cremated him, read a few poems," said Nikka as she stuck her tongue out at Sums.

"None of this is funny!" said Stella indignantly. "People are going to think that Nikka is psychotic."

"No," said Tristan, irritably. "The psychotic thing is hanging a dead rat on someone's easel." Nikka smiled at the way he said *easel.* She loved listening to him talk; his Irish accent made everything sound warmer, prettier than it was.

"That's true," said Sums more seriously. "It's a good thing you aren't the actual *rat*. Imagine what Violet is going to do to whoever it is when she figures it out." Sums swallowed another giant mouthful of taco. *Violet*, the name rang in Nikka's head and filled her with rage. Of course, she knew it was *her* who had put the rat there, it had to be, but it felt weird to have it confirmed out loud. Stella dropped her fork halfway to her mouth, food splattered across the table on impact. Stella began to shake as tears streamed down her face.

"Was it something I said?" asked Sums. He stared at the sobbing Stella, dumbfounded, as if the crying girl were a strange species he had never seen before. He glanced over at Tristan for help, who shrugged his shoulders in response.

"I'm the rat," Stella hiccupped in between sobs. A wave of shock registered on the faces of her lunch companions. Nikka looked around, making sure that no one had overheard her.

"Why would you do that?" she whispered back urgently. Stella sobbed quietly into her scarf. Her eyes were shut, thick mascara streaks trickled down her cheeks.

"The Dean said he would expel me for drinking if I didn't give him a name," she explained. Sums' large blue eyes filled with sympathy, but Tristan's and Nikka were decidedly cold.

"And is *Eloise* the name you gave?" asked Nikka angrily.

Stella nodded. Nikka pushed her plate away in disgust. The last thing she wanted was to participate in Violet's witch-hunt, but this new development had upset her. Just because Stella couldn't live with missing a single party, just because she couldn't abstain from drinking, and just because she was slow enough to get caught, a girl as talented as Eloise had lost her spot at Wildwood. *What if it was her dream school? What if she loved it here as much as I do?* Nikka thought, bitterly. It had just been taken from her, taken by Stella and her loose tongue. Stella looked up at Nikka pleadingly.

"Are you upset with me?" she asked, her brown eyes glistening with guilt. Tristan and Sums shifted awkwardly as the tension at their lunch table continued to rise. Nikka got up without a word, picked up her tray and left a sobbing Stella behind. She knew it was cruel, but she did it anyway.

×

There were only a few hours left until the Halloween party, and Nikka still had nothing to wear. She had complained about it to Daria on the phone, but her mother had just said, *you're creative, you'll come up with something.* Nikka couldn't very well borrow something from Stella anymore, since she wasn't technically speaking to her. Stella had only appeared in the bedroom once, to pick up her pirate costume, and she had avoided eye contact with Nikka. Nikka looked around her room - curtains, pillows, drapes and carpet - nothing she could cut up or sew. She spotted something red tucked away on Stella's desk, *duct tape.* At the beginning of the semester Stella had wanted to cover her side of the wall with magazine cutouts of models and clothes, but the student store was sold out of regular duct tape so she had bought and used a red roll. Nikka picked up the packet. The red duct tape was cool, she could always replace it, and there was enough left for what Nikka had in mind.

With newfound purpose Nikka walked over to her closet and pulled out a corseted dress her mother had given her a few years back. She had never liked it. She grabbed a pair of Stella's fabric scissors and sliced through it, then pulled the bone structure out of the fabric, like pulling a skeleton out of its skin. She slipped the carcass of the dress onto Stella's mannequin and started taping over it. The tape was mendable and sturdy. Nikka did not know what she was going to be yet, but the occurrences of the week - the dead rat, Stella's confession, Violet's threat - had all left her feeling dark. Halloween was a good time to feel dark.

Three hours later, Nikka finished the dress and tried it on. It fit her perfectly; the corseted bodice tapered her every curve and created a sharp, daring silhouette. Nikka gave a satisfied twirl in front of the mirror. She painted her eyes coal black and her lips dark red, then she straightened her signature curly hair; the long blond streaks now reached down to her waist. Out of the last of the remaining fabric and tape she made herself a pair of red wings and attached them to her back. She looked at herself in the mirror again; she was every inch the dark and dangerous demon, just as she had intended. She smiled and walked out the door.

On the other side of campus, at the end of a long, uninterrupted path, stood a large, imposing modern mansion. The mansion was used for events, board meetings, and dinner parties meant for entertaining and persuading Wildwood investors. It was also rumored that Stamos took up residence in one of the master bedrooms upstairs. Nikka found the mansion easily and as it came into view, intimidating and lavish, she could tell from yards away that this would be better than any Halloween party she had ever been to. Tiny orange lights were strewn throughout the grass; ghouls hung dispersed through the lower branches of the trees, and carved pumpkins lined the entrance. The porch was made to look like a cemetery, littered with fake moss and erect tombstones. A hidden smog machine spilled smoke over the veranda and cast the entrance into an eerie fog. Nikka could hear the music coming from the inside of the house; it shook the walls and thumped like a heartbeat.

Of course, there was also a guard, clad in the usual Wildwood red and black, stoically standing next to the key slot. Nikka had to step through a wall of fake spider webs to enter the foyer. She crossed a hallway and ended up facing another closed door. Next to the door was a large toy clown sitting in a rocking chair. The clown looked sad and murderous. He opened his mouth and spoke:

"If a party you seek
Heed my warning - beware
You will scream, you will shriek
And find death on the way there."

The clown raised his animatronic arm and pointed at the closed door. Nikka took an anxious step back; she wasn't fond of clowns.

"What are you waiting for?" challenged a voice from behind her. "Don't be scared," he whispered into her ear.

Nikka recognized the smooth and callous voice instantly. She felt him breathing down her neck and winced as he put his hand on the small of her back and gently nudged her forward. Nikka sighed, there was no getting out of it now. She pushed the door and Izaya followed her into the first room of the haunted house. They found themselves in a dark space, lit by a single dangling light bulb that flickered and swung from side to side. Nikka could see another door at the end of the room, *the way out*. She took a cautious step forward and heard Izaya chuckle at her. Suddenly, a dark masked figure jumped out at Nikka and screeched. Nikka let out a scream, followed quickly with an embarrassed laugh, as the figure retreated back into the darkness. Out of fear she had grabbed Izaya's hand, and Izaya squeezed it, holding on. Surprised, she turned towards him and in a brief flicker of light she caught him smiling. A second later the light was switched off completely and they were plunged into darkness. Someone grabbed Nikka's leg, then her shoulder. The light went on again, and for the briefest moment, they saw that they were surrounded by five more masked figures, and then the light flickered off again. The effect was terrifying. Nikka screamed again and the pair bolted forwards, out the door at the end of the room. On the other side they found themselves in a hallway; the door behind them swung shut and a child's screechy laughter echoed through the room.

Nikka laughed hysterically and took a moment to catch her breath, she clutched her side with one hand, painfully aware that Izaya was still holding the other. The hallway was lined with skinny side tables, which were covered in skulls, fake pearls, and jars of goo full of submerged distorted specimens - bugs, eyeballs, lizards. The pair traversed the hallway slowly. There were fake Victorian portraits fixed onto the walls; their eyes blinked red as Izaya and Nikka walked by, setting off the motion sensors. Ominous music played in the background. Nikka was glad to leave the creepy hallway behind as they found themselves at another door.

The next room was bathed in red light. In the corner, a man dressed as a doctor was working on a severed head on a surgical table. Recorded screams and squeals echoed through the air, turning Nikka's stomach inside out. The doctor looked at Nikka and Izaya, and then smiled, a wicked smile, before slicing right into the head. The head squealed loudly and blood sprayed everywhere. Nikka screamed again and Izaya laughed at her; it was the first time Nikka had heard him laugh so genuinely, a warm laugh, doughy and unpolluted. Nikka wasn't scared anymore, she held onto Izaya's hand as he led her through the rest of the haunted house. The next room had witches chanting over a smoking cauldron, the room after that was a torturer's den, followed by a skinny hallway lined with black candles and moving skeletons. Finally, they made it into the last room; Nikka could tell because she could feel the bass thumping through the wall on the other side. The door behind them closed; the room was dimly lit, the walls covered in velvet, and Nikka couldn't see a way out.

"You look beautiful tonight," said Izaya, his manner easy and confident.

"Thank you," said Nikka. She was nervous, her voice cracked; he was so close to her. *And why are we still holding hands*? She wondered, pink creeping into her cheeks. The room was dark, but Nikka could make out a figure in the corner, just sitting there, not moving. Nikka tried to relax; she figured whatever trick was coming her way it would be over soon enough. Izaya squeezed her hand.

"How come you're not wearing a costume," she asked him.

He was wearing a black V-neck and tight jeans. He

pulled back his plump lips and showed her his fangs.

"Points for effort," Nikka joked sarcastically. She stood still and Izaya pressed closer to her. Nikka felt like her blood would bubble up through her skin. With jittery anticipation they both watched the dark, immobile figure in the corner.

"I didn't think you were so easily scared," he whispered into her ear. Nikka didn't know how to tell him that it was *he* who was having that effect on her, not the haunted house. Suddenly, the lights went out and something dropped onto Nikka's face. It was moving and felt like slips of fabric and bits of goo-like spiders and intestines. The lights went on again and a man with a knife sticking out of his eye appeared before her.

"Welcome to the party," he said in a creepy, nasal drawl. "This way, please."

The man lifted up a sheet of velvet to reveal a door. Izaya let Nikka's hand go, and for a moment she felt a pang of regret, but she willed it away. Nikka went through the door first and emerged into a large decorated reception room full of people.

There were people dancing everywhere, laser lights blinking through the air, and a band dressed as skeletons was performing on a stage at the front of the large room. Suddenly, Nikka was enclosed in someone's arms. *Tristan.* She smiled at him and he kissed her cheek. Sums was right behind him. Tristan was wearing a black cape, a Venetian outfit and a black hat.

"Hey there, cool costume," he yelled over the music. He let her go and was looking at her, impressed. Nikka beamed at him. Sums was dressed as a Jedi and he eagerly waved at Nikka with his lightsaber.

"Thanks," Nikka yelled back. "I know Sums is a Jedi, but what are you?" she said, tilting her head at Tristan. Tristan pressed a white, angular mask onto his face.

"I'm Casanova. The infamous rake," he said. Tristan pulled Nikka back into his arms.

"So you were stuck going through the haunted house with Izaya, huh?" He nodded in the direction where Izaya was already standing, encircled by a group of friends. Nikka nodded and shrugged her shoulders as if to say, *so what?* Sums shot her a knowing, slightly disapproving look.

"I was stuck with Stella," complained Tristan. "She screamed even when there was nothing happening." Tristan rubbed the inside of his ear for emphasis. "My ears still hurt," he added.

"I can imagine," said Nikka and smiled.

"Well, I was by myself, so I was doing all the screaming," said Sums. Nikka and Tristan laughed, then Tristan grabbed Nikka's hand and pulled her to the dance floor.

Nikka danced and studied the room. As well as the amazing skeleton band, there was a full Halloween-themed buffet and the ceiling was covered in spiderwebs and suspended bats. The Dean and Stamos were nowhere to be seen, but the party was littered with guards, who occupied all four corners of the room and kept a watchful eye over proceedings.

Nikka was dancing with Sums and Tristan. Amber stopped by quickly to greet them, and then went to talk to another art student by the buffet; a tall, handsome boy with dreads. Amber was dressed as mother nature; sticks, shrubs, leaves, and other greenery were fixed to her green dress; it looked odd, but not too odd for Amber. The pair remained engaged in conversation for the better part of an hour. Sums kept risking nervous looks in their direction.

Nikka noticed that Marcus Jenkins was dancing with and kissing one of Violet's friends. Across the room, she saw Stella gawking at them unhappily. Violet's other friend seemed to be comforting her, she had her arm around her shoulder and Nikka saw her sneakily give Stella a swig from a flask. At the other end of the room Violet was dancing around Izaya, who looked bored. Violet looked beautiful dressed as Medusa, clad in a long toga paired with golden necklaces and tiny snakes attached to her hair. She swayed seductively near Izaya and Nikka felt a hatred rise up in her. She knew the rat was Violet's doing, she just didn't know how to prove it, or what to do about it. She didn't want to risk anything, whether it was caution, or maybe cowardice, her place at Wildwood was worth more than petty revenge. Nikka carried on dancing.

When Nikka looked back to Stella half-an hour later, her roommate was swaying sloppily. Stella stumbled forward a little, Jordan caught her and they laughed. *She can be friends with whomever she wants,* Nikka reminded herself with irritation. The music was loud, all Nikka could do was dance, but she kept sneaking looks at Stella, something about her behavior was *off.* Nikka just couldn't put her finger on it. The song changed and the band began to play a slow number. Sums looked awkwardly at Tristan, then at Nikka, and then back again.

"Go ask her to dance," said Tristan warmly. He cocked his head in the direction where Amber was standing.

"She's busy," said Sums sullenly.

"You're making excuses, buddy," warned Tristan.

Nikka felt a hand loop around her arm and she was tugged backward.

"Nikka, I need to talk to you, now," urged Izaya who had suddenly appeared behind her. Nikka took a step back, and instinctively looked in Violet's direction. Violet was gone.

"Can I help you?" said Tristan, with challenge in his voice. Izaya turned towards him slowly; his green eyes glowered with annoyance.

"Sure, why don't you go fetch me a drink?" said Izaya dismissively, and then he turned back to Nikka. Tristan grabbed Izaya by the arm and Izaya faced him, ready to pounce. The boys were clearly about to fight, so Nikka wedged herself in between them.

"Stop it!" she yelled. "What, Izaya? What is it?"

"You need to get your roommate home," he said.

"What? Why?" Nikka looked over at Stella, who was swaying to the music by herself in a corner.

"Just trust me, take her home, now," Izaya urged.

Nikka looked around, she didn't want to leave. She looked back at him, expecting Izaya to elaborate, but he looked uncomfortable.

"There's still an hour left of the dance, why should I take her home?"

"Violet knows she's the rat," explained Izaya.

"So what? No one here is scared of your tiny girlfriend," said Tristan defiantly. Izaya ignored him.

"They have this thing, Violet and her friends, about poisoning rats. They've done it a couple of times in the past... It's this pill from Mexico, it makes you really drunk..." Izaya struggled to find the right words. He hesitated and stuttered. Nikka had never seen him like this. Her brain shot back to the flask in Jordan's hand, and finally she understood what was going on. She looked at Stella; her dancing was slow, messy, her eyes half-closed.

"They...they drugged her?" Nikka's voice shook.

There was the faintest nod from Izaya. He didn't meet her eyes. A moment later Nikka was at Stella's side, leading her out, back through the haunted house. Sums and Tristan followed close behind. Stella looked up at Nikka hazily, and leaned into her. Stella moaned in discomfort and tried to say something, but couldn't form any words.

"Shhh, everything is going to be okay. We're taking you home," Nikka soothed.

Halfway down the candlelit hallway Stella's body went suddenly limp and she passed out. The gang stopped and looked at each other in panic.

"There are guards at the entrance, if they see her like this she'll be expelled for sure," said Sums.

Nikka looked around the hallway and spotted a window at the far end, half-covered by a velvet curtain. Tristan followed her gaze. He approached the window, shoved the decoration and curtain aside, and propped the window open. Stella's eyes were still open, but they were glazed; she look confused and her body was completely limp. Tristan and Sums carried her over to the window as best they could. Nikka jumped through the window first, Sums went second, then Tristan lifted Stella through the window, and with his hands between her armpits carefully lowered her down, where Nikka and Sums could receive her.

Under the cover of the woods the boys carried Stella all the way to Roseland. Then they snuck her in while Nikka distracted the concierge. Once in the room, they laid her down on the carpet. Sums grabbed a bottle of water, and Nikka grabbed a rag. She tried to wake Stella up, but it wasn't working. Desperate, she pressed the button on her bedside table and minutes later Magda came bustling in.

Magda took one look at the boys, and then at Stella on the floor.

"Someone gave her something; I mean, she was poisoned," explained Nikka, for lack of a better explanation. "Please help," she implored.

"I know what to do," said Magda determinedly. She left, and reappeared moments later with a few little black pills; she crushed them up in a glass and mixed them with water.

"She needs to drink all of this," explained Magda. "Even if she spits it out." Magda propped Stella up and forced the liquid down Stella's throat. Stella's eyes jerked open and she immediately spat out the vile looking black sludge. Magda forced more down her throat. Stella threw up, again, and again, and again. Finally, she stopped and looked better; some of the color had returned to her face. With a few incoherent mumbles, Stella rolled over on her side and went to sleep. Magda looked up at the boys and Nikka. Her eyes filled with a quiet disappointment.

"We will talk about this tomorrow," she scolded. Then she walked out. The room was silent. Nikka looked at Tristan, and then at Sums; both boys looked defeated.

Nikka began to shake, the rage inside her rose, higher and higher, like smoke.

"I'll be back," she said, her voice shaky. She didn't wait for the boys to respond. She walked through the hallway, out of Roseland and down the hill. Suddenly, she was running. A light drizzle was coming down. Her dress was falling apart, but she didn't care. Nikka ran into the forest, trekked up a hill, through a clearing and arrived by a meeting spot called *The Point*. She walked quietly, listening to the distant voices of Violet's gang; a while back Stella had told her that *The Point* was Violet's preferred spot.

For a moment Nikka's rage was gone; the physical exertion had dissipated it. There was sweat at the nape of her neck, and it had turned cold. The icy air of the mountain chilled her to the bone, though her blood ran hot. She spotted them - Violet, Jordan, Marcus, Izaya, and four more familiar girls and boys that she didn't know by name. The group was sitting on the boulder, continuing the party. The sight filled Nikka with a fresh wave of anger. Decidedly, she walked towards them. Izaya saw her first; he rose from the boulder in one swift motion and watched her cautiously. Jordan saw her next.

"This is a private party," Jordan called out snidely.

Violet looked annoyed to see her. "What are *you* doing here?"

Nikka climbed onto the boulder where they were all

sitting. She was well aware that everyone was staring at her, confused. Violet was sitting at the furthest edge of the boulder, right next to the cliff's edge. Her feet were hanging off of it. Nikka grabbed Violet by the sides of her jacket and dragged her up. Violet screamed. Nikka held on tight and pushed Violet to the very edge of the boulder. She was holding her, but Violet's entire body was leaning into the abyss, toward certain death. The only thing stopping her falling was Nikka. Violet screamed again.

"What...what are you doing?" she stuttered in wild fear.

Jordan and Violet's other friends approached Nikka from behind, cautiously.

"If you touch me, I'll let her go," said Nikka. Violet's friends took a step back. Jordan gasped. Violet was shaking and holding onto Nikka's hands for dear life, her nails dug into Nikka's skin.

"Nikka, what are you doing? Let me go! Please!" she begged. Her tone was no longer authoritative. The dainty girl was terrified. Nikka smiled.

"You should know, Violet, that some bad things are irreversible," Nikka said calmly; she intentionally let her grip on Violet slip just a little bit. Violet squealed with fear. Nikka continued.

"Do you know what will happen if I drop you off this cliff, Violet?" asked Nikka icily. Violet shook like a leaf. "If I do this, this *bad* thing, I will be expelled, arrested, imprisoned, but it won't matter, because you will be dead, and the damage will be done." She spat. "Some bad things can't be undone, Violet."

Tears spilled from Violet's face, she was shaking and grasping Nikka's hands, which were wound tightly around her jacket. Nikka let her slip a tiny bit more. She heard movement behind her.

"One more person moves and Violet goes off the cliff," snapped Nikka, trying her best to sound menacing. Whoever it was stepped back. Nikka couldn't risk the two of them falling off the cliff. She turned her attention back to a weeping Violet.

"What you did to Stella was *bad*. It can't be undone. You took away her free will, just like I'm taking away yours now. I've got your life in my hands; I can control what happens. Just like you tried to control what happened to Stella. It doesn't feel nice, does it?"

Violet shook her head.

"Does it?" growled Nikka; she shook her one more time.

"No, no it doesn't. I'm sorry," Violet stuttered. "I'm really, really sorry."

Nikka moved her face closer to Violet's.

"Bad things can't be undone," Nikka repeated. With those words she pulled her back from the cliff and let Violet drop onto the boulder. Violet fell to her knees, sobbing. Jordan rushed to her, and put her arms around her. Nikka didn't look at anyone, but knew they were all watching her with terror as she left.

Nikka walked fast, down the path through the forest that led back to campus. The moonlight lit her way. The wind lashed at her, and she was suddenly conscious that she had no jacket. She heard steps behind her, but she wasn't going to run. Instead she braced herself for a fight and turned around. Izaya stood in front of her. He closed the distance between them and, unexpectedly, took her face in his hands.

"Are you alright?" he asked softly.

Nikka felt relief at his reaction. With that question she also felt tension, fear, confusion, and the weight of the realization of what she had just done crash down on her. She started to cry.

"I don't know why I did that, I...I... was just...so angry," she explained through sobs. Her whole body was overcome with the cold and with waves of tears. Suddenly, there was the sound of people approaching. Nikka looked up in fear. Izaya grabbed her and pulled her into the cover of the woods, he was hiding her, just as he had done after the townie party. He opened his jacket and enveloped her in his warmth. Nikka sobbed hard into the warm leather. The people that walked by were talking animatedly and didn't hear her. Once they were gone, Nikka regained her senses and pushed Izaya away.

"Get away from me," she snarled. She could not

control her crying; it was getting worse and worse. Her body was shaking irrepressibly and she was so cold she couldn't make sense of anything that had happened.

"No," he said simply.

Izaya pushed her against a nearby tree, so hard it scratched her exposed back. Then he kissed her. This was different from the kiss at the townie party; it was rough, hungry and passionate. Half-heartedly Nikka hit him, again and again, but he didn't stop kissing her. He pushed himself against her, with a passion that was almost violent, and in that moment Nikka let herself go, and kissed him back, completely, fully. She could taste her own tears on him. Could feel his cold cheek against hers. She felt his hands exploring her back, and then cupping her face, as if he could never get enough of her.

Nikka withdrew from him. She wiped her eyes.

"This won't happen again, any of this," she managed coldly. She tried in vain to catch her breath.

"Why not?" he asked softly. He leaned against a tree opposite her.

"Why not?" repeated Nikka angrily, "Why not? Are you serious? I just held your girlfriend over a cliff. *Your* girlfriend, you know, the one who poisoned my friend? Who apparently has done this kind of vile thing before, and yet is still *your* girlfriend. Whom you cheat on with her friends, and with *me*." Nikka paused and collected herself.

"Labels are stupid, Nikka," he said evenly. "They mean

nothing in the real world."

"I don't want to be part of any of it anymore, Izaya. It's all...dirty," she said, for a lack of a better word. Izaya looked up, his eyes shined under the moonlight, with guilt, and desire.

Nikka turned and walked away. Izaya did not follow her.

10

Gratitude

The Wildwood Academy shuttle bus was as comfortable as the Academy itself: new seats, shiny surfaces, large tinted windows, and a flat screen TV. All for a 15-minute drive into town. The Academy had scheduled a field trip for the first weekend of November, as a treat. This was their first *official* outing, although for some, like Tristan, who snuck into town at least once a week, it was far from their first visit. Nikka spotted Izaya and Violet occupying the back row, surrounded by friends, as always. Violet noticed Nikka and quickly looked away; she had not made eye contact with Nikka since the incident at The Point. Nikka could tell Violet was scared of her, and after how she had treated Stella, Nikka didn't mind. Izaya let his eyes linger on Nikka for a short moment, and then looked away. They hadn't spoken since the incident either; he was doing what she'd asked, he was leaving her alone.

Amber, Tristan, Stella and Sums were already on the bus. Nikka waved at them, and plumped into a seat next to Stella. The bus jerked and took off. Tristan reached his head over the seats and into Nikka's row.

"Hey, Nik," he said affectionately. "Stella, how are you on this fine day?" he asked carefully. Stella hugged her pink purse close to her torso.

"Fine, thanks," she said dimly. She looked out the window and watched the passing scenery. Tristan raised an eyebrow and shot Nikka a concerned look. Nikka shrugged her shoulders. No, Stella wasn't *fine.* She hadn't been fine since she had woken the day after Halloween without any memory of the previous night. Nikka had filled her in, of course; it was the right thing to do. Stella was embarrassed that Sums and Tristan had carried her when she was unconscious, embarrassed that Magda and the boys had force fed her charcoal, and then seen her get sick all over the floor, but most of all she was wounded that her supposed 'friends', Jordan and Violet, had been the cause. Rumors had spread, the whole school now knew that Stella was the rat, and some of their less tolerant classmates sucked air in through their front teeth and made rat noises when Stella walked by. Stella had sulked the entire week after the party, said very little, ate very little, and stopped accessorizing her uniform. In Stella's mind, she had involuntarily committed social suicide, and being expelled might have been a better fate.

Nikka played Stella's favorite music each morning, and even asked her for style advice, but it did nothing to cheer her up.

The bus traversed the woods and shook a little over the bumps in the road. Amber was knitting something; she paused and glanced over at Stella.

"I'm knitting you a hat," she declared cheerfully. Stella looked over the seat. There was a mass of something fuzzy, misshapen and turquoise resting in Amber's lap, like a curled up cat with mange. Stella smiled weakly, but it was unconvincing, more like a grimace. Sums stuck his head over and into their row, like a giraffe.

"So, Stella, are you excited? Shopping *is* your favorite activity, isn't it?" asked Sums. Nikka shot him a reprimanding look, as if to say, *You are not helping.*

"There's nothing to buy here," said Stella grumpily. She continued to stare out the window, her expression lifeless. Sums sat back down, defeated.

"There is a cupcake shop on Main Street," he said defensively. Nikka knew that Sums was very excited. She and Sums, the full scholarship kids, got an allowance of 50 dollars for each school outing. Magda had delivered the freshly printed bill in an envelope and Nikka had folded it neatly into her coin purse.

Fifteen minutes later, the bus pulled into the town square off of Main Street. The gang dismounted and gathered under the shade of a nearby tree. Nikka watched

Izaya, Violet and their friends walk off away from town and towards the residential houses. Nikka told herself that she didn't care where they were going.

"I'm thinking cupcakes?" Nikka suggested.

"I need the tech store, the supermarket, the comic book store..." Sums began to list things off on his fingers.

Amber chimed in. "And I want to go buy some new crystals, candles, beads..."

"Guys," said Stella nervously. "If it's alright with you, I'm just going to go get my nails done." Stella looked sad, vulnerable and broken.

"Sure," said Nikka, disappointed. "Do you want me to come with you?" Stella shook her head and walked off. Tristan shifted in place for a few seconds.

"I kind of need to go take care of some *stuff* too," he said, uneasily facing Nikka. Nikka pretended to rummage in her pockets. She didn't want to know what that *stuff* was. They had never talked about the details of their first meeting, or about what Tristan did when he went to town on his own. Nikka didn't want to ask questions; she wasn't sure she'd like the answers, but she liked whatever it was that she and Tristan had.

"No problem," she said, and smiled. Tristan pecked her on the cheek and tucked his hands in his pockets.

"I'll meet you for a cupcake later," he said and walked off.

"It's just us then," said Sums. He looked at Amber

nervously, as if she too were about to leave them.

"At least we have one gentlemen to accompany us ladies into town," said Amber in a fake southern drawl. Nikka laughed. Amber linked one arm with Sums and the other arm with Nikka, and the trio set off towards the shops.

×

They had been walking around for two hours and Nikka's feet were hurting. They had stopped at the comic book shop where Sums searched the shelves for a good half hour, then they visited a run down tech store that didn't have a single one of the items Sums wanted in stock, then a jewelry shop where Amber bought beads for her knitting, and a woodwork shop where Nikka had purchased a small wooden bracelet that said *Wildwood*. They had ended up at *The Moon Goddess*, a messy, metaphysical store filled with incense, crystals, birthstones and self-help books. There was even a complex-looking machine that could tell you the color of your aura for a 20-dollar fee. Amber was in the back room getting her palms read. Nikka examined the arrangement of crystals sprawled before her. She read the description of what the stones were meant to bring - *health, happiness, love, peace, energy, and courage.*

Nikka picked up one that said *Prosperity* for her mother. After all, that was what Daria wanted most right now- a job and some money, because despite many job interviews, she was still unemployed. She wondered if there was one she could get for Sonya, maybe one that said *Sobriety.* Instead, she picked out one that said *Health*, a close second. Thanksgiving was in two weeks, and she wanted to get a little something for them both. Nikka paid the cashier and walked over to Sums, who didn't see her. She leaned in to peak at what he was examining in between his thick fingers. He noticed her and stepped back, startled. He tried to shove the item away, but it was too late, Nikka saw it: a silver chain with a small fairy pendant. Sums turned a bright shade of red. Nikka grinned at him.

"I'm going to get some air, I'll wait for you outside," she said. "I think she would really like that," she added encouragingly, and headed outside. Amber was very bouncy after her reading; she skipped along merrily as they headed to their next stop, the supermarket.

"The psychic told me I have a trip coming up. That I will either be leaving a place behind, or going somewhere new," explained Amber happily. "I think she means my trip to Peru with my mother over Thanksgiving."

Sums looked like he wanted to say something along the lines of *"That's not fortune telling, it's deductive reasoning."* But he refrained because Amber looked so pleased. As they approached the gritty exterior of *Wildwood Produce*, Nikka noticed a familiar face. Alex *the townie* walked out of the store, clutching a six-pack of beer in one hand and a bag of groceries in the other.

"Hey!" Nikka yelled sunnily at the boy. She sauntered over to him.

Alex looked behind him, as if he thought she was calling to someone else. Then he looked at Nikka skeptically, searching his memory, trying to figure out where he had met her.

"We met at your party," offered Nikka. "I saw what happened to your uncle the other day. I'm sorry. Is he alright? I don't know how the guards get away with treating him that-"

Alex interrupted her.

"How did you know that was my uncle?" He snapped. Nikka was taken aback by his tone, which was angry and savage.

"I just put two and two together. That boy, Zac, told me your uncle is a journalist investigating the school," Nikka explained timidly.

"I'm going to kill Zac," Alex grumbled under his breath.

"Is he okay?" asked Nikka.

Alex was momentarily distracted.

"What?"

"Your uncle, is he okay?"

Alex's features softened a little. He looked around them, as if to make sure that no one could overhear. Amber and Sums were standing a dozen feet away by the store entrance, talking and waiting for Nikka.

"Look, no offense, you seem like a nice girl," said Alex, "but I can't be seen talking to you." Alex turned and walked off, leaving Nikka stumped. She didn't tell the others what Alex had said, but she thought about it, mulled it over in her head in the store whilst Sums was buying junk food, then later in the cupcake shop as she shared a raspberry vanilla cupcake with Tristan, and again on the bus on the way home. It was the only stain on an otherwise wonderful day in town.

×

"You should really eat something," said Nikka sternly. Stella looked at her untouched muesli. Amber, Sums and Nikka shared a concerned look across the lunch table. Tristan was absent-mindedly eating his cornflakes.

"You should try the chocolate chip pancakes, they're amazing," offered Sums.

"No, thanks," said Stella mildly. Her eyes travelled to the other side of the cafeteria where Marcus, Jordan and Violet were having breakfast. She pushed her bowl of cereal away and picked up her tray.

"I'll see you guys later," she said softly.

"Jeez, is she going to be like this for much longer?" asked Sums, once Stella had left.

"I hope not," Tristan echoed grumpily. Nikka scowled at them both.

"Healing takes time," she said. "What Violet did to her

was terrible."

"Speaking of healing," said Amber. "I found this great ritual in one of my holistic healing books. It involves the forest, crystals, and a full cleanse of the soul; I think we should do it this coming weekend, for Stella," said Amber thoughtfully. Sums frowned.

"Does this healing ritual have any umm... scientific basis?" he asked, politely holding back. Amber smiled at him.

"Not everything is based on science, sweetie," she answered. Sums looked like he was prepared to argue, but being called *sweetie* had momentarily thrown him off. He smiled shyly.

"What is everyone doing for Thanksgiving?" asked Nikka, in attempt to change the subject.

"I'm going to visit my folks in Massachusetts," said Tristan. He shifted uneasily in his seat, as if the notion of visiting his parents for Thanksgiving wasn't something he found particularly pleasant.

"Sounds like fun," said Nikka flatly. She didn't want Tristan to get the idea that she wanted to come with him. She and Tristan had spent a few weeks tittering on the brink between being friends and just a little bit more, and that brink was where she felt most comfortable.

"I'm going to Peru, as you already know," said Amber dreamily. She bit into a strawberry. Nikka shifted her attention to Sums, who was eating quietly.

"And I'm doing family stuff, you know *the usual,*" he said airily. Nikka didn't press further; she knew Sums hated talking about his family. Sums plopped the last bite of pancakes into his mouth and rose quickly.

"We are going to be late for class," he urged Nikka. Sums' classes had finally been redesigned just for him, so he no longer shared basic math or science with Nikka, but they still had their first class in the same building. They said their goodbyes and made their way down the hill.

"Can I make a quick call?" asked Nikka. She wanted to call her mom and confirm their Thanksgiving plans, and aside from Izaya's, Sums' was the only phone that could break the dead zone. Somehow, hearing everyone else's plans had made her nervous. Sums pulled out his phone in front of the math building and looked around hesitantly.

"Be discreet," he stressed.

Nikka nodded and hid the phone up her sleeve. She found a supply closet at the back of the math building and dialed the number. The line rang through.

"Hello," Daria's voice sounded from the other end.

"Hey, Mom," said Nikka excitedly. "I don't have much time, I just wanted to ask what we are doing for Thanksgiving. What time are you picking me up?" There was a static silence, and for a second Nikka thought the line had cut out.

"Mom?" she said.

Nikka heard Daria sigh into her receiver, a heavy, loaded sigh. "The thing is, sweetie, Sonya has this new boyfriend," explained Daria carefully. "He's got a drinking problem, and they are spending a lot of time in the apartment building; so it's not exactly *ideal* circumstances right now to be making a turkey and giving thanks," Daria paused, waiting for Nikka to fill the silence, like she always did. "I've been trying to find a new place, but no luck yet."

"That's alright," said Nikka with forced gaiety.

"You've made a lot of friends there," said Daria confidently, as if she knew this first hand. "Could you ask one of them if you could spend Thanksgiving at their house?"

"Sure," Nikka lied, and tried to keep her voice perky for her mom's sake.

"Great!" exclaimed Daria, "I'm so happy you don't have to spend it *here*. I'll find a new apartment for us by Christmas, I promise!"

On her way back to class, Nikka panicked. Where would she stay? She didn't want to ask Tristan, Stella was leaving for another state and Amber was going to Peru. Sums would have been perfect, but any time Nikka inquired about his family or home life he made it clear that it was not up for discussion. Nikka was out of options.

×

"I still don't understand what we are doing," whined Stella. She kicked a piece of moss out of her way. Nikka and Stella, spearheaded by Amber, were headed uphill and into the woods. It was close to sundown. Nikka looked around; she didn't recognize this part of the woods, it wasn't like the woods of pine leading up to The Point, or the dense wood that she and Izaya had crossed on their way back from the party. The trees here grew a little further apart, letting more sun in, and the uphill climb was steeper.

Nikka had reluctantly agreed to go along with Amber's wild idea of performing a healing ceremony for Stella. Stella's sadness had become unbearable, and Nikka could no longer remain a spectator to it. The way Nikka saw it, if this holistic exorcism didn't help Stella, at least it might make her laugh.

"It's a surprise," said Nikka. She saw a glimmer of excitement cross Stella's face.

They came upon a creek and followed it upwards. Amber walked with purpose and Nikka wondered how she had found the place that they were headed to, whatever *it* was, it was located up the mountain, with no roads or paths leading to it. They followed the creek further. Amber clutched her large duffle bag with both hands. Nikka wondered what was in it. They arrived at a large boulder and abruptly, Amber stopped.

"Climb up and lay down," she instructed. She pointed at the massive boulder. It was large, smooth, and majestic. Stella threw a hesitant look at the large rock, then at Nikka. Nikka smiled encouragingly. Stella climbed up the boulder and lay down. The two other girls followed suit. Amber sunk to her knees beside Stella, opened the bag and pulled out a few crystals, a candle and a tied bunch of sage leaves. Stella stared sideways at the items with suspicion, as if they were surgical tools. Nikka sat down and watched.

"Close your eyes," Amber whispered to Stella. Stella obliged. Amber began to line the crystals up on Stella's body, one on her head, and then in a diagonal line down her body. Stella giggled when the first crystal touched her forehead.

"It tickles," she chuckled.

It's working, thought Nikka with a sly smile. *It's cheering her up.* It was the first time she had seen Stella smile in weeks. Amber lit the sage and waved it over Stella's body. The sage left trails of smoke rings in the air. Nikka found the smell comforting, especially when it mixed with the crispness of the forest air. The sun continued to set and the woods were getting pinker.

"Repeat after me," said Amber. "Bad energy be gone. Bad energy be gone. Bad energy be gone."

"Bad energy be gone," said Stella hesitantly. It sounded more like a question when she said it. "Bad energy be gone, bad energy be gone,"

Amber made Stella repeat this twice more, and Nikka joined in. Stella giggled again, at the sheer silliness of the whole ordeal. They sat there in silence a few moments, whilst the sky turned from pink to red. Amber pulled the crystals off of Stella and put them back into her bag. Then she pulled out a yellow candle.

"This is a healing candle. I'm going to light it and leave it here," she said. Stella nodded. One thing Nikka liked about Stella was that she wasn't stubborn; you could take her to the woods and perform a healing ceremony on her, and she wouldn't stop you. Amber melted the bottom of the candle a little, so that it would stick to the boulder, and lit the wick. Then she pulled out a blindfold.

"Turn around," she said to Stella. Nikka raised a brow as if to say, *There's more?* and looked at Amber uncertainly. She and Amber hadn't discussed anything beyond the candle, and she felt a little nervous. Stella stared at the blindfold in Amber's hands, dumbfounded.

"Why do I need to be blindfolded?" she asked warily.

"Just trust us," said Amber. Her soothing voice was hypnotic. Stella turned and allowed Amber to fix the blindfold into place.

"Can you see anything?" she asked. Stella shook her head. Nikka shot Amber a worried look, but Amber just winked at her. She took Stella's hand and helped her climb off the boulder. Nikka followed as Amber guided them further up the forested hill.

The woods were getting darker, and Nikka found herself worrying about how they would find their way back. Amber held on tightly to Stella's hand and led her uphill for a while, then downhill. Stella was hesitant; she took each step as carefully as if she were crossing a floor of cracked glass. Nikka was so focused on Stella that she hadn't noticed where they were. She looked up and gasped.

"What is it?" asked Stella worriedly. She stopped walking.

They had emerged from the woods, into a clearing on a small cliff edge. The view here was different to what Nikka had seen at The Point or anywhere else in Wildwood; it was panoramic and revealed everything, from the desert at the foot of the mountains, to the rolling hills of the forest, and even the resting snow high on the neighboring peaks. The black of night was pushing in on the dusk, washing it away.

In the middle of the clearing there were water holes. Steam rose from them like escaping smoke. *Hot springs,* Nikka realized with a start. She couldn't speak. It was all so breathtaking, it had knocked the words clean out of her. Amber met her eyes and put a finger to her mouth, *Don't say anything*, she signaled. Amber guided Stella closer to the foot of the nearest hot spring. Stella breathed nervously.

"I need you to undress down to your underwear," said Amber calmly. Amber silently signaled for Nikka to do the same. Nikka obliged.

"Excuse me?" said Stella indignantly. Amber let go of her hand for a short moment and undressed herself, quickly. Then she regained hold of Stella's hand again.

"You were hurt. Someone betrayed your trust. Now you need to let go of that pain, and the only way to do that is to trust someone completely, let go, and surrender yourself to the elements," said Amber serenely. Nikka was in awe of her.

"What? Nikka are you there? I'm not sure about this," Stella's voice shook as she grappled blindly for Nikka with her free hand. Stella was terrified of being humiliated yet again.

"Trust us," said Nikka gently. Unconvinced, Stella let go of Amber's hand and took her clothes off. Then she stood there in a t-shirt and underwear, quivering from the cold.

"This is really scary," she complained as Amber led her one step at a time towards the hot spring. She signaled for Nikka to get in. Quietly Nikka climbed in, trying her best not to make a sound. The water welcomed her, hot and amazing.

"Are you ready to let go?" cheered Amber. Stella whimpered in response, but leaned into Amber's hand anyway.

"Yes," she declared confidently. With those words Amber slowly led Stella into the water. At first Stella yelped, surprised. Then she moved her arms a little, steadied herself, and smiled wide.

"Oh my god, are we in a Jacuzzi?" she asked excitedly.

"Better," said Nikka, as she pulled her blindfold off. Stella shrieked and then gasped as she took in the view around her.

"Wow," she whispered, awestruck, as Nikka had been. Amber cannonballed into the hot spring and covered them both in water. A splash war erupted, mingled with joyous screams and laughter.

Amber had thought of everything; she had brought towels, spare clothes, soda and even a small portable radio. The light was gone now. A blanket of black had stretched over the sky, and moments later it was studded with stars. The stars were brighter and more numerous than Nikka had ever seen. She sighed and moved around in the hot water.

The girls lounged in the hot spring for a little while, splashing and laughing. Then they sat watching the sky. There was a satisfied grin plastered on Stella's face and she looked happy, *truly happy*. Amber and Nikka shared a knowing grin. Amber's idea was genius, to heal Stella all you had to do was give her a new memory, vivid and wonderful, to replace the bad one she was dwelling on. A new story to tell, one that made the bitter night of Halloween pale in comparison. Here, on top of this mountain, nothing mattered. Nikka's mind too was cleansed by the hot water; she leaned back and grinned at the star-dotted sky. Nothing mattered when you were looking up at eternity.

×

The three happy girls made their way back to the dorms, laughing and skipping along the creek. They had changed into the dry clothes that Amber had packed for them, but their hair was still wet. Stella was back to her usual self and excitedly talking about her plans for Thanksgiving. They were about to exit the forest and cross the wide road that led back to campus when they were intercepted by a large truck. It passed them, and something fell off the back and onto the road. Nikka and the girls withdrew back to the shadows of the wood and watched as a man exited the truck, cursing under his breath. Nikka recognized the voice. Alex the townie grabbed the fallen bag and loaded it back onto his truck. He turned to walk away, but as he did, Nikka followed him. Amber and Stella stayed back.

"Hello, Alex," she said.

The boy turned, startled. He observed her curiously- the girl with wet hair, emerging from the forest at night, in the middle of nowhere.

"What are you doing here?" he asked. "You shouldn't be in the woods." Nikka instantly resented his condescending, authoritative tone.

"I could ask you the same thing," she said pointing at the car, which had the Wildwood logo stenciled on the side. For a second, Nikka wondered if he had stolen it.

"I run a laundry service for the Academy," he admitted through gritted teeth.

Nikka felt like he had slapped her in the face.

"Let me get this straight." she said measuredly. "You can't even exchange two words with me because the mere fact that I go to this school *disgusts* you, but you feel just fine renting your house out for Wildwood parties and working *for* the school?"

Nikka could tell she had surprised him with her bluntness. For the briefest moment Alex looked like he wanted to tell her something. Then his features hardened. He turned angry again, his tattooed arms flexed with tension.

"You know what they say, keep your friends close-" he muttered, and without finishing his sentence he turned, got into the truck and drove away, leaving Nikka standing in the middle of the street looking foolish.

"And your enemies closer," Nikka finished his sentence long after the truck had gone. She rolled her eyes. Amber and Stella emerged next to her.

"What's his problem?" asked Stella. Nikka stared at the road where the truck had just been.

"I have no idea," she said. "But I'm going to find out."

×

Nikka watched the procession of cars that crowded the street next to the dorms. Taxis, limos, town cars, and civilian cars queued on the long winding road that lined

Chadbourne, Roseland and Becks, as Wildwood students departed for their Thanksgiving holidays. Nikka was observing one person in particular. She had avoided looking at him for the last few days, but today she allowed herself to watch. He was wearing suit pants and a white button-down. Today, he looked older than everyone around him, groomed and serious. A fancy black town car pulled up in front of him. Violet was nowhere to be seen. *Have they already said goodbye?* Nikka wondered. She felt a sinking feeling in her gut. A driver emerged from the car and put Izaya's luggage in the trunk. Izaya lit a cigarette in broad daylight, perfectly unafraid of the consequences, and then got into the town car. Nikka watched it leave. She found herself wondering where Izaya was going, what his family was like, what he would be grateful for that weekend.

Nikka was going to stay at the Academy; after Daria canceled their plans, Nikka had been relieved to find out that staying was an option offered to all the students. She spotted Tristan walking towards her, pushed thoughts of Izaya away, and forced a quick smile. Sums and Amber caught up to him. Amber skipped over to Nikka.

"Hey!" she beamed. "My mom is at the back of all those cars. I just came over to say bye. Where are your folks?"

"On the way," Nikka lied.

Amber pulled Nikka into a hug. Nikka squeezed back.

Amber yelped out in pain and Nikka let her go instantly.

"Sorry," said Amber through a grimace. She rubbed her shoulder. "Nurse Smith gave me some shots the other day, my shoulder is still sore!" she explained.

"I know how you feel," said Nikka sympathetically.

"Well, have a good Thanksgiving," said Amber. She hugged Tristan and then Sums and walked off. Sums grinned like an idiot.

"My cab is here too," said Tristan. He hugged Nikka. For a moment she nuzzled into his neck. He smelled musky, of soap and oak.

"I'm grateful to have met you," he whispered nonchalantly in her ear. Nikka smiled. "Same," she whispered back.

"Have a good Thanksgiving, mate," he called to Sums. Tristan walked off and got into a taxi, and suddenly Sums and Nikka were left alone.

"So what time *is* your mom coming?" Sums asked suspiciously.

"Any minute now," said Nikka innocently. There was a pause, Sums observed her. Neither of them moved.

"You're staying here, aren't you?" asked Sums. Nikka prepared to argue, but Sums was smiling ear to ear.

"What are you smiling about?" She said defensively.

"I'm staying too!" he yelped. Nikka shrieked and tackled Sums into a bear hug.

×

On Thanksgiving Day a knock resounded on Nikka's door. She threw an excited look at Sums, who was curled up on her bed with a comic book, and then opened the door. Magda was on the other side; she smiled brightly, revealing her gold tooth, and carried in her heavily loaded silver tray table. The room was instantly filled with an intoxicating smell. In awe, Nikka gawked at the tray loaded with nearly a dozen foil-covered plates.

"Will you join us?" asked Nikka, eagerly facing Magda. Sums was busy lifting up the foils and inspecting all the delicacies on offer.

"No, I can't," said Magda, but she smiled at Nikka's invitation, and gave her shoulder a quick squeeze. Nikka realized with a sudden pang of guilt that Magda probably wasn't allowed to join them. It was probably *against the rules*. Magda was working on Thanksgiving, just like any other day, and Nikka's heart weighed heavy.

"Are you sure?" said Nikka, knowing the answer already.

"Some other time," said Magda reassuringly, as if she were reading Nikka's thoughts. "Have a nice dinner. And you," Magda pointed at Sums sternly, "Back to your own dorm before curfew!"

"Yes, Miss Magda," answered Sums dutifully. Magda left the room, and Nikka stared at the closed door for a moment. She loved Wildwood; it was a beautiful, magical place, but one thing she hated were the unforgiving *rules,* and the suffocating hierarchies that were the iron backbone to the school's fancy way of life.

"Time for a feast!" said Sums excitedly, pulling Nikka from her melancholy train of thought. He and Nikka began to unload the tray industriously. They pulled back the foils and laid out the plates on the floor, buffet style. Nikka had made a little decorative Thanksgiving table setting earlier that day- dry yellow leaves, a few origami swans that she hoped would resemble turkeys, and orange doilies, which she had cut out herself. She had also put pillows down for them to sit on, set out brown and orange napkins, and arranged a vase full of pinecones and twisted branches, which she had spray-painted gold.

Nikka and Sums had already had a great start to their Thanksgiving holiday. They had gone to the observatory and used the school's massive telescope, and Sums had told her the names of all the constellations. They had watched old scary movies and taken coffees and croissants up to *The Point* early that morning.

"Yes! They gave us pecan pie! They make the absolute best pecan pie. Just the right amount of cinnamon," said Sums knowingly. He unpacked the pie carefully, like it was something precious, and put it down on the ground. Nikka looked at him questioningly. He shrugged his shoulders.

"They had apple last year," he explained casually. "It's not as good." Nikka could no longer hold back the question that had been lingering at the back of her mind, but she waited till they were sitting down and serving themselves before asking it.

"Sums," she treaded carefully, "Did you spend all three of your Thanksgivings here?" she asked. Sums was loading up his plate, forming a tall tower of food. Nikka was doing the same. The school chef had thought of everything: turkey trimmings, stuffing, cranberry sauce, gravy, Brussels sprouts, mashed potatoes, string beans, pie, and Nikka's personal favorite - mashed yams covered in marshmallows.

"I never know why they add *this,*" he said, pointing with distaste at the yams. "It's like baby food," he said, trying to change the subject.

"Are you kidding? It's my favorite," said Nikka, "it's such an odd dish, and you would only eat it on one day of the year, that's what makes it special. Answer the question," she added stubbornly.

Nikka took her first bite of food- it was delicious. For a moment she felt bad that Daria was stuck at Sonya's, probably with nothing more than turkey cold cuts and half-drunk beer, but she also knew that by not coming home she was making Thanksgiving easier for her mother. Sums took his time, treading water, chewing slowly - as if he needed to enjoy himself to the fullest, because answering this question would put an end to the pleasure.

"I've spent every *single* one of my holidays here," he said simply, after some time.

"How come?" Nikka urged, softly. She couldn't drop it, it seemed too important to ignore.

"I don't have anywhere else to go," Sums explained in between mouthfuls of turkey. Nikka had half-expected this answer, but it shocked her anyway. She felt awful that she was such close friends with Sums, yet had never thought to press this issue about his family further. Sensing her guilt, Sums continued.

"Look, it's not like I was trying to hide it or anything," he told Nikka as he topped off his plate with seconds.

"Hide what?"

"The fact that I don't have a family, or a home. *Technically,*" said Sums so flatly that something stung inside Nikka's heart. She bit her lip, feeling guilty that she had forced the subject, and on Thanksgiving of all days!

"I'm sorry, Sums," she said.

"It's alright." He paused as if deciding whether or not to go on. "I was put in an orphanage when I was still a baby, then later in foster care. I moved around *a lot* and my 5th grade math teacher thought it would be fun to give me a mock SAT test - I got a perfect score on the math section. A few months later I got an invite from Wildwood. I mean, I could still go stay with my foster family for the holidays, since they technically still get paid for fostering me, but they're not very nice. And I would miss out on *this,*" he gestured at the spread. "String beans glazed in a pomegranate vinaigrette," he said, as if that were family enough. Nikka nodded, searching her brain for something comforting to say and coming up empty. What could possibly be said?

"Oh, come on, don't look at me so sadly," said Sums, his tone cheery again. "You've lost a parent too, it's not like you can't relate." Nikka nodded, she was starting to feel like a turkey, nodding away to everything he was saying, without saying anything much in return. She stroked his arm and for a brief moment held his hand, as if to say, *I'm here for you, you have me now.*

"So, tell me, how did you come to be such a gastronome?" asked Nikka. Sums smiled nostalgically.

"That part was always there, only the means weren't. At the orphanage, I once asked the chef if he could add a little fresh basil to the tomato soup. It was from a can. He almost hit me with the ladle!" Sums said, and Nikka laughed.

"One Thanksgiving," Nikka started, "My mom had just lost her job and we were really broke. She couldn't cook at our house because the electricity got shut off when we didn't pay the bill, so she came up with this idea that we could warm up the cans in the living room by making a small fire and cooking them over it... well, we set the house on fire." Sums laughed so hard he choked on his mashed potatoes.

"So, what did you do?" he asked once he had recuperated.

"We moved to another state," said Nikka. Sums tipped his head back and roared with laughter. Nikka pulled a bottle of sparkling apple cider from the tray and poured them two cups.

"When I was around eight years old I went on my own into one of those fancy organic stores, you know the ones that do the free tastings? I started sampling everything: Brazilian chocolates, Serrano ham, French cheese, Greek olives. I stayed there so long that they called the police because they thought I was a missing child. When the police took me home I asked if I could have some samples to go," Sums recounted with a grin.

Nikka laughed so hard her stomach hurt.

"Well, happy Thanksgiving," said Sums.

"Happy Thanksgiving," repeated Nikka. "I'm grateful for your friendship."

"I'm grateful for yours," he countered, "You're my first *real* friend here."

"I'm sure that's not true, but thanks anyway." Nikka beamed. She knew there was an age gap, but she still didn't understand how someone so wonderful could have been there for two years without making friends.

"You had a *Doctor Who* patch on your bag the first day I saw you. It's been my favorite show since I was little," said Sums. "I figured if you like Doctor Who, you couldn't be a bad person, so I decided to try my luck and introduce myself," he added playfully. Nikka smiled warmly. She decided not to tell him that her bag had come that way, from a thrift store.

Nikka cut up the pie and served an extra large piece to Sums. He smiled, smelled it, and dug in. Nikka felt the hot sugary mass make its way down her throat and sighed indulgently. *Sums was right*- it was the best pecan pie she had ever tasted. She took another swig of her cider to wash it down.

A moment later Nikka began to feel hot. She pulled off her scarf and then, still not feeling any cooler, pulled off her socks. Nikka looked around, her closet was swaying a little. Her neck was itchy and suddenly she was having a hard time swallowing. Nikka put a hand down on the carpet to steady herself. Sums stared at her.

"Nikka"- his voice wavered. "You don't look so good. Are you okay?" Nikka looked around her, at the pie, and then her eyes drifted to the bottle of cider. Lightheaded, she pointed at it.

"Allergic," she stuttered "*allspice*." She pointed at the cider bottle again. Sums looked at her, then at the bottle, then back again.

"You're allergic to allspice?" he said in a panic. "Didn't you fill out the meal request card?" he shrieked, almost yelling at her. Nikka shook her head. Magda had brought her the meal request card that week and Nikka had discarded the small piece of paper without reading it, deciding that whatever Wildwood chefs made was good enough for her. She completely forgot about her random allergy to a rarely used spice. The room was spinning; the edges of the furniture blurred. Sums had opened her nightstand and was anxiously digging through her things, throwing stuff down on the floor.

"EpiPen," he said urgently. "Where do you keep your EpiPen?"

"I don't have one," she managed. *My mom doesn't like doctors,* she wanted to add, but she was too hot. The room was too hot. Sums gawked at her in disbelief. A second later he pulled her to her feet and dragged her out of her dorm room. Sums shouted for Magda as he and Nikka made their way to the first floor, but she was nowhere to be found. Sums cursed under his breath and kept one hand tightly wound around Nikka's waist, the other under her arm as he led her out of Roseland. The fresh air outside made Nikka feel better. Sums looked around desperately and cursed again. There was no one in sight, just a parked security guard golf cart, red and black, standing outside the entrance to Becks.

"Just stay here for a moment," he instructed Nikka, and leaned her against the wall. Sums scurried off towards Becks. Nikka heard him yell, searching for the guard, and then curse again. She rested her face against the cold stone and tried to resist scratching her neck and face. Suddenly, she heard the low roar of the golf cart. Sums pulled up next to her and helped her into the front seat.

"Don't ask!" said Sums as he sped off down the serpentine paths. Sums cut corners at speed and Nikka almost flew out of the passenger seat. She looked at him in awe, her vision still blurry; it was the bravest she had ever seen him. It only took them a few minutes to get to the Health Center. Sums parked at the top of the hill out of fear the sharp descent that led down to the Health Center. As he half carried her toward it, Nikka spotted something, and pulled on Sums's sweater so hard it forced him to stop.

"Nikka, we have to keep moving," he urged, but Nikka was transfixed by the figures that had just emerged from the Health Center: Madame Grenoble, Nurse Smith and Stamos. There was a limo waiting for them. Grenoble gestured wildly with her hands and pointed at Nurse Smith. Nikka couldn't hear what they were saying, but it looked like they were arguing. A moment later the three of them boarded the limo, and drove off.

What are they doing here? She wondered, but then she stumbled forward, feeling lightheaded again. Sums sighed, picked her up and carried her all the way down to the Health Center. Inside they found a nurse, who quickly administered a dose of antihistamines into Nikka's arm. Sums and the nurse scolded Nikka for her inattentiveness, and half an hour later a guard drove them home. When they got back to the dorm, a worried Magda put Nikka to bed and made her a hot chocolate, she even allowed Sums to stay and keep her company until she fell asleep. Right before she dozed off, Nikka thought about how, despite the medical emergency, this had been one of her best Thanksgivings ever.

11

I'll Dance Forever in the Snow

The December air was chilly. Nikka zipped her coat all the way up to her chin and waited outside of her *Bataillisme* class for Madame Grenoble to arrive. Grenoble appeared into view a moment later, clad in an unbuttoned fur coat that revealed a black skirt suit underneath; she looked fabulous, as always.

"Hello, darling," she cooed in her heavy French accent.

"Good morning, Madame Grenoble," said Nikka sweetly. Inside the dome Nikka took her coat off and settled in front of her giant easel.

"Did you have a nice Thanksgiving?" asked Nikka. She hadn't had a *Bataillisme* class since before the holidays.

"Yes, it was really nice, I visited family in Manhattan," said Madame Grenoble distractedly. She was fiddling with the projector buttons.

For a second, Nikka thought she had misheard her.

"Oh, so you had a real *American* turkey dinner in NYC, and on Thanksgiving night, how cool. Did you spend the entire weekend in New York?" she pressed on.

"Yes, I did," said Grenoble growing irritated with the small talk.

"I visited my family too," lied Nikka.

"That's wonderful, darling," said Grenoble without the slightest bit of interest. "Now, back to the drawing board."

Two hours later, Nikka left Bataillisme feeling unsettled. Why would Madame Grenoble lie to her? Why would she want to hide the fact that she had been with Stamos and Nurse Smith on Thanksgiving night? *There could be a myriad of reasons*, thought Nikka reasonably, but still curiosity gnawed at her like a tiny rat trapped inside her brain. She had half an hour to kill, so she headed towards The Valley and sat down on the damp, downhill slope. She stared up at the yellow parachutes above - they swayed, intermeshed masses of different shades of yellow, rising into the air and falling back towards the ground, as if The Valley were taking large, yellow breaths. The beauty of it calmed her, as it always did. Nikka spotted a figure emerge from the woods. Izaya walked out into The Valley and stood in front of her, silent and statuesque. His hair was wet; it looked like he had been out in the rain for hours. His eyes shone bright green against the grey, overcast daylight, like emeralds embedded in stone.

"Hello," he said. Nikka couldn't help but notice that his mouth was also wet from the rain.

"Hello," Nikka answered.

"I was wondering if we could talk?" he asked, and cocked his head in the direction of the path that led up to The Point. Nikka looked at the path hesitantly, then at her watch.

"Fine, but I don't have much time," she conceded.

Wordlessly, Nikka followed Izaya uphill, through the cliff side clearing and up to a large boulder. They sat down on the boulder, side by side, their feet dangling off the precipice. Nikka noticed that her dog tags were peeking out from under her shirt, and she gently tucked them back in, but it was too late. Izaya reached for the nape of her neck and gently pulled the chain free. Nikka shuddered.

"Why do you always wear these?" he asked.

Nikka was surprised that he had noticed, she normally kept her dog tags well hidden.

"They were my dad's," she answered.

"I had family in the army too," he said tensely. A silence followed. Nikka wanted to ask why he had brought her there, but doing so would also bring them closer to parting, so she deviated instead.

"Why are you still with Violet?" she asked, finally. Izaya had not cared when Nikka held Violet over the cliff, he had kissed Nikka – twice - and he had kissed Jordan too. It didn't make sense. Izaya smiled, it clearly pleased him that Nikka cared enough to ask. For a minute, Nikka reprimanded herself for having given him that satisfaction, but then a flash of sadness crossed his smug face.

"I've known Violet since we were children. Our parents were friends. Violet knows all the skeletons in my closet, and sometimes, for people like *us,* that makes life easier."

It wasn't a clear answer, but it was an honest one. Nikka had hoped he would justify himself, or maybe lie. But he did neither, and she had to respect that. She wondered what the skeletons in his closet were, and felt suddenly envious of Violet for knowing them.

"One more question," said Nikka. Izaya chuckled.

"Don't get greedy now," he joked warmly.

Izaya stared over the precipice at the woods that stretched out before them; Nikka was momentarily entranced by the strict lines of his profile-his strong jaw, his sharp nose, his pronounced cheekbones.

"Why are you always hanging out in the woods?" she asked.

He shifted his gaze towards her and looked at her with that same conflicted expression he had when looking at the horizon.

"That's an easy one," he said. "Sometimes Wildwood

can make you feel trapped," he explained. "It's almost like they own you, in a way." Nikka thought back to the guards at the party, at their key cards, the Dean and she nodded in full agreement.

"But here in these woods, they can't own you. No one can. They can't watch or control you, it's too big to contain. It's the ideal hiding place." He smiled at her. Nikka smiled back, but she got the impression that Izaya wanted to hide from more than just the school.

"It's my turn to ask you a question," he said, his voice low and serious.

"I've done some bad stuff in the past. I know that, but I would really like it if we could start fresh, *Nikka Mason*," he said her full name softly and Nikka was surprised that he knew her last name. "I would like it if we could be friends?" he concluded.

Nikka smiled. She had never expected Izaya to take her up to The Point for this. She reached her hand out to him and he shook it. She tried to push down the feelings his touch gave her, and she smiled at this new simplified relationship they had entered into.

"I would like that very much," she answered.

×

On her way to lunch, Nikka was starting to feel a little guilty about her trip to The Point. Granted, there was nothing romantic about it, but Nikka felt like she had been doing something wrong. She didn't see Tristan often, and suspected he was always off somewhere doing something slightly illicit in town, breaking the rules one way or another. So it was his fault they didn't spend much time together, not hers. Sums, who shared a hallway with him in Becks, reported seeing him leave campus several nights a week and returning late, whistling happily and playing with a poker chip in between his fingers.

Nikka met with Stella, Sums and Amber for lunch.

"I'm excited to actually remember *this* party," said Stella enthusiastically at the table. She was referring to the Winter Ball that Stamos was organizing. They had received their invitations a few days prior.

"I'm excited to not have to carry you this time," said Sums cheekily.

"I'm looking forward to it too. I didn't get to spend any time with you guys at the Halloween party," said Amber. Today she had paired her uniform with colorful bangles lined halfway up each arm.

"Don't forget to save me a dance," she added and winked at Sums.

"Yeah, save me one too," cooed Nikka. She elbowed him teasingly in the ribs. Sums turned scarlet, and chuckled.

"What is everyone wearing?" asked Stella with great interest.

Nikka and Sums looked at each other and burst out laughing.

"Oh, right..." said Stella as she realized the futility of her question in present company.

"Well," she rose from the table indignantly, "if anyone is to require *my* expert fashion help, you know where to find me," she said huffily. Stella collected the remnants of her salad and fruit smoothie and stalked off. Nikka and Sums giggled like school children in her wake.

Minutes later, when Sums had finally polished off all that was left of his lasagna, they headed for the door. When the gang emerged from the cafeteria, they found that the entire school grounds had turned an ethereal shade of white. Large flakes of snow fluttered lazily to the ground all around them. The paths were already covered in it. Nikka stretched out her hands to the sky and felt the wet flakes fall and dissolve on her hands and face. She stretched out her tongue and tasted the fresh snow. It had been six years since she had seen snow, and Nikka began to dance around in it, relishing the feel of snowflakes sticking to her eyelashes. Amber joined her, and the pair twirled round and round. Sums watched them happily and laughed. Nikka was so caught up in the moment that she didn't see the fat snowball hurtling towards her face, until it hit her square in the jaw. She turned to look around and caught a fleeting glimpse of a flat cap disappearing behind a tree. *Tristan*. Nikka ran after him, stopping to arm herself with a snowball in each hand. She missed the first throw but the second got him in the ear. He shot one back and got her in the arm. Sums and Amber joined in. Nikka ran after Tristan but Amber derailed her with a snowball before ducking behind a tree. Nikka hid behind another tree and gathered a small mound of snow with the tip of her shoe. Her hands were frozen numb, she was wet down to her tights and her flushed cheeks burned against the icy cold, but she was having too much fun to stop. She picked up the small mound and was preparing to launch it when Tristan appeared from behind the tree, his arms full of snow. He tackled her to the ground. Nikka landed with him on top of her and Tristan began to shovel snow over her. She fought back laughing, shoving a pile of snow back at him, causing his hat to fly off and land a few feet away. She tussled his brown hair with a handful of snow. The pair rolled around wrestling for a bit until they were both on their backs, laughing and exhausted.

When Nikka brushed the snow and tears of laughter from her face, she saw that there was a group of people watching them. Violet and her friends were staring at them from a few feet away. A panting Sums and Amber, both covered in snow, came and stood next to Nikka. Nikka noticed Izaya standing reluctantly behind Violet, Marcus Jenkins at his left. Izaya looked sad. Nikka was suddenly painfully aware that she was lying on the ground next to Tristan. She sat up.

"Hello," said Izaya, who was looking only at Nikka.

"Hey," she said back amiably. Tristan and Violet

seemed surprised by this exchange. But Nikka and Izaya were honoring their agreement - they were being *friends*. Violet looked furious, any fear she had after The Point incident seemed to vanish in that moment.

"It must be really fun being *simple*," said Violet sweetly. "You get excited by things like snow and mud. Kind of like dogs," she added snidely. Her girlfriends laughed. Izaya's face didn't move. Margaret, an oil heiress voice major, laughed the loudest.

"You should associate more with your own type," said Violet, she looked down at Tristan and batted her eyelashes.

Tristan rose and brushed the snow off his jacket. He reached down and lifted Nikka up with ease, then laced his hand around her waist. Nikka noticed Izaya's eyes narrow. Nikka understood that by *simple* Violet had actually meant *poor*, and by Tristan's *type*, she meant *affluent*. Her hand instinctively balled into a fist.

"See, I would," said Tristan, "but unfortunately there aren't many Buddhists at this school." He grinned at Violet madly, which made Amber laugh. Violet looked annoyed, she rolled her eyes, turned on her heels and walked away. Marcus said something to Izaya and the pair walked off towards the woods. Izaya threw a regretful, backward look at Nikka.

"What a load of pricks," Tristan mumbled. He faced Nikka, "So, the dance...." he said suggestively. "I'll pick you up at six?"

It was more of a statement than a question. Without waiting for her to respond, Tristan kissed her on the cheek and disappeared.

×

Amber, Nikka and Stella spent the afternoon sledding in The Valley, then got ready for the dance together back at the dorm. The boom box was blasting hits in the corner. Amber, despite Stella's resistance, lit her favorite sandalwood incense. Stella coated her face with multiple layers of make-up and then lay down on the carpet and attempted to squeeze herself into an extra small, black sequined dress. The dress matched her fake eyelashes, which, as Stella repeatedly pointed out, also had tiny sequins glued on. Nikka helped Amber make the final alterations on her outfit, which, to Stella's great horror, was actually an eighties powder blue suit. Amber then mixed a tin of hair gel with a bottle of blue glitter and generously slathered the mixture on top of her red hair.

"You look like a very glamorous Smurf!" complimented Nikka. Stella didn't say anything.

"You'd better hurry," Amber coaxed a still half-dressed Nikka. Nikka obliged and pulled out a plastic parcel from her armoire, which contained a purple fascinator. It was a beautiful shade of deep purple, with a short lace veil that just covered her eyes. There was a delicate bow positioned at the side and a few delicate strands of feather escaped from it, each one a different shade of purple. Daria had spent days making this piece for Nikka's last birthday.

Nikka undid her hair and brushed through her thick golden curls, which reached down to her chest. She put on a knee-length lilac dress, which left her back and shoulders exposed and was gathered tightly at the waistline. She topped it off with some light pink lip-gloss and rimmed her lids with cat-eye liner. When she walked out of the bathroom, Amber and Stella were in awe.

"You look really chic," said a surprised Stella. Amber echoed the sentiment with wolf whistle.

There was a knock on the door. Stella opened it and in walked Tristan, without his usual flat cap, wearing a tweed suit and a pink bow tie. He was followed by Sums, who was wearing a velvet suit and a yellow tie patterned with the infinity symbol. Both boys were holding what looked like Tupperware; Sums was holding two boxes, one in each arm. Tristan popped his open and revealed a white corsage made of lilies. He slipped it on Nikka's wrist expertly, and then looked her up and down.

"You look like rock and roll royalty, " he said, looking pleased.

"And you look very handsome," she said, low so that no one would hear. Sums struggled briefly with his two boxes. Finally, he managed to open them and nervously reached out a corsage to both girls simultaneously -

rainbow colored for Amber, and pink peonies for Stella. Stella snatched hers eagerly.

“Corsages!" she shrieked excitedly. "We will be the only girls there with corsages.”

"Thanks, Sums," said Amber dreamily and gave him a soft peck on the cheek. Sums’s apple-shaped cheeks turned, as they did whenever Amber touched him, a deep shade of red.

"No problem," he stuttered. "It was all Tristan, really."

Tristan shrugged his shoulders.

"What can I say, the village florist is a really bad poker player," he joked, his eyes still fixed on Nikka.

"Shall we?" he asked, and stretched out his arm for her to take.

Nikka linked her arm in his and followed him out the door. Stella and Amber theatrically wound their arms into each of Sums’s.

"Shall we, luvs?" said Sums, emulating Tristan’s Irish accent.

"Oh yes, Sire, take us to the ball!" quipped Stella in a terrible rendition of the same accent. The group continued to laugh and joke all the way down to the Campus Center.

It was easy to see why the student body had dubbed Stamos the ‘King of Parties’. The Campus Center, previously a large auditorium with a stage, was now void of all chairs, and instead there was a large glittering dance floor. On all sides of the circular room were long rectangular tables, covered in sparkling silver tablecloths and platters of exquisite food. There were tall bejeweled cakes, pheasants with the feathers left on, fruit platters in the shapes of flowers, and silver trays of finger sandwiches stacked in fluffy pyramids.

Next to the dance floor was a bar serving fruit cocktails, and waiters in penguin tuxes sauntered around the room carrying flutes of sparkling lemonade that looked like champagne. Above them, expensive overhead lights were projecting lasers all around the dark room, flooding the dance floor with color.

The speakers were blasting a rock song and Nikka dragged Tristan to the dance floor. Tristan grinned as he wound his hands tightly around her waist and began to guide her to the beat. Sums and Amber danced next to them; Amber seemed to be leading Sums in an odd type of waltz. Stella swayed next to them, back and forth in what she must have thought was a highly seductive manner, all the while scanning the room to see who was looking. But even Stella couldn't resist laughing when Tristan dropped to his knees and performed an air-guitar solo for Nikka.

Nikka mostly danced with Tristan, but she also did the robot with Sums, and a samba with Amber and Stella. After fifteen or so songs, Tristan excused himself, mouthing the word *cigarette* and heading out the door.

Nikka flashed him a grimace, in disapproval of the filthy habit. Sums and Amber went off to the buffet and were soon busy sampling different delicacies. A few moments later, Stella was invited to dance by an unfamiliar boy; overjoyed, Stella followed him to a different part of the room.

Nikka lingered, dancing on her own. Suddenly, Izaya appeared at her side. He towered over her, dressed in a crisp black button-down with three buttons left casually undone, revealing a thin silver chain that clung to his chest. Izaya looked at her intensely; his green eyes boring into hers. His plump lips were, as always, pursed into a slightly disapproving bow, which at that moment expressed both want and displeasure. He was wearing tight black jeans that hung low on his lean frame. His cheekbones stood out in the dark, creating shadows on his pale, flawless face. He didn't smile; he just stared at her. Izaya closed the last step between them, took hold of her hand and gently placed it on his shoulder. He grabbed her other hand and firmly began to lead her in a slow dance. Nikka followed his swift slow steps across the floor, as the voice of the country singer wailed in a southern drawl through the speakers. He looked into her eyes, past the small veil, and then lifted it away so that he could see her fully.

Her dress swayed back and forth, and in her peripheral vision she could see that people were stopping and beginning to stare. Nikka's blond curls bounced as Izaya twirled her with ease. His hands clasped tighter around her waist and his face was so close that she could feel his breath on her ear. Suddenly she felt very exposed, all too aware of his fingers tracing lazy circles on her bare back. She felt the heat from his fingertips burn like matches. He twirled her again and again, making her dizzy. As the song came to its swift end, he dipped her low, then brought her back to face him, inches away from his face. She felt the involuntary pull towards him in her bones, and for the briefest moment his chin rested on her cheek, affectionately. She felt him sigh in her ear before he suddenly separated himself from her. He let go of her hands, almost aggressively, as if he were waking from a dream and realizing what he had done. His own hands dropped to his side and wordlessly he stalked off. Nikka stood there alone, dumbfounded as people stared at her. When she scanned the room she saw Tristan, by the door, watching her, unhappily.

For the next hour or so, Nikka avoided him, feeling embarrassed and not quite understanding what had just happened. *It was just a dance,* she thought to herself with forced innocence, *just a dance between friends - no big deal.* But then she recalled the burning feel of Izaya's long fingers on her back and she felt ashamed. Nikka wandered the room, and avoided the rest of her gang. She also stayed away from the corner where she could see Violet dancing with her friends. If Violet, like the rest of the room, had witnessed her and Izaya's display, then Nikka was in for a world of pain. Nikka took refuge at a fruit cocktail stand in the furthest, most anonymous corner of the room.

"Well, look who it is," came a familiar voice from the barstool next to hers. Nikka turned around and was surprised to find Stamos sitting at the bar. He was slouching slightly; looking rather disheveled compared to his usual perfectly manicured self. His shirt was unbuttoned and un-tucked.

"Hello, Mister Lederman," answered Nikka, politely. "What a great party you've organized."

"You don't look like you're having fun," he countered, slurring his words. He took a shot and chugged it. The barman, who seemed to instinctively appear out of nowhere, poured him another, and it dawned on Nikka that Mr. Lederman was drunk.

"No, I *was* having fun, it's...complicated," she said wondering why she was explaining her feelings to a drunken school official.

"It's only going to get more complicated from here," declared Stamos bitterly. He glanced at Nikka, his slanted eyes filled with sympathy, pity and something darker that Nikka couldn't pinpoint. The barman refilled his shot glass again, and Stamos downed it gracefully. His mouth was wet and glistening with liquor.

"This could have been a very different place," he said melancholically. He gestured at the room. "A simpler place," he added sadly. There was a long pregnant pause, during which Nikka could only shuffle wordlessly on her barstool.

"A happy one," he elaborated, before downing another shot.

Stamos got up with a sudden sense of urgency. "Excuse me, my dear," he said, his usual elegance returning to him. He walked away, swaying lightly. Nikka stared after him, confused. Glumly, she decided that men were far more difficult to decipher than she had thought. She drained her fruit cocktail and surveyed the room. The music was blaring, the students were dancing, everything was as it should be, and for a brief moment Nikka relaxed into her seat- until she spotted Izaya.

Izaya was standing next to Violet and kissing her. His eyes were open, and when they met Nikka's he gave her an almost imperceptible wink. Nikka was instantly furious; she hopped off her barstool, her head a muddle of bewilderment and rage. *Why did Izaya dance with her in that way? What was Stamos rambling on about?*

Izaya was still kissing Violet, and still throwing looks in Nikka's direction, as if watching for her reaction. The song came to an end and the dance floor cleared a little. Nikka saw Tristan sitting on the other side of the room by himself. He was shuffling a deck of cards. Nikka felt even more furious now, she knew that she had hurt Tristan by dancing with Izaya in that way. Izaya was a jerk; he had lied to her, he never wanted to be friends, he just wanted another way in, another way to play with her, and she had let him have it, yet again

Determined, and aware of Izaya's gaze, Nikka walked across the room to where Tristan was sitting. Tristan stood and prepared to walk away, but Nikka was quicker. She put one hand behind his head and kissed him, deeply, furiously, pouring every inch of her regret and rage and apology into that kiss. Tristan was momentarily stunned, frozen in place. Then, having regained his composure, he pulled her closer and kissed her back. Nikka broke the kiss first; flustered and out of breath, she felt herself blush and Tristan chuckled.

"Apology accepted," he said. He smiled and led Nikka in the direction of Sums and Amber. Nikka held his hand and giggled when Sums and Amber mocked them by blowing kisses to one another. Nikka danced and kept her eyes glued on Tristan for the rest of the night. She decided she simply no longer cared about *his* reaction, but still she knew that, somewhere behind her, Izaya was no longer looking smug.

12
Broken Amber

By the end of the following week the wave of excited gossip that had followed the dance had died down, and everything at Wildwood was back to normal. The student body was busily preparing for their mid-year consultations. The first snow had turned to ice, making sledding and snowball fights impossible. Nikka hadn't spoken to Tristan in days, not since he had walked her back to Roseland after the Winter Ball. She had secretly hoped that he would join them in the cafeteria, or that she would run into him on campus, but nearly a week had now gone by without so much as a glimpse of his flat cap. Wildwood Academy had a big campus, huge even, but there were only two paths that led from the cafeteria down to the general campus, and only one path that led back up to the dorms, so this was not the type of place where one could go a week without running into a fellow classmate, which could only mean... *he was avoiding her?* This thought had left Nikka feeling sour all week.

The following Thursday morning, Nikka ate breakfast with Sums. She munched on oatmeal and papaya whilst Sums restricted himself to a humble single serving of French toast.

"I'm not in the mood," he explained, enigmatically. Nikka thought that Sums' uncharacteristic lack of appetite stemmed from the fact that Amber too had been absent from their cafeteria table for the fourth day in a row.

After breakfast, Nikka made her way to figure drawing. Amber wasn't inside the studio when she arrived. Nikka sat down in front of her usual easel and unpacked her pencils. A few more students bustled in, including Violet and her friends, and two robed figure models appeared through the service entrance. The slender middle-aged white woman and young, exceptionally muscular man sat down on the podium and chatted to each other quietly, waiting for the class to settle in.

The overheads dimmed and a bright light illuminated the models. The pair stood up, on cue. A few remaining students shuffled through before the doors swung shut for a final time. The man and woman disrobed, and they stood still and naked before the class. At the beginning of the semester Nikka had always blushed slightly during the disrobements, but after a few weeks she had grown accustomed to the professionalism figure drawing entailed, and she had come to love the class and the art form.

The pair assumed their first pose, and Professor Camden switched on a classical music station on the radio. Nikka picked up her thinnest pencil and began to draw. First, she drew separate body parts frozen in pose- an arm curving to the side, a flexed leg, veins lightly protruding from a muscular calf. Then, with a piece of coal that stained her fingertips black, she perfected the shading of their muscles and the folds of the small, nearly non-existent deposits of fat on the woman's thighs and arms. She drew the dents and details of their skin, and filled in the skillfully relaxed expressions on their faces as they sat, unmoving on the podium.

Nikka was so caught up in the moment that she hadn't noticed Amber walk in late and take her place at the easel next to hers. When Nikka finally took note of her friend she smiled to her brightly and raised her hand to give her a small wave, but faltered, momentarily stunned as she took in her friend's appearance. Even in the semi-darkness she could see that Amber's wide brown eyes were heavy, and her red hair looked dirty and greasy; she had come in from the blistering cold without a jacket on, and looked as if she hadn't slept or eaten in days. Nikka observed her friend with unease, whilst Amber laid out her pencils with a shaky hand and stared vacantly past her easel at the posing figures.

"Amber, are you okay?" whispered Nikka, but Amber did not look at her.

Amber reached for a pencil, inched it towards her canvas and drew a single crooked line. Then she squealed and let her hand drop. The distraught girl took a few steadying breaths. She grabbed hold of her wrist, and with the help of her other hand inched it towards the canvas. The same thing happened again. Amber began to sob quietly as she tried again, and again, and again to draw something on her canvas, but all she could manage were nonsensical lines veering to the left or right. After the sixth or seventh failed attempt she dropped both hands to her sides and looked down at the floor. She performed what looked like a meditative breathing exercise, and then resumed her attempts.

The rest of the class were deeply absorbed in their drawing, and no one noticed Amber's peculiar struggle. Nikka reached out to her friend, but Amber pulled away and got up from her chair. She began to sob uncontrollably, and in a sudden fit of rage flung her easel halfway across the room. Startled, the figures broke their poses, and seconds later the overheads roared on. Everyone was now staring at a lost and furious looking Amber.

“What is going on?” Came Professor Camden's concerned voice from the back of the class.

Nikka rushed towards her, but before she knew it, Amber was tearing through the room, flinging easels left and right, tearing up drawings and crying hysterically. Nikka tried to grab hold of her, and screamed her name, but Amber was quickly destroying the room. Professor Camden managed to grab her from behind and tried, in vain, to restrain her.

"Calm down, sweetheart," she cooed soothingly, but Amber continued to thrash around, like a fish out of water.

Nikka wasn't sure how they had been alerted, but at that precise moment two guards burst into the room, pushed Nikka and Professor Camden aside, and took a hold of Amber. They immobilized her from both sides.

"Be careful!" Nikka screeched desperately.

The rest of the class pressed against the wall in shock. Unnoticed by anyone but Nikka, who was standing mere feet away, the larger of the two guards pulled out a syringe and plunged the needle expertly into Amber's arm. Amber jerked a few more times, before her hands fell limply to her sides, and her eyes fluttered and then settled, half-shut. Nikka watched in horror.

"What did you do to her?" she yelled at the guards, through gritted teeth.

"She was having a violent panic attack, we sedated her. Standard procedure," said the larger guard, so that only Nikka could hear him.

“Don’t worry, she will be perfectly fine," announced the smaller guard, addressing the entire class. Each guard looped one arm under Amber’s armpits, as if she simply needed help walking. Amber’s fiery locks spilled over the guards’ muscular arms, and her eyes remained vacant. She looked broken and frail as they effortlessly half carried her out of the room. Nikka made to follow them, but a third guard appeared and blocked her way out the door.

"She’ll be taken to the nurse. Get back to class," he commanded coldly. Nikka stood up on her tiptoes and tried to see past him, but his bulky shoulders blocked her entire field of vision.

“Now,” barked the guard.

Unwillingly, Nikka returned to her easel, which had already been repositioned. A flustered Professor Camden asked the frightened figure models to resume their positions. She assured the class that Amber would be fine, and explained that panic attacks were not uncommon in children their age.

Nikka was distressed, and she couldn’t draw for the rest of class. She kept replaying the scene in her mind: Amber’s expression, her clenched wrists, her frantic tears. Nikka couldn’t chase these images from her mind. As soon as class was over she would run to the nurse’s office and check on her friend.

×

When class let out Nikka sprinted all the way to the clearing where the Health Center stood. Nikka asked the concierge to call the nurse, and a minute later Nurse Smith opened her door, seeming busy and annoyed at the interruption.

"I wanted to see how my friend, Amber, is doing..." said Nikka. She was out of breath and impatient for Nurse Smith to let her through. The large woman observed her from head to toe, but did not budge.

"Amber has been signed out," she declared with disinterest, "sadly she has suffered a mental breakdown and will be temporarily suspended until her condition improves."

Nurse Smith began to close the door, but Nikka shoved her foot in the way.

"What do you mean *temporarily suspended*? It's not like she broke any cardinal rules," demanded Nikka, defiantly. Nurse Smith observed Nikka's protruding foot with surprise, as if she were not used to being challenged. She smirked, her thin lips spread widely across her square face.

"You might still have a chance to say goodbye," she paused. "If you run," she added maliciously. She flashed Nikka a sweet parting smile, pushed her foot from the threshold, and slammed the door shut. Nikka turned around and ran as fast as she could, all the way to Chadbourne.

By the time Nikka made it up the hill her sides were aching and her throat throbbed from the cold air. With the last of her strength she quickly climbed the steps up to the third floor and sprinted down the hallway to Amber's room. When she got there she found it empty. All that remained was the bed linen and the furniture provided by the school. The benefactors who had funded Chadbourne were modern art enthusiasts, so the furniture in the dorm was mostly made of glass and fancy plastic, geometrically complex shapes and colorful, minimalist patterns. The furniture was untouched, but Amber's vintage propaganda posters, the mosquito net she hung over her bed, the Tibetan flags that had lined her room, and her giant incense stand, along with all of her other personal possessions, were gone. Nikka stared at the empty room and sat down on the bed, dumbfounded.

She searched her head for reasons Amber could have had a breakdown. *Did I miss the signs?* Wondered Nikka ruefully. Amber had been fine a few days ago, and it wasn't like her to turn violent or hysterical. *Why would the school suspend her for this? And if it's just a temporary suspension, why did she take all her things with her? Why did she not say goodbye?* After a while Nikka left Amber's room feeling empty.

Izaya, Violet, Jordan and their gang were sitting on the red couches shaped like lips that adorned the large, loft-style common room of Chadbourne. Nikka tried to hurry past them unnoticed, but as soon as Izaya saw her he stood up.

"So, it's true?" he asked; his eyes glimmered with concern. Nikka nodded. From behind him Violet stared malevolently at her, and Nikka tried to muster up some bravado - the last thing she wanted to do now was cry.

"I'm sorry. You must be really upset," said Izaya. He reached out and tenderly put a hand on her shoulder.

"It's just a temporary suspension," said Nikka trying to sound confident. Izaya nodded sympathetically, but his look suggested what Nikka feared, that temporary suspensions at Wildwood were rarely temporary. Violet's nasal voice resounded behind them.

"Izaya, honey, why are you *acting* so concerned? They had reason enough to throw her out, she's dangerous!" The girls from Violet's entourage were vigorously nodding their heads in agreement.

"You don't know what you're talking about! " spat Nikka.

"I was sitting right there," said Violet with the tone of a victim. "She looked like a fox with rabies when she tore through that classroom. It's lucky none of us got hurt," said Violet wickedly. Her entourage nodded in enthusiastic agreement again, like a hoard of bobble-heads.

"You're an idiot, Violet," said Nikka weakly. She didn't have the energy to take it up with the girl, even her name tasted dirty on Nikka's tongue.

"I guess she was going through something," said Nikka, more to Izaya than anyone else. Her voice came out pained; she hated that she did not know what that *something* was.

"It's not fair for them to just throw her out," Nikka reasoned out loud, to no one but herself.

"Well then, why don't you organize a protest?" said Violet mockingly and shot her a cold, condescending glare.

"Maybe I will, " said Nikka angrily.

"Good, maybe then they will throw you out too. The less poor, psychologically unbalanced students we have, the better," spat Violet hatefully, and her little gang broke out into a fit of vicious snickers. Izaya whirled on them.

"Violet," he announced loud and calmly, "I can forgive a lot, but I cannot forgive stupidity and pettiness. I have no desire to date you anymore, nor talk to you for the time being, and frankly I think you should stop talking altogether until you learn some manners," Izaya gave Nikka a parting look of solidarity, before swaggering off and leaving a stunned Violet and her entourage behind. Nikka, who was pretty stunned herself, managed to linger just long enough to watch Violet's face turn purple with humiliation as tears began to make their way freely down her face, before she too headed out the door.

×

Nikka had briefly stopped by Sums' room to check up on him, but he wasn't there. Wherever he was, Nikka suspected that the news would reach him soon enough, and she regretted that she would not be there to comfort him. She ditched her next class and instead went to her room where she lay on her bed, staring up at the ceiling. She quickly grew fidgety, and failed to distract herself with drawing or cleaning. Violet's sarcastic remark came back into her head. Her restlessness escalating, she rifled through her art cabinet and pulled out a large neon green poster that she had kept for a project. On it, she wrote in thick, sharp letters 'UNSUSPEND AMBER' in black marker pen. She rolled the poster up and shot out the door.

The Dean's house was too far away and too out of sight for what she had in mind, so instead Nikka occupied the curb outside the Student's Lounge, the epicenter of campus. She sat down on the ground and proudly held up her sign. In the first hour only a few errant classmates walked by and stared at her curiously, but, like most gossip at Wildwood, news of Amber's suspension and Nikka's one-woman protest spread like wildfire and after the last class of the day was let out Nikka was joined in solidarity by a number of Amber's classmates and friends. Some she had never talked to before, others she had met in passing; a few brought signs of their own. Sums joined them too, he smiled weakly in Nikka's direction but kept from looking straight at her - his eyes were red from crying.

Sums held up his own sign, which read: 'Discrimination x invalid suspension = malpractice.' Stella showed up too, shyly holding a small sign that simply read 'Totally unfair." Many more students showed up and joined their ranks. They held up signs, complained to one another about friends who had been suspended or expelled in the past, and joined in a loud communal chant. The protest continued to have a snowball effect on the student body, mostly because people wanted to socialize and be involved in the drama. Eventually, even Izaya appeared; in his own icy-cool manner he sat down on the curb and wordlessly wrapped one arm around an exhausted Nikka.

Shortly after eight o'clock the chanting began to die down, as most of the protesters abandoned their cause in favor of dinner. By nine, the buzz had completely dwindled, and just a few protesters remained. They had all been expecting a reaction, Nikka especially. An inciting appearance from the guards, a warning, a few words of explanation or comfort from Wildwood staff or authorities - anything. But no one came. Nikka knew that every inch of Wildwood was under watch. Yet no one came, and no one reacted to their spontaneous protest. *They were being blatantly ignored.*

After hearing his belly growl repeatedly, Sums left for the cafeteria looking utterly defeated. Stella went after him, while Izaya offered to walk Nikka home. Nikka politely declined; she simply had no energy left. No energy to look at him, or to think about what he had said to Violet. She had no energy to feel anything at all. For that reason, she pushed away the thought of Tristan's continued absence, and the fact that he clearly couldn't be bothered to join them. Most of all she didn't want to think about when, or if, she would see Amber again. She thanked Izaya and, without looking back, she headed to Roseland, to her room, where she curled up numbly under her covers and cried herself into a dreamless sleep.

×

The next morning, Nikka was woken by Magda. Her House Matron sat at the foot of her bed and smiled at her warmly. Nikka smiled back and looked at her nightstand, on which rested a tray loaded with all of her favorite breakfast foods: poppy seed rolls, lemon tea, a bowl of strawberries, and an assortment of fancy jams.

"I know you had a hard day yesterday," said Magda, gesturing at the tray. Magda, like many Eastern European women, believed that food could make all worries go away.

"It's alright. Today is a new day," she said mildly, more to comfort Magda than herself. Magda smeared a poppy seed bun with peach jam and handed it to her. Then she looked worriedly at Nikka through her heavily hooded eyes.

"I'm afraid today will not be much better," she said. "You have an appointment. Car already waiting outside."

Nikka cringed. She had expected some sort of reprimand after the protest, but she had hoped it would come in the form of a counselor's meeting or a detention. Magda laid out her freshly pressed uniform for her and made her way to the door, then she stopped, walked back and gave Nikka a quick kiss on the forehead. Nikka smiled up at her appreciatively; at that moment, the small motherly gesture gave her more strength than the most lavish breakfast could. Magdalena walked again to the door, but turned around once more.

"Miss Nikka, try to not make *him* angry," she said warningly, before disappearing. Nikka knew exactly to whom she was referring.

At the Dean's office, Nikka waited fifteen minutes before she was allowed in. The Dean sat back in his luxurious chair and regarded her closely. He looked tan, fit and even more powerful and wealthy than the first time she had seen him. A faint smell of cigar smoke permeated his glass office.

Nikka mumbled "Good morning, Sir," and sat down, pretending to pay close attention to the Zen garden outside the window.

"I am not pleased with the stunt you pulled yesterday," came his icy drawl from across the desk. Nikka forced herself to meet his black beady eyes.

"It was a protest, it's my first amendment right," she responded, and was instantly angry at the lack of conviction in her voice, which made her statement sound like a question.

"Protest against what, exactly?" asked the Dean, looking amused.

"Amber's suspension. It wasn't fair. She's just going through something; she shouldn't have been suspended so quickly," said Nikka trying to sound convincing.

The Dean's expression was unchanged. He observed Nikka with interest.

"Nikka, we didn't suspend Amber. She has been sent home for a brief rest period," he said in the most soothing of tones, but even then his extremely articulate, dry speech dripped with mockery. As Nikka stared into his black eyes and images of Amber's barren room danced before her, she knew he was lying.

"It's not fair," Nikka repeated slowly, holding her ground.

The Dean was beginning to look aggravated. He opened a drawer in his desk, pulled out a stack of papers and gently slid them over to Nikka.

"This is your acceptance contract," he explained. "It is identical to every other contract that governs Wildwood students whilst they reside on campus. If you turn to page 22, clause B you will see that *any* violent behavior in or outside of the classroom will result in an immediate suspension, commencing from the day of the offense. Re-acceptance after such an offense is at the discretion of the school board, and is decided at a disciplinary hearing." Before Nikka could challenge him, the Dean continued.

"Amber has pre-existing conditions that we were aware of before her acceptance, which might result in her not having a disciplinary hearing at all," he explained matter-of-factly.

"It's all up to the board; I'm afraid my hands are tied on this one," he added. Nikka was concentrating intently on not crying. The Dean resumed.

"If you turn to page 27 paragraph 2 clause B you will see that organizing a protest on campus is also grounds for expulsion." Nikka's head shot up and she prepared to recite a few lines about freedom of speech but the Dean was quicker again.

"Page 24 paragraph 4 clause D says that all Wildwood students, upon signing their contracts, are bound by school rules and, since you are all minors and under our supervision, you thereby relinquish your rights to such luxuries as free speech," he continued, lightning fast. Nikka was struggling to locate each page from which he was so perfectly reciting.

"Page 9 paragraph 1 clause B explains that any student who is dissatisfied or displeased with Wildwood rules has a right to leave."

Nikka smirked sarcastically; at least they were

allowed to leave when they wanted to.

"However, if you turn your attention to page 13 clause D paragraph 1 you will see that regardless of whether you are expelled or sign yourself out willingly, if you leave before the end of the calendar school year you are legally obliged to pay the school's full yearly tuition, whether you are a scholarship student or not."

The Dean paused, taking a short, triumphant breath.

"And if you turn your attention to my favorite page, page 37, you will see your and your mother's signatures at the bottom," the Dean's eyes burned coal black.

Nikka remembered something she had never really thought about, that she and her mother had been so excited about Wildwood that neither of them had bothered to read so much as a few paragraphs of the contract they had signed. She sat still, feeling stupid.

The Dean observed her sympathetically. "Perhaps your mother's financial situation has improved of late, but I think our fifty-two thousand dollar annual tuition might still burden her a tad. Don't you?" he asked contemptuously. Nikka looked away, she felt like she had been slapped in the face.

"Do we understand each other?" he asked, and flashed a cruel smile. *Yes,* she understood him. If she were ever to object to the school's methods again, she would be expelled, and her mom would be ruined. *Again*. Nikka suddenly realized why the Dean always looked at her liked she was a possession of his. Because she was, at least till school let out in June. Nikka felt a light hand on her shoulder.

"I think we understand each other," concluded the Dean. Nikka rose without a word, and made her way out the door.

"And don't forget, mid-semester evaluations are two weeks from now so, study, study, study!" called the Dean jovially, as if nothing had transpired between them. Nikka was speechless as she left the Dean's office. Her head spun wildly until she finally made it back to her room. That day she attended class as usual, and tried her absolute best to study, just as the Dean had instructed. Every now and then, the memory of his winning smile sent shivers down her spine.

13
Christmas

Nikka stood in front of Roseland, a suitcase by her side. A line of cars had again formed outside the dorms. A queue of parents and pick-up services awaited the students departing for the Christmas holidays. Nikka saw Sums walking over to her from Becks. He was dragging two large suitcases behind him, which were so heavy that they left trails in the grass.

"Are you sure you packed enough *stuff*?" said Nikka sarcastically.

"It's mostly my computers and game consoles. Does your aunt have a TV?" asked Sums excitedly. Nikka nodded, *if she hasn't pawned it.*

Granted, it was not the best idea to take Sums home with her for Christmas - there was no room, no money, and it was *Sonya's* home - but Nikka felt even that would be better than Sums staying on his own at the Academy. At least, she hoped it would be better. It pained her to think about Sums having been alone in his dorm room for the last two Christmases, just him and a gourmet meal wrapped in foil. Either way, it was too late to rescind the offer now. Sums had been so excited when Nikka had suggested it, and her mother had approved, after making sure that Sums was in no way Nikka's boyfriend. Moreover, Amber lived on the outskirts of Los Angeles, so both Sums and Nikka were motivated by the prospect of finding out where she lived and visiting her.

As Sums busily checked his jacket pockets and made sure he hadn't forgotten anything, Nikka glanced around - there were still a few clusters of students waiting to be picked up. She wondered how her mother would be collecting them, and hoped that Daria hadn't got the pick-up time wrong, which it would be like her to do. Nikka watched a limousine pull up and a pretty blond girl, who looked so polished it was like she had been Photoshopped, climbed out. The girl approached a huddled group of students next to Becks and asked them something. To Nikka's surprise the students turned and pointed at her and Sums, and the girl walked over.

"Hello," she said flatly, when she was close enough for Nikka and Sums to hear.

"Hello," the pair echoed in response.

"I was told *you* would know where Tristan McMally

might be?" asked the girl. She looked at them doubtfully, as if she was unconvinced that they were the type of people who would know where Tristan was.

Nikka and Sums looked at each other. Which one of them was she addressing? *Is this one of Tristan's sisters?* Nikka wondered, as she sized up the manicured stranger. She looked nothing like him, and had an American accent. Sums saw the hesitation on Nikka's face, so he answered first.

"No, we haven't seen him in a couple of days, actually," he answered. The girl looked at Sums suspiciously, as if she suspected him of lying to her. She pulled out a phone.

"Crap," she mumbled when she realized there was no service.

"Well, if you see him, could you tell him Cassie, his *girlfriend,* is looking for him," she said angrily, as if Sums and Nikka were somehow at fault for Tristan's absence. She turned and strutted away, without so much as a thank you. Sums gulped and slowly turned to look at Nikka, as if scared of her reaction. Nikka felt like someone had punched her in the gut. She couldn't breathe for a moment, and felt nausea creeping up on her, then drowning her. She felt like she was on a plummeting rollercoaster. In that moment it struck her how odd it was that something emotional could cause such a physical reaction. Sums stared at her, concerned.

"Nikka, I..."

"Don't," said Nikka gently. "I don't want to talk about it. I'm not going to let this ruin our break," she said, with forced nonchalance but the sinking feeling inside of her was quickly taking over. Nikka was fed up; fed up with boys, with games, with lies, and with the drama and intrigue that seemed omnipresent at Wildwood. All she wanted was to see her mother and to spend Christmas with her best friend. *Tristan and I are not together, he's free to do what he wants,* she reasoned. *But maybe there's a logical explanation?* Countered the part of her that was still close to tears. Heartache was quickly spreading through her like a stain, and her internal monologue did little to ease the ache. Sums tried to comfort her, awkwardly tapping her on the back. Nikka smiled at him.

"I'm fine," she said. "I promise."

Nikka spotted a large yellow Jeep drive up the road, narrowly missing a few town cars. She hadn't even considered that Daria would ask Sonya to take her - not such a long way, and not through the precarious mountain roads. Although now that she saw the car, it made sense - Daria didn't have any other option. She looked at Sums, his baby blue eyes narrowed in worry as he watched the erratic car approach.

"You're in for one wild ride," Nikka warned.

×

They arrived at Sonya's apartment three hours later. As they entered the apartment, Nikka carefully watched Sums' face for any signs of shock or disappointment, but there were none - Sonya's dire living situation and her drunken state didn't seem to shock him in the least. Nikka attributed this to the fact that Sums had probably seen worse in foster care. As he looked around the apartment, the only emotions on Sums' face were excitement and traces of fading nausea. Three hours of Sonya's drunk driving had caused him to throw up twice - once on the side of the road, where Nikka had patted his back and Daria held back his curls, whilst Sonya laughed at them all hysterically, and once again into a plastic bag in the back seat.

The apartment was cleaner than it had been when Nikka and Daria first arrived. Daria had hung up some Christmas lights by the windows, and there were fewer empty bottles strewn about. Daria had also washed Sonya's Greek garden statue so that it was no longer grey but a yellow shade of white.

It took Sums an hour to settle in. He connected all of his gadgets to one another, plugged them all in, and sat on the couch with his laptop. His brows furrowed and he typed quickly. Nikka had seen him in this position many times before. Daria left to get some groceries and Sonya happily passed out in her room. Sonya was excited to have guests; *misery loves company*, thought Nikka, as she sat down next to Sums.

"What are you doing?" she asked, peeking over at his computer. Nikka looked at the screen but could only make out a scroll of letters and symbols glowing against a dark background.

"I'm trying to find Amber's phone number and address," said Sums without breaking his focus.

Before leaving Wildwood Nikka had asked the School Center for that same information, but they had denied her request and lectured her on school policy and confidentiality. Nikka and Amber had never exchanged cell numbers; there was no need - their phones didn't work and they lived next door to each other.

"We could try the Yellow Pages?" offered Nikka. Sums rolled his eyes.

"Nikka I'm a hacker, I'm above the Yellow Pages. And I looked it up online, she's unlisted anyway."

Nikka knew that Sums could disarm the school alarm, and that he had found a way to get his phone to work in the dead zone, but aside from those facts she didn't *really* understand the extent of Sums' 'hacking' abilities. She just took his word for it when he boasted that he could "access most embassy files in under ten minutes." Whether or not his abilities were exaggerated, she wasn't sure.

"Any luck?" Nikka probed.

"So I found her previous schools and I'm going through her records as we speak."

"That's amazing," said Nikka earnestly. Sums' brow furrowed again, creasing his forehead like a wrinkled sheet.

"Strange..." he mumbled, more to himself than to Nikka.

"What?" she asked nervously. Sums kept clicking.

"Well, you said that the Dean told you Amber had a history of *mental illness,*" said Sums, choosing his words carefully. Nikka nodded.

"Last week I found her insurance information and I looked through it," Sums admitted, a little hesitantly. Nikka shot him a disapproving look.

"There were no psych evaluations, no treatments for mental illness, no prescriptions, no trace of her ever having had any issues in the past," he explained.

"Get to the point?" urged Nikka, growing impatient.

"Her previous school *does* have a record of her having a breakdown, and of violent behavior, and also of her visiting the psychiatrist numerous times," said Sums. "Her file was amended a month ago," he elaborated. There was a brief silence as Nikka contemplated the implications of Sums' words.

"Why would they amend her file months after she had left the school?" Nikka wondered out loud.

"My question exactly. I can't see what was changed, only that the file was amended internally," said Sums. He grabbed a piece of paper from the table and scribbled something on it.

"That's her number," he said, handing it to Nikka. "Can you call, please? I'm too nervous." Nikka sighed, picked up Sums' cellphone from the couch and dialed the number. It rang through.

"Hello?" answered a women's voice.

"Umm, hi," Nikka stammered. "My name is Nikka Mason, I'm a friend of Amber's..."

A silence followed.

"Would it be possible... Can I talk to Amber, please?" said Nikka hesitantly into the line. There was another silence that stretched long enough for Nikka to wonder if the line had been disconnected.

"How do you two know each other?" asked the woman suddenly. Her voice was weary and tired. *Must be her mom,* thought Nikka.

"We met at Wildwood Academy, we were in the same class," she said gently. "I just wanted to see how she's doing." There was another pause.

"Amber is not available now," said the woman. Her voice was weighted with hesitation and a kind of deep buried anger. Sums looked nervously at Nikka. He inched his head closer to the receiver to try and overhear.

"Well, could you tell me when she might be available? You see, my friend Sums and I really wanted to visit her. We are in Los Angeles right now, on winter break," said Nikka sweetly, the way you ask your parents for an extended curfew. There was a sigh on the other end.

"She's in a recovery center," admitted the woman.

"Maybe we could visit her there?" Nikka pressed on, knowing from the woman's tone that she was pushing her luck. Sums looked at her, his blue eyes hopeful.

"It's not a good idea," said the woman sternly. "You can see her in a few months. When she is..." the woman faltered, as if she didn't know how to finish the sentence.

"Healthy," she said, finally. And then she hung up. Nikka stared at the wall dumbfounded. *Had everything with Amber really been so bad?* It made no sense. Sums pushed his computer away in disgust and went to the window. The idea that he might not see Amber for a few months seemed to greatly upset him. That night he skipped dinner.

×

Nikka was determined to give Sums the full Christmas experience that he had missed out on in the previous years. First, she took him to visit Santa's grotto at the Los Angeles Grove, then they drank hot chocolate in various parks around town, and spent their evenings cooking up apple cider and making decorative garlands and paper snowflakes. Sums had a giant smile plastered on his face during any and every Christmas activity that he partook in. Especially, when he noticed that Daria had sewn little Christmas stockings from scrap fabrics, initialed them, and hung them off the windowsill. The only thing that was missing now was snow, but in Los Angeles a snowy Christmas was too much to ask for; instead, Nikka surprised Sums by taking him to an outdoor mall where machines blew fake snow over the crowds in the evenings leading up to Christmas.

They tried to spend as much time away from the apartment as possible, to avoid drunken, unpredictable Sonya and to try and forget the Amber situation, which depressed them both. During their outings there were three banned topics of discussion: Wildwood exams, Amber's whereabouts, and Tristan's girlfriend. Nikka was grateful for this unspoken arrangement.

Instead of dwelling on these, Nikka put all her energy into having the best Christmas break possible. Sums had grown up in Arizona, and had never been to Los Angeles before, despite its proximity to Wildwood. So Nikka provided him with the full tourist experience: the Hollywood Boulevard walk of fame, a visit to Santa Monica Pier, and a hike up to the Hollywood Sign, which Sums barely survived, but seemed to enjoy nonetheless. Despite their troubles, it had been a wonderful few days.

On Christmas Eve, the pair sat side-by-side on the couch in Sonya's living room and played traditional Christmas songs from Sums' computer. Sums was wearing a Santa hat that he had bought at the *99 Cents Only Store* and he sat there happily, swaying to *Jingle Bells*. Nikka curled the ribbon on her mother's Christmas gift and then set it down under the Greek statue, which was serving as their Christmas tree.

Nikka had saved a large part of her Wildwood weekend allowance over the fall semester to buy Christmas presents for everyone. Sums too had added a few sloppily wrapped parcels to the foot of the Greek statue.

Nikka walked into the kitchen, popped a tray full of cookie dough chunks into the oven and set the timer. Despite the oily, decrepit oven, the small apartment quickly filled with the smell of freshly baked cookies, and in response, Sums' face stretched into its hundredth grin that week. Suddenly, the front door opened and a breathless Daria stumbled through it.

"Sums, some help, please?" she directed, pointing back at the door. Sums followed her into the hallway and Nikka watched from the kitchen with interest. A few seconds later Daria's face appeared in the door, sweaty and red, followed by something large and green; it took a moment for Nikka to realize what it was. Daria and Sums carried the pine in and set it in the corner against the wall.

"A Christmas tree!" yelped Nikka. She walked over and examined it excitedly. "It's beautiful, where did you get it?" In response to her question, a drunken Sonya waltzed through the door, a small seesaw in hand.

"You cut it off yourself?" asked Sums, his voice full of admiration. Daria nodded.

"Where there's a will, there's a way," she said, breathlessly.

"Where there's a Jeep there's a way," rectified Sonya, and burped loudly. "We had to go off-roading for this baby," she said and patted the tree in a proud, manly sort of way.

Nikka shot her mom a reproachful look. Daria stared back hard and pointed at the tree, as if to signify, 'the end justifies the means.' Sums had already steadied the tree in a bucket and tied the trunk down, and was now happily draping popcorn garlands around it. Daria looked pointedly at the clearly overjoyed Sums, as if he further justified her point. Nikka scowled.

"Thank you, Daria, Sonya, this is so cool," said Sums. Nikka reluctantly picked up the packed parcels from under the Greek statue and put them under the tree. Sonya disappeared into her bedroom just as the cookie timer rang. Nikka went to get them out and Daria followed her, leaning against the greasy kitchen wall as Nikka transferred the cookies onto a plate.

"How often do you get in the car with *her*?" reprimanded Nikka.

"Almost never," reassured Daria. "I just wanted to make sure you had a good Christmas, despite the *circumstances*." Her eyes wandered around the derelict kitchen.

"This Christmas is wonderful," Nikka said reassuringly,

but Daria didn't look convinced.

"So, tell me more about Wildwood, are you looking forward to going back?" Asked Daria. It was a loaded question, and Nikka knew that Daria was probing, hoping that Nikka was happy where *circumstances* had landed her, that she wanted to remain there for the time being, and that Wildwood, in some way, made up for everything that had happened that year. Nikka gave her the answer she wanted without hesitation.

"I love it; it's the most amazing place I've ever been to," she answered – she was being honest, too. So much had happened in her four months there, good and bad, but nonetheless, being there made Nikka feel inspired and alive every waking moment. Reluctantly, Nikka thought about Izaya and Tristan, something else that had made her experience at Wildwood so special. She felt herself sadden a little.

"So, I finally did something right?" said Daria playfully. "Who would have thought?"

"Thank you, Mom. For everything," said Nikka. She hugged her mother and buried herself in Daria's strawberry-blond hair. She smelled her mother's grown-up perfume - a sharp and floral scent. Daria squeezed her daughter back.

"Merry Christmas," she whispered in her ear.

"Merry Christmas," said Nikka.

Sums came in and hesitated awkwardly by the door,

worried that he had interrupted an intimate moment.

"I was just going to ask what's next?" he said, like an excited child waiting for his birthday itinerary to be revealed.

"Cookies and presents," answered Nikka, and Sums beamed. He picked up a cookie and popped it in his mouth. In the living room Sonya was sitting on the floor and staring at the Christmas tree like another large expectant child, except with a bottle of vodka next to her. She picked up a present and shook it ferociously.

"Oops. Sounds like glass," she said and laughed coarsely before tossing the packet aside. Sums picked up a parcel and gave it to Nikka. With a smile she opened it and found some paintbrushes and a set of oil paints.

"I thought you might want to paint while you're away from Wildwood," he said timidly. Nikka wrapped her arms around Sums and gave him a big hug, and then handed him his present. Sums unwrapped it breathlessly, and with complete disregard for the wrapping paper. He froze as his eyes settled on an autographed comic book he had shown Nikka when they had first visited the shops in Wildwood during the fall.

"Thank you, Nik," he said, a little choked up. He carefully laid down the comic book by his side.

Nikka handed the rest of the presents out. Daria received a quartz crystal and an antique thimble from Nikka, and a book on the history of hats from Sums. Sums got a mug from Daria that read, *'Coffee first, hack second,'* which made him laugh, and Nikka received a small antique pocket mirror compact, embedded with mother of pearl engraved with the words 'You're beautiful' - a gift from Daria. Sonya hadn't yet touched her gifts.

"Sonya, it's your turn," said Daria loudly, and shook Sonya's shoulder to break her out of her near comatose state. Sonya slowly came back to life, like a bear waking up from hibernation. Daria placed three parcels on her lap. Sonya opened the first one - it was a flask. She smiled and opened it, but her smile faltered.

"There's nothing in it," she said, shaking the opened flask up and down, and looking around at the three of them as if they were playing a practical joke on her. Sums gave a nervous cough.

"I'm under the drinking age, so I umm... couldn't fill it..." he said nervously. Sonya threw the flask over her shoulder with disinterest and opened her next present, which was another flask. Again, she unscrewed the top and smelled it, and then she smiled and took a swig. Nikka gave Sums and Daria reprimanding looks that said, *really, you both got her flasks?* And they both shrugged their shoulders in response. Sonya opened her last present, which was from Nikka - a book on self-discovery and health accompanied by a small set of healing crystals.

"Those crystals can be used for different types of healing, and the shopkeeper really recommended that book," said Nikka proudly. But that look quickly faded when Sonya grumbled "Thanks," and proceeded to use the book as a coaster as she filled the first flask with vodka. Sums chuckled, and then tried to pass it off as a cough.

"I'm going to go get *my* presents," Sonya slurred unexpectedly. She disappeared into her room and reappeared with three tin foil packages, which contained a salt shaker for Nikka, a sweater for Daria, and a small porcelain statue of a pug for Sums - all items that had been on display in Sonya's apartment a day prior. Sums laughed so hard at this that his hot cocoa almost came out through his nose. Once the laughing died down and the last of the presents had been unwrapped, Daria suddenly remembered something.

"I forgot to tell you that some mail arrived for you yesterday, it's on the window sill," she said, addressing Nikka. On the window sill Nikka found a postcard and a brown package with her name on it. Nikka stared at it, dumbfounded - she couldn't think of a single person who knew where she lived, except for Stamos. She went into Sonya's room for some privacy. The postcard was of a snowy alpine peak and the back read: *'Merry Christmas, girl! Missing you here in Aspen. P.S. Sums gave me your address, see you soon xoxo - Stella.'*

Nikka smiled and set the postcard aside. She examined the parcel. The return address was a P.O. box in

Los Angeles. Nikka ripped the parcel open and shook the contents out onto the bed. It was a photograph and a handwritten note. Nikka read the note first:

'I wanted to give you something special. Like I told you before, my family is well connected in the army... This is the last official photo taken of him in service - it was classified. I hope it makes you smile. Merry Christmas.'

The card wasn't even signed. Nikka turned the photo around with the level of care one reserves for the most delicate glass - she was irrationally afraid it would disappear from her hands before she had a chance to look at it. On the photo were two rows of men, all in neat uniforms. She spotted him instantly, shy and stern, standing proudly on the left side of the top row. The men looked relaxed, suggesting that this was the photo taken after the official one, but he, *her father,* stood proudly anyway. At the bottom of the card it said 'Regiment 13' and the date.

Nikka's body reacted before her head had a chance to catch up. Hot tears spilled down her cheeks, the kind of tears that don't hurt or strain the muscles in your face, but instead flow freely and naturally in a blend of sadness and joy. She was happy to have a photo, sad for the man in it, who was lost to her, and deeply touched by Izaya's thoughtful gesture. She held the photo to her heart for a moment and let the tears run their course. Then she put it back into the envelope and tucked it into her pocket.

She would show it to her mother eventually, but that night it would be just hers, a small piece of him that she had never seen. She wiped her tears and went back into the living room.

Sonya, Daria and Sums had dimmed the lights, and Sums had found a way to make the music from his computer blare through the TV. Sonya was dancing with a bottle in her hand, Sums was doing the robot, and Daria was swaying back and forth, spilling her canned eggnog on the carpet.

It was an odd scene; a happy, misfit, hillbilly Christmas. Nikka grinned widely and joined in.

14
A New Beginning

The bell rang, releasing Nikka from the prison that was her math class. Nikka collected her things and walked out. The icy cold January air hit her in the face and blew her curls backwards. At Wildwood Academy, January was considered the glummest month of the year – the skies were always grey, the temperatures dropped below zero, and the majority of the student body was consumed with post-holiday blues. The students sat at their desks and stared at the walls morosely, filled with nostalgia for Gluhwein and skiing, whilst classes resumed where they had left off. In the week since she had returned to school, Nikka too had been reminiscing about her holiday. Somehow, against all the odds, she and Sums had had an amazing Christmas. They had finished their Holiday off with a New Year celebration on the beach, the cherry on top of an already perfect sundae.

Nikka looked up at the sky; there was promise of rain. Sluggishly, she walked downhill towards her next class, science, and suddenly she spotted him, a few yards down the path. It was the first time she had seen Tristan since before the holidays. He was walking uphill, towards her, with his flat cap tilted forward over his eyes. At the sight of him, Nikka's heart hurt a little and her stomach clenched with anxiety. She felt a strong urge to turn and walk the other way, but decided it was better to face this problem now rather than later. Nikka swerved a little so that she was right in his way. Tristan trudged up the muddy path unknowingly, then he stopped and looked up at the unexpected obstacle in his way. His blue eyes met hers, but there was something odd in his look; it was blank and glazed. He observed her, but there was no hint of recognition there, his gaze wandered past her, disinterested.

"Hello, Tristan," she said coldly. She wanted him to feel the same rejection she had felt, or at least take note of the coolness in her voice.

"Hello," he replied, slowly, as if the words were an effort. He was still looking at her like he couldn't quite place her. Nikka, who was growing angrier by the second, took a moment to look him up and down; his eyes were slightly bloodshot and dull, he was slouching, and looked weak. For a moment Nikka was concerned for him, then the feeling washed away and was replaced by rage. How could he just stand there and act as if he didn't even know her?

"So, did your *girlfriend* ever find you?" Nikka ventured, trying not to sound bitter.

"What?" he asked, confused.

"Your *girlfriend*. I met her right before the holidays, she was trying to find you," Nikka explained. Tristan seemed to come to a little; he stared at Nikka hard, as if the pieces of the puzzle were coming together in his head.

"Nikka," he said slowly. His voice was soft, full of tenderness and recognition. Then he paused, weighing up his response. Nikka waited for the carefully crafted explanation or excuse she thought was headed her way.

"I don't feel very well, could we talk about this later?" he asked. Tristan fidgeted, as if he were late for something important. He looked past her again, his expression growing anxious. Nikka could admit that he did not look well, *not at all*. In fact, she had never seen Tristan look this bad, or this uncomfortable before. But whatever was causing his discomfort, it was not the fact that Nikka had found out about his girlfriend. Nikka bit her lip to stop herself from crying. Tristan wasn't even trying to explain himself, or comfort her, or make things right. When Nikka had imagined this situation during winter break she thought that Tristan would be upset, that he would stutter an explanation of what had happened; but he just stood there, leaving them both to bask in the silence and awkwardness. Then he nodded at her, as you would a passing acquaintance, and walked on.

Nikka felt shaky. Tears, free and hot, made their way down her cold cheeks. The blistering wind whipped them away and left her face feeling dry and raw. Nikka ducked off the path before anyone could see her. She was already late for her science class, but she didn't care anymore; she made her way deeper into the forest. She stopped after a few minutes and leaned against a large tree.

Nikka slid down the tree trunk and sat on the frozen pine-littered ground. She couldn't tell what hurt more, the fact that Tristan hadn't bothered to explain himself, or that at this point it didn't seem like they were even friends. Nikka opened her backpack and pulled out a familiar envelope. She slid the photo out and stared at her dad's face - young, strong, full of promise. The photo didn't make her cry anymore; now it injected her with courage, and she had Izaya to thank for that. She held onto this thought, and sat there in the forest for a few minutes more, alone with her father.

×

"Popcorn?" asked the woman.

Nikka was in a fog. Enveloped in thoughts of Tristan, and for some reason, of her father. She had been staring at the pink wall of her dorm community room and ignoring the cafeteria employee in front of her.

"Popcorn?" asked the woman again. There was no sign of irritation in her voice; some members of the Wildwood student body were too important, too rich and too influential to be on the receiving end of staff attitude. Wildwood staff rarely showed signs of irritation or displeasure, just in case. Sums nudged her and Nikka snapped back to reality.

There was a 'welcome back' Talent Showcase that night in the community room of Roseland. It was a small and intimate affair, and not mandatory. In normal schools, non-mandatory events would be poorly attended, but that night at Wildwood the candlelit community room was packed to the brim, and the line to the popcorn machine was long and impatient. Nikka met the eyes of the cafeteria woman in charge of filling the retro popcorn buckets.

"Yes, please, sorry, I zoned out," said Nikka.

"Extra butter on mine," said Sums from behind her.

Nikka and Sums collected their popcorn buckets and sodas and made their way to the folding chairs at the back of the room. Nikka spotted Stella siting with the guy from the Winter Ball and winked at her.

Nikka felt someone hovering over her, and as she looked up caught Izaya smiling down at her in a manner that was so open and so warm, so unlike *him*, that for a moment she thought it was a trick of the light.

"Hey there," he said to her softly, then he turned to

Sums.

"Hi, Sums," he said and smiled another rare smile. Sums attempted to answer, but he had choked on a popcorn kernel from the shock.

"Hey," said Nikka. "Did you have a nice Christmas?"

"It was alright," he said, shrugging. There was something reluctant about his tone.

"Did you get any nice gifts?" Nikka asked, for lack of anything better to say. His presence made her nervous, she could feel the adrenaline coursing through her bloodstream. It was a redundant question, a boy like Izaya could afford to buy anything he wanted, he didn't depend on Christmas.

"I got a new car," said Izaya with vague disinterest. "How about you?"

"Yeah, I did. Thank you by the way," Nikka started shyly. "For my present, I mean. It was...There are no words," she concluded, unable to express just how much the photograph meant to her. Izaya nodded, and smiled.

"Don't mention it," he said warmly. It was the same thing he had said to her in the forest after their first kiss, but this time his request was soft and humble. Nikka smiled back at him. Sums gawked at them both, perplexed by the friendly exchange; Nikka hadn't told him about Izaya's gift.

"I'll see you later," Izaya said softly before sauntering off.

He went and sat down next to Marcus Jenkins, who was preoccupied with kissing Jordan. Nikka checked her showcase program and frowned; Jordan was going to start the evening with a song.

The noise in the common room died down and the overhead lights dimmed. The whole room glowed with flickering candlelight. Miss Evans, whom Nikka recognized as Eloise's voice coach, took the stage and introduced Jordan. There was some cheering and scattered applause in the room. A moment later, Jordan took in a big gulp of air and began to sing. It was an Italian opera piece - rich and complex. Jordan's voice reverberated, hitting the high notes and plunging back to the low ones with what seemed like little effort. Nikka's skin rose in a layer of goosebumps. She had to admit, Jordan's voice was magnificent.

She looked over at Sums, who seemed just as surprised. Nikka felt irritated; she saw talent as something beautiful and pure. It felt unfair, wrong even, that someone as vile, as closed-minded as Jordan, could be *this* talented. Nikka pushed her thoughts away; it was juvenile to think that only good people could be talented, naive. That wasn't how the world worked; bad people had gifts too, and plenty of them. She let herself go and tried to enjoy the show.

~

"I know you don't want to hear about Tristan," said

Sums at breakfast the next day. Nikka shot him a warning look. Sums seemed to deflate a little.

"But I hadn't seen him since before Christmas, and I was worried about him," he admitted guiltily. "So I asked his House Matron about him, and it turns out he's *sick*."

Nikka looked up with interest. It was a reflex that she instantly regretted.

"Sick with what?"

"He had some rough infection over break and when he came back he was quarantined in the Health Center," said Sums. *Quarantined,* the word seemed alien to Nikka; it was something done to animals with rabies, or to humans in a Zombie apocalypse movie. The word sounded harsh and unforgiving. Nikka didn't want to be, but she was instantly worried for Tristan.

"Apparently, it's pretty bad," said Sums.

A sickly Tristan wasn't something Nikka could imagine. It wasn't something she ever wanted to imagine. He was so full of life, so strong. He had seemed *off* when she had encountered him on the path, but Nikka had assumed he was faking illness to avoid giving her an explanation. *Maybe he really was too ill to explain himself,* she thought, but instantly felt annoyed that she was allowing Tristan's poor physical state to excuse his treatment of her. The two situations were completely unrelated.

"Maybe, we should go visit him? Maybe they will let

us talk to him, through a glass or something," Sums suggested carefully. Nikka realized that Sums was asking for her permission, and felt bad. She had never meant to drive a wedge between Sums and Tristan, who had become close friends. She looked up at Sums, who was clearly trying hard to stay loyal to her, torn between wanting to check on Tristan and not wanting to hurt her feelings. Nikka smiled at him.

"Of course. Let's go as soon as we have a free period," she said.

That afternoon Nikka found herself in front of the Health Center. She wasn't sure how it had happened; she had been thinking about sick Tristan all afternoon, and suddenly she was running towards the Health Center, without Sums, without a plan, and with a sudden burning desire to make sure that he was okay. Nikka walked through the familiar hallway that led to Nurse Smith's office. The receptionist wasn't in her usual spot, so Nikka crossed the waiting room and knocked right on Smith's office door. A few moments passed, and Nurse Smith opened the door. The bulky woman looked at Nikka with surprise and then smiled, just a few moments too late.

"Why hello there, Nikka," she said sweetly, then she looked past her at the empty reception desk with exasperation.

"You know if you feel sick you need to call the Wildwood emergency line, and they'll come and pick you up. There are no evening walk-ins," she said softly.

"My friend, Tristan, I heard he's in quarantine," said Nikka. "Can I please talk to him?" Mrs. Smith's eyes narrowed and she looked at Nikka speculatively.

"What relation do you have to Tristan O'Mally?" asked Mrs. Smith.

"Just a friend," said Nikka awkwardly.

"I'm afraid only family are allowed to see patients in quarantine," said Mrs. Smith, her voice full of feigned regret.

"Well, what does he have?" urged Nikka. "Maybe I have it too. Maybe you should examine me," she said. She threw a quick sideways glance towards the examination room, which was next door to the patient intake rooms, but Mrs. Smith didn't miss a beat.

"It's time for you to go back to the dorms, sweetie," she said, her voice saccharine, yet strict. Mrs. Smith began to close the door in Nikka's face but Nikka shoved her foot in the way. She had a brief flashback to a similar interaction when Amber had been suspended. Nikka stared up at Mrs. Smith defiantly; the anger she felt towards the large woman coursed through her body like a hot current.

I know what you did on Thanksgiving!" she burst out. The door swung back open and Mrs. Smith eyed Nikka, her expression emotionless.

"I know *whom* you were with, and *what* you were

doing," Nikka added, in a desperate attempt to provoke the nurse. Nikka was counting on the fact that Madame Grenoble had been covering up the details of her Thanksgiving for a reason. Mrs. Smith gave a knowing, winning smile.

"I know you came in for your allergy that night," she said impassively. "I was having a staff meeting with a few colleagues, if you must know. It was a disciplinary hearing for a certain blue-haired friend of yours. Those things are usually kept secret," she explained sweetly.

Disciplinary hearing.... Blue hair...Eloise! Nikka realized. That was why Madame Grenoble had lied; she knew that Nikka would have been probing her for the results. Madame Grenoble wasn't the type to burden herself with the trivial emotions of others. Nikka shrunk away from the door.

"Such a pity, she was a very promising girl," Nurse Smith lingered on her words, savoring each one of them, enjoying herself. Nikka hated the way Mrs. Smith spoke of Eloise as if she had died.

"I am not your enemy, sweetie," Nurse Smith added. Her voice was lukewarm again, calm. She took a step back and let the door close, shutting Nikka out, this time for good.

×

Nikka sat opposite Sums in the library. It was a beautiful sunny day, so naturally the library was empty. Sums and

Nikka loved it here; the glass walls, the complete silence, and access to the Internet, but today the majestic library wasn't enough to distract Nikka from her inner monologue. *What's wrong with Tristan? When will I see him again?*

Sums had his nose buried in one of the library laptops. There was no Internet anywhere else on campus, so the library kept a stock of computers available for the students to rent. However, both the one hour time limit and the internet usage rules were heavily enforced; any site that could be considered distracting - or worse, fun - was rendered inaccessible. But Sums, of course, had found a way around the block, and so for at least one hour a day, the library was his haven. He typed away at lighting speed whilst Nikka absent-mindedly leafed through a random art history book. She had given up on asking Sums what he was up to, she rarely understood his answers.

She stared out of the glass wall of the library then tried to read a few dry passages from the heavy set book, but her brain was like a drain pipe; the information went in one end and out the other. *When will Tristan be out? What could he possibly be sick with that is severe enough for quarantine? Is it chicken pox? Bird flu?* Not knowing was wearing Nikka out. She slammed the book shut.

"I'm going out for some fresh air," she told Sums. He half nodded in response, preoccupied with the screen.

Nikka walked out, past the librarian and out into the

Zen garden. She checked her watch, *half past 4 - snack hour*. She considered walking up to the cafeteria and grabbing a few snack bars or finger sandwiches. *Sums would appreciate that,* she thought decisively, and she trudged up one of the smaller uphill paths. Halfway up, her leg caught on something, and she tripped and fell. Her knees hit the ground hard, and she was disoriented by the sudden fall. When she tried to get up she found that her foot was stuck. *A root,* she reasoned. But suddenly, the root was pulling her. Before she could figure out what was happening, Nikka felt herself being dragged quickly into the bushes. A hand covered her mouth and her scream was muted. Her elbows and hands had scraped against the rocks and branches on the ground. She tried to claw herself away from the pulling force when suddenly it lessened, and then stopped, though the hand on her mouth remained firmly in place.

"Relax, Nikka," she heard a familiar voice whisper into her ear.

Nikka tried to blink away the dirt that had gotten into her eyes. Cautiously, she looked over her shoulder and in the blur she found Tristan. The boy in front of her was a different Tristan to the one she remembered - he was skinnier, tired and sickly. Tristan pulled his hand away from her mouth, but Nikka couldn't speak. His appearance was terrible; there were deep rings of purple under his eyes, his freckles stood out like iodine drops on his skin, which was far paler than it had been before. His hair was unwashed and he looked small, defeated.

"Hey, Nikka," he mustered feebly.

Nikka threw her arms around his neck and hugged him close. He exhaled a sigh of relief into her ear. A moment later Nikka pushed him away, her relief had faded, overruled by the pain in her knee.

Nikka sat up and indignantly brushed the dirt off of her uniform. Her knee was bleeding. She pointed at it.

"What the hell did you do that for? Have you lost your mind?" she asked. Tristan didn't answer her right away. He stared past her, looking frightened.

"I didn't want anyone to see us," he explained. Tristan shifted in place then he started to scratch the inside of his elbow with manic force. Nikka reached out and steadied his hand.

"You weren't supposed to leave the Health Center, were you?" she said softly. "How are you feeling?" Tristan shook his head to say 'no,' and suddenly he started laughing, a frenzied delirious laugh. Nikka shrunk away a little, wary of his odd behavior.

"How am I feeling? I had to bribe the nurse so she would let me out for an hour before Mrs. Smith came back. Do you know how much she wanted?"

Tristan laughed again. Nikka couldn't see what was so funny. Tristan's expression was wild, like an animal caught in a cage.

"I kept offering her more, and more... She only agreed once I offered her 10,000 dollars, can you believe it? I don't have that kind of money!"

Nikka had no idea what Tristan was talking about, the money, the bribery, it all sounded so fabricated. Perhaps he was feverish? Tristan stopped laughing.

"Nikka, I think *they* are making me sick," he said slowly, carefully, as if he were speaking to her in code. As if we were trying to tell her a lot more than just the words he was saying. Nikka put a hand on his shoulder.

"What do you mean? Start from the beginning."

Tristan's curly russet hair was a tangled mess, and his beard had grown out. Nikka stroked the side of his arm rhythmically, in an attempt to calm him down, to anchor him.

"I was called to the nurse's office a few days after the dance," he began.

"At first I blew it off because I had a few poker games lined up, and had better things to do, but when I got back, my House Matron insisted I go see *her*..." Tristan quivered and Nikka knew he was referring to Mrs. Smith.

"I went in. She gave me a shot and I started feeling sick instantly. From then on I just kept getting worse and worse. They kept giving me shots, but I just got worse after each one. I didn't even know where I was half the time," he said, in a panic. "They said I was sick and had to stay there."

Tristan looked disoriented and tired; he squeezed Nikka's hand, desperate to cling on to something real.

"You're burning up," gasped Nikka when she felt his hand. She touched his forehead, and then his neck, and found it hot and dripping with sweat.

"You're sick, you need to go back," she pleaded, concerned.

Tristan flipped Nikka's wrist and checked her watch. When he saw the time he closed his eyes. He took a few deep, heavy breaths, trying to regain his composure, to gather the courage to go back.

"Can you please do me a favor?" he begged, his blue eyes locked on Nikka's.

"Anything," she said, swallowing the lump of worry that had formed in her throat.

"Can you explain the situation to Sums, just ask him to look into it. If anyone can help me make sense of this, it's him."

Nikka nodded, but Tristan pressed on, as if he didn't trust that Nikka would believe him.

"I need to find out if there is any reason that they would be making me sick. I'm sorry, I know this sounds crazy, but I need to know," he croaked desperately.

Nikka nodded. It did sound crazy, and in that moment Tristan *looked* crazy, wild with fever. Tristan stroked her hair off her face, a gesture so intimate and warm that it brought Nikka right back to the night at The Point.

"I will," she said softly.

Whatever Tristan was experiencing, whether or not he was right, Nikka knew that this wasn't the moment to doubt him, not while he was in such a state. It wasn't the moment to tell him that he was probably having a mental breakdown, or a psychotic episode. Nikka squeezed his arm one last time.

Tristan smiled, a smile so weak it nearly brought her to tears.

"Thank you, and I'm sorry for scaring you," he said, his voice low and grateful.

"Go back to the Health Center now," Nikka urged, gently. Tristan got up and pulled Nikka up after him. Nikka prepared to turn and walk away, but Tristan called after her.

"By the way," he said. "I *don't* have a girlfriend. It was a big misunderstanding. I know it's hard for you to believe me, but I'll explain everything as soon as I can. I'll prove everything," Nikka's heart skipped a beat. Tristan's gaze was sincere and pained, drained of all former joy. He smiled at her weakly before turning and walking off.

Nikka ran all the way back to the library. Breathless, she found Sums and slumped herself into the chair in front of him, her chest heaving. Sums barely noticed.

"I just saw Tristan," she whispered. Sums looked up from his laptop, his interest piqued. His round face was flushed, no doubt from a tense hour spent hacking.

"They let you see him? How is he?"

"No, they didn't, and he's not doing well at all."

Sums frowned.

"What do you mean *they didn't let you*, is he out?"

"Not exactly," said Nikka carefully. Sums raised an eyebrow.

Nikka looked out of the window, searching for the right words to explain what had just happened, when she noticed something through the glass wall. In the distance, she saw a Wildwood laundry truck. The thought struck her like lightning.

"Sums," she said, "I need you to come with me."

×

An hour later, Sums and Nikka were standing in the dark, overgrown backyard of the wooden cabin where they had both attended their first townie party.

"How on earth did you find your way back here, Nikka?" asked Sums.

"I just remembered," Nikka shrugged her shoulders.

"It's been months, we walked at night," Sums continued, incredulously.

"I have a good sense of direction," mumbled Nikka. She made her way towards the back of the silent house and gave the back door three confident knocks. Nikka had filled Sums in on Tristan's state and claims, and it was shortly after that she had led Sums through the woods without giving him an explanation as to why.

"What are we doing here?" Sums asked looking around uncertainly.

"Do you believe in coincidences?" asked Nikka. She gave two more frustrated knocks on the faded wooden door.

"Coincidence?" repeated Sums thoughtfully. "According to Aristotle, it is probable that improbable things will happen, so yeah, I do believe coincidences can occur,'" he explained. Nikka rolled her eyes.

"What I'm trying to say is, do you agree that if two or more people have conspiracy theories about the same school, then it might be good to weigh them against each other, and that whatever they have in common is possibly the truth?" she asked.

Sums gulped. "You want to speak with the journalist," he said with shaky realization.

Nikka nodded. Tristan thought the school was making him sick; the journalist thought the school was doing something illegal; Alex thought that the school was his enemy - it made sense to start *here*.

"Just pretend we are detectives," she said cheerfully, to try and calm Sums down. Nikka tried to keep her own nerves at bay; perhaps they were on a wild goose chase, but she felt like she owed it to Tristan to at least try and get some answers.

"Nobody's home," said Sums a few moments later, seeming relieved.

Nikka looked around, and through the patio window. In one smooth sweep she removed the screen frame, jiggled the old window and pushed it open. With a deep breath she swung her leg over the ledge and pushed herself into the house. Sums yelped.

"What are you doing?" he whispered furiously, his voice filled with an electric panic. Nikka ignored him and climbed into the familiar living room. It smelled of cigarettes and felt stuffy, just like the night of the party. She walked over to the back door, unlocked it and opened it. Sums stared at her, mouth ajar.

Nikka turned away from Sums and wordlessly went deeper into the quiet house; she could not afford to wait until answers found her, she had to find them herself. A few seconds later she heard Sums' hesitant footsteps follow her, his breath heavy with anxiety.

"We shouldn't be here," he whispered. "This is called breaking and entering."

"And that's different from hacking and entering how?" asked Nikka sarcastically.

Nikka found her way to the basement door. It was slightly ajar, and the padlock was open, as if the journalist had just left for a glass of milk, with the intent of returning in minutes. Nikka shot Sums a mischievous glance, then entered the basement. Sums sighed in defeat and followed her down.

"We shouldn't be here," he repeated. He looked over

his shoulder up the creaky stairs.

"We will be quick," assured Nikka. She plunged into the darkness, one hand tracing the wall.

"I think I just felt something crawling on me," Sums grunted.

Nikka found a switch and a white light flickered on to the side of the room, followed by three sets of large industrial overheads above them. Nikka squinted and looked around the room. The basement was completely plastered in newspaper clippings, pictures, maps, diagrams and highlighted pieces of paper - thousands of them. Sums let out a low whistle. They appeared to have stepped right into the mind of a mad man.

"It's like a serial killer basement on one of those crime shows," said Sums with a shudder.

There wasn't much furniture in the basement: a run down armchair in the corner, and a stained and bare mattress plumped unceremoniously on the floor. There was also a desk, above which hung an elaborate collage of Wildwood-related newspaper clippings. Nikka ran her finger across an old article that announced the ribbon cutting ceremony of Wildwood Academy twenty years ago.

"He's obsessed," she said with apprehension. A small fear started to creep up her spine. Sums was right, *they shouldn't be here*.

"*Journalist Jake Manning*," Sums read the name off a

piece of paper on the wall, "*obsessed* is putting it mildly..." he continued.

"He's got pictures and maps of the whole campus, and over here," Sums pointed at a corner on the wall, "is a list of all the staff names, and the whole student body."

Nikka examined another wall, one that seemed entirely dedicated to clippings and pictures of the Dean. Some of the photos Nikka recognized from his office; pictures of him with the President, of him smiling alongside various senators, and one of him with the Dalai Lama. There was a flash of light and Nikka thought she saw something reflected on the wall, like a streak of oil in a puddle. There was a pearlescent ray of something hidden there, camouflaged, but the light had given it away. *The light,* thought Nikka suddenly. She ran over to the light switches and hit each of them in turn. First, there was darkness, then more light, less light and finally, a light in the corner grunted and came alive, a black light. Nikka switched everything else off and swiveled the black light around so that it was facing the wall. It lit up writing previously unseen to them; all the pictures and clippings in the room were connected by sprawling, web-like lines, and hastily scribbled notes.

Nikka walked over to what looked like a timeline with marked points - *Chess Championship, Nationals, The accident, Court date,* and *First arrest.* The timeline had an arrow pointing from it and at a picture of a beautiful young girl. Nikka traced her fingers over the picture of the girl, who was posing gracefully in a black and white newspaper photo, a chess trophy in her hand. Under the photo there was an annotation: *expelled in 2008*. Sums, whose investigative instincts had now overruled his fear, was rifling through the desk drawers with interest.

"Nikka, you might want to see this," he beckoned, "*Manning* might be crazy but he is good with technology. There's a folder here with all of the Wildwood expulsions in the last decade. That's private information, even I would have a hard time accessing that."

"This girl was expelled too," said Nikka pointing at the black and white picture on the wall. She tilted her head back to look at the pretty girl.

"Who do you think she is?" asked Sums, sounding only half curious, his attention on the folder. It was not Nikka's voice that answered him from the top of the stairway.

"She was my sister."

Alex towered in the doorway, his silhouette black against the incoming light. He had a takeaway cup of coffee in his hand. Nikka froze, well aware of the fact that Alex was blocking their way out. The tattoo-covered townie walked down the stairs and faced them calmly.

"My sister Alexis was an award-winning chess player," he added bitterly. "My uncle got her into that cursed academy of yours. She was brilliant, received a full scholarship. Then, one day, she fell down the stairs, got a severe concussion. She wasn't able to play after that." Alex set his paper cup down on the table and Nikka noticed now that there were many others like it. She realized that Alex was the one who had left the basement door open. Alex had been spending time in the basement... *but why?*

Nikka felt her shoulders tense; her fight or flight instinct was kicking in, but she and Sums didn't dare move. Nikka tried to decipher Alex's demeanor, was he angry that he had found them trespassing in his house?

"She was expelled right after that. My family sued the school but it was no good, we lost. We lost all of our money in the court battle too." He snickered, a miserable empty shell of a laugh. His handsome face looked haunted and tense.

"Two months later, she killed herself," he said finally.

Nikka inhaled sharply and Sums gasped. Neither of them dared speak.

"Our family learned to live with the pain. After the court battle my parents divorced and moved away so that they could have a chance to forget, I stayed because I didn't want to forget - but *Jake...*" said Alex, glancing around the plastered, senseless walls. "He just couldn't go on after losing his niece. He dedicated the last six years to trying to take that school down. He lost his wife, his job and his house in the process. This basement is all he has to show for it." There was a pause. "Which reminds me.

What the hell are *you two* doing here?" Alex sounded angry now. His pained face had become feral, and Nikka felt Sums shrink away a little at the sight.

"Where is your uncle now, Alex?" Nikka asked. *Why are you spending time drinking coffee in his basement*? she wanted to add, but didn't.

"I'll be asking the questions," Alex snarled.

Nikka spoke softly, "Alex, I am so sorry. I understand that this is something very private and painful for your family, but we only came into the house..."

"Broke into it," Alex cut her off.

"Yes. Broke in," Nikka admitted freely, "to find some information that could help our sick friend..." Nikka looked at a hesitant Sums for help.

"We agree with your uncle," Sums stammered nervously. "We think the school is up to something. We're just not sure what..." Sums kept himself from looking at the pretty, dead, chess player in the pictures on the wall.

"I think *they,"* Nikka stressed the word, "did something to my friend, Tristan. I think they're making him sick," she said, hoping she could reason with Alex. "It sounds crazy, I know."

"My bar for crazy is pretty high," said Alex, seeming to relax a little.

"We're really sorry about what happened to your sister," Sums added quietly.

Alex's eyes met Nikka's, he seemed to soften a little.

"You should go," he urged suddenly.

"Okay we will, but maybe we could just ask your uncle a few questions," Nikka pleaded. Sums nudged her in the side, as if to say *you're pushing your luck; let's get the hell out of here.*

A loud knock resounded on the front door upstairs. Nikka and Sums exchanged a frightened look, and Alex sighed.

"I called the police," he said. "I thought it was a break-in."

Another knock echoed followed by someone shouting, "Police! Open up!"

Sums squeezed Nikka's shoulder in fear.

"You'd better run. *Trust me,* you don't want them finding you here. They are close to Wildwood," said Alex. He shifted his gaze to the small basement window. Nikka nodded and she and Sums shuffled over to it quickly.

"Nikka," Alex called out. She turned and his eyes locked on hers. "You might find what lies at the bottom of the pool, but you'll drown at the same time," he said.

"This isn't a battle you can win," he added softly, and with that he was out of the basement. Sums helped lift Nikka through the small window and Nikka struggled to pull Sums' weight through it.

Nikka could hear Alex talking loudly with the police at the front of the house; he was speaking in an abnormally loud voice, in attempt to give them cover. *Smart boy,* thought Nikka gratefully. As she took a last look at the house she was overcome by a sense of sadness for what his family had gone through, for the uncle mad with grief, and for the boy who had lost his sister. She had the brief flickering thought that, had things been different, the two of them might have become good friends. There was something more familiar to her about Alex than any of the friends she had made at Wildwood, he was simple, courageous and carried the weight of his family's pain on his shoulders. Nikka and Sums tiptoed to the edge of the forest and ran, all the way back to Wildwood.

15
Love is Everywhere

"In middle school I always got the most Valentines in my class," said Stella proudly. Her eyes sparkled with enthusiasm as she looked up from her organic oatmeal. "Do you think they do Valentines *here?*" She asked sullenly. Stella always said the word *here* melancholically when in reference to Wildwood Academy, as if she pined for her days in middle school. Nikka and Sums had not heard Stella's question, they were both perched over their breakfasts, plagued by similar thoughts about the basement, about Alex, about the journalist and about Tristan's worsening condition, thoughts they had agreed to not share with Stella.

"Guys, I'm not a ghost," said Stella crabbily.

"Sorry, what did you say again?" Nikka asked foggily. She and Sums exchanged a guilty look and Stella repeated herself.

"I'm sure you will get a lot of Valentines," Nikka placated her. Sums rolled his eyes, but Stella didn't notice, she just smiled dreamily and went on.

"Maybe you will too," she whispered to Nikka and she suggestively cocked her head in the direction of Izaya and his friends. He sat a few tables away from her, upright, formal and elegant as always, a half-smile plastered on his face. It was his usual disinterested half-smile, a social obligation that his face fulfilled whilst his head was off somewhere else. Nikka desperately wished that she could know where his head went to in those moments of disconnect. She tried to swallow those thoughts away; they caused a nagging heaviness in her chest. She and Izaya hadn't succeeded at becoming friends; but then again, neither of them had really tried.

Nikka turned her focus back to Tristan, her sick friend Tristan, that was where her loyalty lay now, and she wasn't going to let anything distract her from helping him. She looked away from Izaya just as his head turned in her direction.

Stella checked her watch, said her goodbyes and scurried off. The moment she was out of earshot, Sums let out a heavy sigh of relief. Nikka shot him a chiding look.

"What?" said Sums defensively. "It's not like I don't *enjoy* having breakfast with her." Sums eagerly dug into his backpack, and pulled out a USB stick. "It's just hard to not talk about *this,"* he tapped at the small object affectionately. Nikka knew that the USB contained all of Sums' Wildwood-related research thus far, protected by a series of passwords and PINs. The pair hadn't told Stella that they were researching Wildwood and its history; firstly, because Stella had a tendency to panic, and secondly, because there was nothing to tell, not yet. The basement, Tristan, Alex's sister - these were all odd, suspicious occurrences. Nikka and Sums were just grappling in the dark, trying desperately to connect the dots, and so far they had been unsuccessful; it was like a puzzle with only the edges in place. They had no proof other than the journalist, and all he had were lines in his basement that connected random events in search of the elusive truth. Nikka looked at Sums and the stick with concern. She should have anticipated that seeing Amber's name on the long list of expulsions would lead Sums to an obsession. It had been four days since the basement discovery and Sums' collection of data was becoming fatter every day, thanks to hours of fruitless research. Nikka was growing weary of it, and more than that, she was surprised to find that she was inwardly defensive of the academy. Deep down she didn't want there to be anything truly wrong with the school that she had come to love.

"What did you find now?" she asked. Sums began to tap on the table out of nervous habit.

"So, I've been going to the library, masking my IP address, and looking up the articles that we saw in the basement. The few titles that I could recall from memory, that is."

Sums said this lightly, as if it were the most normal thing in the world to spend one's days researching conspiracy theories, and for a moment it worried Nikka. She decided she wouldn't tell him that she remembered the title of every single article clipped to the walls of the basement.

"The odd thing is, quite a few of them are missing from the archives," said Sums pensively. "That can happen sometimes due to filing errors, but still, there are just enough missing to completely discredit anything the journalist might have drawn connections between. It's as if he either created those articles in Photoshop... or they were *removed.*" His tone lowered on the final word and Nikka nodded, feeling tired. This new discovery was odd, but it didn't sound like it would help Tristan.

"There's something else," said Sums carefully. Nikka's head shot up. She could see the alarm in Sums' gentle blue eyes, and she could hear it in his voice.

"Someone slid this under my door during the night." Sums pulled out a tiny crumpled piece of paper from his breast pocket and pushed it across the table towards Nikka. She picked it up, unfolded it and read:

"It's getting worse, please help me. –T"

×

Nikka skipped her last period and went straight to the nurse's office. She was determined; this time she wouldn't let Nurse Smith send her off so easily. She signed her name on the waiting list for sick pupils, and sat in the waiting room until the receptionist called her name. A nurse, who introduced herself as Nurse Lisa, led Nikka to a small office in the back.

"Cough for me," said the plain lady sweetly once Nikka had made herself comfortable on the doctor's chair. Nikka had lied to the woman and told her she had been suffering from flu symptoms all week.

The sweet woman pressed a stethoscope to Nikka's chest. Nikka in turn gave her best impression of a bad cough.

"Describe your symptoms to me, please," coaxed the lady after she had taken Nikka's blood. The woman labeled the vial and put it away.

"I've just been feeling *really* ill lately," Nikka lied. "I get shivers. My stomach hurts and my head feels like it's going to explode," she whined. The nurse nodded along sympathetically.

"When did the symptoms start?"

"About a week ago," said Nikka, in a pathetic drawl, as if she were too weak to speak properly.

"I hope I don't have that bug that's going around," she added innocently. "I have a science exam next week, I can't afford to be *quarantined*."

The nurse looked up, surprised.

"Oh no, darling," she cooed reassuringly, "The boy who is quarantined has a rare bug. You are unlikely to have it," she said dismissively.

"That's terrible," said Nikka trying her best to sound surprised. "I had heard rumors. How is he now?"

The nurse smiled. "He's a lot better. He's just recuperating down the hall," she said. "It sounds like you have a bad case of the flu," she added smartly, "I'm just going to get you some medicine. I will be right back."

Nurse Lisa walked out the door, leaving Nikka behind. Nikka didn't hesitate to take her chance and bolted towards the door. Carefully, she slid out of the small office and checked the hallway - *no one*. Then she tiptoed quickly down towards the last few doors. She could hear Nurse Lisa gossiping with the receptionist at the end of the hall and she was grateful for the woman's momentary lapse in professionalism.

Nikka opened the first patient room gently and peeked in- there was nothing, but two neatly made beds and an array of medical equipment. The second room was empty too. Nikka stopped when she found the third door locked. She yanked it a few times and tried the doorknob - nothing.

"You shouldn't be here!" came a sudden, panicked voice from behind her. Nikka spun around and faced

Nurse Lisa, who looked as terrified and appalled as if she had caught her breaking into the prescriptions cabinet. She grabbed Nikka's sweater and tugged her away from the door, her grip gentle but firm. Nikka tried to push the door open one last time.

"I said you need to leave, now, before someone-" Nurse Lisa didn't finish her sentence; she looked to both ends of the hallway afraid that someone would see them. This gave Nikka the confirmation she needed - *the woman was lying to her, Tristan was not okay.* She gave the door one last desperate yank.

"I'm looking for the bathroom," said Nikka feigning flu-induced delirium.

"Well *that* is not it," said the woman heatedly, and pointed in the opposite direction. Nikka smiled groggily and went into the bathroom. Nurse Lisa waited for her outside the stall like a prison guard, and when Nikka came out she wordlessly handed her a medicine pack and ushered her back out into the foyer, huffing and puffing unpleasantly as she went. Before parting she mumbled some remarks about behavior and inappropriateness under her breath, but Nikka could tell that Nurse Lisa was more relieved that no one had seen them than angry. And Nikka got the distinct feeling that the person she was afraid of was none other than Nurse Smith. Nikka put the unnecessary medicine in her bag and left the Health Center feeling worse than when she had gone in.

×

The next morning Nikka woke up to violent shaking. Stella hovered over her bed and was roughly shaking her awake. She looked as excited as a child on Christmas morning; her large chocolate eyes were stretched wide in delight. Nikka rose and rubbed the sleep from her eyes.

"Get up already, sleepy head!" Stella whined. Nikka yawned in response.

"What's going on?" she asked groggily. Stella beamed and pointed to the corner of the room. Nikka saw something big and pink.

"You got flowers, and I did too. Oh, and we both got Valentines," declared Stella triumphantly. She carried over the small pile of tiny envelopes and dumped it on Nikka's bed. Sleepily, Nikka dug through the contents. There were three cards - the first one was from Stamos. Stamos had also sent her a small, delicately wrapped box of French chocolate truffles. Nikka held up the fancy box in the air and arched her brow at Stella.

"Don't worry. I got one too. I think every girl in school did, how amazing is he?" gushed Stella. Nikka smiled, relieved. Stamos really was the classiest school official Nikka had ever met. Nikka tugged the luxurious box apart and popped a truffle in her mouth. The next Valentine was from Sums; it read, *"Valentine's Day sucks"* and there was a picture of a sad looking pug in a cupid outfit on the cover. Nikka chuckled, then opened the third card which read; *"A friend is the best Valentine,"* it was signed by Stella. Nikka grinned at Stella, who was hungrily watching her reaction to each individual item.

"Now, check your flowers," Stella urged. Nikka looked at the beautiful pink peonies on her table. It reminded her of when Tristan had gotten them the corsages before the Winter Dance. She got up, flipped the tiny card attached to the flowers and read it.

Never thine. Never mine.

But somehow still my Valentine.

The card wasn't signed. Nikka looked at Stella.

"My flowers are anonymous too!" she yelped with excitement. "Can you believe it? We have secret admirers!" She pointed at a bouquet of tulips by her bedside.

"Just like middle school!" she announced with great satisfaction. Stella bathed in her sense of holiday euphoria as she proceeded to re-read all of her Valentines out loud. Nikka nodded, but she wasn't listening. She flipped the tiny flower card in between her fingers. The card was anonymous but the words weren't. Everything about it spelled *Izaya*; it was aloof, riddled and secretive. Nikka's heart ached painfully, but she felt like she could fly at the same time. *Never thine. Never mine. But somehow still my Valentine.* A knock resounded on the door, and Magda walked in. She smiled brightly at the girls.

"Happy Valentines Day," she said affectionately.

"You too, Magda," the girls returned in unison. Magda looked at Nikka, her pale blue eyes betraying a trace of concern. She folded a few things and only spoke again when Stella had disappeared into the bathroom to get ready.

"*Alex*," she said to Nikka knowingly, "nice boy from laundry service." Nikka nodded in confused acknowledgement. "He asked me to tell you that he is selling his house and thought that you should know."

The basement, panic coursed through Nikka's veins as she made sense of Magda's message. *Why would Alex suddenly be selling his house? Why now?* Before Magda could say anything more Nikka changed into her uniform and jetted out the door.

×

It was after breakfast and Nikka was hiding in the bushes outside the Academy laundry facilities. As she watched the trucks arrive, unload and take off again, she realized that hiding in those bushes was probably one of the oddest things she had ever done. She was distracted by the thought, when suddenly she spotted the face she was looking for. A few feet away from her, Alex was slowly pulling his truck out from the garage. Nikka walked over and knocked on the side window. The truck came to a screeching halt, and for a moment, Alex just stared at her through the window, startled. Then he got out and leaned against the truck, his hands tucked into his Wildwood staff uniform. Tattoos wound up his collarbone and halfway to his neck, his head was clean-shaven, and his eyes were bleak.

"What the hell are you doing here?" he asked harshly.

"Sorry to bug you again," said Nikka carefully. "I got your message, I thought we could talk about it," she ventured.

"There is nothing to talk about," Alex shot back.

"Why are you selling the house? When did this happen?"

"A realtor came by the other day, said that my area was becoming very desirable and that she had a few clients looking to buy as soon as possible, then she showed me a figure..."Alex lifted his heavily tattooed arm and scratched the top of his head, avoiding her gaze. Nikka got the sense that the *figure* in question was a sizable one.

"And you didn't think that was suspicious? Just out of the blue, someone wants to buy your house?" She asked.

Alex looked towards the forest.

"Who am I to question gentrification," he said with a dark smile.

"You're not convincing," said Nikka with frustration. She crossed her arms reproachfully.

"Nikka," Alex said her name softly, which took her by surprise. "I've spent years thinking that everything was a sign, that everything was suspicious, that everything was a clue. I became afraid of my own shadow," he admitted.

Nikka nodded, she knew exactly what he meant. She was starting to feel that same way, and it had only been a few days since she had begun to question everything. Nonetheless, she couldn't stop questioning now, for Tristan, for her own peace of mind.

"I'm done," said Alex. "Done with all of it."

"What about the basement? All of that proof?" said Nikka.

"Proof of what?"

Of something, something important, Nikka wanted to shoot back, but she realized that wasn't enough to convince him. She also realized that she wouldn't want to convince him to change his mind, even if she could. There was nothing but pain in that house; if it were hers, she would sell it too.

"I'm just done, I don't have the energy to go on," said Alex.

"When does it sell? Maybe Sums and I could take some pictures first," Nikka ventured carefully.

"Escrow closes tomorrow," said Alex. "Nikka, you need to give up," he added after a pause; there was a trace of warning in his voice. Nikka moved out of his way so that he could go back to his truck. Alex lingered for a moment, there was a pregnant pause.

"I keep a key under my mat. I've already moved all my stuff out, so if you wanted to go snoop around one final time, there's nothing to stop you," he said quietly.

"Thank you," Nikka whispered.

Alex sighed, got back in his truck and drove away. Nikka watched him drive off. She had an overwhelming urge to give up, but then she had an even better idea.

×

It took some convincing, but by lunchtime Nikka had successfully dragged Sums to the Wildwood Police Station. The pair entered the small log cabin, which was so quaint and pleasant, that it looked more like a maple syrup store than a crime-fighting hub. The pair entered the lobby, and decidedly approached the front counter. A single heavy-set officer sat at the front desk, talking on the phone, and in what seemed to Nikka like a fatal cliché, the man was eating a glazed donut.

"No, Susan, I don't want meatloaf two days in a row," he said into the receiver with gravity. His eyes narrowed in on Sums and Nikka when they walked in, and he hung up the phone without saying goodbye.

"How can I help you?" he asked. His multiple pink chins jiggled like strawberry Jello when he spoke.

"Good afternoon," said Nikka trying to sound composed and adult-like. "We would like to report a crime."

"What sort of crime?" asked the officer, sounding very tired. His eyes darted to the side of his desk to an unfinished croissant. Nikka hesitated; she hadn't planned this bit. Next to her, Sums fidgeted, shifting his weight from one leg to the other. She shot him an expectant look.

"We would like to report a break-in," Sums offered hesitantly, which made his statement sound more like a question.

"Uh huh," said the officer lazily. "And what was stolen?" he reached for a piece of paper in his filing cabinet.

"It's not so much that anything was stolen," said Nikka carefully. "But these *thieves,* they wrote things on the walls. *Strange things.* We thought we should show you so that you could maybe make sense of it," she concluded.

"Maybe it's gang related," offered Sums. The policeman raised an eyebrow.

Sums was starting to sweat, Nikka could tell that he was afraid they'd be called out on their lies. Nikka knew that what they were doing was wrong on many levels. She shouldn't be using Alex's key to let the police in to see the journalist's notes, but she had no other choice; this felt like the best way to help Tristan - the only way. Maybe the police could make better sense of the journalist's notes than she and Sums ever could, maybe, just *maybe,* they would take over. But as Nikka watched the large man throw a second glance at the half-eaten croissant on the other end of the table, she realized that her idea of police competency was based on living in big crime-ridden cities her entire life.

"Vandalism," said the officer pensively, as if he had just heard the term for the first time.

He got up, which seemed difficult for him, grabbed the croissant decisively and put it in his mouth.

"I'm the only one on duty now, you can show me and I'll file the report, but first I need to see some ID," he said importantly, spittle flying.

ID, realized Nikka - she and Sums exchanged a rattled look. This was something else they hadn't thought of when Nikka made the rash decision to go and report the journalist's basement to the police. Nikka couldn't be sure, but reporting fake vandalism in a house that wasn't yours seemed like a very illegal thing to do. As they stood there looking at the fat policeman, chewing, they both realized not a single part of their plan had been thought through.

"Our IDs are at the house," mumbled Nikka figuring that they could lead the officer to the house, let him in and ditch him there, counting on his investigative instinct to take over - if he had any, that is. The policeman walked past them and out the door. The pair followed him.

"But who will watch the station when you leave," asked Sums worriedly when they were on the curb. Nikka realized he was trying to backtrack, and she quickly stepped on his foot. Sums stifled a cry.

"Nothing ever happens in Wildwood," said the officer, his mouth full of croissant. Sums shot Nikka a *'This is all your fault'* look before reluctantly climbing into the backseat of the cop's car.

The drive only took five minutes. Nikka guided the cop to Alex's house while silently going through the multiple unplanned-for scenarios that could unfold when they got there. When they arrived at Alex's door, Nikka saw to her surprise that it was already ajar. A moment later a fresh-faced woman emerged. She fumbled with the latches of her fancy briefcase, heard them approach, and raised her head.

"Hello, you must be *their* mother," said the officer smartly. He reached a hand out to the woman.

"Umm, no," said the women incredulously. "I am the realtor for *this* property," she pointed behind her. "It just sold," she added self-importantly. The confused officer looked back at Nikka, and then at Sums, who looked like he wanted nothing more than to sink right into the ground.

"My brother lives here. *Lived* here, I'm Alex's sister," Nikka improvised to the lady. "We had a case of vandalism recently in the basement and I just wanted to report it before escrow closed," she continued insouciantly. "No crime should go unpunished," she concluded with a pointed look in the direction of the officer, who instantly straightened up. Nikka smiled innocently, hoping there was some minute possibility that they would believe her story.

"There is nothing in the basement," said the realtor lady, perplexed. "And escrow closed yesterday- the whole house has been refurbished."

"Overnight?" asked Sums, stunned. The woman nodded.

"The buyer wanted the house ready upon purchase; it's rare, but they can afford it so, hey, who am I to stand in the way of good money?" The realtor laughed with delight. Nikka disregarded the woman and pushed past her into the house, and, ignoring her calls, ran all the way down to the dark basement. She fiddled with the lights and a moment later the basement was illuminated. It was just as the women had said - everything was gone, the basement had a fresh coat of paint, and the rest was wiped clean. Any theory the journalist might have had, any morsel of evidence he might have found, gone with the stroke of a brush.

×

Nikka and Sums had painstakingly endured a 15-minute lecture from the policeman about wasting valuable police time and resources, whilst the realtor simultaneously ranted about her busy schedule and how she couldn't afford to waste time on "silly games." The officer then headed to lunch, and the realtor to her next meeting, with both parties writing the incident off as a case of teenage stupidity.

On her way out, Nikka had noticed the sales contract

lying on the living room desk unattended, and she had quickly and discretely flipped through it and committed the contents to memory, which included Alex's new, temporary address and the final price the house had sold for. The document also revealed that the house had been purchased by a company call *Americall,* for triple the estimated market value.

Alex was staying at a motel on the outskirts of town. Nikka and a very unwilling Sums found it easily – it was a boxy, slightly decrepit building with a lobby, blinds and pool that all appeared to be unchanged since the fifties. The building was easy to find because it was an eyesore in the otherwise flawless Wildwood scenery, it was an ugly mix of faded pastels and browning edges.

"He's in room 47," said Nikka to Sums whom stomped on grumpily like a child headed to the dentist.

"This looks like something straight out of a horror film," he complained, sounding unnerved. "You take me to the nicest places."

They made their way up the concrete stairs and along the second floor. Nikka stopped at door 47 and knocked. There was a moment of silence, followed by some fumbling around. The door opened and Alex looked at them, shirtless with a can of beer in his hand.

"Long time no see," he said sarcastically towards Nikka. He nodded at Sums and walked back into his room without closing the door, which Nikka and Sums took as an invitation to come inside. They walked into the small shabby room, which looked a lot like the exterior of the motel, and smelled of mold and cigarette smoke. The bed was covered in an old quilt, the curtains were lacy and timeworn, and the kitchenette had a yellowish tint, framed with peeling wallpaper.

"Nice room," said Sums politely. Alex laughed.

"I'm a fan of Hitchcock's," he said somberly. Sums forced a chuckle.

"Is this where you're going to live now?" asked Nikka, trying not to sound judgmental. She wasn't about to admit that she had seen the price the house had sold for and that she knew Alex could definitely afford better than *this.*

"I'm going to move soon, but the money hasn't come in yet," said Alex, He opened an old mini-fridge in the corner and pulled out two cans.

"Beer? Orange soda?" he asked. Sums nodded and Alex knowingly threw him a can of soda, which Sums caught with great effort.

"Are going to leave town?" asked Nikka.

"My parents are gone, my uncle is gone, my sister..." Alex paused, sounding numb. "Is *gone*. When my contract runs out at Wildwood next month I'm going to leave this town and forget about it once and for all."

Nikka was instantly filled with compassion. She could understand why the boy wanted nothing more than to run away.

"Did you take any pictures of the basement before you left?" asked Sums. Alex snorted.

"So that's what this is about?" he asked. He took a sip. "I told you where I left the key, you can go take pictures yourself."

"But they..." began Sums before Nikka cut him off. Alex didn't need to know that the information his uncle gathered was gone forever, before they had even had a chance to document it.

"Do you know who Americall is?" she asked instead. Sums shot her a questioning look.

"Someone with a lot of disposable income," said Alex. He polished off his can of beer and tossed it in the bin.

"I told you, I'm done asking questions," he added sternly. He rose from his chair without a word, and walked to the door. Nikka and Sums followed his lead, and interpreted this as a goodbye. Once by the door, Nikka turned to him.

"Alex, I hope everything goes well with you, and your move," she offered; she felt guilty. She and Alex weren't even friends and she had broken into his house, cornered him at work, questioned and judged him when he had been through more than she could ever imagine. Alex's features softened, his neck tattoo bobbed as he swallowed hard.

"And I hope you guys stop asking questions, before

you end up in the same place as my uncle," he said frankly. This wasn't a threat; he really meant it. Alex started to close the door.

"Where is your uncle, by the way?" asked Nikka nonchalantly. Sums sighed with exasperation; all he wanted to do was go home, back to the safety of his dorm. Nikka was doing exactly what Alex had just warned her not to do, and the faux nonchalance in her voice wasn't fooling anyone. Alex stared at her hard. Then he groaned.

"You're not going to give up, are you?" It wasn't a question this time. He reached into his pocket and pulled out a card then handed it to Nikka.

The card read. *'Idlewell Psychiatric Facility,'* and there was an address.

"Be safe," said Alex, and he allowed the decrepit motel room door to swing shut.

×

It was late in the afternoon; Nikka carried a small basket with her as she headed towards the Health Center. Magda had helped her pack it; it was filled with chocolates, cake, fruit and a handwritten note for Tristan. When she got to the Health Center she nearly collided head first with Izaya, who was exiting, a paper bag with a prescription tucked under his arm.

"Nikka," he exclaimed, seeming happy, or as close to happy as Izaya could look. "What are you doing here? I was just about to look for you."

Look for me? Thought Nikka flabbergasted. She didn't answer right away.

"Are you sick?" she asked, concerned and she pointed at the packet. Izaya shrugged his shoulders.

"Just some vitamins," he said cheerily. "Are you..." his voice trailed off mid-sentence just as he was about to ask her, for the second time, why she was at the Health Center. His eyes narrowed in on her basket.

"On your way to grandma's house?" he asked. His demeanor had changed; his voice was suddenly icy again. Izaya reached towards the basket and Nikka recoiled a little, but he was quicker.

"*For Tristan*," he read from the basket tag, and Nikka's face flushed a bright shade of red. Izaya let go of the tag with distaste and looked past Nikka at the trail.

"I should get going," he said evenly.

"I was going to come find you too, to say thank you for the flowers," said Nikka, but she couldn't muster any more than that. The awkwardness she felt overruled anything smart she could say to make the situation better. Izaya snorted.

"Flowers?" he said incredulously. "And you just assumed they were from me," he laughed again, an airy laugh laced with mockery and pity, as if Nikka were a silly little girl, letting her fantasies get the best of her.

"It's Valentine's Day, Nikka, and even though you think you're the only worthy girl on this campus," he said in his most arrogant, condescending tone, "I've got more interesting fish to fry," he concluded coldly, and walked off. Nikka was dumbstruck as she made her way into the Health Center. She felt sullen, and empty, any happiness she had felt that morning was gone, evaporated over the events of the day. The receptionist let her leave the note for Tristan but not see him. This time she didn't insist.

×

Nikka tiptoed through the weeds that grew over the entrance to the Wildwood cemetery. She had the chills, and she wasn't sure whether it was from the cold or from her present location. She made her way through and across the rows of headstones, reading them as she went. It felt strange to spend the evening of Valentine's Day in a moonlit cemetery reading off the names of people who were long gone, but it also felt right, as if these souls were in need of a visit on this day more than any other. A few minutes later Nikka found what she was looking for. It was a humble tombstone, half-swallowed by the poorly manicured lawn around it, it read: *Alexis Manning - Daughter, Sister, Niece, Protégé.*

Nikka had assumed that she would find it there, since Alex's family were all from Wildwood. Looking at the large piece of stone, Nikka was suddenly happy that her father didn't have a grave. There had been no remains when he met his end, and Nikka's mother was too disorganized and grief-stricken to organize a symbolic funeral, so instead they got on the road and drove on. The infinite road trip they embarked on was his only memorial. Funerals were about closure, and that's what Daria was looking for every single time she zipped another suitcase shut and closed another door.

Nikka wouldn't have wanted her father tied down to one place. She liked that his memory and presence was always with her, everywhere she went. She knew that if anything would make it hard for Alex to leave, it would be the location of his sister's tombstone. She let her fingers run over her dog tags. She would never want to feel like Alex must be feeling now, like he was leaving Alexis behind. Just as Nikka had expected there would be, she found a crudely wrapped gas-station bouquet of white lilies lying on the headstone next to a tiny wooden chess piece, a queen. Nikka knew it was from Alex; his apology for selling the house they had grown up in. His apology for moving on.

Alex was right to sell the house, he was right to move on, and Nikka hoped he would find peace wherever he went. At least one person in his family deserved to find peace. She placed her pink peonies next to the bouquet of white lilies, then she pushed some of the weeds back, and tore some of them out. She didn't stop for a while, caking her fingernails with dirt as she polished the place clean. Nikka ripped out weeds and let them flutter in the wind like dandelion seeds. The plot looked a lot cleaner now. Nikka smiled; she wanted Alexis to know that there were two people thinking of her that Valentine's Day.

16
SUSPICION

Nikka was in the middle of her English class when suddenly, chipper and with a large smile spread across his face, Tristan waltzed through the front door. Class had already started, so Tristan nodded in acknowledgement to the professor, handed him a note, and without taking a further look around, hurriedly occupied the last free seat in the back row. Nikka turned and gawked at him in astonishment, as if he were an alien life form. She couldn't believe it. His cheeks were flushed; his eyes bright and alive- Tristan was the very picture of health. He sat a few rows away, grinning ear to ear at her. Nikka smiled back. *He's all better now,* she concluded, with a mixture of relief and confusion as she turned back to face the board. Stella, who was sat next to her, cranked her neck all the way back like an ostrich. She looked at Tristan, then at Nikka, and then back again; this new development was far more interesting to her than 18th century literature. Nikka couldn't focus either. *How can he just be better overnight?* She wondered suspiciously.

A painstaking hour later the bell rang. Nikka squeezed herself out of her desk and found Tristan. She threw her arms around him and hugged him hard. Tristan pulled her in, his arms wound tightly just below her shoulders blades. He smelled her hair, and exhaled nostalgically. She could feel the curious stares on her back, classmates analyzing their display of affection, but she didn't care. Nikka suddenly remembered that Tristan had never explained the girlfriend situation to her, and she willed herself to pull away.

"You're okay," she reaffirmed softly.

"I woke up this morning and I felt better. So they let me go," Tristan explained cheerfully.

"That's... amazing," Nikka stuttered trying to disguise her uncertainty.

She gathered her stuff and followed Tristan out of the classroom and into the clearing outside. The doubt that had nagged at her during class didn't fade. Nikka replayed the events of the past week, all that worry, all those theories, all those attempts to uncover something that might not have ever really been there, *and for what? Did Tristan really just have some rare form of flu? Had they imagined everything? Had it all been a massive waste of time?*

No, it wasn't. Nikka reminded herself as she looked at the back of Tristan's russet hair. She had done it all for Tristan, to comfort him; to help him through a tough time; she had done what he had asked. Once they were outside Nikka hugged him again, as if for confirmation that he really was there and okay. Tristan chuckled into her ear. As Nikka withdrew from him she accidentally caused something to fall from his back pocket. She looked down. A notepad had landed open on the ground. The open page revealed a pencil sketch of an apple. Curious, Nikka picked it up and leafed through it. The notepad pages were filled with pencil sketches, portraits, landscapes, and doodles. The drawings were rough, erratic but promising. Nikka handed the notepad back to Tristan, feeling embarrassed for prying.

"I didn't even know you could draw," she pouted, feeling left out. Tristan reached for the small notepad and tucked it into his messenger bag, looking self-conscious.

"I can't, *not really*. I just started. It helped me get through the sickness. Maybe I was inspired by you," he said smiling.

"Those are really good," said Nikka trying to mask the surprise in her voice. She looked at him again, as if she hadn't seen him in years, as if he were an entirely new person standing in front of her.

"I'm so glad that you're alright," she said resolutely.

"Nik, at some point it felt like I was going to die," he

admitted. The sun shone through his brown hair, making it appear red. He grinned his crooked smile and in that moment Tristan was transformed back to his cheeky, carefree self. Whatever had made him sick, Nikka could tell there wasn't a trace of it left now.

"I was worried I wouldn't have a date to the prom," she teased.

Tristan's face turned serious. His gaze darkened and he looked away from her.

"Listen, Nikka," he started, his voice cautious and stern. Nikka interrupted him.

"It was a joke, Tristan. I don't even think they have a prom here," she said, mortified. Tristan shook his head.

"It's not that," he continued awkwardly. "It's just, in light of recent events, I think it's best if I leave Wildwood, for good. If I'm able to, if they let me," he explained guardedly, and just like that all of his nonchalance was gone. His voice went low and his paranoid eyes darted around the clearing, making sure that no one could overhear them. Nikka's head spun a little at what he had said, she could hear the words loud and clear, but she couldn't make sense of them. *In light of recent events...if they let me,* she replayed the phrases in her head. *Tristan was talking about leaving Wildwood as if he weren't free to just walk out the door? As if he were trapped, again?*

"I don't understand," said Nikka meekly.

Then suddenly Nikka realized something. She had

assumed that Tristan's return to health meant that they could now drop all of the suspicion that they had harbored against Wildwood for the past few weeks. That his return meant that he really had just been sick. But Nikka could tell by the grave expression on Tristan's face that he believed otherwise; he was still convinced that *they* had done something to him - and worse even, that they wouldn't let him leave.

"I want to explain, Nikka, but I can't. Not yet," he said cryptically.

Tristan noticed something behind her and gritted his teeth. Nikka turned and found a school messenger standing in front of her, clad in the usual red and black uniform that Nikka had come to find menacing.

"Nikka Mason," said the bland man coolly. "Please report to the nurse's office for a follow up - you are exempt from your next class," the man handed her a summons and walked off.

×

Nikka decided she didn't want to do anything that would further jeopardize her residency at Wildwood, so despite Tristan begging her not to, she headed towards the Health Center for her summons.

Nikka sat in the waiting room of the nurse's office. She looked up at the familiar anti-bullying poster on the wall and decided that she was getting to know the four walls of the waiting room a little too well. Nurse Lisa came out and called her in.

"Hello again," said Nurse Lisa cheerfully.

"Good afternoon," mumbled Nikka, less than cheerful. She followed the woman into the first office in the hallway and took her place on the bed.

"How's that fever doing? Did the medicine help?" enquired the ordinary woman as she took Nikka's blood pressure.

"I'm fine," said Nikka, more irritably then she had intended. This was the last place she wanted to be; she wanted to be with Tristan, trying to convince him to stay at Wildwood. In the corner of the room Nurse Lisa unpacked a small box of cylinders, then she attached a small cylinder to a needle and turned to face Nikka.

"We didn't get a chance to finish your vaccinations last time, there's only one left on the list," she explained pleasantly. Nurse Lisa bent towards Nikka's arm and Nikka instinctively recoiled from her. Every paranoia, every theory, and every bad thought she had ever had about Wildwood pumped back into her brain like raw adrenaline.

"No! I can't have a shot. I refuse," she said assertively. The nurse took a step back, surprised.

"Why not?" she asked softly. Nikka looked around the room in a panic, as if that would help her procure a valid excuse. Nurse Lisa smiled warmly, then she inched closer, as if she could physically close in on Nikka's doubts.

"Sweetheart, it's completely normal to have the jitters," she pacified.

"It's against my religion," Nikka sputtered back in a panic. She tried to keep her face straight and resolute. Nurse Lisa's eyes whizzed nervously from side to side, perplexed.

"What exactly is against your religion?" she asked patiently.

"Medical intervention," answered Nikka without skipping a beat. She was sure that she had read about a religion that didn't allow medical intervention, somewhere, at some point, now she just hoped nurse Lisa wouldn't have the sense to ask her exactly which religion she was referring to.

"But you've had shots done before," said the puzzled nurse.

"I'm recently converted," explained Nikka with great importance. Then she said very loudly, "I do not give you my permission to administer this shot into my body."

Nurse Lisa's resolve was starting to melt, and Nikka could see it. Her mousy eyes muddled over with perplexity. The shot just hung in her hand, her wrist limp, unsure of what came next. Nikka was certain she had hit the nail on the head - this was the perfect excuse, no one could challenge it. Nurse Lisa put the syringe back on the shelf.

"I'll be right back," she said amiably, before walking

out the door. Nikka waited a few minutes- a feeling of satisfaction and empowerment filled her like hot air. *No one can make me do something if I don't want to do it,* she appeased herself, and pushed away Tristan's words of warning. A few minutes later Nurse Smith walked through the door, and with it Nikka's resolve melted like ice cream on a hot pavement - her large frame alone instantly made the room feel small and suffocating.

"What seems to be the problem here?" she barked sternly. Nurse Smith casually picked up the syringe and leaned her hefty back against the counter.

"I told Nurse Lisa that medical intervention is against my religion," said Nikka calmly. She held her head up high and willed her body to fake the confidence that had evaporated when Mrs. Smith had entered the room. There was a moment of silence, and then Nurse Smith smiled.

"And what religion is that?" she countered, seeming entertained.

"I don't feel comfortable discussing it," said Nikka self-importantly. "I don't want to become a victim of discrimination," she added, knowing that political correctness would be a key weapon in her arsenal.

"I see what's going on here," cooed Nurse Smith as tenderly as she could manage. She walked up to Nikka and stroked the side of her shoulder. Nikka shuddered.

"You don't need to be scared," she added caringly.

"I'm not scared," started Nikka but before she could finish her sentence, and before she could truly grasp what was happening, Nurse Smith had plunged the syringe into her shoulder. She pushed the liquid through the skin, removed the syringe and discarded the cylinder in a perfect, robotic, flawless set of motions.

Nikka yelped and her other arm shot up to the tiny rupture in her shoulder. She gaped at Nurse Smith, rendered speechless by what had just transpired. Nikka caught her reflection in the metal cabinet door; she hated the expression that had formed on her face, a look of betrayal, of helplessness. Her eyes spread wide with shock and humiliation, like a dog that had just been kicked for no reason.

"I know a case of the jitters when I see one," said Nurse Smith. She took off her plastic gloves with an audible slap. "But it's a very important shot sweetie. Lisa will put a bandage on that for you," she added indifferently, and on cue Nurse Lisa entered the room. Nurse Smith smiled and walked out the door, leaving a still speechless Nikka behind.

Nikka was overcome with rage as she made her way to the cafeteria twenty minutes later. She held onto her bruised, bandaged arm and cursed vengefully under her breath. *She will pay*, Nikka thought. Nikka didn't know how Mrs. Smith would pay, but she promised herself that she would. Plots and schemes formed in her head, but she dismissed them because they were, for the most part, irrational and half-baked. Nikka kicked a trashcan in her way and sent the trash rolling halfway down the hill; for a split second she felt guilty for littering, then she thundered on. A few passing students stared at her, intrigued. Nikka felt like an animal, and she had been treated like one. *How dare she?* Nikka hissed, to no one in particular.

Nikka arrived at the cafeteria, red faced and fuming. The anger that coursed through her felt unfamiliar, she couldn't remember the last time she had been this angry, this violent and this defenseless at the same time. She threw herself into the chair facing Sums and Tristan so aggressively that the pair stopped eating and watched her.

"You look *very* angry," said Sums warily. "What happened to you?"

Nikka told them the entire story.

"I'm not surprised, Nik," said Tristan softly when she had finished. "Do you have any idea how many procedures they administered on me without my consent? I told you not to go," he said, seeming more concerned than accusatory. Nikka felt like her face was on fire.

"We need to go see the journalist," she said authoritatively. Nikka reached over and grabbed a piece of bread off of Sums' plate, and swallowed it without tasting or chewing it. The boys shot each other an uncertain look.

"We were just talking about that actually," admitted Sums.

"But we have no way of getting there," concluded Tristan.

"Well, I have a way," said Nikka heatedly through a mouth full of dry bread. Her eyes shot to the back of the cafeteria and then to Tristan.

"I have a way," she repeated, her eyes intently set on his. "But *you* are not going to like it."

×

Izaya leaned back against his shiny sports car. His hands were tucked into the pockets of his casual Saturday clothes: tight jeans, white t-shirt, and a jet-black blazer. He was wearing dark sunglasses, his black hair was disheveled and his white low-cut T-shirt revealed his pronounced collarbones. Nikka tried not to stare as she walked towards him. Tristan followed, unhappily flanking her side. When his eyes settled on Izaya, he instinctively tucked his own hands into his pockets and glowered. Just as Nikka had predicted, Tristan did not like the idea of spending a day with Izaya, but he nonetheless had accepted that it was their only choice. Izaya was the only Wildwood student any of them knew with a car.

Nikka had not told Izaya about Sums and Tristan coming along. Instead she had followed another of her mother's famous mottos - *do first, apologize later*. All she told Izaya was that she needed to visit the sick relative of a friend and, to his credit, he promptly agreed to drive her. Sums too seemed unhappy about the arrangement; he trailed behind Nikka, shuffling his feet uncomfortably and kicking up small clouds of dirt. As she made her way down the hill towards him, Nikka couldn't tell whether or not Izaya was upset too, there was a glimmer of a curiosity in his gaze and his eyes stayed intently focused on her; he didn't look in Tristan or Sums' direction at all.

"Hey," he greeted Nikka and nodded at Sums, when they had made their way to the bottom of the hill.

"Good morning," said Nikka cheerily.

Izaya opened the front passenger door for her and Nikka dutifully climbed in, but secretly wished she could have sat in the back to avoid being that close to him. Before getting into the driver's seat, Izaya cleared his throat and grunted in Tristan's direction in greeting. Tristan retorted in a similarly barbarian fashion before squeezing himself into the tiny back seat, which was already three quarters occupied by Sums.

"I like your car, very spacious," said Tristan sarcastically.

"I'm guessing you don't see many of these back in your Irish village," said Izaya coolly as he pulled away.

"On the contrary, they were voted the number one choice of car for Leprechauns in a mid-life crisis," said

Tristan spitefully. Nikka rolled her eyes.

"Do you always use humor to compensate for lack of class?" asked Izaya unemotionally.

"Ironic, a man with a red sports car accuses someone of compensating," Tristan muttered bitterly. A long and tense silence followed.

"Thank you for this," said Nikka once they had passed the threshold of Wildwood Academy. "I owe you one," she added casually, and she lightly patted Izaya's gear-changing hand in gratitude. From the backseat she heard Tristan give a discontented snort.

"I'll bear that in mind," said Izaya smugly. He threw a quick look in the rear view mirror to bask in Tristan's irritation.

Izaya drove fast, expertly shifting and swerving along the serpentine roads. The boys in the backseat kept quiet.

"How is that new upgrade working out for you?" asked Sums, twenty minutes into the journey, at a stoplight in a town eerily similar to Wildwood. Nikka realized that Sums was referring to Izaya's phone, the only thing, aside from *her*, that the two of them had in common.

"Good," said Izaya. The light changed and he pulled off. "I got a hacker in L.A. to rehash a few things. No one can track me now. Want to see?"

"Oh, yes please!" said Sums with the glee of a six-year-old boy discovering a slingshot for the first time.

Izaya continued to speed through the forest, swerving away from the cliff edges that appeared every now and then to dangerously frame the forested road. He reached over Nikka's legs and opened the glove compartment. He pulled out his phone and in the process grazed her exposed knee. Nikka modestly pulled down her skirt, coughed and pretended to be interested in the view whizzing by her window. Izaya threw the phone backwards to Sums. In her rearview mirror Nikka saw Tristan glare at Sums for his excessive show of excitement. *No one can trace me now,* Nikka replayed Izaya's peculiar words and made a mental note to ask Sums about what they meant later. Izaya caught her eye, and smiled at her, focusing his gaze on her for a second too long.

"Maybe try watching the road, *mate,*" Tristan grumbled nervously. Izaya ignored him yet again. Fifteen minutes later the GPS announced that they were nearing their final destination. Izaya pulled off the highway and followed a small road similar to the one that led to up to the Wildwood campus. At the end of the path was a gated building, with an intercom mounted by the entrance. Izaya pulled down his window and pressed the call button. Seconds later a voice answered.

"Hello?"

"We're visitors," said Izaya out of his window.

"Who are you here to visit?" asked the women's voice.

Izaya looked at Nikka expectantly. Unwillingly, Nikka leaned her body over him and spoke out the window.

"Jake Manning," she said to the loudspeaker, hoping that by some miracle Izaya didn't remember the journalist's name. As Nikka sat back in her seat she was met with a displeased look from Tristan, a worried look from Sums and a raised eyebrow from Izaya. The gate opened and Izaya drove through.

"*So*, you're here to see the journalist," said Izaya, seeming intrigued.

"I'm friends with Alex, and he asked me to check up on his uncle," Nikka lied.

The psychiatric institution was a large Spanish colonial building that could easily pass for a spa or a fancy wedding venue. The territory itself was littered with groomed lavender clusters and encircled by a high, intimidating fence. In front of the building was a gravel-covered roundabout, drenched in sunlight. Izaya parked his car in an adjacent lot, and the four of them disembarked and made their way up to the front door. An oval silver plaque on the building read *Welcome to Idlewell, An Institution for Mental Health and Improvement.* Nikka rang the buzzer by the front intercom without hesitation. Behind her, Izaya looked at the plaque and froze, the blood drained from his sharp face.

"Nikka," he said abruptly, his voice almost too low to hear. "*I think...* I think I will just wait for you guys outside, if that's okay with you," he said faintly. Nikka nodded.

"Of course, we won't be long," she promised.

Nikka was happy that Izaya didn't want to come inside; there would have been too much to explain, or too much to lie about. Izaya did not look well as he made his way towards a shaded area across the lot. Nikka decided that she would find out why the place had shaken Izaya up when she had the chance. Tristan chuckled as he watched him go.

"What do you think *that* was about?" asked Sums. He looked back at the sign, then towards Izaya, who was lighting a cigarette under a willow tree.

"He got spooked," said Tristan with great satisfaction. Nikka glowered at him reproachfully, as if to say, *this isn't the place or the time to beat your chest.*

The door buzzed and the three of them entered. Beyond the entrance was a lobby with wooden floors, a large opulent aquarium and suede waiting couches. Nikka made her way over to the concierge's desk, where an older woman in scrubs sat, busily typing away on a desktop computer. The woman looked up and smiled.

"Welcome to Idlewell, can I have your names, please?" she said, her voice Zen, as if she were welcoming them into a Buddhist temple. Nikka found her tone and the rest of the pleasant décor in the place irritating; it seemed like a façade, meant to deceive visitors into thinking they were in a happy place. It reminded her of the candy house from *Hansel and Gretel*.

"Nikka, Simon and Tristan," Nikka listed. "Here to visit Jake Manning. We're *family,*" she lied.

Nikka kept her tone even and cold, not leaving any room for the woman to question her. The woman eyed her and the boys carefully, and typed something into her computer.

"Oh dear, I'm afraid you're not on the approved guests list," said the woman, her voice now full of professional regret. Nikka dawdled for a moment before she felt Tristan place his hands on her hips and move her aside gently.

"Could you check again, *luv'*," he asked sweetly, once he was facing the woman. "We are somewhat distant relatives, but I don't think good old Jake would forget to put us on the list."

He rested his elbows on the counter and leaned in towards the woman, as if the two of them were having a private conversation. The elderly concierge smiled up nervously and righted her scrubs. Tristan's accent had that effect on people; Nikka had seen it put to use on more than one occasion. Obligingly, the woman typed a few more things into her computer.

"I've been to Dublin," she said to Tristan in a shy, matter-of-fact way.

"Dublin is a marvelous city!" he exclaimed.

The woman seemed to forget about her computer for

a moment.

"Yes, I absolutely loved it," she said dreamily.

"My favorite thing in Dublin is the beer of course," said Tristan.

"Oh, don't remind me," quipped the woman. "I gained 10 pounds from all the ales I drank that week!" Tristan took a step back, as if he were surveying the woman's figure.

"Well, it seems those were 10 pounds that needed gaining," he said jovially and the pair of them laughed.

"Pity about the list," said Tristan when they had both stopped laughing. "We drove four hours just to get here. *Uncle Jake* will be so upset when he finds out." Tristan put a hand on his forehead as if in exasperation. The nurse looked around to see if there was anyone watching them. She pressed a little buzzer on the side of her desk and a glass door to their left opened.

"Oh, just this once," she whispered cheekily. "It's room 32, straight through the hall on your left. Here are your visitors' badges," she said quietly and winked at Tristan. "For a fellow Dubliner at heart," she added in a tone, which, if it weren't for her age, Nikka would have assumed was meant to be flirtatious. The woman handed them three badges, and Tristan clasped her hand in between his.

"Thank you, Linda, thank you," he cooed, reading the name off her nametag.

Nikka and Sums mumbled their *thank yous* quietly; afraid to break the spell Tristan had cast on the poor woman. Then they walked through the door that led to the rest of the institution.

"And that's why it pays to be Irish," said Tristan cockily.

"Or to be a good liar," said Sums. Tristan thought about it for a moment- "Yeah, that too," he agreed, and smiled at Nikka. Nikka thought back to the girlfriend he supposedly didn't have, and the explanation he still owed her, and didn't smile back. A hallway led from the lobby through to the rest of the building, with a sliding glass window embedded in the wall. The window opened onto another office, and sitting behind the glass was a dainty man reading a tabloid magazine. The man looked up and slid the small window open.

"Welcome to Idlewell," he said cheerily. "Please deposit any scarves, long jewelry, shoelaces and belts in here," he said, and handed them a plastic box. The trio paused for a moment, taken aback by the man's request. Then slowly, like shifting gears, the dark meaning behind the man's cheery words clicked into place. Obligingly, they undid their belts and shoelaces and put everything in the little tray the man provided.

"Thank you," said the man. Wordlessly Nikka and the boys turned towards the other door.

"Just a moment," he called. The man pointed at

Nikka's neck. "Leave the chain please." Nikka's hand flew up to her dog tags.

"I don't really part with them, *ever*," she pleaded childishly.

"Rules are rules," said the man and he tapped the plastic tray. Reluctantly Nikka pulled off her tags and gently put them in the tray. Then she walked towards the other door and waited for the man to buzz her in. Nikka ignored Sums and Tristan's curious glances.

The three of them walked through the doors and made their way down a hallway past a foyer, a games room, and a small library. As they followed the signs that led towards the patient rooms, Nikka looked around and noticed a few peculiar things. Firstly, the clinic seemed expensive - *too expensive.* From the perfectly manicured front lawn to the marble flooring. Idlewell dripped with money, and judging by the sad basement where the journalist had spent most of his time, money wasn't something that Jake Manning had a lot of. As she took it all in, Nikka had a creepy hunch as to who was footing the bill for the journalist's gilded cage.

Secondly, Nikka found that the institution had a lot in common with a senior home. She had only been to one, and she was little then, but she could still remember bits and pieces from visiting her grandma all those years ago. As she walked through the fancy sterile halls, the institution gave her flashbacks to that day. She remembered that the senior home was mostly silent except for sudden, sporadic bursts of sound that didn't belong- a scream, shattered glass, a walker smacking against the linoleum floor. Idlewell was quiet too. A few patients passed by Nikka and she realized that just like at the senior home, the people here had no light in their eyes- the lights and sounds of everyday life seemed to be eclipsed, blanketed by an eerie silence.

Nikka passed another luxurious foyer; the people in it were playing a tepid game of bingo. *Bingo,* another common feature. There was a faint, bland smell of cooked food permeating in the air and a few half -asleep patients in wheelchairs, none of whom seemed old or sick enough to need a wheelchair. Sums kept close to Nikka whilst Tristan tried his best to look brave as he led the way forward.

"Here it is," he said, stopping at door 32. Nikka knocked, and the three of them stepped back in anticipation. A moment later, a middle-aged nurse in turquoise scrubs opened the door. She had a half-folded towel in her hand.

"Hello, we are here to see Jake," said Nikka timidly. She attempted her most innocent smile.

"Well, hello there," replied the woman.

She looked uncertain, but quickly moved out of their way and allowed the three of them to pile into the room. The room was pristine and spacious. The journalist lay in a large queen bed with a blanket neatly drawn and folded halfway up his body, as if someone had made the bed with him still in it. As she took in the sight of the man lying there, Nikka suddenly realized the weight of what they were doing- what if Manning cried out that he didn't know them? Of all the things she had done in previous weeks, trespassing at a mental institution under false pretenses seemed like the most dubious. Nikka felt guilt and heaviness weigh down on her.

"You won't get much socializing out of him," said the nurse half-heartedly.

"Could we have some privacy, please?" Tristan asked sweetly. Sums had instinctively backed up against a nearby wall like cornered prey. The nurse nodded and happily left them. Sums, Tristan and Nikka looked at the man on the bed, then at each other. The man seemed to be asleep; a little bit of drool escaped the left side of his chapped mouth, dampening the high tower of pillows that was propping him up. Nikka approached slowly and looked him over. She felt a sting in her heart for Alex, for Alexis, and for the entire Manning family. She reached out, squeezed his arm lightly and the man opened his eyes. The journalist looked so much older, so much more tired, than he had that day back at Wildwood.

"Hello Sir," said Nikka steadily. "I'm really sorry to disturb you, my name is Nikka. I came to ask you a couple of questions about... *your work*, would that be alright?"

Nikka stuttered; her resolve had dissipated as she looked down at his vacant gaze, void of any reaction. Tristan hovered over the man, studying him.

"We wanted to know if you could maybe tell us more about Wildwood Academy, and about your research? About what they might be up to," said Tristan cutting straight to the point. The man's eyes narrowed, but quickly lost their focus again, as if he were coming to, and then fading out again in bursts.

"They are drugging him," said Tristan. "There is no point."

Sums looked petrified and he shrunk further to the wall. "Maybe we should just leave," he implored. "This feels wrong."

"Let's try some pictures first," said Nikka. She held her hand out to Sums for his phone. They had agreed on this beforehand; if the journalist wasn't in a fit state to answer questions, they would try to jog his memory with a few visual cues. Nikka didn't want to bother the man any further, but she tried to push her compassion aside in order to get what they had come for. She pulled up a picture of the Wildwood campus first and held it in front of the man's face.

"What can you tell me about this place?" she asked softly.

The journalist muttered something unintelligible and turned away from her.

"Let's go," whispered Sums, his eyes darted to the door every few seconds.

"Just a few more minutes," said Nikka. The journalist drooled a little again and then he pointed at the window. Unrelenting, Nikka walked over to the other side of the bed so that she could face him, and then showed him a picture of Mrs. Smith. The man's eyes narrowed and for a moment he was still. Then he looked at the window again and pointed at it idly. The man's movements were slow, foggy, and sickly. Nikka felt angry that a place that was meant to heal had instead debilitated the passionate, loud man she had seen on campus.

"CH4563," said the man sleepily. Nikka looked at Tristan and Sums. They both shrugged their shoulders.

"CH4563," repeated the journalist, this time more persistent. A man pushed the door open and walked in with a tray.

"Sorry to disturb," said the male nurse jovially. "It's time for his meds."

The man smiled and Nikka had a sudden urge to slap the smile right off his face, and the tray out of his hand. *This medicine is clearly not helping him*! She felt like screaming. The journalist swallowed each pill dryly, in a practiced motion. *How many times a day does he have to do that?* Nikka wondered bitterly, and how much convincing had it taken until swallowing those pills had become second nature? She could see by their expressions that Tristan and Sums were disgusted too.

"CH4563," said the journalist after he had swallowed the last pill. "CH4563, CH4563,"

"CH4563," he voice grew louder and louder each time.

"Yes, we know, CH4563," repeated the nurse condescendingly, and patted Jake dismissively on the shoulder, the same way you would a child throwing a fit.

"He says that all the time," explained the nurse cheerfully as he turned towards Nikka, Sums and Tristan, as if Jake were a senile old man saying funny things, not a middle-aged man losing his mind. The nurse took his tray and left.

"CH4563," repeated the journalist once the nurse was gone and the door was closed. He sat up and let his feet dangle from the bed. He looked down at the floor speculatively, then at the door, then back again, as if in his half-dazed state he were weighing up whether or not he could physically traverse the space before him. Nikka pulled up another photo on the phone and showed it to him.

"Can you tell us anything about this man?" she asked.

Jake looked at the photo and screamed.

The screams ripped through the stale air, as if the windows had been broken and at that moment air rushed in, panic rushed in, and all the things the place seemed so intent on keeping out, rushed in like a flood wave.

Nurses appeared as if out of thin air, rushing into the room like a raid party. They grabbed hold of different parts of the journalist's body and pushed him onto the bed. The man screamed, grunted and thrashed, taken over by his invisible demons, just as he had been that day on the school grounds. One of the nurses injected him with something as they pushed him back onto the bed. Nikka launched towards her instinctively, just as she had done at the Academy, but a strong nurse held her back. She felt a pain in her arm as the man dragged her backwards.

"Don't touch her!" growled Tristan, and pulled the nurse off of her.

It was a moment of pure chaos, of painful commotion, and as quickly as it had come, it dissipated. In a fog, Nikka felt herself being ushered out of the room; the door closed behind her, the screams stopped and a crisp clean nurse came and told them delicately that it was time for them to leave. A moment later, they were being led through the hallway, out the lobby and suddenly, they were again standing on the lovely sun-drenched roundabout outside.

A minute later, a nurse came and brought out the plastic tray with their belongings. Silently, Sums and Tristan put their belts back on and Nikka slipped her dog tags back over her head, holding onto them as if at that moment they were the only thing grounding her to the earth. She felt shaken up, afraid and guilty, like she had hurt Jake, like she had brought back ugly memories into his world, and in doing so had taken away the sliver of peace he may have found. Although Nikka suspected that the man had not found any peace at Idlewell.

The trio gravitated silently towards where Izaya was sitting by the willow tree. Nikka sat down next to him on a bench and pulled her knees up to her chest. Sums sat down on the ground and planted his head in his hands.

"What happened?" asked Izaya as he looked at his three troubled peers.

"He was... in a very bad state," said Nikka for lack of better words. Her voice came out tired and drained. Izaya didn't say anything. He reached over to the side of the bench and pulled up a small bunch of peonies, which he must have gathered somewhere from the grounds while they were inside. Gently, he placed them in Nikka's hand. Nikka smiled at him weakly. *Never thine,* the words echoed in her head.

Izaya was calling her mind away from what was happening and giving her something else to cling to. He was also confirming what she already knew, that the note and the flowers had been from him. Nikka couldn't bring herself to look into his green eyes, full of secrets, apathy and somehow tenderness at the same time. And she couldn't look at him because she felt like that would be the last straw, and she would cry, over Jake Manning, and over what was happening in the building behind her. She closed her hand around the peonies.

"What are you two smiling about?" demanded Tristan sounding appalled. Izaya smirked at him, relishing the fact that he and Nikka shared secrets that Tristan wasn't privy to. *How many other people share secrets with him?* Nikka wondered jealously.

"I'm glad you can still smile after that horrible experience," Tristan hissed accusingly, before stalking off towards the car. The small smile that had formed on Nikka's lips melted away, and she felt guilt and sadness creep back in its place. *Tristan was right.*

"Can we please leave now," whined Sums, seeming depleted.

Nikka looked back at the institution. As she thought of the broken and undone man behind those walls, she could understand why Alex wanted to leave. Most of all, she could understand why he hated Wildwood. Sums walked off to the car. Izaya and Nikka followed.

"It was horrible in there," Nikka whispered as they walked.

"It's over now," said Izaya and he brushed his hand along her shoulder blade.

"Earlier," said Nikka, "what was it that scared you so much about this place?"

Izaya hesitated.

"Maybe someday I will tell you," said Izaya dryly. "But not today."

"You never tell me anything," complained Nikka. It was partially a complaint, and partially a desire to know more about him.

"It's an old habit," admitted Izaya, "I let other people fill the silence," he said. "Then they hear what they want to hear, see who they want to see." They were almost by the car now. Nikka stopped and faced him.

"For what it's worth, I already see what I want to see," she said, tenderly. Nikka was taken aback by her own boldness. This was hardly the place or the time, but she felt the overwhelming need to say it.

"That means more than you can know," said Izaya softly. "Now let's get out of here."

Nikka was relieved to see the asylum shrinking in her rearview mirror. She hated that place; so peaceful on the outside, so wrought with unhappiness on the inside, like a colorful birthday cake rotting from the inside out, its decay hidden by layers of sweet frosting.

×

Nikka took a large, eager bite of her burger. Recent events had lessened her love for the Academy, but they hadn't, by any means, lessened her love for its food. The same was obviously true for Tristan, despite believing that the Academy had poisoned him and made him sick, he sat across from Nikka and dug into his lasagna feverishly.

Nikka smiled at him.

Nikka was halfway through her sweet potato fries when she spotted Sums walk into the cafeteria, sweaty and out of breath. Nikka happily waved him over and Sums sat down with her and Tristan without bothering to load up his tray first. Nikka surveyed her friend with concern. Sums had dark circles under his eyes, his lips were dry and chapped, his curly hair was oily, and he looked distressed.

"Have you been researching again?" she asked reproachfully.

Tristan turned his attention from his lasagna to Sums and his eyes widened.

"You look like you haven't slept in days," exclaimed Tristan. "Or eaten," he added trying to hide his surprise at the latter statement.

Sums smiled weakly. He pulled out a folder, and after a quick look around, placed it on the table between them.

"I have what some people might call an obsessive personality," he said sheepishly. "Once I started to pull at the threads, the whole sweater started to unravel," he added mysteriously.

"Can we do without the riddles? I'm too tired for riddles," complained Tristan, grumpily returning his attention to his lasagna. Nikka pushed her fries towards Sums and he gobbled a few of them up.

"Sums, this is not healthy, what you're doing," she

said softly.

"That thing the journalist kept saying, *CH4563...*" said Sums in between mouthfuls.

"Was a load of drug-induced gibberish?" Tristan interrupted him, crabbily.

"At first, yes, but then I dug a little deeper. There was an experiment in the '70s, it was named after its creator," said Sums.

"A scientist named *Carole Hem*, she died a few years ago. It was filed as 4-5-6-3 in the system." Tristan had stopped chewing; both he and Nikka hung onto Sums' every word.

"Basically, it was shut down. All the information regarding the experiment is classified because the government funded it. I couldn't access any of it," admitted Sums.

"That just sounds like a coincidence," said Tristan. "For all we know the journalist was calling out the number of his car plates," he added sourly, but there was a glimmer in Sums' eye, a surge of excitement or triumph-he knew something else, something he was keeping for last. For the second time, Nikka wondered if she had done the right thing in letting someone as brilliant, as fixated as Sums, participate in this wild goose chase, but she reminded herself that it was Tristan who had dragged Sums into this in the first place. Sums pulled out a piece of paper from his pocket and placed it in the center of the table. It was a newspaper clipping, a grainy photograph of a group of people standing in a lab.

"I couldn't find any information on the experiment, except *this*, a photograph of the team of scientists who worked on it, taken by a small local newspaper. I guess they forgot to remove this one," he added cryptically. "Anyone look familiar?"

Nikka scanned the photo. Tristan craned his neck around to look at it upright. She studied each face, one by one, distorted and pixilated in the poor quality print. Her eyes scanned the rows twice until one face in the back looked slightly familiar. He was younger in the photo, but his features were the same- a full head of '70s hair masked a face that she otherwise knew very well.

"*The Dean*," whispered Nikka horrified.

"Okay, so not a coincidence," said Tristan sounding half-sarcastic, half-frightened. There was a quiet pause, and once the information had sunk in Sums continued.

"We now know the Dean worked on this experiment. We know that experiment was funded by the government and later classified. We know the Dean founded the Academy in the '80s. An academy that may or may not be making some of their students *sick*," Sums summarized, as if providing Nikka and Tristan with the Cliff Notes version of their discoveries. Nikka's heart sank a little as she stared at the photo, irrevocable proof that the Academy was not a questionable place.

"So what now?" she asked unwillingly. Nikka swallowed back the sour taste that had materialized in her mouth.

"Nothing," said Sums looking exasperated. "It's a hacker's dead end." He leaned in towards her and lowered his voice a few octaves.

"I've been trying to get into the Dean's computer, but it's just impossible. His security is so heavy you would have to break into the actual computer," he explained. Nikka pushed away her plate in irritation.

"I think it's pretty obvious what we need to do," said Tristan, tapping his fingers on the grey folder. Sums and Nikka looked at him, dumbstruck. Tristan smiled his signature, mad, mischievous smile.

"We have to break into the Dean's office."

×

The Dean's office building looked just as striking and grand as it had the last two times Nikka had been summoned there; the only difference this time was that Nikka was there and the Dean wasn't, or so she hoped. At that late hour, the grounds were dark, but the inside of the Dean's office was illuminated by moonlight; it pierced through and reflected off the many windows and glass walls of the two cube-like buildings. The three of them scaled the white boundary wall and tiptoed to the back of the building.

"Are you sure?" Tristan asked severely as they

approached the back of the office building. Nikka could only see half of Tristan's face, the other half was in the shadows.

"I'm sure," came Sums' shaky voice from behind them. "I can get us a thirty-minute window from the internal security system."

"And the guards?" whispered Tristan.

"Let's just say I've created a diversion," said Sums enigmatically.

"Over here," called Nikka. Through a window, she had spotted the kitchen, which she assumed was where Emily had disappeared to when she went to fetch elderflower lemonade at Stamos' request. There was a service door, Nikka pointed.

"That's the kitchen," said Tristan.

"It leads right into the waiting room," whispered Nikka.

"That's way better than going through the front entrance," Tristan seconded and he grinned at her.

"Here goes," he said. Tristan pulled out a few lock picks from his pocket, and inserted them. After a little shimmying, the lock gave. Tristan covered his hand with the sleeve of his sweater and turned the knob.

"Don't leave finger prints on anything," he warned as the pair stared at him. The door swung inwards. The trio didn't move; they stood on the threshold as still as they could and waited for the aftermath of their break-in, but nothing happened - no alarm, no guards. Tristan turned to Sums and stared at him in awe.

"He's one of a kind," said Nikka nodding in Sums' direction.

"He really is," Tristan agreed, mouth ajar. "So what kind of distraction did you create for the guards?" he whispered eagerly as the three of them made their way through the dark and spacious kitchen.

"There was a prank two years ago where the seniors tried to set the yellow fabric at The Valley on fire. I put that footage on the current feed. The guards will have called for back up, which would lead the night guards away from here. They will search around The Valley and then The Point...we have at least 30 minutes till they realize nothing happened. "

"Blimey, mate," said Tristan admiringly. "Now *that* is talent!"

The three of them exited the kitchen slowly and cautiously, as if they were walking on thin ice. Nikka pushed the exit door and the three of them walked into the Dean's waiting room. Nikka looked around at the familiar setting; the cubist painting behind the secretary's desk; the bonsai trees that lined the window; and the octopus-like chairs. The frame and TV that normally projected images of Wildwood were turned off. It felt eerie looking at a bunch of blank frames.

"What about the cameras?" Nikka whispered,

noticing a black orb on the ceiling.

"I programmed them to play footage from two hours ago, when no one was here," explained Sums. Nikka was impressed; even though she knew Sums was brilliant, in these moments the word *genius* came to mind. Without him they wouldn't have even made it over the boundary wall before being caught. Tristan threw his arm around Sums' shoulder.

"You know what, you and I, we could really do business together once we leave Wildwood. I mean, I can use a hairpin on most old locks, but disabling complex security systems like that? And wiping camera footage? That's talent!" Tristan whispered excitedly. "You should come to Dublin with me, we could have some fun."

The moonlight hit Sums' face and Nikka could see that it was scarlet, both from the compliments and from fear that Tristan was serious- breaking into the Dean's office was one thing, using his talents to rig casino footage, which is probably how Sums imagined Tristan's life, was quite another.

"It's all about cyber security nowadays," was all Sums said in justification of his impressive talents. He shrugged his shoulders and sloppily pushed his glasses up the bridge of his nose. Tristan ran his finger over the gold frames on the wall.

"I'm glad the pictures are off, it would make me throw up seeing that man next to the Dalai Lama again," he scoffed. Sums and Tristan started to walk up the spiral staircase that led to the Dean's office. Nikka whistled and pointed at the door next to the staircase, the one that simply read *Files.*

"That room is a better bet," she said.

Sums and Tristan walked up to it and Sums examined the doorknob.

"There's a code- I can't unlock it," he said resentfully.

"Me neither," said Tristan.

"I remember the combination," said Nikka timidly. The pair stared at her in surprise.

Nikka pulled her sleeve over her index finger and punched in the same access code she had seen Stamos use on her very first day at the Academy, 624376. The door clicked and gave way.

"You remember it from when exactly?" asked Sums incredulously as he followed Nikka through the door.

"My first day at the Academy," she admitted.

Tristan looked at her then at Sums.

"Wow, when they say 'Academy for Talented Youth,' they're not kidding," he joked. Nikka blushed.

Behind the door there was a small staircase. Cautiously, the three of them wandered up it, and walked through another door. They ended up in a room that was so plain it didn't look like it belonged. Just a room, wallpapered in pictures of the redwood forest, and lined with high-end filing cabinets. There was also a desk with a computer, and on the furthest wall hung a large oil portrait of the Dean.

"Okay, you guys, search the filing cabinets. I mean, storing valuable information on paper is totally medieval, but you never know. Meanwhile, I'll tackle this beauty," Sums said, and took a deep breath as he approached the massive desktop computer. Nikka stifled a chuckle as she watched him survey the dormant machine with a mixture of awe and fear, the same possessed look he got when he was doing his math homework or tackling his latest cyber challenge.

Tristan used his little tools to open a set of filing cabinets for her. Nikka began to leaf through the names.

"I found my file!" said Tristan a few minutes later. Careful to not touch it with his actual fingers he leafed through it hungrily, using his sleeve as a protective barrier between the paper and his skin.

"There's nothing in it," he said, sounding disappointed.

"We don't have much time. Read as much as you can," urged Sums as he continued to type on the computer.

"So, what exactly are we looking for here?" asked Nikka as she opened the second set of cabinets and began leafing through the files of students whose names began with 'F.'

"Anything that is abnormal, or objects clearly related to evil conspiracies," joked Sums.

"How's about a self portrait?" whispered Tristan, "only the evilest of people commission self portraits to hang in their office, if you ask me." He pointed at the large oil painting hung above the cabinet, in which the Dean was posed aristocratically with an American flag behind him. His head was titled upwards, his little eyes glowing with self-importance. Nikka put a hand on her mouth to stifle a laugh.

"I bet there's a safe behind it too," she chimed in lightheartedly. There was a sudden silence. Her eyes met Tristan's. A moment later Tristan was removing the painting from the wall, which revealed, just as Nikka had jokingly predicted, an embedded safe.

"Huh," shrugged Sums, "Now *that,* I did not expect, safes are even more archaic than filing cabinets. If it were me I would store everything on secure servers."

Tristan stared at the safe, wondering whether or not he had the capacity to open it. Sums too was sizing it up, while Nikka leaned back against the wall, feeling useless.

"Maybe I can unlock it," declared Sums, after some deliberation. He pulled out a cellphone and shone a light on the lock, which revealed grease prints on the numbers.

"We don't have time to try a gazillion combinations," hissed Tristan.

"Obviously not..." said Sums and he rolled his eyes. "This kind of lock will shut down after three wrong tries," said Tristan impatiently.

Sums frowned, consumed in thought. Then he put his finger behind the bottom of his T-shirt and started to press a combination, speaking as he did so.

"24-45-63," he said. The safe clicked and opened.

"CH-45-63," repeated Nikka in understanding. Tristan looked at them both with confusion. "When you dial 24, that's CH," Nikka clarified. Tristan grinned in return.

"Brilliant!" he yelped triumphantly as he pulled the door open.

Inside the safe were a few black leather boxes and a stack of eggshell-colored folders. Nikka and Tristan began looking through the boxes carefully. The largest contained bonds, credit cards, multiple passports, and an excessive amount of travel checks and cash.

"That's a get-away box," Tristan declared.

"A what?" asked Nikka. Her eyes locked on Tristan's and she asked herself the question she had been pushing to the corner of her mind for months. How did Tristan, a trust-fund baby from Massachusetts, know so much about breaking and entering? Tristan looked down, and away from her.

"A get away box, for when you need to be ready to leave the country at the drop of a hat. I saw it in a movie once," he whispered unconvincingly.

Nikka turned her attention to another box, which contained a red address book filled with sequences of numbers. Nikka flicked through it with interest. The sequence of numbers did not make any sense to her; she threw the item on the desk.

Tristan avidly dug through what Nikka presumed were expensive collectibles: coins, a few medals, jewels and an array of boxed watches; white gold, yellow gold, diamond studded. Meanwhile Sums was leafing through one of the folders from the safe, nodding to himself. He closed one folder, reached for another, and suddenly he muttered a quiet and nervous “uh-oh.”

“What’s wrong?” asked Nikka and Tristan in unison.

Sums looked up at them with a mixture of panic and disbelief. He stared hard past them towards the door, thoughts visibly racing through his mind at a mile a second. He stared back at the safe. His baby blue eyes burned with silent panic.

“Uh-oh!” he repeated this time more urgently.

“What, mate! The suspense is killing me!” whined Tristan, nudging Sums hard in the side to bring him out of his stupor. Sums pointed silently into the empty space in the safe where the file had just lain, and where lay what even Nikka knew to be a motion sensor connected to an alarm. Just then, they heard voices coming from outside.

17

Departure

"Sir, I assure you this is just a false alarm. We have very competent security procedures in place, and there is no reason for you to personally get out of bed at this hour," Stamos was assuring someone loudly from somewhere outside.

The icy voice that answered kept Nikka, Tristan, and Sums rooted to the spot.

"I suggest you demonstrate your competency by figuring out where the night guard is, Mister Lederman," said the Dean, with slow and menacing articulation. A moment later, Nikka heard a distant pair of doors open.

In mere seconds, Tristan closed the file cabinets, wiped down the computer keys, and shut the safe. Gently, he opened the furthest window in the room and without a sound, he beckoned Nikka and Sums towards it. Sums tiptoed after Nikka, an expression of terror contorting his plump face. As gently as he could muster, Tristan swung his blazer over the edge of the window and climbed over it, careful to not leave any prints on the glass. Then he dangled down from the ledge and let go. He landed swiftly on both feet. In turn, Sums stumbled awkwardly out of the window, hung off the ledge with great effort, then finally let himself go. He landed on his feet hard, instantly lost his balance, and toppled to his knees. Nikka heard him stifle a cry. After a moment, both boys turned around and reached their arms out, urging her to jump. Just then something red in the corner of the room caught Nikka's eye. Without a moment's hesitation, she discreetly pocketed the small red leather notebook from the desk, *the Dean's address book,* and made her way back towards the window. She knew she shouldn't take it and leave behind another trace of their break-in, *but it was already locked out of the safe! And she wanted more information...needed more.* The fact that it was clearly written in code told her that something very important was hiding in between the lines.

She heard the first door in the small hallway open, followed by approaching voices and the panicked whispers of the boys outside. Quickly, Nikka climbed over the window, balanced on the ledge, and gently pulled the window shut from the outside. She threw the blazer on the ground and jumped. Tristan caught her firmly, placed her on the ground and grabbed hold of her hand. The light above them went on in the files room and Nikka pressed herself tightly against the wall of the building to remain unseen. Tristan looked around, and signaled for them to follow him. Carefully, the three of them crept along the wall and around the bend of the building; they kept at it until they could no longer be seen from the filing room window. Tristan was still holding Nikka's hand as he leapt away from the building and sprinted towards the boundary wall. Nikka cranked her head to make sure Sums was still in tow. The three of them climbed the wall and, on hands and knees, crawled through the surrounding hedges.

Tristan checked to make sure the coast was clear. On his signal, the trio emerged from the bushes and ran as fast as they could in the direction of the main campus. Nikka snagged and dirtied her uniform as she collided against the branches and thorny bushes in her path, but she wouldn't allow herself to slow down. The adrenaline pumped through her, pushing her body forward, her legs aching in response. Finally, they hit a wide clearing and stopped to catch their breath. Tristan, looking frazzled and sweaty, sat down on a nearby boulder and buried his head in his hands.

"This is so messed up," he said anxiously, his voice muted by the flesh of his palms.

"Don't...worry," Sums managed in between greedy

breaths. The heavy boy clutched his aching sides and squinted up into the moonlight. "*I told you*, there won't be any security footage. They might not be able to pinpoint where exactly the alarm was triggered and we didn't take anything." Tristan didn't look up or respond.

"Sums, did *you* find anything useful?" inquired Nikka in between her own pants. She threw a concerned look in Tristan's direction, who now had his head buried in his knees and was rocking himself back and forth on the boulder, muttering some form of mantra under his breath.

"Well, yes," Sums hesitated, pausing to choose the right words for what he wanted to say. He tried and failed to catch his breath a few more times.

"Inside the safe there were these medical records. There was one with Tristan's name on it, and it said he was scheduled for something two weeks ago," Sums continued.

"Scheduled for what?" asked Nikka.

"A procedure of sorts," he elaborated. "I recognized some of the terms from when I studied genetics but that's it; it's very advanced stuff. I couldn't decipher it. I didn't get a chance to access the other materials on the computer," he said weakly. Sums seemed to struggle with admitting that something was beyond his understanding. Nikka looked at him, and then nudged her head in the direction of Tristan. She widened her eyes at Sums, as if to ask, *what does this all mean for him?*

"All I can say for certain," said Sums quietly, "is that they carried out some kind of genetic procedure on Tristan, and that in their opinion it was a success. That's all I got out of it," he added, sounding guilty. They heard a muffled, desolate moan come from the boulder behind them. Nikka walked up to Tristan and put her hand on his shoulder.

"Tristan..." she cooed, soothingly, but there were no words for what he was going through.

"My name is not Tristan," he hissed, and pushed her hand away abruptly. Tristan rose and walked to the edge of the clearing. He began to pace back and forth, cursing as he did so.

"Tristan, what the hell has gotten into you?" demanded Sums. There was a long, pregnant silence.

"I'm not Tristan," he barked suddenly. Then he looked at Nikka, his blue eyes blurry with regret, and bolted back into the woods.

×

Nikka woke up the next morning feeling heavy, as if her neck couldn't quite support the weight of her head. All night she had dreamt about the Dean's office, about his voice, about what would have happened had they been caught. It was not just the possible repercussions of their break-in that weighed on her mind that morning, it was the meaning of what they had found: a safe full of passports, riddled folders, and a little red notebook filled with code, a notebook that, at that very moment, was stashed under her mattress. And then there was Tristan's inexplicable breakdown.

A knock on the door of her bedroom made her jump. Nikka jolted upwards and looked over to the other side of the room, where Stella was still fast asleep. The door opened and Magda came in, causing Nikka to sigh in relief.

"Expecting someone else?" said Magda teasingly, registering the relief on Nikka's face. Magda smiled warmly, her wrinkled face radiated kindness as always.

"No, I'm just jittery," admitted Nikka. She got out of bed. Magda carried in a tray loaded with a kettle and an assortment of tea and set it on her nightstand.

"Then you should have herbal tea, chamomile calms the nerves," said Magda wisely. Magda rolled her 'Rs' as she always did, and Nikka found herself thinking that she would miss it when she left Wildwood, whenever that day would be. That thought opened the door to a whole slew of other questions that Nikka didn't want to think about. She blinked the thoughts away and instead pulled a yellow sachet out of the tea selection, set it inside the mug, and tried to put her mind to rest. Nikka smiled at Magda gratefully as she sipped on the steaming cup. For a moment Magda watched her, the way a grandmother adoringly watches her grandkids do something mundane, then she got back to work. She opened Nikka's wardrobe, pulled her uniform out, and tucked it into a dry cleaning bag. Nikka didn't mind the slight invasion of privacy that came hand in hand with having a House Matron; Magda had been so mothering and so comforting to her that, despite the archaic nature of her position, Nikka wouldn't have traded her for anything. However, when she saw Magda pull out her second uniform and pack it into a plastic bag with the other one, she protested.

"That was dry cleaned last week. What will I wear if you take both?"

"Because of recent quarantine, school wants to re-wash all uniforms," explained Magda, sounding tired. "Today and tomorrow will be social dress code," she elaborated. Nikka thought it odd that the school would choose to re-wash all of the uniforms just because one student had fallen ill. *And it wasn't even a real sickness,* she lamented silently. Her face turned sour at the prospect of two days of social dress.

"Don't be so sad. The sun is shining, it is a chance for you to wear some color for once!" said Magda joyfully. Nikka smiled back at her and looked out the window. It was true, there were rays of spring sunshine spilling in through the window, and maybe it *was* time to focus on the bright side - if Nikka could find one.

×

Nikka waited outside her *Bataillisme* class and listened to Madame Grenoble close down the room. She heard her draw back the curtains, pull up the projectors and finally switch the light off. Grenoble reemerged looking happy, or as happy as her botoxed face would allow. She was dressed in another fancy navy pantsuit and wearing large diamond earrings - a strange touch of cosmopolitan luxury against the backdrop of the wild woods. Nikka was wearing a pale pink dress with blue shoes and a light floral jacket; she had taken Magda's advice and worn her most colorful ensemble.

"That was a great last class," said Madame Grenoble in her thick French accent. "I am very impressed with your progress."

"Thank you," said Nikka. A sense of pride filled her from within, warm and gooey like hot chocolate. "Do you have any idea which studio class will be replacing this one?" she asked. There was a loaded pause. Grenoble examined one of her rings against the light.

"No, I don't, not yet," said Grenoble. There was something odd about her overly cheery tone, like when someone uses floral perfume to cover up the smell of sweat. This was Nikka's last *Bataillisme* class and Nikka was sad to see it end. Even though the class had disturbed her at first, it had been one of the most intense learning experiences of her life.

"I'm sad for it to end," she admitted.

"Ooh *Cherie*, all things must come to an end. *C'est la vie,*" said Grenoble, her voice entirely lacking in either sympathy or commiseration.

"I will see you next week," she added and waved elegantly at Nikka as she strutted off. Nikka watched her professor leave before setting off on the path to her next class. She found Sums waiting for her when she got there. Her friend was sweating, despite the crisp spring air, and he looked nervous, even more anxious than usual.

"Can you skip your next class?" he urged quietly. Nikka looked over his shoulder at the building that contained her classroom.

"Yeah, but what for?"

"We need to talk, let's go to The Point. I've already told Tristan, he's waiting for us."

"What now?" Nikka moaned under her breath. Reluctantly, she followed Sums.

When Nikka and Sums arrived at The Point Tristan was sitting atop one of the boulders and sketching. Nikka stopped and watched him; his wide blue eyes were locked on the sketch pad, his hand moved quickly, and his messy russet hair fell around his face; he looked handsome and broken, if one could be both. He spotted them, and his eyes lingered on Nikka for a second too long. He gazed at her, looking sad and unsure.

"Pink really suits you," he said, referring to her dress; Nikka's cheeks turned a matching color. She smiled, and climbed up on the boulder to sit next to him. Tristan grinned at her and for a second she felt all the warmth she associated with Tristan flood back into his face. He ran his hand along the side of her arm; a greeting that was just a touch more intimate than an exchange between friends.

"We don't have time for flirting," Sums complained dryly, as he pulled himself up onto the boulder.

"Just tell us what you found," Tristan retorted irritably.

Nikka rolled her eyes at Sums. "He kept me in suspense the whole walk here. As if that was necessary," she said accusingly.

Sums sat down on the boulder facing them, his face grave. He twiddled his thumbs.

"Umm, so I did *something…*" he said, struggling to find the right words. His small blue eyes darted over the precipice of the boulder and he inched away from it, as if scared he might fall. "That I shouldn't have," he concluded.

Sums was sweating profusely now, his curls were wet and stuck to his hairline like tiny blond vines. Nikka and Tristan stared at him in anticipation. Sums tugged at the neck of his casual day T-shirt as if it were cutting off his circulation, and then opened his backpack and pulled out a familiar grey file. Tristan recognized the grey file and gasped.

"You took it?" hissed Tristan in disbelief. Nikka tried to feign shock too - she didn't want the boys suspecting that she had also taken a souvenir from the Dean's office.

In truth, she wasn't the least bit shocked; she was used to the extent of Sums' curiosity.

"It looked important!" justified Sums. "I couldn't figure out what it meant on the spot, and it's not like I had the time to photograph each page!" he added defensively. The wind blew and Nikka's hair flipped around her like golden whips. She knew what *this* was about; Sums simply couldn't back away from an intellectual challenge.

"Haven't you heard, curiosity killed the cat," said Tristan grumpily.

"Maybe we can put it back?" Sums offered weakly, although he knew that was impossible.

Many emotions danced across Tristan's face. He pulled his flat cap down, and then huffed angrily; his face shifted a little when he threw a curious sideways glance at the file. A second later, his expression melted into panic.

"Hold on," he said cautiously. "The Dean won't be able to tie *this* back to us, right?" Tristan pointed at the file as if it were a ticking bomb, Nikka's head shot up to hear the answer and her pulse began to race.

"You disabled all the cameras," said Tristan with forced certainty, trying to reassure himself. Nikka could tell that this behavior was instinctual for Tristan; he was worried about the punishment, about the physical repercussions of being caught. But Nikka was like Sums, and what she cared about most were not consequences, but the answers that were in the folder Sums was clutching to his chest.

"I did," said Sums defensively, "But there *is* another problem. I lost a button from my blazer, and I think I lost it in the Dean's office," he said; his hand slid past the part of his chest where his blazer buttons would normally be.

"So what, it's just a button - we all have them," said Tristan.

"They're collecting everyone's uniforms so that they can find the missing button!" Nikka yelped in terror as the realization dawned on her. "The uniforms all have our initials sewn in!"

Tristan turned a pale greenish color, the shade of an unripe cucumber, and Sums let his head hang in shame.

"Precisely," he said, confirming Nikka's worries.

"How could you let that happen?" said Tristan angrily. Nikka shot him a furious look and guided his gaze towards the desolate, guilty-looking Sums. Tristan looked like he wanted to say more, but then he sighed, scooted over next to Sums and put his hand around his shoulders.

"Don't worry, mate," he said with forced nonchalance, "if they find out you were in there, they'll just expel you. That's the most they can do, you're a minor." Nikka met Tristan's eyes and they both looked away quickly, because neither really believed in what he was saying.

"They will do worse than that if they know I took *this,*"

said Sums, he clutched the file tighter to his chest. Nikka pulled the file from his grip and flicked through it; numbers, dates crisscrossed across the pages like some twisted Sudoku, there was nothing she could make any sense of. Tristan looked at her questioningly and she shrugged her shoulders in return.

"So what's in this precious folder?" asked Tristan. Sums lifted his head from his arms.

"Another schedule," he said heavily. "One that definitively proves that Wildwood is carrying out medical procedures on their students," he explained. The side of Nikka's arm stung at the mention and she thought back to the shot that had been forced upon her by Mrs. Smith.

"A schedule for what?" said Tristan.

"I'm not sure," Sums said even more guiltily. "It's all very vague, deliberately so I imagine. It talks about genotypes, blood groups, that sort of thing. Then one page has the schedules for this year, who is scheduled for the procedure and when. It says Tristan successfully underwent the procedure in January, Amber in November, and *you,*" he signaled uncomfortably towards Nikka, "Are scheduled for tomorrow."

This last bit of information took Nikka's breath away, as if she had been punched in the gut. *She was scheduled.... for what?* She breathed in deeply at first, then her deep breaths turned into short pants as she felt a black, creeping panic closing in on her, filling her lungs like sawdust. Nikka tried to calm herself- *they can't do anything to me if I don't let them; I'm in control.* Her hand shot back to the part of her arm that told her otherwise.

"What kind of procedure?" she asked, once the initial fear had liquefied into anger and confusion. Tristan looked fine, Amber had had a meltdown, but what was there aside from that? What were they missing? The boys weren't listening to her anymore. Sums was hunched over the file, dissecting it. Nikka turned to look at Tristan but he had gotten up and was standing a few feet away from her, gazing over the rolling mountains. Nikka could tell that Tristan was agitated just from looking at his tense back and the way he folded his arms.

"Tristan...it will be alright," she said. There was a long pause. Nikka looked at Sums. Sums stared up at Tristan.

"Tristan," Nikka repeated, she was beginning to grow tired of him ignoring her, no matter how upset Sums' news had made him. She got up and tugged on his shirtsleeve, then tried to turn him so that he would face her.

"What's your problem?" she snapped. Tristan turned and gawked at her, a shadow of doubt crossed his face, then hesitation.

"I told you," he said slowly, softly. "My name is not Tristan." He turned and stared over the precipice again. His proximity to the edge, his bewildered eyes, and his nonsensical words made Nikka nervous. She reached out and tugged at his shirt, making sure that she could grab hold of him if need be. She threw a pleading glance backwards at Sums.

"Please just try to explain, we have no idea what you're talking about," she pleaded.

Tristan turned and faced Nikka. The wind blew her dress and hair back and he watched her, taking in every part of her greedily and intently, as if he thought he would never see her again. His sky-colored eyes filled with regret, fear and shame.

"My name is not Tristan," he repeated, as if the words would suddenly make sense to Nikka after she had heard them for the third time. She took a step back, and when he saw her withdraw, Tristan began to talk fast, as if he were desperately trying hold onto her, like a fisherman pulling back his line.

"I come from a farming family in Ireland. I was in Dublin last summer, playing poker," he paused, but after neither Sums nor Nikka interjected he continued.

"One night, I ended up losing in a high stakes game in this basement of a club. It was a *bad* night," he stressed. Nikka looked at Sums, his mouth ajar, his brow creased, and a faint look of irate confusion spread on his face. Tristan's voice grew more animated, more passionate, and the words spilled out of him in a defensive and aggressive manner, as if he were defending himself in court.

"I was 150 thousand down and I already owed my buy-in to a local loan shark..." Tristan paused in an attempt to pick the best words to weaken the blow of what he was saying.

"One of the guys I played against, this rich American bloke, looked a lot like me - brown hair, green eyes, same height. The resemblance was uncanny, Nikka, you wouldn't believe it. After the game we got to talking-"

Tristan stopped and took a moment to observe Nikka and Sums' reaction. Upon seeing the blank expressions on their faces, he continued.

"Turned out he was of Irish descent, from a very rich family in Massachusetts, old money. His dying grandmother's last wish was that he attend this prestigious boarding school in the States. Problem was, he didn't want to go. He didn't have any talent or interest. He had inherited a bunch of money and just wanted to travel around the world, gamble, drink, and spend it," Tristan explained. "And there was I, about to lose a limb, maybe even my life to the loan shark, penniless, in debt, in danger, and the spitting image of *him*."

Tristan spoke quickly. The words buzzed around in Nikka's head feverishly and made her temples ache. He spoke in fragments, letting more and more of the truth pour out in large chunks, spilling out of him wildly after months of being forcibly kept in.

"I told him jokingly that I would take his place in a

heartbeat. I don't know if it was the alcohol, or the fear or what, but next thing I knew I was at his king suite in the Dublin Residential. A week later, I was on a plane, and now here I am. *Tristan Blake*, a wealthy American boy from Massachusetts." There was another pause, and then Tristan sighed easily, as if a massive weight had been lifted off his back.

"All expenses paid, two years and all your debts paid off in exchange for doing two years at a boarding school *he* didn't want to go to," Sums reasoned out loud. Tristan nodded, but his eyes were on a shocked Nikka, watching her every move. Sums, like Nikka, seemed flabbergasted, but more preoccupied with putting the pieces of the puzzle together than thinking about what they meant. He no longer looked upset or confused, just fascinated. Nikka was a different story. She felt sick and anxious; *did she not know the boy standing in front of her at all? Had she cared for a complete stranger? Had she kissed a complete stranger?* Nikka felt as if she were trying to swim out of a pool of dirty water, but didn't know whether the world was up or down.

"You believe this crap?" she said, suddenly furious with Sums.

"It makes sense, all elements considered," Sums answered temperately.

Tristan walked up to a still stunned Nikka and tenderly clasped her face in both of his palms. Sums looked away, uneasy.

"I'm so sorry," he said. The wind was beginning to blow more heavily as evening approached, it whistled past them. Nikka's mind felt like a chain so badly tangled that you would rather give up than undo it.

"What's your real name?" Nikka stuttered, barely able to squeeze the words out.

"My name is *Quinn*."

"Quinn," Nikka repeated, feeling the taste of the foreign word in her mouth.

"I'm so sorry I didn't tell you the truth earlier. *You*, of all people, Nikka," he said tenderly.

Nikka felt cold. She pushed away his hand. This was too much to take in all at once. *Quinn* looked down at the dust-woven ground beneath the boulder. He didn't look anxious or scared anymore, instead he looked liberated, but miserable at the same time.

"Whatever they did to me, they did it to the wrong guy," he said.

"It's like a real life prince and pauper story," said Sums sounding engrossed. Nikka was irritated that Sums was so intrigued by this when she couldn't make sense of what was happening around her, while her notion of reality was being challenged and flipped on its head. Sums was looking at it like a math problem, and not as if they had just learned that their friend wasn't who they thought he was.

Nikka tried to push away her own creeping feelings of doubt and shock. Her stomach lurched with unsettling feelings and she thought she might be sick right there on the boulder. She stared off into the distance and curled her arms around her torso, trying to find warmth and safety.

"How old are you?" she asked. Quinn seemed hesitant.

"19," he said. *Old enough to go to prison,* thought Nikka, and suddenly things began to make sense. It was like wiping away the steam from a bathroom mirror, and she could suddenly see the reflection more clearly. The accent, why Tristan had never come across as someone who'd had a privileged childhood, his ability to picks locks, the way he had hidden from his girlfriend at Thanksgiving - because she wasn't his girlfriend at all, she was the girlfriend of a wealthy Massachusetts boy who was somewhere out there, traveling the world and avoiding a boarding school sentence. Tristan's extreme wariness of authority made sense now too; he was old enough to go to jail, he was committing fraud just by being at Wildwood.

"You might hate me now," said Quinn slowly. "But the fact remains, we have to leave this place, and we have to leave it tonight, before they trace the folder back to Sums. Otherwise, whatever they have done to me, they will do to you next, tomorrow."

Nikka nodded weakly - *Quinn* was right.

×

Nikka, Quinn and Sums attended dinner that night as usual, partly to keep up appearances and partly because it might be the last Wildwood meal they would ever have. After dinner Nikka stood in her room and felt her previous resolve melting away. None of it made sense; *why would the school conduct experiments on them? To what end?* Nikka wondered. Her hands trembled as she packed her old backpack full of what she considered necessities: toothbrush, a couple of T-shirts, a warm winter jacket, matches and the hat her mother had made for her. She heard the door creak open and jerked around in fear. Upon seeing her reaction, Magda raised an eyebrow, then walked in with a tray loaded with different sandwiches and packaged snacks, and put it down on her nightstand.

"I thought you might be hungry," she said.

Nikka didn't stop to analyze why Magda would bring her snacks after she had already had dinner; Magda was always overly attentive.

"Thank you, Magda," she whispered gently.

Magda's eyes widened when she saw the backpack sitting by Nikka's knees, a pair of pants spilling out of it, and Nikka wondered if she should even bother making any excuses. Nikka opened her mouth to speak, but Magda put one thin finger to her mouth to silence her. Nikka noticed the threat of tears glazing the old woman's translucent blue eyes.

"You should hurry to assembly, Miss," said Magda. Her voice was loud and clear, but her gaze said something else. Her misted eyes darted back and forth around the room, and she looked slightly panicked. Magda pointed a long wrinkled finger at her ear, which had a cluster of colorful earrings hanging off the lobe, and then she pointed all around the room. *They're listening*- Nikka realized what her House Matron meant as the truth hit her like a bolt of lightning. She looked at Magda's kind pale eyes, earnest and afraid.

"Okay, Magdalena, I'm going to head out to assembly. I'll see you afterwards," she answered loudly, taking Magda's cue. Magda gave a weak smile, and nodded her head. Nikka got up and hugged the woman close. As quietly as she could muster, she whispered into her ear, "Thanks for everything, Magda." The House Matron hugged her, and whispered back.

"*Run* Nikka, and take loved ones with you." These were the final words Magda whispered to her before Stella's shrill voice interrupted them from the bedroom door.

"What the hell is going on here?"

×

Nikka bent low and snuck right past the Becks House Matron's window. She dodged into the first stairwell and sprinted up to the fourth floor. Then she checked the hallway - *no one* - and ran into Sums' room.

Nikka had told Stella to wait outside. She hadn't told her where they were going, or why; she had told her only to pack some clothes and that they were going on a fun outing. To speed up the process she told her there would be boys there. She had not told her that the boys were just Sums and Tristan, and that their 'fun outing' was running away from the Academy, *indefinitely*. She also left out the fact that they had no idea where they were running to. Nikka didn't know how to form any of that information into a realistic argument without sounding like one of those people who wandered Hollywood Boulevard barefoot threatening the impending apocalypse. So instead she lied to Stella, and bought herself some time.

Nikka clutched her backpack straps to her ribs. She was leaving some of her stuff behind, but the way Nikka saw it, if they were wrong about the Academy, then they could bear the detentions for breaking curfew and return for their things; but if they were right, then getting caught because they were trying to escape with massive wheelie suitcases just wasn't worth the risk. Lastly, *if* they were right, and the Academy was hurting the students and conducting experiments on them, then she couldn't well leave Stella behind. She couldn't leave anyone she cared for behind.

Sums didn't have a roommate; instead he had a small

room all to himself. He was sitting on the bed looking exasperated as he surveyed a tangled tower of his belongings laid out on the bed. Quinn had one hand on his shoulder, as Sums stared sadly at an array of black wires, a few comic books, and gizmos Nikka couldn't name. Nikka closed the door quietly behind her, and when her eyes met Quinn's, she grumpily looked away. She noticed a small backpack next to his foot.

"Sums isn't really understanding the notion of packing light," said Quinn.

"Shhh," Nikka pulled one finger to her lip and gestured around the room the same way she had seen Magda do. Quinn raised an eyebrow. Nikka ignored him. Sums was playing sadly with one of his wires, like a child stroking a dead pet.

"Maybe we can come back for it," Nikka whispered trying to sound hopeful. "If we find out we were wrong."

"And if we don't come back?" said Sums. His large blue eyes spread wide with fear.

Quinn checked his watch; his previous sympathy had drained from his face.

"It's just *things* Sums," he urged quietly. "*Things* aren't worth becoming a lab rat over. Right, Nikka?" Quinn looked to her for support, but Nikka didn't look back. Nikka didn't mind leaving her own things behind. After living with her mother all these years, leaving material possessions that were too heavy to carry had become second nature to her, but as she looked around the room, at the books, the gadgets, the tattered comic books, she knew exactly why it was so hard for Sums to let go. Sums didn't have a home, or a family, anything he had been able to purchase with Wildwood's generous allowance over the course of two and a half years; that was his home; that was all he had in the world to hang onto. Nikka sat on the other side of Sums, her backpack pressed to the wall.

"Either we come back," she whispered softly. "Or I will personally help you replace every single item you have here, and I'll put *these*," she pointed at the comic books, "in my own bag."

Sums stared at his possessions, unconvinced, but half-smiled at her. Quinn unceremoniously grabbed two fistfuls of Sums' possessions off the bed and stuffed them in his already full backpack. This time Nikka looked at him, and smiled a little.

"I'll help you too, mate," said Quinn. He nudged Sums in the side in a brotherly way.

"I get a five-finger discount at most stores," he added playfully.

Sums and Nikka stared at him, confused. He waved his hand in the air, showing them five fingers. Nikka realized what he meant and glared at him. Sums chuckled.

"Alright," Sums said dimly. He rose from his bed and calmly picked out the items that were most important to him. Nikka felt terrible that she was forcing him to do this; Sums had an empty, pained expression. Despite Nikka and Quinn's help, Sums still ended up with the largest backpack of the three.

A few minutes later, Sums was teary-eyed, but packed and ready to leave. Nikka checked her watch, and chucked a few extra comic books in her backpack when Sums wasn't looking; she figured she could surprise him later.

"An hour left until curfew, we'd better hurry and get off campus," said Quinn. "Once the school checks the ID card logs they'll realize we're gone."

"How will we get off campus exactly?" Sums whispered. "If we take the woods it will take us an hour to get into town, and it will be hard avoiding the guards. And it's ten miles at least," said Sums sounding very reluctant at the prospect of walking such a distance.

"I have a plan," said Nikka. A vague plan of action had begun to form in her head when she left Roseland; it was feeble, but it was all they had for now.

"Give me your phone, I'll call Alex," she said to Sums. Sums frowned, having instantly figured out her plan - nothing ever escaped him.

"Fine," he mumbled. "And I know where we should stop first, if he agrees," he added cryptically. Nikka nodded, again understanding him without anything being said out loud. Quinn sighed at them.

"I'll go first so that it doesn't look weird, see you down

there," he said as he walked out. Sums stopped for a second and surveyed his room.

"It will be okay," Nikka whispered. "This is just a precaution."

Nikka wasn't sure if she was convincing Sums, or herself. She glanced around to make sure there was no one in the hallway to see her sneaking out of the boys dorm, then Sums took a step back and let the door close. Halfway down the hall, Sums stopped abruptly, as if he had hit an invisible wall.

"There is one thing I haven't told you, and I won't forgive myself if I don't," he said. He threw a brief look towards a specific door at the end of the hall, then he whispered hastily.

"Izaya was on the procedure list too. He was scheduled for the week after you."

×

"I can't believe you brought *them*," Quinn moaned under his breath. He eyed Stella and Izaya with blatant disdain as the five of them marched through the dark woods.

"I heard that," said Izaya calmly.

"You were meant to," hissed Quinn.

"Sorry to ruin your hopes for date night," Izaya retorted in a bored tone.

Nikka had wanted to take Izaya with them from the very beginning; she wanted to protect him, but she didn't know if he needed protecting. Once Sums had told her that Izaya too was on the procedure list, it was the final push she needed. Strangely enough, Izaya didn't require a lot of convincing; maybe he was just along for the joy ride, maybe he knew his actions never had any consequences and it was just another way to break curfew, or maybe because he would use any excuse, no matter how far-fetched, to leave the Academy behind.

"Izaya, please don't start," Nikka warned. "And stop complaining, *QUINN!*" she scathed, dragging his name out for emphasis, showing him that she was still mad about his concealed identity.

"First of all," came Stella's high-pitched voice from behind them, "What are we all doing here? How much further to the party? Secondly, why are you calling Tristan *Quinn*?"

Nikka didn't answer.

"Let's go, I'll explain everything later," she said authoritatively, "we have a lot of wood to cover."

Nikka and Sums tried to fill Stella and Izaya in as best they could whilst keeping their story believable, which was no easy feat, so they did it gradually. They reminded them about Eloise and Amber. They told them about Alex's sister, the journalist's basement and meeting Manning in person at the asylum. Nikka told them about her forced shot. Quinn told them about his sickness, about how he had been treated, and Sums filled them in on his research and findings. Nikka finished by telling them about the Dean's office and Magda's warning. They left the issue of why Quinn was no longer Tristan for another time, fearing it would just distract from the immediate situation. During the briefing, the five unwilling companions slowly trudged further through the woods, towards a different side of campus.

"Are you sure you guys didn't just imagine this?" Stella asked guardedly, as if suspicious they were playing a prank on her.

"Did I imagine being medicated and tested against my will for weeks on end, well let me see... *No*, probably not," Quinn snorted sourly.

"I can easily call my uncle and figure all of this out," said Izaya with great self-importance, as he tried to shake off the weeds and mud that were clinging to the soles of his Italian sneakers. "He's on the Academic Board."

"We can't call anyone until we've figured out *what* exactly is going on," responded Nikka calmly. "No one would believe us. What are we going to tell them? That *the* Academy is doing something bad- and what exactly? And how? And when? And why? We don't even have enough proof to convince our own parents," she said, exasperated.

"Why don't we just call the police!" piped up Stella, as smartly as if she had just invented the telephone.

"We've tried involving the police; it's pointless, we don't have enough information and the police are probably on their side," said Quinn.

"I don't think they would believe your story anyway," agreed Izaya.

Stella looked embarrassed and shut down. Nikka squeezed her arm to comfort her. A few minutes later they emerged from the wood and into the familiar clearing of the Wildwood truck depot. Alex was standing there, leaning against his black truck. He smiled at Nikka-a tight, forced smile. He was waiting for them, just like he and Nikka had agreed on the phone.

"On the run to nowhere?" he said mockingly. He looked at Izaya then at Stella, observing them one by one, as if they were odd shop window displays. "Not the road companions I would have chosen, but each to their own," he added.

Izaya rolled his eyes at the snarky comment.

"We do have *somewhere* to go," rectified Sums. He handed Alex a piece of paper. "That's the address."

Alex read the paper and frowned, a muscle in his tattooed neck twitched.

"You're lucky I'm taking you past the gate, they've tripled security in the last three days," he said crossly. Nikka, Sums and Quinn looked at each other knowingly - *they tripled security since the break-in.*

"And *this,*" Alex pointed at the piece of paper that Sums had handed him. "Is in another town. Get in before I change my mind," he said cocking his head in the direction of his truck. Today it was the garbage truck, a change from the laundry truck he usually drove; the open back was loaded with swollen black bags full of trash. Izaya made the first move towards the front of the truck.

"Oh no, no, no," cooed Alex, the way a governess would reprimand a child reaching for a cookie before lunch. Nikka could tell that he was relishing every moment of the plan they had agreed upon, a plan to get them safely off of campus. Izaya stared back at Alex. Alex pointed at the back of the truck, and smiled widely; the first natural smile Nikka had seen on the boy. He said the last phrase in a buttery, satisfied tone.

"*Everyone* rides in the back."

18
THE MUSCLE

Nikka was not comfortable. She was all too aware of being pressed against Quinn's legs and Izaya's back at the same time. She was also being crushed by the weight of the lumpy bags on top of her, and suffocated by the sweet stench of rot. They were buried under trash for a mere half an hour, but the black plastic eclipsed the light and made the journey feel like three. No one spoke during the drive, partly because they weren't sure at which point they would be clear of Wildwood territory, and partly because they were trying to keep the smell at bay by breathing through their mouths. Every now and then, Nikka could hear the boys grunting and shuffling a millimeter this way or that, in a futile attempt to get more comfortable, and what felt like every few miles, Nikka heard Stella whimper unhappily. She regretted the way they had treated Stella. Stella had initially refused to get into the garbage truck, so Nikka had climbed in first, followed by the boys, and had called her a coward. It was shameless peer pressure, but it had worked like a charm, and it was the only way - *the end justifies the means.* As the truck trudged along, Nikka was surprised by how sure she felt of her decision to leave Wildwood, and with each mile the truck put between her and the school grounds, she grew even more certain.

She felt the wind whipping the top of the bags and wondered why Alex hadn't yet pulled over and let them sit in the front, then she realized it was because Alex was thoroughly enjoying every minute that Izaya spent lying under a pile of trash. A little thread of panic unraveled in Nikka's head, *what are we going to do next? How can we prove our theories to anyone? Maybe we can just go back home, resume normal life... Would the Academy even look for us?* She pushed these thoughts away; they were useless and did nothing except cripple her with fear.

The truck pulled to a slow stop and Nikka held her breath. A few moments later a bag was lifted from above her head and she could see the night sky, dotted with stars. She breathed in the clean air and let it pull some of the garbage stench from her nose. Alex lifted a few more bags off of them. Nikka sat up and looked around. They were parked on a quiet residential street lined with large upmarket houses. Izaya climbed out quickly, dusted himself off and ignored the smug smile on Alex's face.

"Hurry up," Alex urged them. He looked around the suburban street nervously, like a teenager about to steal a car. Nikka found it strange that he would feel the need to be cautious *here*, in a completely different town, on an empty residential street. But then again, it would seem odd to anyone seeing a bunch of teenagers climbing out of a trash truck marked with *Wildwood Academy.* She landed on the asphalt. Sums, Stella and Quinn followed suit. Stella jumped onto the sidewalk and started hysterically brushing off her clothes and shaking out her hair in a dramatic fashion. They stood in front of a large house with a carefully manicured lawn, full of eerily shiny garden gnomes. Nikka faced Alex.

"I guess this is it," he said quietly.

"When will you leave Wildwood for good?" Nikka asked, concerned.

"I have a flight tomorrow. I decided I'm going to travel across Asia," said Alex. He stuck his hands in his pockets indifferently and tried to sound less excited than he was.

"Sounds amazing," said Nikka. "Be safe, and good luck."

Alex looked past her at where Izaya, Sums, and Quinn were still brushing off their pants.

"Good luck to you too, you're going to need it," he said, signaling towards the boys. Nikka knew that Alex didn't mean it in a snide way; he meant it literally - *they were going to need luck to get out of this mess.* Nikka contemplated hugging him, but decided he was not the hugging sort. Instead she smiled up at him and said one last thing-

"For what it's worth," she said. "I think *this* is what Alexis would have wanted for you."

Alex paused and looked at Nikka with disbelief. His eyes glazed over just a tiny bit and he blinked hard in an attempt to cover it up. He gave her a grateful, boyish nod.

"Thanks," he grunted quietly, before turning to the others.

"Bye bye, boys and girls," he said condescendingly. "Hope you have a dry cleaner on speed dial," he said towards Izaya. With those words, Alex got in his truck and drove away.

"Charming guy, really," Quinn muttered sarcastically as he watched the truck disappear down the street and around the corner.

"Oh yes, I must make a mental note to invite him to my next dinner party," Izaya added grumpily.

"You just don't get him," said Nikka. Izaya's normally composed green eyes flashed with a trace of jealousy. His lingering gaze was interrupted by a sudden ringing sound, which Nikka faintly recognized, and which was followed by a persistent sequence of buzzing.

"My phone!" Nikka exclaimed excitedly as she reached into the pocket of her backpack and yanked it out. The screen read *16 messages from Mom*, and more were coming in each second, as her phone caught up with finally being in a serviceable area. Nikka looked down at the phone and smiled at the silly notion that her mother had continued avidly sending her texts despite knowing that she wouldn't receive them. She began to read through them.

"Oh my god, we're out of the dead zone!" Stella screeched with the excitement of a child spotting a pony through the car window. Greedily she pulled her pink phone from her own backpack and instantly her well-seasoned fingers began to dance across the keyboard.

"No!" Sums yelped with sudden urgency. He launched himself forward and pulled Stella's phone from her grasp, then just as quickly he grabbed Nikka's.

"Hey- what the hell?" Nikka cursed in irritation whilst Stella was doing her best impression of a spider monkey as she tried to climb over Sums and snatch her phone back.

"Give it back this second!" she squawked wildly as he wrestled out of her grip.

"Phones are traceable! We have to switch them off immediately," said Sums with cold rationale.

"I'm sorry," he mumbled a moment later in Stella's direction, but she had already stormed off crying. Sums handed Nikka's phone back to her with an apologetic look. "Switch it off," he said softly.

"My phone is about to die anyway," Nikka mumbled grumpily.

"Tristan, uhh- *I mean Quinn,*" Sums rectified, "switch yours off too."

"I left mine in the room," he answered. Izaya, Sums and Nikka all stared at him in surprise.

"I know phones are traceable, this isn't my first rodeo," he explained and flashed them a cheeky grin.

"Okay, well that problem is settled," muttered Sums, as if he were ticking off boxes on an invisible list. "Izaya and I can keep ours on for emergencies, since they're not traceable."

"Well that's fair," said Nikka sarcastically as her eyes locked on Izaya's. *The rules don't apply to some* - the phrase replayed in her head again, but this time the distant memory did not make her smile.

Subtly, Nikka tucked her phone back into her bag without switching it off, hoping that perhaps she would get a quick moment to check her texts in secret before the phone died. She turned and faced the house.

"What are we even doing here?" asked Quinn.

"We're here for answers," said Nikka as she walked past him and opened the gate to the house.

"A less vague answer, please?" said Izaya as he walked after her. Sums cleared his throat.

"*Okay*, we've established that the Dean is at the root of our problem," he explained as he wobbled after Nikka.

"*He* is the king and Wildwood is his twisted kingdom. Now, to find more information in a kingdom you go to the person who executes the King's wishes, *the muscle,* if you will, the henchmen. Since we've established that the problem is *medical* in nature..." Sums let the sentence trail off and linger in the air, like a professor waiting for his class to fill in the blanks.

"So, what you're saying is you play too much *Dungeons and Dragons,*" joked Quinn.

"Or is it *World of Warcraft*?" added Izaya. The pair shared a laugh, but when their eyes met, they both stopped and looked away irritably, as if they'd overstepped a boundary by laughing at each other's jokes.

"Oh, for Christ's sake!" said Sums in a huff. "We're here to ask Nurse Smith a few questions, *she's the henchman*. It's a metaphor, you Neanderthals." At these words, Quinn shrunk away from the gate, as if it had burned him.

"The nurse," he stuttered. "I don't want to see *that toad*."

"Fear of shots?" Izaya asked snidely. Quinn glowered at him.

"This is our last chance to get some real information," Nikka pleaded.

"And what do we do after we get it?" asked Izaya.

"We decide whether or not we leave for good. Or go back to the school and forget any of this crazy stuff ever happened," said Nikka sounding a little uncertain.

At a sluggish pace, the four of them progressed towards the front door. Nikka turned and noticed that Stella was still standing by the gate, like a displaced kitten. She was whimpering a little and looking around uncertainly.

"This is not a *fun* adventure, you lied to me, and now Sums has taken away my phone! Just when I had finally gotten service," Stella whined bitterly. Quinn rolled his eyes. Nikka reached out and put an arm around her roommate's small frame.

"I know, and I'm sorry about that. This is almost over, just bear with me," she lied, yet again. Ignoring them, Sums knocked on the front door - nothing. He knocked again. The five of them listened to the silence, paralyzed with anticipation. Nikka looked around the gnome-littered, perfectly manicured lawn and felt her dormant hate for Mrs. Smith rise up and spill over like black ink on wet paper, drowning any sense of reason she might have otherwise had. She checked her watch; the Health Center wasn't closed yet, not for another hour.

"Pick the lock," she said decisively, in Quinn's direction. Quinn looked stunned for a moment, then his mouth curled into a delighted smile. He pulled out his lock picks and bent over by the door.

"Are we breaking into her house?" Stella asked, as she peeked over his shoulder. Her voice shook like a leaf as she spoke.

"It's going to be fun, or are you scared?" said Nikka, again using peer pressure to her advantage. Izaya smiled at her with unkind amusement, but Nikka didn't return it. She hated acting this way, but playing on Stella's need to fit in was the easiest way to get her to agree to something quickly. Of course it wasn't fair, but leaving her to fend for herself at the Academy didn't seem fair either. If Wildwood was doing something to its students, then surely taking *all* of her friends with her was the right thing to do. *It's the least I can do,* thought Nikka. The lock clicked as it yielded and Quinn stood up looking satisfied and proud, he pushed the door and it swung open. He looked back at Izaya, smirking. Izaya rolled his eyes.

Quinn entered first, followed by Sums. Nikka threw a final glance at the suburban street to make sure it was empty before entering the house. Mrs. Smith's house was spacious, modern, and *fancy.* Fancy was the best word Nikka could think of; it wasn't too full or too empty, but there was nice furniture, long leather couches, a large flat screen TV, and everything seemed new, expensive, and unused. It reminded her of those show houses they used to sell apartments in yet-to-be-built complexes. Everything was coordinated, the same shades of navy blue and beige, and it was spotless throughout. There were no creases on the couch, no tears or smears on the carpets.

"She doesn't spend much time here, does she?" said Sums.

"Separate, and search different areas," commanded Quinn. "We need to work fast." He checked his watch; just like Nikka, he too was overly familiar with the Health Center's hours of operation.

His voice was so sure, so calm, but Nikka knew that a deeply rooted fear was concealed underneath his bravado. She wondered about Quinn, about the man behind Tristan. The man whom she sort of knew, the man whose expressions she could read, whose emotions she could feel, but also the man whom, in theory, she knew nothing about. It was a conflicting sensation; like recognizing someone on the street, but not remembering where you know them from. *How many times has he broken into places? How much has he stolen in his life?* She wondered.

"What are we looking for?" asked Izaya.

"Anything suspicious," said Nikka. Sums' stomach growled loudly.

"I'll start with the kitchen," he said. Everyone in the room looked at him.

"What?" he said defensively. "That's where I would hide things, no one would think to look there," he said smartly and he headed to the kitchen behind the living room. A moment later Nikka heard the fridge door open. She chuckled and her hand shot up to her mouth.

"That's not what I meant when I said we should get out of here fast," yelled Quinn. He smiled at Nikka warmly and she smiled back. Gently, he traced the chestnut ring on Nikka's finger.

"You still wear it," he said, sounding relieved.

"For now," she answered coldly. She wanted him to know that she was still mad and would continue to be for some time, but as she turned away from him she smiled. *Yes*, she didn't know Quinn, but she knew his voice, his smile, and until she learned more, that would have to be enough.

"I'll take the living room," said Izaya.

"I'll see what other rooms there are," offered Quinn. "Remember to keep everything as it is. That includes eating stuff," he said loudly.

"I'll take the bedroom," Nikka volunteered.

"I'll come with you," said Stella anxiously.

Quinn followed Nikka and Stella into a hallway, where she presumed she would find the bedroom. There were a number of doors and Quinn went to the end of the hallway to start there. Nikka pushed the first door open - it was a guest room, clean and seemingly untouched. The bed was made up as perfectly as if it were a hotel suite. Nikka moved onto the next room.

"This is it," she said as she observed the almost identical room, the only notable difference being the dog-eared tabloid magazines by the bed. Nikka walked in, careful not to touch anything, Stella followed.

"I don't know what to look for," she whispered.

"Anything that is *odd*, out of the ordinary." Nikka whispered back.

"The décor is odd," said Stella crankily.

"Try the closet," suggested Nikka, trying her best to not sound irritated. Nikka checked under the bed. Nothing. She started to ruffle through the nightstands. They were filled with mundane, everyday things: a crime novel, a night cream, and spare candles. There wasn't a misplaced item, nothing private or odd to be found. Nikka lifted the mattress gently. Again, *nothing*.

"Her taste in clothing is horrible," said Stella with disgust.

"Not everyone can afford amazing clothes," said Nikka, irritated again. She was checking the windowsill and the bookshelf. Stella was leafing through the hangers as if flipping through an old, tattered magazine.

"I know that!" she said defensively. "But all of this stuff is really expensive, like these are the brands my mom wears. So there's no excuse, really," she said huffily.

Nikka spun on her heels and turned towards her.

"That's a clue," she said.

"Really?" said Stella excitedly. Nikka nodded.

"She can't afford *this*. Any of this," said Nikka, certain of the fact. She walked out of the bedroom and towards where Quinn was, in the room next door. Stella followed her eagerly. Nikka walked into what seemed to be the study. Quinn was hunched over something on the luxurious, leather-lined desk.

"Stella found something," said Nikka. Quinn looked up, surprised.

"This school must be overpaying her for whatever she's doing to the students. She can't afford any of this, not on a nurse's salary," said Nikka.

"I'm not sure how much a *geneticist* makes, but probably a lot more than a school nurse," said Quinn. He held up a piece of paper for the two girls to see. It was a degree, printed on parchment paper and finished off with an embossed stamp and a signature. Nikka looked closer - a degree in the study of genetics from the Berlin University, awarded to a Ms. Gertrude Kampf.

"That's not her name," said Stella blankly.

"It is according to this," said Quinn and he held up a plum-colored German passport in the air. Nikka gasped. Suddenly they heard a sound erupt from the living room, something like tin colliding against glass.

"I found something," Sums called a second later. Quinn hastily rolled up the degree and put the passport in his back pocket. Nikka wanted to warn him to not take anything, but she was already hurrying towards the living room, where they found Sums, who was holding a cookie tin in his hands, as gently if it were a newborn baby. There was a moment of silence.

"*Cookies*?" said Quinn incredulously. "Really?"

Sums looked at the tin in his hands.

"No, no. I *was* looking for cookies, then I dropped this and it spilled. But there are no cookies inside it," said Sums. Nikka and Quinn gawked at him.

"*Please* tell me there is more to that story," said Quinn.

"Of course there is more to the story!" said Sums indignantly. He opened the tin and spilled the contents of it on the kitchen island - an array of small colorful Polaroid pictures toppled out.

"It's full of Polaroids of students. With dates on the back," he explained.

Nikka looked at the pile. She pushed a few photos aside with her hand, brushing them to the ends of the table. Amongst the faces she recognized Alexis, Eloise, Amber, and Quinn. She picked up Quinn's Polaroid and flipped it around; there was a date on the back.

"That's the day I went into the Health Center for treatment. She took a photo of me for my file that day," said Quinn weakly.

"Put that down now," came a sudden sickly-sweet voice from the main entrance. Nikka froze; she felt her blood turn to ice. Then she slowly turned her head and her eyes locked on Mrs. Smith, who stoically occupied the front door. She towered in the doorway, a Taser gun in hand, aimed straight at Nikka's chest.

There was complete silence except for the breeze coming from the door, which Nurse Smith had left open. Nikka took a step back and Mrs. Smith took a step forward, like a predator closing in on its prey. Time seemed to stall and Nikka could feel Sums shaking lightly next to her. Nikka wanted to move, but she was frozen in place; she wouldn't give Mrs. Smith any excuse to use the weapon in her hand. She took a sharp breath in and let the Polaroid flutter to the floor, like a dying butterfly. Mrs. Smith smiled and readjusted her posture, two legs spread apart, ready to fire.

"Well, what do we have here?" said the nurse sweetly. She kept one hand on the Taser gun, and with her other bulky arm she knocked over a nearby vase, it shattered on the floor. The noise shocked Nikka out of her temporary stupor, making her painfully aware of the situation they had gotten themselves into. With her other hand Mrs. Smith knocked over a nearby lamp, it too shattered on the ground. Quinn took a step forward and the stun gun was quickly aimed at him. They all stared at her, speechless.

"What a cruel, horrible student prank," said the nurse with theatrical distress.

"To come here and trash the poor lonely nurse's home. What do they call that? Oh yeah, *breaking and entering*," she said and she knocked another vase to the ground. "*Destruction of property*," she said, and smiled at them cruelly as she let it sink in - they were busted, she could accuse them of whatever she wanted to. Her smile faded, but her teeth still showed. "Get on the ground," she spat. Nikka did not move.

"I said, get on the ground," she screamed. "You filthy, stupid, annoying little-"

Nurse Smith didn't get the chance to finish her sentence. There was a thump. A blow to the head, and the nurse was lying on the ground, sprawled like an awkward sack of potatoes. Izaya stood over her, a gnome in his hand. He looked at her with distaste, as if she were leftover trash. Nikka, Sums, and Quinn stared at him, their mouths ajar.

"She was going to taze you," said Izaya dispassionately when he caught them staring. He let the gnome fall to the ground. Quinn took a step forward and observed the nurse carefully. He prodded her lightly with his foot, as if she were a dead rodent. She didn't move.

"You knocked her out," he said, seeming impressed. Izaya shrugged his shoulders.

"That's it, let's get out of here now," said Quinn.

"No!" yelped Sums. His voice was shaking, but determined. "We should tie her up. We need more information."

Somewhere in the corner of the room, Stella began to cry. Nikka looked at Sums, stunned at his brazen proposal, but she knew he was right. It was too late to ever return to the school after what they had done, but if they left now they would be going onwards with very little information.

"Quickly, before she wakes up," Nikka agreed.

"Oh my god," blubbered Stella. "Oh my god! What are you doing? I have no idea what's going on? Are you all crazy?" Stella started to sob loudly, everyone continued to ignore her; there were more pressing matters at hand. Quinn and Izaya grabbed Nurse Smith's arms and Sums took her feet. They lifted her up with extreme difficulty. Nikka grabbed a nearby chair, and they pulled her into it like a crash test dummy. Her large head cocked to the side and sank onto her shoulders.

Tying someone up turned out to be a lot more difficult than Nikka had imagined; she scoured the rooms and pulled out all the scarves, hairbands and belts from Nurse Smith's bedroom. Then they tried to bind her arms in whichever way they could, tirelessly looping the fabric over and over her large body until they thought the knots looked unbreakable. Nikka was half-aware of what she was doing, the other half of her was numb and in denial, executing orders. She had learned early on in her life to not panic, to take situations step by step, but still, a small voice inside of her was screaming, *this is madness, this is wrong.* After all, they had broken into and entered her house, and now they were technically kidnapping her. But as Nikka contemplated the woman's motionless face, she felt no pity, there was something fundamentally *bad* about the nurse, a cruelty Nikka had felt from the very first moment she'd met her. She took a step back and felt a pang of satisfaction at seeing the woman restrained. Sums, Nikka, Quinn, and Izaya stood in a half circle and observed her. Stella had stopped crying, she wiped her tears on her shirtsleeve and sat there looking at the wall. Sums picked the stun gun up off of the floor and surveyed it with scholarly interest.

"Why would she carry this on her?" he wondered out loud. The stun gun looked heavy duty, not something the average woman would carry for protection in a bad part of town.

Nurse Smith twitched a little. Her eyes opened, and slowly focused. Her hand jerked, instinctively, towards her head, which must have been hurting from the blow. She squinted a little, jerked her arm again and realized that it was restrained. She started grunting and jerking around in her seat, in an attempt to escape the restraints. Nikka took a step toward her; the nurse stilled and stared up at her calmly.

"We don't want to hurt you," said Nikka carefully. "We just want you to answer a few questions, and then we'll let you go." She tried to keep her tone as level as possible. The nurse looked at her and thrashed violently in her seat. Suddenly, her arms were untied and she launched toward Nikka. Nikka took a quick step back right as Nurse Smith's strong arms closed around her neck. Sums shot the gun and hit Nurse Smith in the chest. Visible currents ran through the woman's bulky body and she shook mid-air before collapsing on the floor. Stella's shrill scream pierced the air. Everyone looked back at Sums, who was clutching the stun gun, guiltily.

"Sums!" Nikka reprimanded, but her hands had shot up to her neck.

"I panicked," he said ruefully, as his four companions stared at him in awe.

Quinn and Izaya got Nurse Smith back into the chair and this time Nikka doubled the restraints and tightened all the belts. A few moments later, the woman came to again, red-faced and even angrier than before.

"You're going to pay for this," she muttered weakly.

"You're going to answer a few questions first," said Quinn. He grabbed the stun gun out of Sums' hand and brought it close to Nurse Smith's face. "Or I will shoot you with this, in the face, repeatedly," he threatened. Nikka grimaced, and turned away so that the nurse wouldn't see her hesitation. The situation was escalating and quickly spinning out of control. From the corner of the room Stella looked on, terrified. Nurse Smith looked at Quinn with hate, but there was also a hint of uncertainty in her cold glare. Nikka could sense that the woman was at least a little afraid that Quinn would come through on his threat.

"You're doing something to the Wildwood students, a

genetic procedure. What is it," demanded Nikka, trying to sound as menacing as Quinn had. The nurse looked at her and there was a flicker of surprise in her face. Then she turned away.

"I don't know what you are talking about," she said evenly.

Nikka got closer to her.

"*Yes*, you do," she said icily. "*Gertrude*," she spoke the name she had seen on the degree. Mrs. Smith met her eyes.

"Tell us what the procedure is. Or I *will*..." Nikka looked around the room in hesitation. She grabbed the Polaroids off the table.

"Or I will burn these!" she said, flashing the photos before Mrs. Smith's eyes. Nikka was going off a crazy hunch that the tin of pictures meant something to the woman. Or else why would she be hiding them in a cookie tin in her otherwise completely impersonal house? The nurse looked upset by this. Her mouth opened, but then closed again.

"I have no idea what you are talking about," she repeated robotically. She started wriggling in her chair, trying to get free again.

"Zap her," said Nikka coolly. Instantly, Quinn obliged. The woman shook again, but this time she did not pass out. She was sweating at her hairline; her face was scarlet and blotchy.

"Untie me," she wailed angrily.

"No, tell us what the procedure is!" Nikka yelled back with all the strength and aggression she could muster. She grabbed a Polaroid of a girl whom she did not know and shredded it through the garbage disposal in the sink. The nurse grimaced as if she had been punched in the stomach. Then she looked back at Nikka, hatred coursing through her like poison.

"You spoiled, rotten brats," she spat viciously. "You think you can do anything you want just because you're privileged, or you have talent. You think you're better than everyone else," she sputtered the last word out so violently that spittle flew halfway across the room. There was silence as everyone tried to digest what she had said. One of the words stuck in Nikka's mind, bothering her, like a pebble in her shoe. The nurse looked suddenly terrified, and she turned away. That's when Nikka knew that the woman had said something she shouldn't have said. Nikka stood in front of her and gazed down.

"*Talent,*" she repeated the word that had bothered her. The nurse looked up horrified, and then looked down at the floor.

"Is that what the experiments are about? All those memory tests you did on me?" asked Nikka. She was still trying to understand what she was saying herself. The nurse was looking past her, for an escape route, her beady eyes danced in a wild frenzy. Her eyes shot to the

Polaroids in Nikka's hand and quickly, too quickly, she looked away. Nikka leafed through the pictures, and stopped on the familiar faces. She thought back to Alexis, who could no longer play chess, to Eloise, whose voice had gone hoarse, to Amber, who could no longer draw.

"You take it," said Nikka, searching the woman's beady, frightened eyes. Nikka looked down at the pictures of students in disbelief. *That was it, the answer. Wildwood was stealing the talent,* she realized, in shock. Her hand went to the little red book in her blazer front pocket- The Dean and the Nurse were hunters, thieves, and the address book and the tin of pictures were their souvenirs, their trophies, their taxidermy. The expression on Nurse Smith's face - terrified, exposed – told Nikka that she was right.

"That sort of makes sense," said Sums from behind her, breaking the silence. "Genetic theft. Illegal, immoral - that must have been what the experiment was." Sums was mumbling fast, and more to himself than to anyone else in the room. He was putting together the pieces of the puzzle far faster than Nikka ever could. Suddenly, Nikka noticed that Nurse Smith's hands were moving. Stella had stood up and she walked up to the nurse, seized by a sudden bout of bravery.

"You were going to steal my talent?" she asked furiously, her brown eyes filled with tears. The nurse smirked, her hand continued to move in an odd way and

Nikka assumed she was trying and failing to get herself out of the restraints. The nurse laughed, a neurotic, maddened laugh.

"You don't have anything worth stealing," she said. Stella took a step back as if she had been slapped. "You don't have any talent, you're nothing-" continued the nurse, just in case Stella was too dim-witted to understand. Nikka grabbed the stun gun out of Sums' hands and zapped the nurse one more time. The nurse shook violently and went limp. Something fell out of her hands and thumped onto the floor.

"Wow, Nikka" Izaya let out an appreciative whistle as he looked down at the limp woman.

"You're the one who hit her on the back of the head," Nikka reminded him. "Besides, she deserves it. All of it."

"Can someone explain what's going on?" asked Quinn. "Because I feel like I'm in a science fiction movie." Izaya shook his head at him, failing to comprehend the details either. Sums made his way to the back of the nurse's chair and picked up what had dropped from the nurse's hands. He held the cell phone up for everyone to see.

"She must have had it in her back pocket," he narrated as he examined the phone. Suddenly, Sums froze. "We've got a problem," he said glumly. "She sent an SOS text before she even came in."

At that moment there was knock on the door, and a

loud voice echoed from behind it.

"Police, open up!" came the thunderous call.

There were a few quiet seconds when everyone in the room looked at each other. Then Quinn put up a finger to his lips, and pointed at the back screen door, past the kitchen. There was another knock. Nurse Smith was out cold. Quinn quickly pocketed the Taser, grabbed his backpack and made his way towards the door. There was another urgent knock - the knocks were like the chime of a clock, signaling to them that they were running out of time, and fast. Nikka pulled her backpack on her shoulders, grabbed Stella by the arm, and on tiptoes they made their way to the door.

Quinn flicked the latch, pulled the glass door open, and then the screen door - he exited first, followed by Nikka, Stella, Sums, and finally Izaya. They walked down the wooden steps that led to the fenceless backyard, past the trash bins, and towards the forest. Nikka felt a little disoriented. She could hear light footsteps, the shouts of the police, and their knocking from the other side of the house. Her uneven breathing echoed in her ears, and somewhere along the way she lost hold of Stella's hand. The boys broke into a quiet run, she saw Sums' back and watched Izaya's coat disappear into the darkness of the wood.

Only Quinn was left next to her. Nikka heard the voices of the officers as they shouted by the front door.

Quinn reached the trees and disappeared in between them. Just as Nikka was about to follow him she risked a final look back at the house, and her eyes locked on Mrs. Smith's. The nurse was standing on the back porch. Her cold eyes bore into Nikka's knowingly, menacingly. She was using the porch to hold her weakened body up, and was holding something long and black in her other hand. As Nikka turned to run she felt the bullet hit her shoulder.

19

Run, Baby, Run

Nikka felt herself drifting out of consciousness. First she saw spots, the way you do when you've stared at a light for too long, then the edges of her vision blurred. She ran, as fast as she could, deeper and deeper into the redwood forest. At some point she felt her body go limp, then she felt herself being dragged across an ocean of twigs, thorns pulling at her skin. She felt the heat of someone's breath on the nape of her neck. She felt herself being carried, cradled, and then dragged again. The world around her seemed intensely real and non-existent at the same time. There was a dull sting in her arm but she could no longer remember why. Images of her mother's face danced on the walls of her closed lids, and when she managed to open them, flashes of moonlit redwood swarmed past her, like a flock of blurry red birds.

Nikka thought back to an artwork she used to make with her mother when she was a child; the pair of them used to put pieces of canvas on a spinning wheel and take turns spinning it really fast whilst the other dropped oil paint on it. The effect was bursts of intermixing colors, exploding on the canvas like fireworks. This is what the redwood looked like now; violent bursts of green, red, and brown swallowed her whole, as if she were lying on the spinning wheel and the forest was paint being poured over her. Slowly, the spinning wheel came to a halt, and so did time. Nikka wasn't sure if hours had passed, or a just a few seconds. The trees melted away and in their place came darkness, complete and total darkness.

"We have to find her," she said to no one but herself.

×

"Find who, Nikka? Who?"

Nikka felt herself being shaken like a ragdoll. She opened her eyes, slowly. The forest spun briefly before settling in front of her, along with a pair of worried blue eyes.

"*Nik,*" he whispered tenderly. Quinn cupped her face with his cold hands. He looked relieved.

"How do you feel?" he asked. Nikka looked past him and spotted Izaya. Izaya didn't look at her. Sums and Stella sat next to him on a collapsed tree trunk.

"Rough," she admitted. She raised herself onto her elbows. Her shoulder stung a little, like it would from a dirtied scratch, and she felt drowsy. With a start, she realized that she was no longer wearing her blazer. Then she traced the spot of the incision. Memories flooded back into her throbbing head - Mrs. Smith's cold eyes, and the flex of her bicep as she pulled the trigger of the tranquillizer gun.

"Did you disinfect it properly?" Izaya snapped in Stella's direction. Stella's upper lip quivered.

"I said that my dad is a doctor, not that I'm a doctor!" she said indignantly. Stella turned away from him and began to sob quietly. Nikka wanted to comfort her but her movements felt restricted and her head still spun. Stella's hair was frizzy, her face dirty, and her head bobbed as she cried. Nikka thought back to the nurse's house, what they had learned there. Stella had no reason to even be with them in the first place. *She is not the target - she has no reason to run. I made her run...I put her in danger,* realized Nikka. Stella's quiet sobs shook Nikka to the core. She wondered which realization would be more painful for Stella - that her beloved school was committing talent theft, or that she had none of it to steal.

Sums put an arm around Stella and she burrowed her face in his shirt. He shot Nikka a look of solidarity. Nikka pulled back her button-down sleeve again and looked at her shoulder; it was bandaged with ripped pieces of fabric. *The bandages are not necessary,* thought Nikka, a dart would probably make a small, clean incision.

"I can't believe she shot me," Nikka thought out loud. She thought back to the small cluster of feathers attached to the syringe-like dart that had hit her and pulled her into unconsciousness.

"Me neither," said Sums. "But the good news is they're not dangerous, just incapacitating," he added quickly. Nikka smiled at him. Where Magda believed that food cured all, Sums put his faith in knowledge, and she loved him for that.

"Does it hurt?" asked Quinn. He stroked the side of her arm and Nikka felt the fine hairs on her arms rise up. She shook her head.

"I'll be fine," she said.

Nikka risked another look at Izaya but he still wouldn't look back at her. Izaya looked somewhere between angry, irritated and confused; there were a number of emotions written across his normally bored face that Nikka couldn't decipher. She took a moment to look around her circle of friends and take in their surroundings. The forest air was cold, the ground too was cold and its dry-packed surface was littered with rocks and pine. Everything, and everyone was illuminated by the silver gleam of the rising moonlight, as if they were floating through a ghostly version of the real world. There were noises in the forest, an infinity of them, and Nikka had to stare hard into the depths of the black wood to make sure that nothing was there. At least nothing that could hurt them.

"Well, now we know *exactly* what the Academy is doing," said Nikka morbidly. Her eyes nervously darted back to the dark abyss of the woods.

No one said anything. Finally, Izaya looked up and met her gaze.

"You've been tranquillized, Nikka, maybe you should just rest," he suggested passively. Nikka lifted herself into a sitting position defiantly. She touched her cheek - her face felt hot to the touch. She flinched from the burn that movement sent through her arm.

"That doesn't change anything!" she said angrily. "It *all* makes perfect sense now. Amber couldn't draw anymore; Alexis couldn't play chess, and Eloise..." her voice trailed off when she looked at her peers and realized that no one wanted to listen to what she was saying, because no one wanted it to be true.

"It does makes sense," said Quinn grimly.

"It's just not possible. Are you hearing yourselves? Have you all lost your mind?" Izaya asked furiously.

Nikka stared at Izaya hard, tying to decipher why there was so much venom and fear in his voice if he didn't believe them. Everyone in the group instinctively turned to Sums, the best judge of what was impossible.

"I know it sounds *improbable,*" he said measuredly, "but I think that Wildwood has found a way to isolate people's talent genes and extract them. I mean *steal* them," he said struggling with the truth.

"And clearly," said Quinn, pointing at Nikka's arm. "That is one secret they would like to keep."

"You know what, this was fun at first, but now it's all getting ridiculous," said Izaya, his voice laced with disdain and feigned nonchalance. "Just because you guys decided to play out an *Isaac Asimov* novel does not mean that your diluted theories are true," he spat. "And *you* just got shot with a tranquillizer gun, it's not like any of us were actually hurt," he added flippantly.

Nikka looked up at him in surprise, feeling more wounded by his words than the dart.

"Are you saying it's no big deal that they kept Quinn medicated against his will? That they tranquillized me? That they experimented on him? That the school nurse is a geneticist who keeps her true identity secret? That they keep secret files and medical documents about God knows what? We didn't *imagine* any of that, Izaya," said Nikka calmly.

Izaya rose from the log, walked over to Nikka, and sat down directly next to her thereby forcing Quinn to move over, which he didn't seem happy about.

"This is insane," he said again to Nikka in a tone of half pity, half plea. "Let's stop these games and just go back," he continued, this time in a more commanding tone. Izaya reached out towards her and Nikka recoiled, like a threatened snake. Behind him she noticed Quinn's hands ball up into a fists.

"Don't touch me," she said.

"Fine," said Izaya venomously through clenched teeth. "Then you guys can play out this little thriller fantasy you have constructed in your heads on your own. *I'm over it*. I'm not fifteen," he said coldly and he got up and went over to the edge of the small clearing to light a cigarette. Sums cleared his throat awkwardly.

"Just suppose it is true," he started carefully. "Then what are all the other students at the Academy for?" He asked and threw a delicate look at Stella who still had her face buried in his shoulder.

"The umm...*less talented*," he added, as nicely as he could.

"I'm not sure," said Nikka feeling drained. She looked at Izaya's tense back.

"A cover-up? Extra funding?" she suggested uncertainly, the pain in her head was affecting her ability to think.

"You're tired, and hurt, you need rest," Izaya pressed on from the edge of the clearing. Nikka moved and felt a pain run through her body, she grunted.

"I thought you said it was no big deal, just a tranquillizer dart; that none of us were actually hurt," Quinn reminded him bitterly. Izaya came back and kneeled next to Nikka, this time he looked concerned.

"Alright, I'm sorry about that part," he said softly. He pulled something shiny out of his blazer pocket - a flask.

"This could help with the pain," he said gingerly, and he gave her a weak, apologetic smile. Nikka caved and smiled back; it was just like Izaya to take a flask with him on the run.

"I forgive you," she said quietly.

His green eyes were cat-like under the silver gleam of the moon. He brushed a hand through his jet-black hair and looked away from her, seeming newly disturbed. Nikka took the flask and knocked back a small swig. The liquid was felt hot and peaty in her throat. Quinn observed them both with revulsion.

"Nikka, are you really that naive?" he said darkly. Nikka looked away from Izaya and raised a brow. For a moment Quinn hesitated, second-guessing himself.

"What do you think they do with the talent once they take it?" his voice was slow and calculating. "Why do you think Izaya was on the list of procedures, scheduled a week after you?" he said. Nikka heard Sums gasp in comprehension. Nikka looked back at Quinn blankly, then at Sums. The thought had never crossed her mind. Izaya was on the list too, and, just like Stella he didn't have anything they would have wanted to steal, not that she knew of anyway.

"Maybe they wanted something else from him," she said meekly. Quinn laughed.

"He was going to steal your talent, and then you were going to be discarded like a used toy. The way Amber was," Quinn barked. Sums winced at the mention of Amber's name. "All so that *he* could feel what it's like to be *special*." Quinn pointed an accusing finger in Izaya's direction.

Izaya got up and clenched his fists. Quinn got up too and although Izaya towered over him a good few inches, Quinn looked up at him with a menacing expression. Nikka gazed up at them, still blindsided by Quinn's words.

"What are you trying to say?" Izaya growled.

"I thought it was quite obvious, *mate,*" Quinn spat vindictively."*You* are the bad guy here. The talent is sold to the other students, the *rich* students. And you're the one on a shopping spree."

Stella gave another loud sob and Nikka noticed that she was no longer burrowed in Sums' sweater.

"I can't believe they were going to steal my design skills," she wailed in between sobs. For a moment everyone just looked at her, confused. Then Izaya turned his attention back to Quinn.

"Take that back," Izaya demanded.

"If I take it back, doesn't make it untrue," Quinn countered.

"At least I'm not the one who actually ended up stealing a talent," spat Izaya.

For a moment Quinn lost his wits and he looked disoriented, as if Izaya had just told him the sky was green.

"We don't know that, maybe they were trying to take

something from me," Quinn stuttered sounding unsure. Nikka knew Quinn was hoping that the real Tristan had some talent worth taking; otherwise it would mean all the experiments Wildwood did on him were about him receiving one.

"Oh yeah, tell that to your new sketchbook," said Izaya cruelly; no detail ever escaped him. Quinn launched himself in Izaya's direction and punched him square in the jaw. Izaya was momentarily thrown back, but he quickly regained his composure and swung. Quinn tried to move out of the way and the blow hit him in the shoulder. The two boys fell to the ground and began to tussle amidst the dry crackling leaves. Nikka's head was foggy; she couldn't think clearly, she was hungry and there was a ringing in her ears.

"STOP," she screamed, so loudly that she momentarily interrupted the boys' fight.

"Sums and I are the ones who were invited to this school," she yelled hysterically, "*Just* so that we could be stolen from. I am the one who has been lied to and betrayed," she looked at both Izaya and Quinn accusingly, "and I am the one who has just been shot with a freaking tranquillizer dart! I haven't eaten, or slept, none of us have, and the best you can do at this moment is fight each other?" she felt thick tears swelling up in the corners of her eyes, turning her vision blurry. All she wanted was to get out of there. *But where was there?* They were deep inside the redwood forest, lost. There was a long silence; even the forest seemed quieter in the wake of Nikka's hysterical screaming.

"What do you mean, *you and Sums*?" said Stella quietly. She had detached her face from Sums' shirt and stared at Nikka. Nikka couldn't even muster a white lie to comfort her friend. She turned away from them all and stared into the wild, unforgiving wood.

×

Half an hour passed in near silence. Sums was busily typing on his small computer, one headphone hanging limply from his ear. Stella, who looked both bored and terrified at the same time, if one could be both, was frantically chipping away at the remainder of the magenta nail polish on her fingernails. Quinn was sketching and Izaya was smoking by the edge of the clearing.

"We are going to have to make a plan... When you feel better, Nikka," said Sums tiredly. She looked up at her friend; there were tiny purple bags under his eyes. She reached into her backpack, pulled out a chocolate bar and handed it to him. Sums smiled widely in return. Nikka knew he was right, they had to get out of this mess somehow; they had to make a plan. She angled herself so that she could face everyone.

"Any idea what we should do?" she asked lightly.

"Well," began Sums as he pulled out a smartphone from his pocket,

"I took the liberty of hacking into the Dean's phone and I have been listening in on him. I now know what he's been up to, I also know that they are very, very unhappy that we are gone, and it is crucial for them to get us back. They will use whatever means necessary to detain us. I guess that was obvious when Nurse Smith shot you," he said and looked at Nikka.

"I think if we turn ourselves in at this point we might get stuck with something worse than detention," he added. Stella shuddered.

"One more thing," Sums paused for dramatic effect. "The Dean has been making a lot of phone calls..." the gang looked up at Sums, suddenly interested.

Sums tapped a few buttons on his computer and the Dean's voice echoed loudly through the speakers. The sound sent shivers down Nikka's spine.

"We don't need your men working on this problem, they've got nowhere to run, Sir," said the Dean.

"If they've got nowhere to run," answered a deep, unpleasant voice,

"Then where are they, *Steven*?" There was a long pause.

Nikka had never heard anyone refer to the Dean by his first name.

"In the woods, Sir," answered the Dean forcibly.

"Considering you've got about 700,000 acres of wood around you, my worries are not alleviated. I'm sending you a search squad."

The Dean sounded displeased. "We will find them," he repeated icily.

"You'd better," warned the man. "I don't have to remind you, there's room enough in the electric chair for both of us," and with that the receiver was thrown down and the line went dead.

"Who is important enough for the Dean to refer to as 'Sir'?" asked Stella sleepily.

"The Governor of California," answered Sums. Izaya snickered at what he perceived to be a joke, but Nikka felt like she had just jumped headfirst into a pool of ice water. She searched Sums' face and her stomach clenched as she confirmed that he was serious. She had only seen the Governor a few times on television, and there was nothing frightening about the short stubby man. He was your usual politician- sly, overweight and a convincing liar. But it wasn't him Nikka feared; what Nikka feared now, was the magnitude of the Dean's connections, the extent of his reach. *What school principal has access to politicians, search squads and... tranquillizers?* She wondered silently.

Quinn spoke as if reading her mind. "The Dean seems to have friends in high places, we're going to need someone quite important to help us," he said thoughtfully, the group nodded in response.

"My mom goes to synagogue with Spielberg's wife,"

Stella offered looking hopeful.

“That’s very useful," Quinn rolled his eyes. “If we want our story converted into a PG thirteen blockbuster.”

“I’m just throwing ideas out there," squealed Stella. She defensively pouted her upper lip and looked like she was about to cry for the 30th time that day.

Izaya cleared his throat. "I’ve known the Los Angeles Chief of Police since I was a kid. He’s a friend of my uncle’s," he admitted unenthusiastically.

“So now you admit we need help?” said Quinn.

“I’m pretty sure *you* need professional help,” said Izaya sarcastically.

"That’s a start," said Sums decisively, "my phone will die in 16 hours so our only chance is to get some sleep, get on our way and then we can..." he shot a nervous look in Izaya’s direction. “Talk to the Chief of Police and hope for the best.”

“Mate, how are we going to get out of these woods?" asked Quinn. His blue eyes wandered across the dense darkness of the ostensibly endless forest that surrounded them.

"That’s what a compass is for, buddy," Sums answered teasingly. He pulled out two phones from his bag and smiled, exposing his small round teeth. Nikka stared at Sums in admiration; his ability to rationalize his way through every situation never ceased to astound her.

"Sounds like a plan," she said, trying to sound

confident.

She glanced around at her mismatched group of friends. Stella looked like a frightened mess, Sums still looked hungry, they were all exhausted, and she couldn't help but feel that this was all her fault. *I brought them here.*

"Are you sure we should sleep here?" asked Stella hesitantly, "Maybe we should go back..."

"No!" Quinn cut her off aggressively, "we are not going back there."

Stella did not look convinced, but Quinn's glacial tone made her turn away and bury her head in her jacket.

Quinn went to fetch more dry wood, and with Izaya's reluctant help they built a fire. Slowly, everyone positioned themselves comfortably around it. Sums was first to fall asleep; he snored loudly, curled up in a fetal position. Stella fell asleep soon after, her head still buried in her jacket. Quinn sat silently and stared at the dancing flames; he shot hesitant looks in Nikka's direction now and then, attempting to fight off sleep, but in the end he failed and his head rested heavily on his shoulder as he dozed off. Nikka's eyes caught Izaya's over the fire, he was still wide-awake and his bright green eyes were fixed intently on her.

"Can we take a walk?" he whispered, quietly enough so that no one would wake.

Nikka shook her head. "No."

"Please?"

Izaya's looked earnest and desperate, for the second time that day Nikka caved in to him, despite knowing better. Without waiting for her to answer Izaya walked over, took her hand, and pulled her up. They strolled in silence through the trees, their unknown path lit by silvery moonlight. When they hit a big clearing a minute or so away they stopped and the pair of them sat down on a patch of grass. Nikka could still see the fire in the distance, which was comforting; this was not a good time to get lost. Izaya was staring at her and she found it difficult to meet his gaze.

"Is it true..." Nikka whispered, she didn't know how to phrase it without it sounding obscene. "Were you really going to *steal* from me?"

Steal my talent, my ability, my life. Nikka had been sketching since she was old enough to hold a crayon, and the thought that this could be taken away from her, the way it had from Amber or Alexis, that the only thing in her unstable life that she had any control of could be ripped away and sold off... The notion drove her mad. Izaya watched the anger flare in her and took his time. He moved closer on the ground beside her, and flinched when she inched away.

"I didn't know anything about this. I promise."

Nikka was silent, she felt like she didn't know anything anymore. She didn't know who Quinn was, didn't know who Izaya was, all she knew now was that this feeling of murkiness, of not being able to tell up from down, was the feeling of betrayal.

"Nikka," he pleaded. "This is crazy. Do you even realize what you are accusing me of?" he reasoned.

She turned away from him, and tucked her knees under her arms.

She felt Izaya breathe deeply beside her. Izaya moved closer again and Nikka could feel the few inches between them shrinking and tensing as if they were made of something tangible.

"I swear, I knew nothing about this," he whispered close to her ear. He closed the final inches between them and Nikka felt feverish. She struggled between wanting to hold him and hit him. She desperately wanted to believe him, but couldn't bring herself to do that, either. The only reason they had met was because Izaya was meant to steal from her, *to steal a part of her.* Nikka reminded herself of what she was accusing him of - something otherworldly, something no one sane would ever believe. Lost in a brew of thoughts, she barely noticed Izaya's face nearing until his lips had found hers. She wanted to withdraw, to slap him indignantly, but she let him kiss her instead. She parted her lips and let the kiss, the softness of it, sink into the places inside of her that had been left hollow from exhaustion, fear and the anxiety of the past few days. This kiss was different to the one he had greedily planted on her after the townie party, or the passionate, rough one he had stolen from her after Halloween. It wasn't hungry, it wasn't forced, or part of a game, instead it was soft and apologetic. At the precise moment when their repressed longing started to creep its way into the kiss and turn it more desperate, Izaya broke it off, as if he wanted to keep its purity intact. He stroked her cheek; his long fingers framed the side of her face as he looked at her sadly from under his long black lashes.

"I had nothing to do with this, I swear to you. If I had, then would I be running? Would I be here in the woods with you?" he pulled her onto his lap and she burrowed her face in his neck. She was too tired to analyze it, and in too much pain to resist. Izaya watched her intently as an inner battle raged on in her head, and for a while they just sat there, without saying a word; both grateful for the simplicity of the silence.

After a while, she slid down from his lap and let her head rest on his shoulder. They both stared up at the black star-filled sky, it looked like a moth-eaten blanket that had been held up against a bright light. Izaya was gentler than he had ever been before; he stroked her hair and the rhythmic sound of his breathing was almost enough to calm her. *The calm before the storm,* she thought to herself, remembering the amount of trouble they were still in. Nikka decided to ask him something she had been wondering about since the beginning of the school year.

“Why did you come to the Academy?” she asked.

“My uncle insisted,” he said bitterly.

"You seem unhappy whenever you mention your uncle..." Nikka attempted to pick her words carefully but couldn’t. "Where are your mom and dad?” she asked bluntly, too tired for tact. Izaya fidgeted in place.

"I never met my dad, and my mom had a lot of problems. She was sick. She died when I was seven.”

There was another pause and Nikka realized that Izaya was opening up to her like this, unhindered, in an attempt to show her how sorry he was. He would never allow himself to be this vulnerable in other circumstances.

“I’m really sorry. How did she die?” Nikka asked quietly.

“She killed herself,” he retorted evenly. “In an asylum.”

Izaya sounded both ashamed and defensive, and Nikka remembered how reluctant he had been to enter the *Idlewell Centre*, how disturbed he had looked.

“That’s horrible,” said Nikka lamely. She couldn’t find the right words, so she just squeezed his hand.

"My uncle took me in. He gave me everything - good schools, vacations, apartments, no expense spared,” he said dryly.

“But you don’t love him?”

“It’s not that. *He* never loved me. Never gave me any attention. I was raised by the constantly rotating staff at one of his villas, and our relationship was supposed to stay secret from the public."

"*What*?" Nikka yelped out in shock.

"His sister..." Izaya continued, digging his nails into the dirt, "*my mother,* and her death, and her whole perturbed existence, for my uncle it was bad publicity. He's a pharmaceutical tycoon; his company specializes in anti-psychotics. The last thing he wanted was for people to know that the meds didn't work on his own *family*," Izaya said the word *family* with loathing.

It was strange for Nikka to realize that Izaya, whom she had thought to be terminally spoiled, had actually lived through so much pain, so much loss. It made her think of her own mother, and her fear of losing her, which was never too far from Nikka's mind, and which seemed a fate so awful she could not even imagine surviving it.

"You've been through so much," Nikka said broken-heartedly. "For what it's worth, I believe that you had nothing to do with any of this," she added charitably.

"Thank you."

"Should we go? Maybe get some sleep," she offered softly. Nikka didn't want to push him further; Izaya had already given her a glimpse into his soul, more than she could have hoped for. Izaya rose and pulled her up effortlessly from the ground. They took a few steps back towards the campfire.

"Nikka?"

"Yes."

"I haven't told you everything," he said, gravely. Nikka felt like a stone was sinking through her stomach. Izaya continued.

"I don't think my uncle would have much use for a secret nephew who was good at art, in fact, he doesn't care about art at all."

Nikka looked on blankly.

"I thought about this at Mrs. Smith's house when you mentioned the memory tests they've been doing on you, and I'd noticed something about you even before that..." his voice trailed off.

"It reminded me about research my uncle has been doing for the past few years, to do with finding a treatment for dementia. He's been looking for test subjects with advanced memory capabilities, and trying to develop medication to suppress Alzheimer's and other illnesses. I realized that you have an eidetic memory because I've heard so much about it; it's a photographic memory that allows you to recall things you have seen, down to the smallest detail, even years down the line," he explained. Nikka nodded numbly; she had always had this uncanny ability to recall things she had seen a long time ago, but she didn't see the correlation.

"I think he was going to take *that* from you, and use it to create a formula," he said, matter-of-factly, "new treatments, maybe new cures."

Nikka cut him off, *"steal it,"* she corrected.

Izaya nodded, without meeting her eyes. "And because he had kept our family ties secret, and because some of my mothers *problems,"* Izaya stuttered, "were hereditary, I would be the best man for the job; the perfect lab rat for the first transplant," he concluded quietly.

"That's not possible," said Nikka abruptly, more for Izaya's benefit than for her own.

"You wouldn't say that if you had met him," answered Izaya. Nikka didn't say anything.

As they walked back to the campfire in depressed silence, Nikka concluded that she would never see Izaya the same way again, and that it was a repeat occurrence during her time at Wildwood that one short walk in the woods could change everything.

×

Nikka woke up the following morning stiff and wet with morning dew. She rolled over on the ground and felt her joints ache. She had slept next to Stella on a bed of twigs; her jacket was laid out beneath them whilst Stella's served as their blanket. Izaya, Quinn and Sums had all offered to relinquish their jackets to the girls, but Nikka insisted that everyone cover themselves with whatever they had; it was way too cold in the woods for gallantry. She was the first to wake and the forest was full of early morning activity; birds chirped, squirrels scavenged through the trees, and shuffling sounds erupted from all corners, like a morning symphony. It was similar to a city roaring to life at six in the morning, and it reminded Nikka of when she lived in Chicago with her mother; if you got up early enough, you could watch the city wake up with you.

She brushed the cold droplets from the jacket and tucked it tightly around Stella, who was still sound asleep. Pale rays of sunlight shone through the dense wood, giving everything around her an ethereal white morning glow. Izaya and Quinn were still asleep, forced to share a clear space a few meters away. In the coldness of night the two boys must have drifted closer to each other because they were nearly spooning. Nikka stifled a chuckle. Quietly she rose, taking care not to wake anyone. She stretched and felt her shoulder throb.

Sums was curled up in a ball like a large cat, and shivering. His jacket lay a few feet away from him; he must have shed it during the night. Nikka walked over, picked up the thick jacket and tucked it around him, or as much of him as it would cover. He opened his eyes sluggishly and upon seeing her hovering over him, gave her a sleepy smile. Then they heard a faint beeping sound nearby, Sums sat up and wiped the sleep from his eyes.

"It's my computer, I set it to record all of the Dean's conversations," he said in answer to Nikka's anxious expression. He pointed at the rucksack from where the muffled sound was coming. Nikka grabbed the bag and threw it to him.

"There's activity at the Dean's office," said Sums through a long drawn-out yawn. "He's up early." Sums hit a few buttons on his computer-

"I wonder who is causing him so much grievance," he added shooting Nikka a playful wink. Nikka chuckled, but inwardly she was terrified.

"Play it," she whispered impatiently. Sums pressed another button and turned the computer towards her. The main screen displayed an array of sound waves, which began to pulsate as the Dean's voice played through the loudspeaker.

"Where are you?" he said coolly; he did not sound tired, he sounded sharp and murderous.

A man's brute voice growled in response, causing Nikka to shudder,

"A local reported seeing smoke in the woods last night, thought it was a forest fire. I'm betting our little friends set up a camp to keep themselves warm, we are closing in on the location in ten boss," the man panted heavily into his receiver. Nikka realized the man was running. *Running...campfire...closing in....in ten boss...* She looked at Sums' panicked expression and could tell he was piecing it together too. They both stared at the now extinguished campfire, which still smelled of smoke. Then the Dean said something that catapulted them both back to reality.

"I need the *girl* alive and the boy, Izaya. I don't care about the rest, but don't get carried away," whoever was on the other line grunted in agreement, he was still panting. *Still running...* Sums threw the computer on the floor as if it were poisonous.

"What does he mean 'I don't care about the rest. Bring the girl alive. Don't get carried away?" Sums wailed, looking petrified.

"We need to get going," said Nikka quietly, trying to control the panic rising up inside her like vomit. *They are minutes away....* In seconds she was over by Izaya and Quinn, shaking each one of them violently, and both woke with a start.

"What's wrong, Nikka?" mumbled Quinn, half-asleep.

"They're coming," was all she said in return. Both boys were up and packed within moments. Nikka looked over at Sums who still sat there, shell-shocked and immobile. Quinn woke Stella and Izaya was frantically packing the rest of their things, shoving them into bags left and right. Sums looked up at her, his eyes round and dazed.

"Do you really think they would..." he gulped, " *kill us?*" Nikka could see that Sums' resolve was starting to melt away. She grabbed him by the shoulders.

"Do you want to stay here and find out?" she said impatiently. It took a few seconds for Sums to shake his head in return. Sums gathered his things and then turned to them.

"I've thought about it; we are an easier target if we run all together, and a slower one. We have to split up. I've put in a meet-up location into the GPS on my second phone; it's an IHOW by the freeway at the border to the woods. We'll go in opposite directions and meet there," he said sounding sure. Nikka was about to protest, but Sums was already walking up to the boys and explaining his plan to them. Stella looked horrified and Nikka tried to meet her eye, to let her know everything would be okay, but Stella was looking away and seemed too wrapped up in her own frightened thoughts. Nikka could not bear the idea of the group splitting up, but she knew Sums was right, and they would be faster, harder to find, if they split up.

"I will go with Stella and Izaya, you and Quinn head the opposite way. It will be safer for everyone, that way one of the *people they need* is in each group," Sums said hurriedly. He threw Quinn his other phone with the final location in it. Izaya looked unhappy about the idea, but he said nothing. Nikka's eyes met Izaya's and she felt a dread that was unlike anything she had ever felt before.

"Nikka, we have to go. Be safe," Sums urged and gave her shoulder a squeeze before leading Stella out of the clearing and into the woods. Stella did not turn around or wave goodbye. Izaya quickly walked up to Nikka and right in front of Quinn, kissed her, briefly. It was quick, a whisper of a kiss. He turned, "keep her safe," he hissed to a stunned Quinn. Then he turned around and disappeared in between the trees in pursuit of Stella and Sums. Nikka heard them break into a run. Quinn was standing next to her, tense. He looked like he wanted to say something to her, but thought better of it. He grabbed her hand rather roughly and they broke out into a run in the opposite direction. Just then they heard the fast approaching sound of a helicopter echo above them.

Nikka couldn't see or hear anything, except for her own breathing, and the dancing light reflected off the propeller above them, which created streaky shadows against the backdrop of the redwood forest. She heard Quinn panting beside her as they sprinted through the woods. Nikka found herself thinking that Quinn ran like someone who had been chased many times before. He darted expertly through the wilderness, dodging branches, and jumping over logs. Nikka caught more shadows in her peripheral vision; thick black shadows on the ground, and realized that these were not the shadows from the propeller; they were now being followed on foot. Just as she let herself wonder what was happening with the others, the helicopter above them backtracked and headed in the opposite direction. With the helicopter gone, Nikka could now hear her and Quinn's light footsteps cracking against the dry leaves below them; behind them she heard footsteps that seemed to crash harder against the ground. Her arm was throbbing and her knees were growing weak from sprinting, but she pushed herself on. She gave Quinn's hand a reassuring squeeze and he began to run even faster. Just as Nikka thought she heard the footsteps behind them slow down, someone grabbed her arm hard. She squealed in pain and felt herself tumbling. Quinn's hand slipped out of hers and she was face down in the cracked dirt. She tried to regain her footing, but someone hit her, and the pain from the blow momentarily blinded her. Suddenly, she felt a heavy mass crashing onto her; then her arms were being pinned to the ground. She looked up through the caked dirt in her eyes and saw a figure on top of her, wearing a ski mask. She tried to fight him off, but his whole weight was on her, rendering her arms useless. She screamed and the shrill sound seemed to resonate through the entire forest like the sound of a firework when it first soars. The figure slapped her in the face to silence her and Nikka could taste blood in her mouth as he tried to turn her around. She thrashed, ignoring the pain in her face and arm. Just as the man was about to cuff Nikka, Quinn came out from behind him and hit him on the back of the head with the Taser. The man collapsed sideways with a big thump. Nikka pushed the man off of her and looked around them, there didn't seem to be any more guards within view, but she could hear the distant voices and footsteps growing closer. Quinn lifted her from the ground and led her in the opposite direction, still clutching the Taser in his hand.

20
International House of Lies

Hours later, an exhausted Nikka and Quinn finally arrived at the border of the dense wood and emerged near a freeway. The two wanderers stood there, panting and clutching their aching sides. Nikka observed the small stretch of desert that separated them from the freeway and searched for the agreed upon meeting spot. A diner. Behind the freeway there was more wasteland, which, to the naked eye, seemed to stretch on forever. They walked towards it under the smoldering sun. Nikka watched as waves of heat rose from the concrete and made the freeway look as if it were evaporating. Cars and massive eight-wheeler trucks whizzed by, leaving trails of dust dancing in their wake. Their meeting point, *the International House of Waffles,* stood about half a mile away, isolated like an oasis. Aside from an old gas station right next to it, the diner was the only thing in sight. Both buildings were rusty, and the exterior layers of paint had burned out and faded from vivid colors to dirty pastel shades. The pair of buildings looked like deteriorating carcasses of their former selves, rotting in the desert sun.

Nikka pointed at it and Quinn, seeming relieved, took hold of her hand. The two of them walked on in silence. They were still petrified by what had happened in the woods, but neither had a desire to talk about it, neither wanted to make it feel more real. They approached the freeway and walked alongside it. Truckers and family cars sped by and each one gave the two teenagers walking through the desert holding hands a quick, curious glance. Nikka was suddenly worried that they were being unnecessarily obvious, but between the expansive desert-like land and the woods they had just gladly left behind, there was no place for them to hide. A car whizzed by behind her; the sound startled Nikka and she instantly searched the sky for signs of a helicopter. Embarrassed, she looked over to Quinn, whose hand had reflexively shot to the Taser in his back pocket. When they caught sight of each other, paranoid and sweaty, the pair broke out in uncontrollable laughter - every inch of the frustration and fear from the recent days was expelled through that one hysterical, gut-wrenching laugh. It felt immensely freeing to laugh like that. The situation was so unreal, so incredibly frightening, and so utterly absurd that there were only two things left to do, laugh or cry. Quinn put his arm around her reassuringly and they continued to walk and chuckle.

“Why didn’t you just taze the guy?” asked Nikka.

“I thought it might hurt you,” he answered. Quinn looked back at the wood.

"I wish someone had warned me that attending school was more of a threat to my future than skipping class," he joked and Nikka grinned.

“Did you skip class a lot back in Ireland?" she asked.

"I would have attended more if *you* went to my school." Quinn grinned back at her. Nikka grimaced, as if to say *how cheesy*.

“Besides, my school wasn’t as strict as Wildwood - tranquillizer guns and Tasers were only used on the upper classmen,” he added playfully. Nikka felt a chill go up her spine, despite the desert heat.

“What is it like back home, where you’re from?” she asked, desperate to change the subject from Wildwood and tranquillizers.

“It’s all fields and cows, luv,” he answered coyly. “Nothing too exciting ever happens there. Safe and boring.”

“That sounds lovely,” she said dreamily. “I would give anything for some peaceful, unexciting times.”

"When we get out of this mess…” said Quinn, his voice suddenly vulnerable, “I could show you my hometown.”

Nikka blushed; she had never been invited to a boy's house, much less to his home country.

"I would love that," she answered and Quinn looked hopeful as they pushed open the door to the cool, air-conditioned IHOW.

A plump, bored-looking waitress stood behind a small hostess stand in the diners' foyer and smiled at them widely.

"Welcome to the International House of Waffles!" she squealed in a hyped energetic voice. "Where the service is sweet and the waffles are sweeter! A table for two?"

The woman looked them up and down and Nikka could tell that their battered appearance was starting to intrigue her. The waitress looked past them curiously and into the parking lot to see what type of car the two bizarre visitors had arrived in. Quinn quickly piped up,

"Umm, we are actually meeting some friends here, so a table for five... *Jennifer,*" he cooed as he read the name off of her nametag and gave her a dazzling wink. Nikka noticed that Quinn's accent was thicker when he needed it, for instance when he needed to make a girl's simple name sound more exotic.

The waitress gave what she must have thought was a very sexy titter.

"You talk funny," she said bluntly and flashed him a bright smile, which revealed a large rhinestone embedded on one of her canines. She fetched five colorful plastic menus and gestured for them to follow her to one of the diner booths. The IHOW was your typical, dusty roadside joint, with a run-down jukebox in the back, aluminum counters, and replica pictures of pin-ups collecting dust on the walls.

Nikka and Quinn squeezed into the cracked red leather seats on opposite sides of the booth. Until that very moment Nikka hadn't had time to think about what they were supposed to do if they made it to their meet-up point first, or how they were going to get from the IHOW to Los Angeles, or how incredibly hungry she was. She inhaled the sweet intoxicating smell of bacon, coffee and waffles, and felt her mouth salivate in response. From one look at Quinn's pained expression she knew he felt the same. She wondered if he had any money on him and if it would be horrible for her and Quinn to eat something before the others arrived. *What if they don't come?* She wondered with a panic. These and other worrisome thoughts circulated in her head, and she tried to distract herself with the Photoshopped images of food on her laminated menu. She was interrupted by the loud creak of the swinging door. Nikka turned around, and her heart lifted when she saw Izaya walk through the door, followed by Sums. She searched behind them for Stella, but she wasn't there. Sums' eyes were red from crying. He was sunburned and soaked through with sweat. Izaya looked a little better, but still disheveled. Sums squeezed wordlessly into the booth beside her and put his head on her shoulder.

"They got her," he mumbled and began to cry softly into Nikka's shirt.

"Oh, would you stop being such a drama queen!" Izaya grunted while he squeezed himself into the seat next to Quinn. "He's been crying for two hours now," he added irritably.

"What the hell happened, where is Stella?" asked Nikka her voice shook a little. Horrified, she looked from one boy to the other; both refused to meet her eyes. She bit her lip to keep from crying.

"Tell me what happened," she repeated this time louder and more hysterically.

"Wildwood has her," said Sums.

The few customers that were in the diner were beginning to turn and look over to their table. Nikka could no longer hold back the tears and they began to spill down her cheeks freely. Izaya didn't look at her.

"They went after you first," he said calmly, "that gave us the advantage, we were getting away for a while, but when they got close, Stella just up and ran in the opposite direction. I ran after her, but she was already disappearing into the distance and running straight at *them*, there was nothing I could do, Nikka." Izaya pretended to focus on his menu to avoid watching Nikka cry. "It's her own fault," he added defensively.

"You don't know that!" Sums squealed, "Maybe she got disoriented."

"It does sound like she wanted to get caught," seconded Quinn, but when he caught a sight of Nikka, he backtracked. "Calm down, Nikka, she's not one of their experiments; they aren't going to do anything to her. Except maybe expel her," he added in his best attempt to sound comforting.

"She ran towards them, *this* is what she wanted," Izaya reiterated, his eyes trained on his menu. Nikka felt her heart slow down a little and her hands relax. A short silence befell the table.

"I really hope you're both right," she whispered after a few moments. There was nothing else she could say. Maybe Stella didn't feel safe with them, maybe she wanted to return and they just hadn't listened, hadn't tried to help. Exasperated, she was trying hard to not think of Stella's desolate face back in the woods; every inch of her upbeat nature gone, swallowed up by fear. She was also trying not to think about the Dean's words, *don't get carried away*. Nikka gulped down the remainder of her guilt and it lingered in her stomach.

"If she does get expelled, it's for the best," added Nikka.

"We should be worrying about ourselves, Nik," said Quinn, "if they caught us they would put me in jail, arrest you guys for assault, and possibly still carry out that procedure on you." Across the table Nikka felt Izaya tense. Everyone knew there was no reason for him to be there either; he, like Stella, would not risk much if he were to go back, except maybe charges for hitting Nurse Smith on the head.

"I wouldn't go back. I don't want to be a part of what they are doing," said Izaya sternly, and Nikka gave him a weak, grateful smile.

"We will report everything to the Chief of Police and take it from there," he added confidently. His eyes fixated on Nikka, "*Stella will be fine*," he said decisively, in a way that both comforted Nikka and signaled that the conversation was over. There was a subsequent contemplative silence; Nikka suspected that everyone at the table was wondering the same thing - what *would* happen to them if they were to go back? What was at stake? What crimes could Wildwood pin on them? It was like playing a game of poker without knowing how much you were betting; not knowing whether you would walk away a few hundred dollars poorer, or whether the casino staff would break your legs in the parking lot. They still didn't know *how* dangerous Wildwood could be, and how deep down the rabbit hole they had already fallen.

The waitress interrupted their cumulative reflection-

"Y'all ready to order now?" she cooed. Her whole attention was now fixed on green-eyed, broad-shouldered Izaya, whom she had just noticed.

"One of each," he said lazily without looking at her and flicked the menu to the side of the table, the others handed their menus in, following Izaya's lead. Sums seemed to perk up at the prospect of food; with his paper napkin he wiped the tears, sweat and dirt off of his face. Nikka heard him whisper, *she will be all right,* while he cleaned himself up.

The waitress emerged minutes later with a series of white plates packed with mounds of crispy bacon, stacks of waffles drenched in puddles of maple syrup, hash browns, sausages, eggs sunny side up, scrambled, poached, and Eggs Benedict, two baskets of toast and pastries, five tall glasses of orange juice, and a large glass pitcher of coffee. The boys and Nikka stared at the food for a few polite seconds before eagerly digging in. Nikka was hungry beyond any etiquette; she crunched bacon loudly and dug into mouthfuls of waffles, gulping them down greedily with the cold orange juice. The others were just as giddy; the table was silent except for the loud noises of slurping and chewing. Nikka noticed a pair of truckers walk by them and sit a few booths down. The chewing and the silence went on until the plates were scrubbed clean. The four of them reclined back into the red leather, visibly full and satisfied. The small monitor in Sums' front pocket began to beep.

"I'm betting that has something to do with us," he said without reaching for it.

"We have to keep moving, " said Quinn urgently, the satisfaction from the meal was already melting from his face.

"I'll be right back," Izaya mumbled as he slid out of the booth and headed for the back of the IHOW. The euphoria that Nikka had felt from the food was also starting to subside; fear and guilt crept into its place.

"You can't blame yourself," said Quinn. He reached across the table and clasped her hand.

"I'm the one who started *this*, it's my fault we are here," he added quietly. Nikka turned her palm over so that his hand was lying on top of hers and looked at him.

"If it wasn't for you," she thought back to the woods, to Quinn hitting the guard over the head, she thought about what might have happened to her had she stayed at the Academy- being suddenly unable to draw - or unable to remember things; if Izaya's theory was correct - would have left her feeling... dead. *Discarded,* like a farm cow being sent to the slaughterhouse once she could no longer give milk.

"I wouldn't have survived it," she finished darkly. She heard the drama in her voice, but she meant every word of it. She stroked his scarred knuckles and looked into his dark blue eyes, trying to show him that, despite the circumstances, she was very happy to be exactly where she was, it was far better than what she presumed to be the alternative. Nikka put her hand on Sums' shoulder.

"I have you to thank, too, you and your brilliant mind," said Nikka and she gave his shoulder a squeeze.

"Without you we wouldn't have even gotten out of those woods, mate," said Quinn before chugging the remainder of his sweetened black coffee. Sums gave a nervous chuckle.

"It's really nothing," he said.

"I'm sorry to interrupt this sentimental moment," said Izaya from behind them. He rolled his eyes when he noticed Nikka's hand glued to Quinn's.

"But while you were busy exchanging praise, I was busy solving *our* problems," he shot them a winning smile as he plumped a pile of clothes on the side of the table. Nikka picked a shirt out of the pile and stretched it out in front of her. *"I heart the Jacinto Mountains,"* was inscribed on the shirt in front of a picture of the redwood forest.

"It's a bit obvious," said Izaya pointing at the insignia on the shirt, "but still less obvious than bloodied school uniforms."

"You're right," agreed Sums pulling a matching navy blue extra large T-shirt out of the pile. "We can wear them inside out, " he suggested. Izaya picked a shirt from the pile and threw it at Quinn.

"Got you one too, *mate*," he said looking smug, "no need to thank me." Quinn pursed his lips and rather unwillingly stretched the t-shirt out in front of him. He looked up at Izaya.

"It's an IHOW staff shirt," he said through gritted his teeth.

"That one cost me extra," said Izaya and he smiled condescendingly, "I thought it would be more believable on you."

Nikka saw Quinn clench his fists, and she didn't blame him, but now was not the time to attract even more attention than they already had. She shot Izaya a disapproving look.

"I'll trade with you," she said softly, and she handed her shirt to Quinn. "Purple is more my color anyway," she added.

Quinn gladly swapped T-shirts with her and threw Izaya a superior look in the process. Izaya frowned, irritated that his jab had backfired and landed on Nikka instead.

"It's all they had in the 'gift shop,'" he mumbled.

Sums was intently staring at Izaya, watching his every move, the way you watch a fly that you're trying to catch.

"Please tell me you used cash," he said, his voice grave. Izaya shrugged his shoulders.

"Yeah, of course I used cash."

Sums let out a sigh of relief.

"But *obviously* I used my card for the ATM. We can't be fugitives without a cent in our pockets," said Izaya lazily. He followed this statement with an arrogant smile.

"Well, I hope you took *a lot*," said Sums his voice small.

"Why?" asked Izaya, his nonchalant demeanor was dissolving, and was quickly replaced by confusion.

"Because ATMs are traceable," said Nikka as she caught on.

"There is nowhere to run in the desert, if they are tracing your cards they will find us in minutes," she said and her eyes shot towards the front door.

"For future reference, fugitives don't use ATMs!" said Quinn, visibly pleased with Izaya's mistake. Izaya glowered at him, while Sums was beginning to hyperventilate in the corner of the booth. He whispered a series of numbers under his breath. Nikka looked at him questioningly.

"I'm trying to calculate how long it will take them to trace the card and then get here, assuming they are still in the woods," he explained.

"Good job, trust fund baby, you blew our cover over a couple of shirts," said Quinn viciously.

"Not just a few shirts," Izaya responded calmly. He got up, pulled two twenties out of his front pocket and flung them on the table amidst the empty plates.

"I also scored us a ride," he said and flashed them a big white smile, "he is waiting for us outside."

×

The ride to Los Angeles was bumpy and hot, but there was

an overwhelming sense of relief amongst the group that made the minor discomfort seem irrelevant. *We got away,* thought Nikka to herself. *For now...* Izaya paid 100 dollars to a beer-bellied truck driver named Bill to transport them for the two and a half hours that it took to get to the greater Los Angeles area. Izaya, Nikka and Quinn sat in the front of the large sixteen-wheeler Coca-Cola truck while Sums lounged behind them in the truck driver's sleeping quarters. For the majority of the ride they stayed silent; there wasn't much either of them could say to each other that they would want truck driver Bill to overhear. The 40-something year old man seemed more than happy with his hundred-dollar bonus and the silence. He didn't ask any questions; instead, he blasted a scratched disk of Lynyrd Skynyrd and only stopped singing to gulp down a can of Coke. Sums had his headphones on and was concentrating on the smaller of his two computers whilst charging it from the truck's dashboard. Nikka locked eyes with him and Sums mouthed the words "*still searching the woods*" and nodded in the direction of his computer. Nikka was relieved to have Sums listening in on the Dean's office; knowing the school's every move was priceless.

"Stella?" she mouthed.

Sums shook his head and Nikka squirmed in her seat. She was squeezed in between Izaya and Quinn, which made her feel restricted. She couldn't move her hands or legs without rubbing up against one of the boys so she sat impossibly still, only rotating her head every now and then to look at Sums. She stared out at the window at the desert and watched the mounds of sand and dry bush disappear. For a second time, she was deeply grateful for every passing mile that took her and her friends farther from the Dean and farther away from Wildwood.

When the freeway signs began to indicate that they were mere miles away from Los Angeles, Bill informed them that his large truck was not allowed into the inner city and asked where he should drop them off. Sums discreetly slipped Nikka a note with the address of the Los Angeles Police Department. Izaya whispered into her ear, "he will help us, I'm sure of it." But just then Nikka saw a passing freeway exit sign that she recognized, *'Cliff Edge Avenue.'*

"Pull over here!" she yelped so suddenly that Bill almost turned right into a ramp.

"There's someone here I need to see."

×

The house Nikka was looking for was easy to find. It was painted olive green and tall over-grown sunflowers lined the small front garden, which was guarded by a matching green picket fence. It was by far the most creative house on Cliff Edge Avenue. Nikka had remembered seeing the address in one of the Dean's files, and of course had instantly memorized it.

"What are we doing here, Nikka?" asked Izaya, dumbfounded. He pushed a few sunflower stems aside and looked at the house as if it were the strangest building he had ever seen.

"Getting more answers," she explained and used the brass fairy-shaped doorknocker to give three loud knocks. A series of shuffling noises resounded from behind it, followed by a clinking and light approaching footsteps. The door opened to reveal Amber.

Her fiery hair was now longer than it had been the last time Nikka had seen her. Amber was wearing a raggedy white T-shirt paired with acid- wash overalls, which Nikka instantly noticed were heavily stained with paint. Amber's honey-colored eyes widened and she smiled from ear to ear before throwing herself into Nikka's arms.

"Hey, girl!" she said, her voice muffled into Nikka's shirt. She smiled past her at the boys that crowded in her doorway. Amber didn't seem at all surprised by their presence at her house, 250 miles away from Wildwood, on a Wednesday afternoon. Amber smiled warmly, as if the group were merely neighbors stopping by for a scheduled tea. She took turns giving everyone a hug, even Izaya, and she kept the longest one for Sums, which made him blush.

"I missed you, Sums!" she beamed.

"I missed you too," said Sums, trying and failing to sound casual.

"I'm so happy you guys came to visit me, my horoscope did say that it would be an eventful day!" Amber smiled and led them inside. Quinn shot Nikka a nervous look as he followed her through the door and into the house.

The decor inside the house was even more flamboyant than its exterior; the walls were covered in various eclectic wallpapers, seventies lamps gave the living room a retro vibe, and a pink Victorian couch covered in graffiti stood in the living room. Every wall in the house was adorned with Amber's artwork. Nikka recognized some of her friend's signature style - an oil canvas of a fairy garden, a meeting of two elves, aquarelles of castles floating in the sky, and a few coal sketches of alien life forms. She was instantly reminded of the admiration she had felt the very first time she had seen Amber draw.

Amber gave them a quick tour of the house, which was a stunningly decorated three bedroom. Lavish accents, expensive artworks and a massive skylight in the master bedroom made Nikka realize that Amber was one of the few Wildwood scholarship kids that did not come from a poor background. Amber led them to her large, modern kitchen, which looked out through a glass wall onto the back garden and its litter of overgrown sunflowers.

"Where are your folks?" asked Izaya.

"They have an exhibition in Norway this week," answered Amber, "but they are almost never here anyway. They travel a lot, and I join them when I can," she explained. Amber's parents were also artists, or in her words 'creators.'

"Must be nice," Izaya retorted with a forced smile. Nikka caught herself thinking that most family dynamics must be nice compared to his.

Amber nodded her head while she pulled out snacks from the cupboards. She arranged the various vegetarian and vegan choices on the large marble island in the middle of the kitchen - cranberries, kale chips, pita, hummus, goat cheese, celery and baby carrots.

"It *is* nice," she said smiling vacantly, "gives me space to make my art."

She signaled to the corner of the room where Nikka had already noticed a set of easels. Intrigued, Nikka walked over and examined the canvases. There was a plastic sheet on the floor, two easels and a huge messy array of brushes and oils by the sink. Amber had obviously turned that part of the kitchen into her workspace.

Nikka observed the artwork on the easels. Both paintings were composed of thousands of little dots and splashes of oil paint. They were colorful, vibrant, and reminiscent of Jackson Pollock. Next to them were a dozen smaller paintings that crowded a nearby desk and the floor. Nikka reached and gently caressed the thick mounds of dry, glistening oil with her fingertips. Amber's pictures didn't show anything in specific, no form or outline stood out amongst the mass of color and thousands of dots, but they were simply...

"Beautiful!" exclaimed Nikka astounded. She looked at Amber with amazement.

"Jeez, don't sound so surprised," said Amber with a giggle.

"I'm not," Nikka lied awkwardly.

"We just thought that after your accident"- Sums started to explain, but couldn't finish.

"Ever since my little accident at Wildwood," said Amber helpfully, "I haven't been able to get figures or shapes right. I don't know why, I just can't. It's like trying to do math when you haven't learned to count yet. *So,* I had to find some other way to express myself. I throw paint at the canvas in different ways, and I see what happens."

"Some accident," snorted Izaya.

Nikka shot him a furious look, but Amber didn't seem to notice. Quinn coughed nervously in the background.

"I...*ummm*... I need to go smoke a cigarette," he stuttered and bolted out the glass door that led to the garden.

"What a strange boy," said Amber. She stared at the garden with a half-smile.

"Not alright up there, if you ask me," said Izaya. He

circled an index finger around his temple as if to imply that Quinn was crazy. Nikka shot him another furious look and he gave her a wink. Nikka looked back at the easels and the artwork.

"Can I see more of it?" she asked.

×

After a lengthy tour of Amber's house and her recent artwork, the gang settled in for some much-needed relaxation. Sums was quietly sitting in a rocking chair in the living room with one headphone in his ear and his eyes closed. Quinn was sitting in an armchair in the garden and Izaya was in the middle of a conversation with Amber about European art galleries. Nikka didn't want to risk asking Sums anything within earshot of Amber; she wasn't quite sure whether it was a good idea for her to discover the truth about her "accident" just yet. So instead she slipped unnoticed out into the garden and joined Quinn.

When he noticed her, Quinn gave his second cigarette, which he must have scored off of Izaya, a few quick half-hearted puffs before discarding it, seeming disgusted. Then he sat up on the green lawn chair and moved so that Nikka could sit down next to him. His eyes were glistening with the threat of tears. Nikka opened her mouth to speak but he raised a silencing hand. He pulled out the sketchbook from his back pocket and opened it to a page that contained a drawing of a fairy.

"Notice anything familiar?" he asking melancholically.

Nikka nodded. The fairy before her was eerily similar to the ones she had seen moments ago on the walls of Amber's hallway.

"I'm a thief, Nikka. I know I am. I was practically born one, my step-dad taught me how to hotwire a car when I was 10, but not *THIS*." He nudged his head in the direction of the kitchen.

"I would never hurt someone like *this*," he said miserably. "I would never take away something this precious, this intimate-" his husky voice cracked.

"You didn't do anything, Quinn, this was forced upon you, "Nikka answered earnestly.

"Besides, did you see those new paintings in there? They are magnificent. They took her physical ability, her technique, *yes*, but her vision remains. Her *talent*...remains. There is still hope. We will figure this out, and whatever they took from her and gave to you, we will find a way to give it back," Nikka said passionately. She put every inch of persuasion she could muster into comforting him.

"Because seeing you draw fairies is very disturbing," she added lightheartedly.

Quinn smiled a little. Absentmindedly he ran his finger across the chestnut ring on her finger.

"*Ahem,*" came Sums' dry cough from behind them, "Nikka we've got a situation."

Nikka's head shot up with worry. Izaya was standing

behind Sums.

"Spit it out," urged Nikka.

"Okay, well the *thing* is... I was listening to the transmission, and Stella turned herself in." There was a pause, and Izaya gave Nikka an *"I told you so"* look.

"We already knew that," Quinn said irritably. Nikka noticed Amber standing behind Izaya, listening in, but she was too distracted to worry about what she might overhear.

"Stella told the Dean *everything*. He called your uncle," said Sums turning to look back at Izaya. "They've warned the Chief of Police to arrest us on sight for breaking and entering, as well as assault," he added. Izaya's expression turned furious.

"It seems the Dean also knows the Chief of Police, they seemed pretty friendly on the phone." Nikka felt her mouth open but words failed her. A second ago she had felt so sure that everything would turn out okay. She had felt safe. She had believed the comforting words she had said to Quinn. But now their entire plan had been pulled from underneath them like a rug. Amber was staring at her, curiously. Nikka's only comforting thought was that Stella, at least, would be okay... She would be okay because she had betrayed them.

"I have to think," she said, rising from her chair and shakily making her way back to the kitchen.

"Nikka!" Sums called, "that's not all."

With a shaking hand he wiped away the mass of sweat that had accumulated above his glasses and in between his brows.

"They are headed to your mother's house."

21
The Last Step

A thousand thoughts ran through Nikka's mind. There was heaviness deep inside her gut, and the prolonged sensation of falling, like when you stumble in a dream and seem to fall forever until suddenly you wake. Nikka had the overwhelming urge to scream.

"I'm sorry," she whispered hoarsely as she faced Amber, "I can't explain now, but I have to go."

Amber's concerned look was the last thing Nikka saw before she grabbed her backpack and bolted through the eccentric house and out the front door. She ran onto the sidewalk and scanned both sides of the empty street; there were no taxis, no bus stops, *nothing*. The thoughts in her mind quickly turned irrational; she wanted to fly, sprint, hotwire a car – anything, possible or impossible, but she needed to get downtown...*fast*.

Sums, Izaya and Quinn had followed her out. The three boys huddled nervously by the curbside and scanned the street.

"Freeway. We can hitchhike," proposed Quinn, pointing at the distant spot where truck driver Bill had dropped them off.

"Taxi?" suggested Izaya. He pulled out his phone, and looked worried as his eyes searched both empty sides of the long suburban street.

“I can call one?” he offered.

"Won’t be here fast enough," mumbled Sums.

"Nikka," Amber’s soft voice came from behind her. Amber stood on the curb with a duffle bag in one hand, and slipping into a purple leather jacket with the other.

"I’m coming with you," she said, determined.

Nikka couldn’t deal with this; she knew it was unfair to not tell Amber what was going on, or about what had *really* happened to her at the Academy, but there was something far more pressing at hand.

"It’s too dangerous, Amber, I’m not going to let you involve yourself. I’ll explain everything later, when I can," said Nikka dismissively.

"Don’t talk to me like I’m a child," Amber replied calmly. Nikka spun around to face her, surprised.

“I wasn’t”- she protested, but Amber interrupted her.

"Do you really think that I don’t understand what *they* took from me?" her honey-colored eyes were unyielding and her voice shook with unfamiliar rage. Nikka looked away, ashamed. The boys stood there- stunned into silence, just as she was. Quinn stared at his feet, unable to bear looking in Amber's direction.

"I DESERVE a part in this, whatever *this* is. I deserve answers," Amber continued adamantly. Nikka sighed, she started to walk away, guilt pulsed through her, mixed with adrenaline, but she was determined to not give in; she would not endanger anyone else that she cared about. She had to get downtown and she had to get there *now*. She heard a clinking sound, metal colliding against metal. Nikka turned again and saw Amber holding a large dangling key chain in front of her. Amber gave the chain a small wiggle.

"Need a ride?" she asked, and smiled triumphantly.

Amber drove her Chevy like a drag racer; she flew over bumps and cut sharp corners, running every red light blocking her way. The boys gaped at her in awe from the backseat, while Nikka barked out directions from the front like a drill sergeant. Sums had calculated that it would take the Dean's men thirty minutes to get downtown from their last known location. Luckily the gang made it to Sonya's house in less than twenty. They parked in the back alley by the recycling bins. Nikka shot out of the car and ran to the front of the dingy downtown building; her four friends sprinted after her. She crossed the dilapidated lobby, with its cracked marble floors, and then called the elevator. The button didn't light up, Nikka cursed loudly.

"Busted," she complained. Sums looked up the flight of stairs like he didn't quite trust them and Nikka heard him whisper a panicked, *"Oh no,"* right before she bolted up towards the fifth floor. By the time she made it to Sonya's apartment, she was panting and her sides were burning. The door was unlocked; Nikka pushed through it and staggered into Sonya's living room. Izaya, Amber, and Quinn stumbled in after her, panting. Sums, who looked like he was about to faint, limped in a few seconds later. Sonya was sitting on the ragged couch in the living room next to the Greek garden statue and watching reality TV on the loudest possible setting. She looked up at them, visibly drunk, her eyes slightly out of focus.

"Hello," she said lazily, unimpressed by the five people who had suddenly barged into her living room. She looked away again to the TV, disinterested. Daria emerged from the kitchen and stared at Nikka, dumbstruck. Nikka crossed the few feet between her and her mother and threw her arms around her. Daria hugged her back tightly and Nikka felt like crying with relief.

"Mom," Nikka exhaled, her voice muffled into her mother's shoulder.

"Hey there, sunshine," Daria soothed softly and after another tight squeeze she released her. Amber stepped forward and hugged Daria too. Daria looked over her shoulder at Nikka with bewilderment; she had never seen the redheaded girl before. Nikka shrugged her shoulders and laughed.

"It's so nice to meet you, Mrs. Mason. I'm Amber," she said as she let go of Daria.

"Nice to meet you too, Amber, call me Daria," she offered hesitantly. She looked past her and raised a brow at Nikka, who had already crossed the room, grabbed one of her mother's duffle bags, and was manically shoving her mother's valuables into it.

"What is going on? Who is *this*?" she cocked her head in the direction of the boys. "And why are you packing my things?"

Nikka didn't answer her right away.

"That's Izaya and Quinn, and you already know Sums," she said breathlessly. Izaya and Quinn both straightened a little as they exchanged their hellos with Daria.

"That's my aunt, Sonya," Nikka explained distractedly half-pointing at the large immobile woman on the couch. Desperately Nikka shoved another handful of clothes into the duffle bag. Sonya's misty eyes drifted towards Sums, whose arm was blocking the TV; she smiled at him with recognition.

"Hey there, fatty!" she said joyfully. Sums reddened.

"I've missed you," she said and burped giddily. Quinn shot him a teasing look and Sums gave the drunken woman a shy wave.

"Hello, Sonya," he said. Daria shot him an apologetic look.

"*Fatty*, she's one to talk," Sums mumbled grumpily under his breath.

Izaya made his way over to Nikka and steadied her hands. "Nikka, time is of the essence. We should get out of here," he urged. Nikka snapped out of her stupor and dropped the last handful of clothes on the ground.

"Are you planning on explaining yourself anytime soon, or are you just going to pack the entire apartment?" Daria asked with irritation. Nikka faced her mother.

"Mom, you trust me, right?" she asked. Daria instantly nodded.

"What if I told you Wildwood Academy is conducting illegal medical experiments on their students. *We* found out about it," she gestured at the others in the room, "ran away and now *they* are after us. They are armed, dangerous, and they are headed here. You need to pack your bags and come with us. *Now*." There was silence in the room as everyone waited for Daria's reaction. Daria's eyes widened, and then settled.

"Okay" she said, her tone final, "I'll get the rest of my things."

Everyone in the room was stumped, as if they were cumulatively thinking the same thought - *what, that's it, just like that?* With an expert set of motions Daria filled the bag quickly, then proceeded to a second one. Nikka was aware that everyone in the room, except for Sonya, was staring at her mother in disbelief. Nikka wasn't surprised though, just relieved. This was the woman who read conspiracy novels, who had seen UFOs on a number of occasions, and was skeptical about the moon landing. Daria had never gotten vaccinations, nor taken Nikka to get any because she believed, *no, she knew,* that pharmaceutical companies put strains of other diseases into the shots. But more importantly, this was the woman who could pack and leave at the drop of a hat, and she had left far more beautiful places behind than Sonya's apartment. At that moment more than ever, Nikka was grateful for Daria's quirks and her ability to believe in unlikely things. Sums leaned his hip against the window and stared out of it. Izaya sat down on a chair in the kitchen, and after examining the variety of cigarette butts and ashtrays scattered around, decided that no one would berate him for smoking indoors, so he lit up. Quinn lingered by Nikka's side.

"Uh-oh," said Sums suddenly. He was looking out the window and down into the street. It was the same type of cautionary *uh-oh* he had uttered in the Dean's office when he had discovered the alarm.

"They're here," he said quietly. Quinn hurried up to Sums and stared out the window alongside him.

"If they are guarding the alleyway it means they have someone up front too, we are surrounded," he said.

"Mom, hurry!" yelled Nikka. Daria's head shot up and she didn't move.

"I will stall them," she said suddenly.

"No, Mom," said Nikka, but Daria cut her off.

"*Yes!* Take the fire escape. I will distract the car at the front. Stay at a friend's house till we figure this out. I'll say I haven't seen you," said Daria decisively. She walked over to Sonya and bent to her level.

"Sonya, sweetie there are some men outside, they wish us harm. Can you help me distract them?" Sonya grunted unhappily in return.

"Make the leprechaun do it," she said her voice hoarse. Everyone turned to look at Quinn.

"That's offensive," he grumbled.

"Sonya, please," Daria urged, blocking the TV. Sonya grunted again but this time she got up. Daria turned and took Nikka's face in her hands, then she kissed her on the forehead. Nikka planted her feet hard on the ground.

"No," she protested hysterically, "This is ridiculous, Mom."

"I have an idea, just trust me," said Daria, as she pointed at the open window. Sums looked out the window and gulped.

"I'm not running away this time," said Daria. There was a glint in her eye and Nikka understood what she meant.

"But Mom, I-" began Nikka.

"No," said Daria, resolved. "Take her, get her out of here," she screamed commandingly at Quinn and Izaya, who quickly scrambled to his feet. Nikka felt Izaya's hand on her back urging her towards the window. She pulled away, and crossed the room to hug her mom.

"I'll call you, let you know where I am. We'll get the authorities involved," Nikka promised desperately. Daria kissed her ear and with those words, she grabbed Sonya by the arm and was out the door. Nikka stood there looking at the closed door, stupefied.

"Nikka," she heard someone whisper gently and Izaya enveloped her in his arms and pulled her to the window. Nikka threw her legs over the ledge. She looked back at the crappy empty apartment. *She will be okay, she will be okay* - Nikka repeated the mantra to herself as she took the fire escape one slippery metal ladder step at a time. She looked up at Izaya and his worried green eyes met hers. *Keep going,* said the voice in her head. *Just keep going*. Quinn was already halfway down, followed by Amber and Sums. A few seconds later Nikka, tailed closely by Izaya, landed on the crowded last level of the fire escape. She crouched down beside Sums. Amber turned and held a hand out to silence everyone.

"Shhh," she whispered and pointed at the opposite end of the alleyway.

There was a parked limo and two guards standing outside of it. One faced the street and the front exit of the building, the other faced the alley; if they took the last drop from the fire escape to the alleyway then they would be in plain view. Quinn hunched down next to her.

Nikka stared around the alley in search of a way out, but Quinn was right, *there was none*. Suddenly, there was a commotion - the grinding of metal. A rusty garage door in the alleyway pulled open with the sound of nails on a chalkboard and Sonya's Jeep burst out of it like a contained animal set free. At high speed, the Jeep crossed the length of the alleyway and crashed into the limo, causing it to drift into oncoming traffic. Nikka could see smoke and hear screams, but could not look back, she was already moving down the last ladder and running to the other end of the alley. All she could do was hope that her mother was okay and mourn Sonya's beloved Jeep. She boarded Amber's Chevy, which was concealed behind the recycling bins, and they were off, speeding out of the alley, leaving the smoke-enveloped scene and Daria behind.

×

For a while Amber drove around aimlessly, then she parked, deciding not to waste more gas.

"That was one hell of a distraction," said Quinn, his tone one of regret and admiration. Nikka nodded numbly.

"What now?" asked Amber.

"We need a place to hide and think this through," said Quinn nervously, scanning the side mirrors of the Chevy.

"Can we go back to your house?" asked Nikka in Amber's direction.

"My aunt comes to stay tomorrow and my parents' cleaner comes today, it would be hard to explain," she said.

"It's also obvious if we go to her house. I'm sure the Dean would think of our connection to her," said Sums dryly.

"My house is off limits because of my uncle," said Izaya.

"My house is in Ireland," Quinn said lamely.

"I doubt my foster family would welcome the five of us, not without a fat check," said Sums, his tone flat.

"What we need is money. Money solves most problems," said Izaya

"Is that your family motto?" Quinn asked crankily.

"It's just a *fact*," snapped Izaya. "Money buys security, lodgings..."

"We can't use the ATMs," said Nikka.

"We could steal some," said Quinn half-heartedly. Nikka looked at him stunned.

"Not from any nice people," he said defensively. "From someone evil, like Izaya's uncle."

"I'm not going to hold back from punching you just because we are in a car," said Izaya menacingly.

"That's a great idea; the accused criminals on the run should commit another crime"- chimed Sums, irritably.

"Izaya is right," said Quinn, "we need money to keep us fluid. We can fly out to Europe."

"We can report the school to the press, or to whistleblower agencies, we just need some funds to tide us over in the meantime," said Sums suddenly excited at the prospect of a solution.

"I can get cash from my Uncle's P.A.," said Izaya. Quinn snorted at this.

"Can you trust him?" Nikka asked carefully.

"*Yes,* I've known him since I was born and he has kept bigger secrets than this. I can get him to bring me a couple of grand, easy," Izaya said lazily. Nikka made a mental note to ask Izaya what kind of trouble he could have possibly gotten himself into that was a bigger secret than *this*.

"Thank you," she said softly.

Izaya smiled at her and cockily dialed a number on his phone.

×

The meeting spot that Izaya and his uncle's personal assistant, Silvio, had agreed upon was a deserted parking lot in Compton, near the airport. The parking lot was behind a half-completed construction site meant for new condos, and therefore unused and out of sight from the street. Amber pulled her Chevy into the vacant parking lot and pulled over. The group of teenagers disembarked the car and waited. The sun was still scorching hot, and Nikka couldn't believe that after all that had happened to them, the day was still going strong. Izaya checked his watch, and surveyed the empty parking lot.

"You're sure Sylvio will be able to find it?" asked Nikka.

"*Oh yeah*. He remembers this place alright. This is where I used to go before I had a fake ID; I threw parties here," he said nostalgically. Nikka didn't look at him; she wasn't in the mood for a trip down memory lane, not after she had left Daria behind. She breathed out and tried to retreat to a dark corner of her mind, one where she wouldn't think of her mom, of the Dean, or of Sonya's beloved car. Everything was too surreal, and she decided the best thing to do was to clear her mind of it all, to just go with it, as if she were playing pretend and not living real life. Amber caught her eye and smiled her warm comforting smile, a smile that said- *everything will be okay*. Nikka sighed and leaned back against the car.

"You partied in a parking lot?" asked Quinn, dumbfounded. "Guess we do have some things in common, you and I."

"My uncle owns the lot. Before he started building here it was empty. We use to put up a marquee *here*," Izaya pointed, "bouncers *there*, DJs, cocktail waitresses - the whole nine yards. But that was years ago," he added nonchalantly. Sums snorted; Izaya had started throwing wild parties years before Sums had ever even been invited to one. Quinn rolled his eyes.

A limo turned the corner and slowly entered the parking lot. Nikka's heart did a little jump; the sight of the slow creeping limo instantly sent ice through her veins and it took a moment for her to realize that it was not a Wildwood car. Izaya's face brightened at the sight of it, he winked at Nikka as if to say, *I told you so*. It came to a halt on the other side of the parking lot. The door opened and a man emerged. The limo was heavily tinted and Nikka could not see whether there was anyone else inside. The man had a thick envelope in one hand, and kept his other hand on the rim of the limo door, as if for support.

Silvio looked just like his name; he was handsome, dark-haired and dark-eyed, with something inherently feminine about him. He was dressed opulently in a green tie and suit, and he had carefully manicured facial hair. He looked like the type of man who would usually be throwing his hands in the air, gesticulating happily, but there was something soft in his eyes as he looked at Izaya, a masked sadness that looked out of place on the otherwise flamboyant, expensively groomed face.

Izaya crossed the parking lot. Silvio closed the door to the limo behind him. They half hugged; the way men sometimes do, half-heartedly slinging one arm around each other. Nikka and the group were silent as they watched Silvio and Izaya exchange a few words, but they were too far away to hear. Silvio's eyes locked on Nikka curiously in response to something Izaya had said, and then quickly looked away.

Nikka felt like something had gone wrong before anything even happened. Her instincts flared, like an animal tenses when it feels a presence behind it. Izaya was shaking his head vigorously and moving his hands. Silvio's face drained of all color and he turned away, with a look of shame and guilt. Izaya turned and for the briefest moment, his green eyes met Nikka's. There was alarm there, fear and a final restricted kind of longing, as if he wanted to cross the parking lot and grab her, but couldn't. A split second later, the limo doors flew open and four masked men emerged. One grabbed Izaya and wrestled him into the open limo door. Nikka screamed and launched forward, but Quinn grabbed her into a bear hug and with Sums' help pulled her back.

Nikka thrashed against him wildly, for a short moment she wondered why Quinn would hold her back; *does he hate Izaya that much?* And then she saw why. The three remaining, unoccupied guards were holding guns, pointed directly at them.

"No one move," grunted a guard to the left. Nikka heard more commotion erupt from the car, she pushed against Quinn's body instinctively, but he was too strong. She had to help him, she had to get to Izaya, she couldn't think of anything else as she frantically pushed against Quinn's strong arms.

She heard a slap, and muted protests from Izaya as he naively screamed, *"Do you know who I am?"* A moment later the commotion in the limo died down, like a loud stereo being muted. Nothing but a terrifying silence came from the black abyss beyond the limo door.

"Please, don't hurt him!" Nikka begged. Her voice was hoarse and pathetic.

Silvio was looking at the ground. *They tranquillized him,* Nikka realized. The parking lot swarmed before her as hot tears clouded her eyes, misting away the view, like rain on a windshield.

"He trusted you," she cried accusingly in the general direction of Silvio. Silvio didn't answer her; he boarded the limo and closed the door. A moment later it pulled out of the parking lot, and disappeared, like a shadow turning a corner. Nikka screamed and felt Quinn's sweaty palm close around her mouth. The sweat and tears mixed on her face and all she could taste was the salt of Quinn's hand. *Izaya, Izaya* - his name danced a panicked waltz in her mind. She felt her knees wobble and she collapsed forward onto them.

"Where are you taking him?" demanded Amber. Her voice wavered and Nikka could tell she was trying hard to stay as calm as possible.

"Shut up," grunted one of the guards menacingly. "And *you*," he pointed at Nikka, who was on her knees. "One more scream and I will kill one of your friends."

Her fear for Izaya melted a little, replaced by fear for her friends, and for her own life, she was suddenly all too conscious of the barrel of the man's gun. Nikka rose slowly, and faced the guards.

"He will be okay, it's not him they want. *Just stay calm,*" Quinn whispered into her ear. Nikka nodded and squeezed his hand. Quinn took a step forward and angled his body so that he was standing between Nikka and the gun. One of the guards pulled out a cellphone and spoke into it.

"I got them. Yeah, *he's* safe. The *girl* is here. Come now," he said roughly.

Nikka felt Sums shake next to her. The guard put the phone away and re-steadied his gun. *There is no way out,* the realization dragged Nikka down like a bag of bricks underwater as she glanced around the parking lot. An abrupt cracking sound erupted around the corner, the sound of an approaching motorcycle. The left guard tensed and pointed his gun in the direction of the sound, clearly recognizing it as alien and uninvited. A second later, a Harley Davidson bike turned and entered the lot at high speed. Nikka heard what to her sounded like fireworks exploding at close range. She was quickly dragged down onto the concrete. Time seemed to stall; Nikka reached out for Sums' arm and pulled him towards her. Sums was holding his ears and screaming. Nikka craned her neck to try and see where Amber had gone. As quickly as it had started the shooting stopped. Slowly Nikka looked up. She could see a stream of liquid, trickling slowly and moving towards her like a snake, shiny against the pavement. The liquid spread onto her hands. She sat up and observed her hands curiously; it was blood - crimson, warm and sticky. For the last time, she screamed.

×

Nikka felt a strong silencing hand mute her screams, but this time it wasn't Quinn's. She looked up and saw the biker. Once he was sure she had stopped screaming, he released her. Nikka stood up and looked around the parking lot and saw the three bodies, lying on the ground, sprawled awkwardly like toppled toys. Quinn, Amber and Sums were standing near her, staring at the bodies, stunned into silence by their first glimpse of death. Nikka looked at the biker again and he smiled at her, a decaying smile of bad veneers and gold. The man looked like he was in his mid-forties; he had a bandana on and his long brown beard had traces of white. He was wearing a leather vest, a jean shirt, and he had long grey hair tied into a greasy ponytail. The gun was gone; he had already tucked it away.

"Hey there," he said. Nikka shrunk away from him in terror.

"Relax," said the man.

He reached into his breast pocket, past a thick chain that held a cross on it and pulled out a pair of dog tags that Nikka recognized instantly. He dangled them before her.

"I come in peace," he said tentatively.

Nikka reached out a shaking hand and steadied the chain, then studied it.

"You served with my dad?" she said weakly reading the tag that was near identical to the one she wore around her neck.

Silently she read off his name - *Chad Rodriguez*, and recognized it as one of the names listed on the group photo that Izaya had presented her with.

"But how-" began Nikka.

"Your mom called me for help. I've known her for many years. She said you were in danger and then she located you through that GPS thing you guys have on your phones."

Nikka nodded, she and her mother both had GPS locators on their phones, a function Daria added once Nikka started walking to school on her own in Chicago.

"So I came," said the man flatly.

"But you killed them," said Nikka dazedly.

"Kill or be killed, darling," said the large and sweaty man. He glanced at the bodies without emotion. Nikka felt the presence of Quinn, Sums and Amber, who had gravitated towards her and were staring at the man with suspicion.

"I'm still a good shot. But not as good as your father

was," he said gaily. Nikka tried to speak but couldn't. She heard Sums suppress a gag and look away from the bodies.

"I don't understand," said Nikka quietly.

"Ask questions later," he grunted. "Now get in the car, and follow me. It's time to move."

×

Nikka stared out of her window. At some point they had left the Compton parking lot behind, but Nikka could no longer build a credible timeline in her head. *Did anyone report the gunshots? Were those bodies picked up? Where did they take Izaya? Izaya, Izaya, Izaya.* His name sent a wave of pain through her. She glanced through the front window at the leather clad back of the man on his Harley, whom they were following. She watched as he turned off the freeway and pulled into a gas station. The man disembarked his bike and walked up to the Chevy. Nikka looked around at the dry bush surrounding the gas station, and assumed that they were somewhere near Calabasas, on the outskirts of Los Angeles. She got out of the car and found the biker waiting for her by a pump.

"How about you tell me everything, from the start, and I'll try to help you," suggested Chad. Nikka looked back at her friends, but Quinn, Amber and Sums' faces were all resigned. Sums especially looked like he was going to throw up.

"Or, we could part ways, and you can take your

chances out *there,*" he said, "If you prefer." Chad signaled in the direction of the freeway in a kind of condescending 'the world is your oyster' way.

"How come I've never met you?" asked Nikka. Chad's brow creased.

"I'm not really a kosher house guest, if you know what I mean - not the type of person you want around your kids," he smiled as if this fact amused him.

"So why would she call for your help?" asked Nikka sounding exhausted.

"Precisely for that reason," said Chad, still smiling. "I owe your dad one. And I'm in the right line of work to help," he added and tapped the place where Nikka knew he kept his gun. Nikka wanted to ask more about her father, about Chad's favor, about his line of work, but she knew it wasn't the time. Instead she launched into a tireless explanation of what had happened to them at Wildwood, and all the other unbelievable events that had brought them to that gas station.

Half an hour later, Nikka was perusing the Mini-Mart with Sums whilst Chad placed calls outside under the watchful eyes of Quinn. Through the dirty window, she could see the sun setting over the dry horizon - pink, pale and cloudless. Nikka approached the register and plopped her items on the counter. A bored attendant was flicking through a TV guide behind bulletproof glass. A mounted TV blared the news behind him obnoxiously. The attendant tallied up Nikka's six-pack of soda and box of frosted donuts that she was purchasing as dinner for her and her friends. Nikka watched the biker on the phone outside. Amber, not too far from him, was washing her windows with one of those squeegees that gas stations provide. Quinn entered the Mart and started absent-mindedly leafing through magazines. Sums queued up behind her, already snacking on an open pack of Cheetos he was going to buy. Nikka pulled the Cheetos away from him and put it on the counter to add to her tally. Suddenly, her ears perked up as she heard a familiar word come from the TV. Nikka turned her head up and watched. The screen was showing a picture of a fire in the forest.

"Cash or card?" said the clerk in front of her through a mouthful of gum. Nikka ignored him; she couldn't look away from the reporter on the screen.

"A small forest fire in the San Jacinto Mountain region claimed two lives this afternoon," announced the woman. The picture on the screen shifted from a picture of a fire to a picture of scorched pine. "The fire, believed to have been caused by a cigarette, was quickly contained by local authorities, but not before killing a local student and a staff member of a local boarding school."

Nikka didn't hear anything else after that. The attendant was yelling at her to focus, she felt her knees buckle and the overwhelming urge to vomit washed over her as Stella and Magda's faces flooded the screen.

22
The Tunnel

It was a long while until Nikka could breathe again. She had run out of the gas station without paying, desperate for open space, desperate for a space in which she could scream. It was like she was made of fabric and ripping at the seams, bursting with the tension of sudden, unexpected grief. Nikka sat down, mildly aware of Sums throwing up into one of the bins nearby, or of Amber holding her, stroking her, or of Quinn cursing loudly, kicking a nearby pump, and of Chad telling them to all shut up.

Nikka felt like the air had been pulled out of her throat. Like she had swallowed a rock and it was lodged halfway between her throat and her lungs, only allowing a small wheeze of air in at a time. She never gave her eyes the signal to cry, the water just pooled in the corners and made its way down her face in heavy, painful bursts. It was as if her body knew how to react before her mind did. Sums was sobbing somewhere in the background. Chad stood by, wordless and unapologetic, as if he were comfortably untouched by the tragedy erupting around him and felt no need to pretend otherwise. He spat on the floor, sat down on his Harley, and watched the street.

Nikka cried and cried. Her eyes and throat ached and she felt like she had been punched in the stomach. She made an odd croaking sound, an attempt to try and breathe again, and as she gulped down the cool evening air a tiny bit of relief poured in. She felt Quinn hug her from behind and then the pain returned full force, it felt like falling down the stairs, each time she thought she could stop she kept falling. The tears dried at some point from the wind, but the shaking and heaviness of her body didn't subside at all. On the other side of the ramp, in between the two pumps, Amber was hugging a crying Sums.

"I'm not surprised," said the biker coldly, "it's a warning shot; it's what you do when someone is fleeing- it's how you silence them," he said calculatingly. Nikka looked at him in disbelief, how could anyone rationalize something as horrible as that? Her fists balled and she tried to settle the gagging in her mouth as she thought of Magda, her kind eyes; Stella's smile. The crying returned as quickly as it has subsided. Nikka vomited on the other side of the gas pump.

"Confirms what I thought," continued the biker obtusely. "We need to get you out if the country. Speaking of *which-*"

There was a roaring sound, like an approaching thundercloud. Chad looked up expectantly as three other bikers on loud spluttering Harleys entered the parking lot of the gas station and pulled to a stop beside them.

The convulsing in Nikka's body eased a little, suppressed by curiosity and fear. She clasped Quinn's hand protectively and pressed the feelings down, storing them away, compartmentalizing them as she had been doing for days. One of the bikers had a duffle bag and he tossed it at Chad with a grin. Quinn stood up, defensive upon seeing the strangers who looked even less *Kosher* than Chad did. Sums flanked his side.

"Relax, *big boys*," said Chad with amusement. "They're with me."

Nikka stared at the man, who was amused, untouched by the pain around him. He may have served with her father, but the brute had nothing in common with her dad, Nikka decided silently. The bikers, a skinny man, a fat bearded one, and a woman, nodded at the group in greeting. Chad opened the duffle bag and pulled out a few jackets, bandanas, and helmets. He tossed them to Amber, then to Quinn, then Sums. The bearded biker disembarked and bent in Chad's direction in order to whisper something into his ear. Chad's eyes instantly narrowed on Nikka.

"Slight change of plans," said Chad. "You're already on a *no fly list*," he said, pointing at Nikka. "You're coming with me. You're going to be 'hopping the border' as our Mexican friends like to call it. The rest of you will go by bike."

Wait, why would we go by bike?" said Sums, his small voice boarded on hysteria as he looked at the beast-like motorcycles.

"We have a car," Amber echoed lamely.

"Because *Hell's Angels* don't get hassled," croaked the bearded biker and his friends roared with laughter in response. He pointed at a faded tattoo sprawled on his neck. Nikka took that to be a sign that he was an *Angel*.

"Let's go, you're running out of time," Chad barked, suddenly irritated. His tone was sharp and commanding.

"You three get on," he pointed at Amber, Sums and Quinn.

"And *you're* with me," he said to Nikka.

"I'm coming with her," Quinn countered instantly.

"Me too," echoed Sums. Before Amber could agree as well, Chad cut them off.

"That won't work," he said coldly as he slipped his helmet on. Then he smiled. "It's more of a one-person vessel of transportation," he said dryly. The fuller biker behind him snickered.

×

Nikka held on tight to Chad's mid-section. Her hands were clammy and they left watermarks on the leather of his jacket. The wind hit her in the neck and pushed against her body and helmet, and she was grateful for it; for a little while it gave her relief and numbed her senses. She tried to focus on the image of Sums in biker gear, clutching the back of the female biker with fear as they drove off and unwillingly left her and Chad alone. She was too weak and in too much emotional pain to smile, but she focused in on that image, knowing that some day in the future, once the pain was gone, the sight of Sums in a leather jacket and bandana would make her laugh.

Twenty minutes later Chad pulled into the parking lot of a liquor store. Nikka dismantled the bike and in the process burned her leg on the exhaust. She squealed in pain.

"Ouch!" she squirmed.

"Careful, it's hot," said Chad. Nikka rolled her eyes at him, but again she was grateful to feel something that distracted her, even if it was more pain. Anything that would distract her from the pain she felt in her heart was a welcome sensation. Cautiously, Chad looked around the empty street and led her into the store.

"Might not be the best time for alcohol," Nikka said sarcastically. She felt the dull burn in her leg.

"It's always a good time for alcohol," Chad answered

dryly. He led her in and through the dusty rows that led to the cashier's desk. A Mexican woman stood there, counting something behind the register. The woman did not greet them. Her eyes narrowed knowingly when she saw Chad and she wordlessly opened the back door to the stock room.

Chad walked through it, trailed by Nikka. They entered the dimly lit stock room and walked past stacked crates of alcohol and litters of bills on a nearby desk. The door closed behind her with the click of a lock, and for a moment Nikka was seized with terror. She was in a stock room with a man whom she did not know, and with no way out. Chad pulled down on a lamp that was mounted on the oily back wall. In the corner of the room, a case covered in dusty bottles of whisky shifted to reveal a trap door, behind which was a long dark hallway.

Chad entered the hallway first and Nikka, eyes wide, followed him. Nikka was terrified, but it was like being stuck halfway down a water slide - there was nowhere to go, but onwards. They arrived in another small, carpeted room. Chad lifted up a dirty carpet; beneath it was another trap door, which he opened to reveal a dark plummeting staircase.

"Some operation you guys got here," said Nikka.

Chad shot her a warning glare.

"You haven't seen the half of it," he said light-heartedly, readjusting his demeanor to a friendlier one.

He started climbing down the stairs, deeper and deeper into the darkness. Nikka heard his feet hit the floor and a moment later hers did too. Wherever they were, it was cold and damp. Chad pulled on something and a swinging light came on above them, which caused their shadows to dance on the concrete walls. Tense, Nikka looked around, trying to find something that could be used as a weapon, *just in case*. There were a few errant liquor crates, but nothing else. Chad walked up to a large open crate. Nikka noticed that there was a square gaping hole in the wall with a large belt on it, meant to transport something and a button by the wall. *For smuggling,* she realized. Nikka thought of asking Chad what the crates were used for, but thought better of it. Whether it was for *people, drugs or worse,* she decided she didn't want to know. The fear inside of her expanded inwards like an endless pit.

"That's useful," she said conversationally. She pointed at the hole.

"It's useful for *deliveries*," he said stressing the last word.

He checked that one of the larger crates was empty and located the lid. Then out of another crate he pulled out something that resembled a sleeping bag.

"Are you claustrophobic?" He asked.

"Does it make a difference?" Nikka retorted darkly. Her lip quivered a little, but she steadied it with her teeth.

"Not really," said the man. "This is your only option as

far as I can see."

Nikka nodded.

"This sleeping bag blocks infrared so that helicopters can't pick up on your heat signature.

"Get in," he said. Nikka took a heavy breath. Under other circumstances this might have been the scariest thing she had ever encountered, but the last couple of days had toughened her up. She put one leg in, then the other, and lowered herself into the bag, all the while thanking some universal power for the fact that she was not actually claustrophobic. The crate felt roomier than she would have thought. She looked up at Chad.

"It takes a few hours to cross the border," he said. "Now it might seem like you're running out of air at some point; but you're not. Trust me, this thing has been *human* tested a number of times. If anything happens, it's all in your head. Whatever you do, don't get out until you've come to a full stop." He smacked the side of the crate for emphasis.

"Your friends are on the other side," said Chad in what he must have thought was a soothing voice.

"Will you make sure my mom is okay?" Nikka stuttered. She stared deep into the biker's dark brown eyes searching for confirmation.

"You have my word," said the man. With that, he zipped her up then shut the crate. There were slits in the crate and the light still shone into it. Nikka could see snippets of Chad as he lifted her to the opening in the wall. Chad pressed the button, there was a buzzing sound as the belt came to life and started moving her in an unknown direction. Soon, all the light was gone.

"Good luck, kid," was the last thing she heard him call after her.

×

Nikka wasn't sure how much time had passed since she left the liquor store basement. At some point she had willed herself to go completely numb, to welcome the darkness, and to pace her breathing in a way that was meditative. She had cried, a lot, and at some point she had even drifted into a light sleep. While she slept, she dreamt of Izaya.

The crate jerked and woke her. After making sure that the crate had come to a full stop, Nikka pushed back the lid and climbed out into what felt like another damp, concrete tunnel. Far away, at the end of the tunnel, there was a swinging light and Nikka walked towards it. There was something lingering in the back of her brain, making her walk slower. There was grief over the deaths of Stella and Magda, there was fear for her mother's safety, and anxiety over being separated from Izaya, but there was something else, too. Under all of the pain and irrationality, her internal logic was working, mapping things out visually, as it always did. With a shock that felt like being zapped, Nikka suddenly realized what was nagging her -

Chad was not familiar. His name was familiar, his dog tags were familiar, but his face wasn't. With closed eyes and heavy breath, Nikka visualized the photo Izaya had given her, every inch of that photo was burned into her memory. Then she cursed loudly.

Nikka threw her backpack on the ground and frantically searched through it until she found the picture. She could barely make it out in the dim light of the tunnel, but in the third row of the photo she could see a young skinny man with soft features, a young man she had never met - *Chad Rodriguez*. Unceremoniously, Nikka dumped the rest of her backpack out on the damp ground. She dug through the contents until she located her phone and held it up to the light - *it was dead*. It had been dead since her visit to Nurse Smith's house. There was no way her mother or anyone else could have used GPS to trace her location.

Whoever the biker was who had saved her, who had put her in this tunnel, who had sent her friends away, *he was a liar* - he had not served with her father, he was not Chad Rodriguez, and her mother had definitely not sent him.

Feeling exasperated, exhausted and hollow, Nikka numbly carried on making her way towards the light. There was no going back now. She didn't know what waited for her on the other side. *Was it safety? Certain death?* All she knew was that she was at a crossroads, not only a real geographical border, but a point of no return in her own life.

There she was. Back on the road, back on the run. In the darkness of the tunnel Nikka laughed to herself - a laugh that bordered on psychotic. She laughed loudly. She laughed at the notion that running, like this, felt so natural to her. She did what she did each time her mother chose to run, she thought about what she was leaving behind. Normally, she would be sad about the odd friend here and there, maybe the great coffee shop in the town center, or a view she was not likely to see for a while, but this time she knew that she was leaving much, much more.

She thought of Izaya, Stella, Magda, her mother, and Wildwood. Then she made her way to the light and found a lever. She pulled on it, hard. It fell on the ground with a metallic thud. There was a stairway and more light at the top. She squinted up and then looked back into the darkness of the tunnel. She knew that somewhere in that tunnel, she had left her old self behind too.

Epilogue

There were no lights on in the Dean's office. The stars illuminated the structure from within. Stamos walked determinedly through the empty lobby and through the glass hallway - there was a sharp echo from the sound of his boots hitting the marble floor. He spotted a flickering light in the Dean's office, a candle. A tell tale sign that his chief was angry - *the day had not gone to plan*. Stamos entered the office and paused by the threshold. The Dean faced the glass wall, and looked out on the forest, as if he were watching it, waiting for something to happen. Stamos cleared his throat; the Dean did not turn around.

"It's done, sir," said Stamos.

"I wish I could congratulate you, *Stamos*. But I think you will agree that this outcome is far from desirable," said the Dean coldly.

"I know, Sir," said Stamos in a tone as close to apologetic as he could manage.

"How?" asked the Dean. Stamos knew what he was referring to. He reached into the breast pocket of his perfectly fitted suit and pulled out a photograph. He set the photograph on the table.

"We ran their Chevy off the freeway outside of Calabasas. It exploded - we burnt the rest of it and had the bodies burned and the remains buried. That photo is the only evidence."

The Dean did not look at the photograph.

"Burn it," he said with irritation. Stamos pocketed the photograph.

"What's the potential backlash?" asked the Dean.

"The fat one won't be missed, we paid off his foster family. Neither will the Irish boy; as you already know, he was an impostor. Amber no longer attended the Academy, so her *disappearance* will not be tied to us; her history of mental illness is a plus. There is still the problem of Nikka's mother, but we are working on that."

"Mitchum's nephew, Izaya?"

"Safely returned home. Mitchum is working on him as we speak."

The Dean reached out a finger and stroked the glass in front of him.

"Three years I kept that math genius around, waiting for the perfect client."

"I know, sir," said Stamos.

"And the girl, she won't be easily replaced," added the

Dean.

Stamos nodded.

The Dean turned towards him slowly. His beady eyes were composed, fixed on Stamos. Black as coal, their usual emptiness was now drowned with silent fury.

"How could this happen, Stamos?" he asked slowly.

"We did not anticipate four of the subjects becoming close friends. Also, the matter of having transplanted to the wrong boy, that exposed us. That is another turn of events we could not have anticipated."

"I don't pay you to *anticipate*," said the Dean dryly. Stamos nodded again. This wasn't the right time to argue with the Dean.

"The situation is under control now," said Stamos.

There was a heavy pause. The Dean turned back to the window. Stamos did not move.

"What are you waiting for?" said the Dean commandingly. "Go get me some new subjects."

Stamos walked to the downstairs kitchen with purpose. He knew that it was the only room in the house that wasn't tapped. His secondary phone had been quietly buzzing the entire duration of the Dean's scolding. Stamos pulled it out and grimaced at the number. He *so* hated talking to the *help*, and considered it beneath him. He picked up. Chad's hoarse, brutish voice echoed from the other end.

"It's done, boss," he said.

"The girl?"

"On her way. The others are already over the border."

"I will transfer the funds as usual," said Stamos coldly, eager to get off the phone with the brute.

"Pleasure working with you," said Chad, but Stamos had already hung up.

ABOUT THE AUTHOR

Jacqueline Silvester is a novelist and screenwriter.

She lives in London with her husband, her excessive YA collection, and a hyper husky named Laika.

Follow Jacqueline online for news on Wunderkids Part 2, advice on writing, and exciting giveaways!

Visit her website at www.jacquelinesilvester.com

Connect with her on Instagram @jchoulji

Follow her on Facebook @authorjacquelinesilvester